Autumn spotted
behind a nearby
Glock was pointe

A Glock? The man definitely wasn't a hunter.

She spotted a fourth man behind another tree. They all surrounded the campsite where Derek and his brother had set up.

They'd been waiting for Derek to return, hadn't they?

Another bullet came flying past, piercing a nearby tree.

"What are we going to do?" Derek whispered. "Can I help?"

"Just stay behind a tree and remain quiet," she said. "We don't want to make this too easy for them."

Sherlock let out a little whine, but Autumn shushed the dog.

The man fired again. This time the bullet split the wood only inches from her.

Autumn's heart raced. These men were out for blood.

Even if these men ran out of bullets, she and Derek were going to be outnumbered. They couldn't just wait here for that to happen.

She had to act—and now.

She turned, pulling her gun's trigger…

USA TODAY Bestselling Author

Christy Barritt
and
Heather Woodhaven

Deadly Trail

2 Thrilling Stories

Mountain Survival and *Search and Defend*

LOVE INSPIRED SUSPENSE
INSPIRATIONAL ROMANCE

LOVE INSPIRED® SUSPENSE
INSPIRATIONAL ROMANCE

ISBN-13: 978-1-335-47598-5

Recycling programs
for this product may
not exist in your area.

Deadly Trail

Copyright © 2024 by Harlequin Enterprises ULC

Mountain Survival
First published in 2021. This edition published in 2024.
Copyright © 2021 by Christy Barritt

Search and Defend
First published in 2021. This edition published in 2024.
Copyright © 2021 by Heather Humrichouse

For questions and comments about the quality of this book, please contact us
at CustomerService@Harlequin.com.

Love Inspired
22 Adelaide St. West, 41st Floor
Toronto, Ontario M5H 4E3, Canada
www.LoveInspired.com

Printed in U.S.A.

CONTENTS

Christy Barritt's books have won a Daphne du Maurier Award for Excellence in Suspense and Mystery and have been twice nominated for an RT Reviewers' Choice Best Book Award. She's married to her Prince Charming, a man who thinks she's hilarious—but only when she's not trying to be. Christy is a self-proclaimed klutz, an avid music lover and a road-trip aficionado. For more information, visit her website at christybarritt.com.

Books by Christy Barritt

Love Inspired Suspense

Keeping Guard
The Last Target
Race Against Time
Ricochet
Desperate Measures
Hidden Agenda
Mountain Hideaway
Dark Harbor
Shadow of Suspicion
The Baby Assignment
The Cradle Conspiracy
Trained to Defend
Mountain Survival
Dangerous Mountain Rescue

Visit the Author Profile page at
LoveInspired.com for more titles.

MOUNTAIN SURVIVAL

Christy Barritt

I will lift up mine eyes unto the hills, from whence cometh my help. My help cometh from the Lord, which made heaven and earth.
—*Psalms* 121:1–2

This book is dedicated to Rusty,
the best Australian shepherd out there.
Thanks for the inspiration, sweet pup!

ONE

"It's up to you, Sherlock," Autumn Mercer murmured as she knelt beside her dog. "You have to find her."

Sherlock barked, his tongue hanging from his mouth as he panted with excitement.

Autumn held a sweater belonging to one of her co-workers beneath her dog's nose. Sherlock sniffed it before sitting at attention and waiting patiently for her command. The dog was practically salivating to get to work.

Autumn paused a beat before saying, "Search!"

At once, Sherlock tugged at his leash and started toward the thick forest on the edge of the small, secluded parking lot.

The dog never looked as happy as when he had a job to do. The Australian shepherd, a red merle with striking blue eyes, was always a sight to behold. In the three years since Autumn had been training him for search and rescue missions, the canine had become like a family member.

She followed behind him, careful to track her steps so she could find her way back later. Every month, Autumn did these exercises with her dog so they could be prepared when needed.

Just last week, she and her team had to track down a missing fourteen-year-old who'd wandered away from his family on a camping trip. Sherlock had also helped with search and rescue missions involving the elderly, hikers who explored off the marked trail and once an entire family who'd gotten lost while geocaching.

Sherlock paused near a tree and sniffed. Then he veered to the left, deeper into the wilderness.

"Good job, boy," Autumn said. "Keep going."

Autumn pulled her jacket closer as she tramped between hemlock and oak trees. Even though it was October, a chill lingered in the air today. It didn't help that the sun was obscured behind gray clouds overhead. A massive storm system was coming this way, but she had at least two hours until it arrived. She planned to make the most of her time.

As Sherlock pulled her, she glanced around. The leaves on the trees around her were gorgeous. There was nothing like fall in Virginia's Blue Ridge Mountains. At least, in her estimation.

She had worked as a park ranger here at the George Washington National Forest for the past five years, and it was her dream job. She'd always been an outside girl, preferring to spend time with nature rather than people. Being out here made her feel peaceful, and peace was something hard to come by at times. Especially lately.

Before sadness could grip her, she turned her attention back to Sherlock.

"Careful, boy," she called.

The trail narrowed, and a steep drop-off on one side

gave them only six inches of slippery rock to cross to get to where they were going. Sherlock had no problem, but Autumn tried to brace herself. Heights had never been her favorite, and the fifty-foot drop made her feel light-headed.

This part of the mountain was no place for a rookie. A gorge cut through the area, and the Meadow Brook River rushed the depths there. If one wasn't paying attention, they might lose their step on one of the cliffs or rock facings. It still amazed Autumn how many people tried to hike this terrain, even without the proper gear or experience.

Kevin used to love exploring this section of the national forest. He'd loved adventure—but only when safety precautions were taken first.

At the thought of him, Autumn's heart squeezed with grief. It was hard to believe he'd been gone for three years now. A heart attack had taken him from this earth but not from her memory. He would always be there with her.

His death was just one more reason she liked being out here. Everyone she'd ever loved was gone. Her parents had died in a car accident when she was a teenager. Then her husband had passed away.

All she had now was Sherlock. Autumn had found the dog on the side of the road as she traveled home from Kevin's funeral. The canine was like a godsend in her time of need.

Though Autumn had previously been a ranger, she and Sherlock had gotten their certification in search and rescue. Sherlock had been a natural and had become a valuable part of her team.

Autumn and Sherlock had been inseparable ever since.

"What do you smell, boy?" Autumn watched as the dog's nose remained close to the ground.

Sherlock continued to tug her through the trees. Autumn watched her steps, careful not to lose her footing on the slick leaves that lined the forest floor. As she moved, a chilly breeze swept over the landscape—a breeze that smelled like rain.

The storm was coming. Maybe it was even closer than forecasters had predicted. They didn't have a lot of time to waste. Thirty more minutes, and Autumn would head back to the Park Service SUV she'd left in the small lot off the windy mountain road. There was nothing else there but a portable toilet, a small display with a map and a wooden box for donations.

Sherlock continued to pull on his leash, leading her through the foliage. But Autumn's muscles pulled tighter across her back with every pace forward.

Steps sounded ahead of her. Twigs broke. Leaves crackled.

Autumn paused. Sherlock's tail straightened, and his hair rose.

Her hand went to her gun, and she braced herself, preparing for the worst.

She held her breath, waiting to see what creature might emerge from the trees in the distance. Whatever it was, it sounded big. A bear? She'd seen her fair share of the beasts out here. She liked admiring them, but only from a distance.

Sherlock let out a low growl.

A moment later, someone darted from the trees. A

big man with broad shoulders and short dark hair. He wore jeans, a thick vest and a knit cap.

As soon as Autumn saw his face, she knew he wasn't trouble. Instead, he was *in* trouble.

Sherlock began barking at him, and the man froze. His breaths seemed shallow. Too shallow. His cheeks were flushed, and his gaze unsteady.

"Heel, boy," she told the dog. Caution lined her voice.

Sherlock quieted and waited for her instructions, but his eyes remained on the stranger. Autumn quickly studied the man. Just looking at him, she didn't see any visible injuries. But the look in his eyes told a different story.

"I'm Ranger Autumn Mercer," she called. "Can I help you?"

The man continued to heave with exertion. "I've been trying to find help. It's my brother. He broke his leg, and I don't have any cell service out here. He needs help."

Based on the desperation in his eyes, the break had been bad. The man was clearly concerned.

Autumn glanced above her at the clouds that were becoming darker and darker by the moment. She didn't have much time to make her choice. She would radio for backup, she decided.

Then she would go and try to help the man herself.

Because if his broken leg wasn't dangerous enough, the approaching storm was.

Before the thought had time to fully develop, gunfire rang out in the distance.

Her back muscles tightened.

It appeared a trifecta of trouble had found them. Autumn braced herself for whatever waited ahead.

Derek Peterson's lungs tightened, and his gaze swerved to the park ranger's as the sound of someone shooting echoed across the mountains.

"It's probably hunters," she said, her voice as calm and steady as her gaze.

"I wasn't aware people hunted around here in October." He wasn't an outdoorsman himself, but he knew that the season didn't start until November.

"They're not supposed to, but that doesn't always stop them." Ranger Mercer plucked her radio from her belt. "I'll call it in, along with a request for help."

Derek found only slight comfort in her statement about the gunfire.

He'd never been so happy to see another living soul as he had when he spotted the ranger and her dog. He'd been rushing through the wilderness for what felt like hours. Trying to quickly navigate these mountains had been challenging, at best. As an attorney, he got his adrenaline rushes in the courtroom.

He observed the woman for a moment.

She almost looked too young to be a park ranger. She had auburn-colored hair that had been pulled back into a neat ponytail. Now that Derek thought about it, her hair and her dog's hair almost matched. Both were a lovely shade of a rusty red.

Ranger Mercer put her radio back on her belt. "Help is on the way, but they're probably thirty minutes out still."

"Thank you."

"Where's your brother?" Ranger Mercer asked as she began walking in the direction he'd emerged from. "I want to see him myself."

"We set up camp down by the river," Derek said. "We've been backpacking through the area for the past three days."

She nodded, but her features still looked tight. She was apprehensive about all of this also, wasn't she? Anyone in their right mind would be.

"How did he hurt his leg?" she asked.

Derek took a deep breath. He usually had an even disposition. He had to for his job as an attorney. Besides, all those years in JAG—the justice branch of the military, also known as the Judge Advocate Generals Corp—had trained him to stay cool under pressure. But seeing his brother hurt and having to leave him... it had Derek rattled.

"He was climbing up some rocks when he fell. His leg got caught between two boulders. He managed to get himself out, but his leg...it was torn up." His voice cracked as he remembered seeing the injury. "Just looking at it, the bone was obviously broken. He's in a lot of pain and can't walk."

Her expression remained even. "How long ago did this happen?"

"Probably an hour." Derek continued walking beside her through the forest. The woman seemed to know where she was going, and she kept a steady pace as she moved. Thank God he'd found her when he did. She was an answer to prayer, for sure.

"You did the right thing by coming to find me."

"That's good to hear, because I hated to leave him."

Derek prayed that William was okay. Derek didn't see how a rescue helicopter could get down to the thickly wooded area. He had no idea how his brother would be rescued, considering there was no way William could walk right now.

"These mountains aren't for amateurs, that's for sure."

Derek frowned at her words. She was right. This trip had been tough, had made both Derek and William dig into their adventurous side. The slopes were steep and rocky. The area was lonely and not well traveled. Plus, the weather had been iffy.

"This trip was my brother's idea," Derek said, squeezing through the trees. "I was just trying to help him out. He had an especially bad breakup a couple months ago, and I think he needed to get away."

None of that really mattered anymore, did it? All that mattered was helping his brother. William had always been the troublemaker of the two.

He was younger than Derek by two years, and something about his little brother had always been rowdy. William had been the one in detention. The one who'd gotten into fistfights. Yet he'd also been the one who was the captain of the football team and homecoming king. Derek, on the other hand, was the responsible one. He'd played baseball, studied hard and worked part-time jobs to save money for college.

"What's your brother's name?" Ranger Mercer asked, clucking her tongue at her dog as the leash pulled tight. The canine seemed eager to move ahead.

"William."

The ranger's dog continued to lead her through the

wilderness, acting like he knew exactly where he was going. As they moved forward, he remembered the sound of bullets just a few minutes ago.

"Where are the two of you from?" Ranger Mercer asked.

"I'm from Washington, DC. I'm a lawyer there. My brother works in finance in New York City. We don't get together that often, but we both thought this trip might be good for us."

"Seems like an interesting choice of places to meet." She glanced back at him, as if trying to study his expression.

"My father used to take us camping and hiking in this area when we were boys."

"Sounds nice." Her voice softened.

"He passed away a couple years ago. We thought this could help us get some closure."

"I'm sorry to hear that."

Derek was also. It had been one of the most challenging times of his life. Only a year later, Derek's fiancée had left him at the altar.

To this day, Derek had a hard time trusting people. When the people you cared about the most let you down, whom could you put your faith in?

He still wasn't sure about the answer to that question.

They continued through the wilderness. Thankfully, Derek had a good sense of direction. Otherwise every path would look the same.

Finally, Derek heard the river in the background. In this section, the rapids skipped and hurried over large boulders. Not far from here was Beaver Falls, a one-hundred-foot waterfall. The rapids grew more turbulent as they inched closer to the drop-off.

Earlier, he'd thought the sound was soothing. Now it seemed a grim reminder of what had happened.

Thankfully, they were almost to the area where he'd left William. Thunder rumbled in the distance, and Derek knew he didn't have much time.

Even though the park ranger had called for backup, Derek knew that getting out to this area was going to be difficult for the rescue teams. It wasn't easily accessible, which was one of the reasons that he and William had wanted to come here.

No, Derek corrected. It was one of the reasons *William* had wanted to come here. Derek would've been just as happy hiking the Appalachian Trail or a path a little more well traveled.

"It's just ahead," he said.

"We should walk a little faster." Ranger Mercer glanced up and frowned.

Her expression seemed to confirm that this was a bad situation all around. The weather would not be their friend.

They quickened their pace, just as the wind began to pick up. Derek knew it was going to storm today. He and his brother had set up camp early because of it, knowing they'd need shelter.

"This is the tricky part," he called to the ranger. She probably already knew this area, but he felt inclined to say something anyway.

But they'd reached a ledge. They had to angle themselves through a small opening, walk along the side of a rock wall and then they'd eventually reach the river-bed. Normally people hooked up safety lines here, just in case they slipped. They didn't have time for that, though.

"Watch your step," she muttered.

Derek wasn't sure if she was talking to him or to her dog. Either way, they all needed to be careful.

They squeezed between the rocks and began the challenge of balancing themselves on the rocky cliff. As the ranger stepped in front of him, the rocks crumbled beneath her feet, and she started to slip.

Derek grabbed her arm and pulled her back up. Her wide eyes met his as she murmured, "Thank you."

"No problem."

They continued walking.

Derek hadn't anticipated any of this happening. A medical emergency while they were in the middle of nowhere. The strange thing was that he'd always been a planner. He liked to know what to anticipate. He didn't like surprises.

All of this was like a test. He knew they were going to get through it. He just dreaded the process.

"It should be right on the other side of this boulder." Derek pointed to the moss-covered rock ahead.

Ranger Mercer nodded and took the lead, her dog walking in front of her.

But just as they cleared the boulder, another sound rang out.

More gunshots.

"Get down!" Ranger Mercer yelled.

Derek ducked to the ground just as a bullet splintered the tree beside him.

What was going on?
One thing he knew for sure: those were not hunters.
They were killers.

TWO

As soon as the gunshots faded, Autumn reached for her holstered weapon. As a park ranger, she didn't have to use it often. But Kevin had taught her how to shoot, and she would defend herself, Sherlock and Derek, if she had to.

After another bullet whizzed by, she turned, trying to get a better view of the gunman. She had to figure out where he was.

"Stay behind the tree," she whispered to Derek. "And keep an eye on Sherlock."

She turned and scanned the landscape around her. Finally, she spotted a gunman crouched behind a nearby boulder. The front of his Glock was pointed at her.

A Glock? The man definitely wasn't a hunter.

Autumn already knew that, though.

Hunters didn't aim their guns at people.

Her gaze continued to scan the area. She spotted another man behind a tree and a third man behind another boulder.

Who were these guys? And what did they want from Autumn?

Backup couldn't get here soon enough.

The breeze picked up again, bringing another smattering of rain with it. They didn't have much time here. The conditions were going to become perilous at any minute. The storm might drive the gunman away, but it would present other dangers in the process.

She spotted a fourth man behind another tree in the distance. They all surrounded the campsite where Derek and his brother had set up.

They'd been waiting for Derek to return, hadn't they?

Why? What sense did that make?

She didn't have time to think about that now. Another bullet came flying past, piercing a nearby tree. She heard Derek suck in a breath beside her.

As far as she could tell, only one of the men had a gun in his hand.

That was good news, at least. She'd take whatever she could get.

"What are we going to do?" Derek whispered. "Can I help?"

"Just stay behind a tree and remain quiet," she said. "We don't want to make this too easy for them."

Sherlock let out a little whine, but Autumn shushed the dog. He lowered his head.

The man fired again. This time the bullet split the wood only inches from her.

Autumn's heart raced. These men were out for blood.

Even if these men ran out of bullets, she and Derek were going to be outnumbered. They couldn't just wait here for that to happen.

She had to act—and now.

She turned, pulling the trigger.

A yelp sounded in the distance.

She pressed herself back into the tree, her breathing labored.

Had she just done that? Her head pounded.

She'd had no other choice. Their lives were on the line right now. That still didn't stop the adrenaline—and some unnecessary guilt—from pounding through her.

Movement sounded behind her. What were the men doing now?

"I think they're leaving," Derek whispered, peering between two trees that practically hugged each other.

Surprise washed through her. Maybe they were taking their injured man back to their own camp to get him help. That's what she could hope, at least.

But it was too soon to leave their shelter. She had to know for sure that the men were gone.

Drawing in the last bit of her courage, she peered around the tree one more time. Just like Derek had said, the men scrambled in the opposite direction. One man had his arm around their injured comrade, and they walked away, occasionally glancing back.

"We'll come up with a new plan tonight," one of the men muttered.

It meant that they weren't done yet. These men would regroup, and they would come back.

That didn't leave her and Derek very much time to form a plan.

She waited several minutes until they were well out of sight. Then she turned to Derek.

"Stay here. I want to go double-check that they're gone before we continue."

"But—"

"Just wait here," she interrupted. This was no time

for him to play the man card on her. She was a trained law enforcement officer, and she had to do her duty.

But she had to admit that a tremble claimed her as she stepped out, trying to brace herself for any danger that might emerge.

Derek's heart pounded into his chest. The last thing he wanted to do was to stand here while the park ranger investigated whatever had just happened. But were the gunmen really gone? What if they had just moved far enough away to keep an eye on them so they could draw fire again?

Dear Lord, please guard us. Be with William. Build a hedge of protection to keep us safe.

He knelt down beside Sherlock and rubbed the dog's head. "It's going to be okay, boy."

The canine let out a little whine, seeming just as worried as Derek felt.

Derek wished he had a weapon with him, but all he'd brought was a Swiss Army Knife. That didn't do much good in a gunfight, as the saying went.

But who would have thought all of this would happen? He certainly hadn't.

Derek waited, listening. He had to be sure that the men hadn't backtracked and come back this way. But he heard nothing but the wind and the rain. He was afraid the elements would obscure any sound of footsteps.

He squeezed his eyes shut and continued to pray that the ranger would be okay. That nobody else would be hurt.

And what about William? Where was he? Was his brother okay?

There were too many questions right now for Derek's comfort.

A moment later, Ranger Mercer appeared again, a frown on her face. "It's clear. For now. But we need to be quick."

He wasn't sure how to read in between the lines of what she was saying. But something was wrong. He was sure of it. Something the ranger didn't want to voice aloud.

Carefully, he climbed down the rocks toward the campsite he and his brother had set up near the river.

They needed to get William and get out of here. Hopefully, his brother had somehow managed to crawl out of sight and to safety. The best-case scenario was that he was hiding out here somewhere right now.

Derek wished he believed that was true. Another part of him knew better.

"William?" he called.

There was no response.

"Look over here." Autumn pointed to the ground in the distance.

Derek headed toward her and frowned. Blood smeared the dirt and rocks. A lot of blood.

"Was this here when you left?" The ranger's eyes crinkled with worry as she stared at him.

Derek shook his head, a throb beginning at his temples as worse-case scenarios played out in his mind. "No, it wasn't. William broke his leg, but there wasn't any blood."

Reality hit him. Something had definitely happened here in the time he was gone.

"I didn't see him with those men," the ranger said, as if reading his thoughts.

"Neither did I. But I don't know where he might be. The only other possibility that I can think of…" He couldn't finish the sentence.

Ranger Mercer squeezed his arm. "I'll look for him. But then we're going to need to take shelter." She glanced up at the dark clouds overhead. "We don't want to be out in this when that storm hits. It won't be safe for any of us. Okay?"

He nodded, but the throb remained at his temples. "Got it."

"Let's stay together," Ranger Mercer said. "I don't know what these guys are thinking, but I feel certain they're going to come back."

Derek followed Ranger Mercer's lead as she walked around the perimeter of the site, examining everything she passed. Sherlock followed on her heels.

His—and his brother's—tent was still there, along with a little circle of rocks where they'd set up a haphazard campfire ring. Inside the tent, there should be William's backpack, as well as some water.

"I need you to grab something of your brother's." Ranger Mercer paused by the tent, looking like the consummate professional. "Maybe a shirt or some socks."

Derek nodded and hurried into the tent. His heart squeezed with worry as he remembered the carefree time he and William had shared just last night. They'd told stories about their childhood adventures. About fishing with their dad. About sneaking out at night. About taking their father's car for a test drive and being grounded for a month afterward.

How could things change so quickly?

Derek looked for his brother's backpack, but it was gone.

Strange.

Had William grabbed it and then run?

He had no idea.

Instead, he grabbed a shirt that had been left beside the sleeping bag. This would work. He jammed it into his pocket before meeting the ranger again. She stood on a boulder, almost as if keeping lookout. The woman might be small, but she seemed formidable.

"We have to find shelter. Now." As soon as she said the words, the sky broke open. Water fell at capacity, it seemed, drenching them to the bone.

Sherlock barked, as if unhappy with the situation.

The ranger was right. It was no place to be during the storm. Between the cliffs and the slippery rocks, there was a little place for them to take shelter.

Even the tent he and his brother had set up would offer little protection in these elements.

They needed a plan. And they needed it now.

"Follow me," Autumn told Derek. "Stay close and watch your step."

The rain came down so fast that she could hardly keep the moisture out of her gaze. Water continued to soak into her eyes, making all of this even more difficult. Still, at least she'd been able to take some pictures to document the scene—just in case.

The only good news she could think of was that the weather might also prevent these guys from coming after them. But the rain also washed away any evidence that may have been left at the site.

The rain may have very well washed away William's trail also.

But they would have to worry about that later. Right now, they just needed to get to safety.

She searched her thoughts for places where they might take shelter. They need to get to high ground, but not too high. At the top of the mountain, the wind would be crazy. But in the valley, there was a chance of flooding.

Autumn knew this area almost like the back of her hand. At least, she thought she did. But there were thousands of acres within this parkland. It was impossible for someone to have explored all of it.

Despite that, Autumn kept moving forward. Maybe they could find a cave or a cove of trees that would offer them some shelter during the storm. Just as the thought crossed her mind, lightning flashed in the sky, followed by a loud clap of thunder.

The storm sounded so close that Autumn felt as if she was a part of nature. The mountains even seemed to vibrate at the loud noise.

More lightning and thunder followed.

Then she heard a crack.

"Watch out!" Derek yelled.

His body collided with hers. They hit the ground.

As they did, a huge tree crashed beside them. Her foot was mere inches from the massive oak.

Sherlock…

She glanced ahead of her and released her breath.

There he was. Sitting on the trail, tail wagging as he stared at her.

Thank goodness he was okay.

They were *all* okay.

For now.

She shifted, realizing Derek's body was still covering hers.

He offered an apologetic smile before rolling onto his elbow. "Are you okay?"

His blue eyes stared at hers before he wiped his hands down his face, clearing the moisture.

"I am…fine. I think. Thank you."

"Of course."

She pushed herself to her feet and tried to pretend like her body didn't ache from where it hit the ground. Her mind reeled from being so close to this stranger. It made no sense.

"We should keep moving," she muttered.

Derek stood as well.

She glanced down. Mud covered her clothing, but she didn't care. They just had to move before another incident like that happened—only next time with worse results.

"There's only one place I can think of where we'll be safe," she yelled over the wind.

"I'm game for whatever plan you can come up with. I realize there probably aren't that many options out here."

The reality only made this situation more precarious. "No, there aren't. This place…it isn't too far away. I think we can make it before it gets too dark out here."

Derek nodded. "Let's keep moving, then."

It wasn't ideal, but it was going to have to work for now.

Autumn felt better just knowing she finally had a plan.

They walked against the rain. The elements made each step feel like they were fighting twice as hard. The rain sloshed inside Autumn's shoes and soaked through her clothes.

They were going to need a fire to dry off or they'd both be sick.

As they reached a craggy part of the mountain, Sherlock barked beside her.

It was almost like the dog could read her mind and knew where she was headed.

She leaned toward him and rubbed his head. "That's right, boy. Let's go."

She followed Sherlock through the wilderness. They wound between trees and over rocks, all while the storm raged around them.

Finally, the rain let up a moment. Their steps slowed. Maybe they could catch their breath.

"The dog seems like a great wilderness guide," Derek said.

Autumn smiled at Sherlock. "He is. He loves it out here."

"So do you. At least, that's how it seems."

She shrugged. "I used to hate the great outdoors, believe it or not. But after working an office job for years, I knew something had to change."

"What did you do?" He pushed a branch out of the way as they continued climbing upward.

"I was an administrator for a health-care company."

She pushed away the wet strands of hair that clung to her face.

"That's quite a career switch."

Up ahead, the dog easily climbed a boulder, taking a shortcut.

But Autumn's short legs were going to have a harder time with this.

"Come on, I'll help you." Derek scaled the boulder before reaching down to help her.

She hesitated before taking his hand. A moment later, he pulled, easily lifting her to where she needed to be.

For a moment, and just a moment, she lost her breath.

It was probably because of this whole experience. It was overwhelming, even for the most level-headed person. It had nothing to do with the man's firm grip or strong arms.

Collecting herself, she pulled away from Derek and tried to compose herself. What had gotten into her? It wasn't like her to react that way around practical strangers.

"Not much farther," she yelled over the wind.

They continued to follow Sherlock until he stopped in front of an old hunting cabin that had probably been on this land for a hundred years.

As soon as they climbed onto the porch, the pounding rain disappeared. A wave of relief rushed over Autumn.

Now she just needed to get inside and recalculate their next steps.

THREE

Derek glanced around the musty old cabin. It was dark in here, and the place looked like it hadn't been touched in years. Cobwebs hung in the corners, and dust seemed to cover everything.

But it was dry. Hopefully, they would be safe here for a while.

"I know it's not much, but it will do," Autumn said, her gaze scanning everything around them also. "For now."

"Do you think it's safe to make a fire?" Derek thought it was, but he would rely on her expertise since she was the professional here.

"It should be. I check on this place on occasion when I'm in the area. It's fairly well maintained. We're going to need to warm up, because the temperature is supposed to drop tonight. Besides, this rain is supposed to last for a while."

"I'll see what I can do to start that fire."

The ranger nodded. "I'll look for some candles or some light so we can actually see. The good news is I don't think these guys are going to chase us in this weather. It's going to buy us some time. Maybe my backup will be here by the time the storm ends."

"We can only hope," Derek said.

As she began to open and close doors and drawers in the kitchen area, Derek went over to the stone fireplace. Some old wood had been left there. He arranged it, almost like a tent, with the kindling on the bottom and the larger logs on the top. Derek looked through a box beside it until he found a lighter. He tried a couple times until finally he had flame.

He would take whatever blessings he could get.

Carefully, he managed to start the fire. A few minutes later, a steady blaze crackled. He sat on the hearth for a minute, watching the flames and making sure it would keep. The warmth felt good.

"Pass me that light," the ranger said.

He did as she asked. A few minutes later, Ranger Mercer had candles and an oil lantern lit around the perimeter of the place.

Derek glanced around at the high wooden ceilings. It wasn't as bad here as Derek thought. In fact, if someone cleaned it up, the place wouldn't be that bad at all.

Two old couches sat along the walls, forming a living room area, and a small kitchen bumped up next to it. A loft stretched above them, probably with a bedroom or two. Around the corner, he'd guess there was a bathroom.

"It's a good thing you knew where this was." He glanced at the ranger as she studied the oil lantern another moment.

She turned away from the light as if she'd deemed it

safe and paced toward him. "Yes, I am very thankful that I remembered it was here."

He looked down at Sherlock, who had lain beside him, probably trying to dry off near the fire. "And this dog seems to read your mind."

"Sometimes I feel like our wavelengths are connected."

She took her jacket off and sat beside him, rubbing her hands near the fire. She shivered, and Derek could see the goose bumps that popped out on her crossed arms.

"I have some dry clothes and socks you could wear," Derek offered.

"Actually, that sounds great. You should change, too."

A few minutes later, they'd both changed. Derek already felt better. They laid out their wet clothes to dry by the fire.

"Thank you," the ranger said.

"It's no problem, Ranger Mercer."

She glanced at him, something shifting in her gaze as she sat near the fire with him. "You know, why don't you just call me Autumn? We might be stuck together for a while. We might as well be on a first-name basis."

"Very well then, Autumn." He liked her first name. It fit with her red hair and freckles and natural beauty. She wasn't the type Derek envisioned wearing a lot of jewelry or makeup or fancy clothing. She didn't need to. Kind of like nature in the fall didn't need to do a single thing to make people's jaws drop.

A moment of silence stretched between them.

Finally, Derek cleared his throat. "What do you think happened to my brother?"

He saw the flash of concern on her face. "I don't know."

"Do you think those men took him?"

"It's hard to say." Autumn frowned. "If they took him, then where was he during the shootout? Did these men seek him out? Follow him? Or just stumble upon him?"

"I have no idea."

"If these men did have him, why did they wait around for you?"

"Again, I have no idea. But I can't stop thinking about the blood…" The words caught in his throat. "Could a wild animal have gotten to him?"

"I didn't see any animal prints close by. I don't think that's what happened."

"But he was bleeding…" Derek pressed his eyes closed, unable to bear that memory and the what-ifs that accompanied it.

Autumn leaned forward again and squeezed his arm. "I know this is difficult for you. But we are going to do everything we can to get your brother back."

He nodded. But, inside, he knew there was much more to this than either of them could ever imagine.

Autumn felt an unusual compassion and connection with Derek. She'd been in plenty of situations where people were in distress. So she wasn't sure why this time felt different.

But when she looked into this man's eyes, she saw the sadness and the worry there. She wished she could take it away.

Just like she wished she could take away her own

grief from losing her husband three years ago. But she wasn't sure that would ever fade. And if it did disappear, would guilt replace it? Guilt that she was no longer mourning the man she loved the way she thought he deserved to be mourned?

She shoved those questions aside. At least she could be thankful they had shelter and fire.

Instead, she glanced out the window. It was already getting dark outside. There was no way they should venture through these woods at night, especially in these conditions. Today had not turned out the way she envisioned.

The storm still raged outside. The winds slammed into the building, and Autumn could feel it practically swaying around them. Lightning electrified the sky, and thunder filled the air.

The conditions were treacherous on so many levels.

"Have you heard back from anyone?" Derek asked.

"Not yet," she said. "I wonder if the radio tower is down. The good news is that my boss knows that I came out here. If I don't check in, they should send a team to check on me."

Even if the towers did come back up, she knew those gunmen could potentially listen in on anything she said through the airwaves. It would take a little bit of technical know-how, but it was possible. It made her hesitant to give out her location, even when she was finally able to reach somebody.

"How about a cell phone?" Derek asked. "Mine doesn't work but maybe yours does."

"There's no signal out here. I have my phone, but I

just use it for pictures, mostly. It's not going to do us any good."

Derek felt Autumn's eyes on him, studying him. There was no need to beat around the bush here.

"What are you thinking?" Derek watched her expression. "I can see it all over your face. You're worried."

She leaned toward the fire, thankful for the warmth. "Like I said earlier, I think we will be safe here for a while, at least until the storm passes. Darkness is falling, my radio isn't working and the terrain around us isn't safe to travel on."

"So we wait here until morning?"

She nodded. "I think so. This isn't what I had planned, but we don't have much choice."

"And then?"

She considered his question a moment. The smart thing to say would be that they should go back to the parking lot where she'd left her SUV and wait for help. But she knew that Derek was anxious to find his brother.

And Autumn had the best opportunity to help him to do that. She'd seen where the man had last been. She had the man's shirt. And she had Sherlock, the best search and rescue dog around, as far as she was concerned.

But she couldn't do anything that would put Derek or Sherlock in danger. She desperately needed backup before they made any moves.

And, of course, all of that was provided they could even get off this mountain.

Would those men still come after them? Based on the look she'd seen in their gazes, the answer was yes.

She didn't know what they wanted, but there was a vengeance in their eyes.

She studied Derek's face for a moment, trying to gather her thoughts. "Any idea why those men may have been at your campsite?"

"I have no idea." Derek swung his head back and forth, his gaze burdened. "Nobody else really knew that my brother and I were out here. The only thing that makes sense is that we happened to be in the wrong place at the wrong time. I heard some people talking at the café I stopped at in town before our hike. They said there are drug runners up in this area. Is that true?"

Autumn frowned at his words. She wanted to think of these mountains as a sanctuary. But that seemed impossible. There was always someone who wanted to abuse what could otherwise be perfect and beautiful. It seemed to be the nature of life.

"Any time you have a secluded stretch of land, there's a possibility that people might want to do illegal things there, out of sight from the rest of the world," she said. "So, to answer your question, yes, there are occasionally drugs that pass hands back here."

"So maybe William got scared, and he tried to find help himself," Derek said, one hand slicing against the other like a lawyer explaining something to a jury. "Instead of finding help, he ran across these guys, and they came back to see if he had left any money at the campsite."

"That's a good theory," Autumn said. "I'm just trying to figure out that blood we found."

Derek visibly flinched as she said the words. "I've

been trying to figure that out as well. Do you have any ideas what it might be?"

She did have one idea, but she hesitated to say it out loud. She didn't want to burden Derek with opinions.

"Go ahead," Derek said. "I can handle it."

She let out a breath and leaned closer to the fire. "If these guys thought your brother had something they wanted, they may have resorted to violence in order to get answers. There's a possibility they pulled a gun on him, threatening him with harm if he didn't fess up to something."

Derek was a lawyer. Certainly, he had a firm grasp on the realities of criminal activities.

"Like where his money or car keys were?" he asked.

Autumn watched as the firelight flickered, softening his face. The look was nice on him, highlighting his strong profile. She looked away and breathed in the smoky scent of the fire, an aroma that brought an unusual amount of comfort.

If only there was any comfort to be found in this situation.

"Yes, something exactly like that," she finally said.

He let out a long breath. "My brother…he's a hedge fund manager. If somehow they found out about that…"

"Then he would be a perfect target," Autumn finished. "And it would explain why he's missing. Maybe these guys grabbed him so they could try to get some money out of him that way."

Derek hung his head, squeezing the skin between his eyes. "I just can't believe any of this. This trip was supposed to bring us closer together, to bring us healing."

She resisted the urge to reach out and touch him, to

offer him comfort. It seemed inappropriate, somehow. "I'm sorry. I know that life doesn't always work out the way we want it."

As soon as the words left Autumn's lips, she realized the truth in them.

No, her life certainly hadn't worked out the way she had wanted it to, either.

But now, more than ever, she wanted the opportunity to rebound, to find happiness again. Given her current circumstances, she wasn't one hundred percent sure that was going to happen.

There was too much on the line.

Mainly, her life.

Derek saw the emotion pass through Autumn's eyes. She understood pain, didn't she?

If he knew her better, he would ask her what she was thinking about. But he hardly knew the woman at all, though in some ways it felt like they had known each other years. What they had experienced today seemed surreal, and it had bonded them faster than normal.

But none of that mattered. Hopefully by tomorrow at this time, they would have found his brother and would all be on their merry ways.

He grabbed his backpack and pulled out some water. "Would you like some?"

"I have enough to last me and Sherlock tonight." She grabbed the small drawstring bag she'd brought with her and found the collapsible bowl she'd brought for Sherlock. Then she twisted the cap off and poured her dog some water.

Once the dog was happy, she took a long sip herself.

Derek tossed her a granola bar. "How about one of these?"

"That sounds great. I didn't realize how hungry I was." She would save part of this for the dog also. She had some treats for him, but they weren't enough to keep the dog satisfied for too long.

"You from around here?" Derek asked, figuring that question was safe enough.

"I grew up not far from here, in western Maryland. How about you? You said you live in DC now?"

"That's right. I grew up in Northern Virginia, though."

"You said you're a lawyer?"

"For a long time, I worked for the military. I was an attorney for JAG."

Her eyes brightened with curiosity. "Were you?"

"I just got out a couple years ago. It was okay. But it was time for me to move on. I can't say I regret it. Now I'm in private practice."

It had been hard to describe the feeling. He'd just known he needed a change. After Sarah had broken up with him, his life had felt out of balance.

He'd hoped the career change might bring clarity, but it hadn't. At least he was able to choose his cases now.

"Do you like being in private practice?" Autumn took a bite of her granola bar.

"It's what I've always wanted to do. My mom died when I was nine."

"I'm so sorry to hear that."

"She was in the wrong place at the wrong time. She went into the bank to deposit a check, and some men came into to rob it. She got caught in the crossfire. I knew after that happened that I wanted to do something to make sure guilty men and women got the justice they deserved."

"It makes sense. Do you and your brother go camping together often?" She stoked the fire.

"No, I can't say that. In fact, we've drifted apart over the years. I thought this trip would be good for us. I had no idea I would be so wrong."

"I'm sorry to hear that." Autumn stood and walked toward the window.

Derek watched her, knowing exactly what she was doing. She was looking for any signs of trouble. They'd be foolish to let down their guard. He knew that also.

More thunder and lightning surrounded them. The sound seemed to echo across these mountains, making the noise seem even louder and stronger than normal.

Sherlock didn't seem to mind. He remained by the fire, seemingly content just to warm up.

"Is there anything I can do?" Derek asked. He hated how things had spun out of his control. Now he was at the mercy of nature, the mercy of this mountain and the mercy of this park ranger.

Autumn shook her head. "I don't know what to do except wait. I'll try my radio again, but I don't have much hope. Not with the storm going on."

Derek understood where she was coming from. Maybe once they both had time to dry off, they could figure out what they were going to do once they left this cabin.

Just as the thought entered his head, Sherlock let out a low growl.

Derek and Autumn's gazes met.

What did Sherlock hear that they didn't?

FOUR

Autumn knew what her dog's growl meant. Sherlock heard something. Probably outside the cabin, something that their human ears hadn't been able to pick up on.

Maybe those men were just brazen enough to come out in this weather to find them.

If that was the case, they must be really desperate for whatever it was that they wanted. She couldn't let on to how much that thought terrified her.

Autumn had to think quickly.

"Derek," she rushed, popping to her feet. "Can you lift up Sherlock and carry him up that ladder to the loft?"

His eyes narrowed with curiosity. "Sure, but what are you going to do?"

"I'll be up there in a moment. Just go."

He stared at her one more minute before nodding and lifting the dog up onto his shoulder. But he still seemed hesitant as he climbed the steps.

As soon as he did, Autumn hurried around the cabin and blew out the candles. She didn't have time to put the fire out, so it was going to have to stay. For now.

One last thing, she went to another door on the other side of the cabin and cracked it open.

She hoped her plan worked.

She grabbed her jacket and backpack before climbing up the ladder herself.

As soon as Autumn reached the top, she pulled the ladder up and out of sight. She leaned closer to Sherlock, who'd been standing near the edge, watching everything.

"Quiet, boy," she whispered.

After moment, the canine seemed to settle down.

She patted her hip. "Come on."

She, Derek and Sherlock quietly shuffled to the back wall, into the shadows there. The space was deep enough that no one should be able to see them—if they planned this right.

Would this work? Autumn didn't know. But she hoped so.

A moment later, voices drifted inside. She held Sherlock to her chest, praying he remained quiet. The dog was usually obedient, but she could feel the tension in his body. He knew danger was close and was poised to act.

The door screeched open, and footsteps sounded inside. Then more footsteps. And more.

Autumn exchanged a glance with Derek, and she saw the trepidation in his gaze as well. He knew how serious this was.

Had all four men come to see if they were here?

Autumn held her breath, praying for the best.

But she could feel the danger in the air.

After several minutes of listening to their footsteps,

one of the men finally spoke. "They must have heard us coming and went out the back door. They must have left fast, because the fire's still going."

"What do you want us to do?"

"Let's search the surrounding area. They couldn't have gotten far."

"The only place in the cabin we haven't checked is up there."

Autumn pressed her eyes closed. If her plan worked, those men wouldn't be able to get up here. The loft was extra high. Hopefully these men would just think that the ladder had been lost.

Hopefully.

Autumn squeezed Sherlock harder, prayed more fervently.

"Maybe if we tip the couch on the side, we could lift somebody up there?" one of the men suggested.

"I suppose it's worth a shot, but I have a feeling they're long gone. Otherwise, why would the door be open?"

"Maybe we could torch the place," one of the men suggested.

Her breath caught. *Please, no...*

"It's a little wet outside for that, genius," one of the men said, the one who appeared to be the leader of the group.

Autumn heard something moving across the floor. Probably the couch. Those men were scooting it closer to the loft, weren't they?

But would her plan work? Even if they tilted the couch, how would they climb up it?

She heard a bang, and then one of the men let out a yell. "Rats. There are rats in this couch."

Scrambling and some cursing sounded below.

Maybe that would work in their favor.

"Let's start outside," that familiar voice said, the one who sounded like the leader. "We're wasting time in here. We can't let them get away."

The footsteps left the cabin.

Autumn looked at Derek and shook her head. They couldn't afford to move. Not yet. Not until they knew if these guys really were gone.

Even if the men were outside, that didn't mean that they weren't going to come back.

She probably had four more bullets in her gun. But she knew that these guys would not come back unprepared this time. She had to save that ammunition until she needed it the most.

Derek could hardly breathe. He'd been in plenty of sticky situations as an attorney, but none like this.

Thank goodness Sherlock was a good dog. Otherwise, the canine could have easily given away their location. One wrong move and…

Autumn put a finger to her lips, indicating they shouldn't move. His thoughts exactly. They couldn't risk anything giving away their presence, not until he knew for sure that these men were gone.

Thank goodness for Autumn's quick thinking when she'd left that door open. She'd probably saved their lives.

Derek stole a quick glance at her. Even though it was

dark in the room, whenever lightning flashed outside, he caught a brief glimpse of her features.

He'd never felt such instant admiration for someone else. Autumn was not only smart, brave and strong, but she was also beautiful. The combination was enough to make his head spin.

Not that right now was the time to think about these things. But he needed *something* to think about, something other than the impending danger they were in.

Survival.

That's what he needed to think about. And, in order to survive, he needed to find answers.

His mind went back to William again. Where was his brother right now? Derek prayed fervently that his brother was alive and that he wasn't suffering too much. But between the broken leg and the bloodstains...

Worry gripped him.

He didn't even want to think about it. How had such a simple camping trip turned into this? It seemed nearly impossible, almost surreal. All of this seemed like a nightmare.

But it wasn't.

This was all too real.

Sherlock continued to sit alert beside them, the dog's intelligent eyes staring forward as if waiting for the command to attack. Autumn sat beside the dog and rubbed his back, occasionally whispering assurances into the canine's ears.

The two were quite a team, and Derek wondered what their story was. He wondered about the sadness in Autumn's eyes. He wondered about her life before this point.

But if he asked too many questions, she might also begin to ask him questions. Maybe it was best if they both kept their distance. Hopefully this would be over soon, and they'd both return to their normal lives.

Hopefully.

He listened. More thunder roared across the sky, just as loud as ever. The fire spilled light in the room in front of them, but the flames seemed to be dying. Along with that would be any warmth that it had offered.

Autumn and Derek remained in the shadows in the corner behind the bed. Out of sight from anyone who might be looking for them from above.

Certainly, those men were still out there. Still searching. If he and Autumn had tried to run, no doubt they would've been found and discovered. The terrain, the storm and those men were unrelenting.

But how were they going to get out of the situation? What if the men didn't leave? What if they simply waited for Derek, Autumn and Sherlock to return? The three of them couldn't stay up here indefinitely.

That was when he heard more footsteps.

His heart rate quickened again.

The men were back. Their voices stretched upward.

"They got away," one of the men said. "I don't know how they did it, but I can't find them anywhere. And the rain is soaked through my clothing. I can't see anything, and I'm ready to call it quits."

"What did I tell you about quitting?"

There was that voice again. The voice of the man who was obviously the leader of the pack. He sounded meaner than the rest, harder.

But his voice was also missing the edge he'd expected. These men almost sounded cultured. They didn't strike him as drug runners.

Derek's curiosity grew even more.

"What do you want us to do now?" another voice asked.

"There's not much else we can do here. We can start tracking them again in the morning, as soon as the storm has passed."

The men didn't say anything for a minute. Finally, someone said, "You're right. Let's get back to the camp and check on our guy there. We don't want to leave him alone too long now, do we?"

Derek's heart lodged in his throat. Were they talking about William? It was the only thing that made sense.

His muscles bristled. They did have his brother, didn't they? The good news was at least William might still be alive.

"Okay, let's get back before it's too late," the leader barked. "First thing in the morning, we're searching again. We're not going to stop until we find these guys and we get what we want."

Derek glanced at Autumn. That didn't sound good.

He had no idea what it was exactly that they wanted. Part of him didn't want to find out. But, for his brother's sake, he would have to.

Autumn released her breath. The men were gone. She was pretty sure this time they were really gone. But she still needed to be cautious.

That had been close. But she, Derek and Sherlock still weren't out of the woods yet.

"What do we do?" Derek whispered. "What do you think?"

That had been all Autumn had been able to think about. How she could get everyone out of this intact and unscathed. She wished there was an easy answer, an easy solution, but there wasn't.

"I think we need to stay here for tonight," she finally said. "Up in the loft. Then, before sunrise, we can sneak out again and go for help. I'm hoping my radio will work by then."

Derek nodded slowly in agreement. "Who are those men? Do you have any idea?"

"None," Autumn said. "I was hoping you might. It sounds like they have your brother."

"That's what I thought, too." He let out a sigh and leaned back against the rough wood wall. "What a nightmare."

She could only imagine what he was going through right now. She wished she could do something to ease his pain, his anxiety. But she was in survival mode. She had to keep them alive and get them out of this situation.

Then she would think more about his brother.

"I know. And I'm sorry that you have to go through this." She rubbed her dog's head as she said the words.

"Does this happen often in your line of work?"

"Missing people? Yes. But a gang of gunmen chasing me through the woods while it's storming outside? No. Never."

He let out another sigh. "At least there's a little bit of warmth up here. And the storm may be passing."

"That is good news," Autumn said. "But there's a

big weather system out there. I'm not sure we've seen the last of it, not if forecasters are correct."

She felt Derek studying her for a minute. She wanted to look away, but she didn't let herself. Was the man curious about her?

"How long have you and Sherlock been together?" he finally asked.

"Three years."

He leaned against the wall, an arm propped on his bent knee. "Did you always want to have a canine on the job?"

How much should Autumn say? The man seemed nice enough. And she had nothing but time to kill right now. Yet, at the same time, she valued her privacy. She didn't usually get personal with people while on the job.

"I actually found Sherlock on the side of the road when I was driving home from my husband's funeral," she finally said.

Derek's eyes widened. "I had no idea. I'm sorry to bring it up."

"It's okay. Sherlock just happened to be in the right place at the right time. I couldn't find his owner, and nobody claimed him, so I decided he could stay with me."

"Sounds nice."

"He seemed to have a knack for finding things, so I started training him for search and rescue. He was a natural. We've been best friends since then." She rubbed the dog's head, and the canine leaned into her.

"It does sound like he found you at just the right time, doesn't it?"

They exchanged a glance, and Autumn felt her

cheeks heat as she realized she'd allowed herself to become vulnerable with this man she didn't even know.

"Yes, you're right." Her throat burned as she said the words. "Sherlock has been a real lifesaver, in more than one sense."

Derek still studied her face. "If you don't mind me asking, how long were you and your husband married?"

"Only a year and a half. He was jogging one day and had a heart attack. He hadn't had any problems until that point. The doctor just said it was a fluke." As Autumn said the words, numbness filled her. For so long, the pain had been fresh. With time, the shock factor had worn off as reality set in.

"It's hard. I can't imagine."

She glanced at his hand, ready to turn the attention away from herself. "Are you married? I don't see a ring, but not everybody wears one."

"No, I'm not. I was engaged, but my fiancée broke things off."

"That stinks," Autumn said. "I'm so sorry to hear that."

"So am I. But everything happens for the best, right? That's what you've got to believe in this kind of situation." He sounded like he believed the words, like he'd lived them.

Autumn had to admire that.

"You have no choice but to move forward, so you have to look for the best in it, I suppose," Autumn said. "Even in this situation."

Could good come from these dire moments? Every obstacle was the opportunity to draw closer to God. That was the case now as well.

"Yes, I suppose even in this situation," Derek echoed.

The two of them shared a glance.

She felt like she'd known this man much longer than she had. Sharing the same belief system could do that. She was grateful to be stuck with someone like Derek.

She shifted her thoughts back to survival, though.

"How about if I take the other side of the loft and you can stay here?" Autumn said. "We should get a little bit of shut-eye for now. Don't you think?"

"Seems like a good idea." Derek drew in a deep breath. "Thank you for everything you did for me today, Autumn. You too, Sherlock."

Autumn offered a smile. Derek was pleasant to talk to. Surprisingly so. But she needed to be careful and not open herself up too much. It wouldn't be wise.

Besides, she was going to need all the energy she could afford tomorrow if she wanted to get them out of this situation alive.

FIVE

Derek couldn't sleep. He'd found some old blankets in a trunk up in the loft and had laid them out on opposite sides of the room, well out of sight of anyone who might come back into the cabin. They were fairly clean, all things considered.

His lack of sleep wasn't because he wasn't comfortable. It wasn't even because he was cold.

It was because his mind wouldn't settle.

It felt unfair that he might rest when he had no idea what his brother might be going through.

That was what it all boiled down to.

Derek let out a sigh.

He couldn't see Autumn across the room, but he would guess she wasn't sleeping, either. Too much was on the line right now.

They could both feel it.

Danger seemed to tinge the air.

Finally, his watch showed that it was 4:00 a.m. Autumn must have been watching the time as well, because he heard her sigh. A minute later, little doggy footsteps clicked across the wooden floor toward him, and Sherlock greeted him with a wet nose.

He rubbed the dog's head, finding strange comfort in the canine. He'd always wanted a dog, but his old job hadn't allowed him to get one. He'd worked too many late hours.

Maybe that would change when all of this was over.

"Good morning." Autumn ran a hand through her hair as she stood on the other side of the room. "Did you get any rest?"

His heart lodged in his throat. Something about the way she looked right now did something strange to his pulse. She seemed younger, more vulnerable. The look made her seem more human and less superhero.

Then again, maybe these odd circumstances were doing something to his mind. He felt an unusual connection with the woman. It would be the same for anyone in this situation, he felt sure.

He remembered her question. *Did you get any rest?*

"Not really," he finally said, stretching out his back. "How about you? Did you sleep any?"

"No. I had too much on my mind."

"I understand."

She held up a map in her hands. She'd obviously been looking at it, planning today's escape.

"I'd like to get a head start back before the sun comes up," she started. "We need to make sure the men don't head back this way."

"Understood," he said. "I'd prefer to get out of here before those guys decide to come back as well."

Derek dreaded thinking about running into those men again. He had a feeling that would be unavoidable, however. If he wanted to get his brother back, he didn't see how that would happen without a confrontation.

As Autumn started to lower the ladder down to the floor, he crossed the space and helped her. She started to go down, but he touched her arm, stopping her.

"Let me," he said. "I'd like to check things out first."

"I don't mind—"

"No, really, let me."

She stared at him another moment before nodding. "Okay, then."

Derek had gotten them into this mess. He preferred to be the one on the front lines in case something happened right now. It didn't matter if this was her job or not. He felt responsible for them right now. Even the park ranger needed someone to watch out for her.

Carefully, he climbed down, trying not to make any unnecessary noise. As he reached the floor, he glanced around.

He saw nothing and no one.

The cabin looked just as they'd left it last night, other than the couch that had been turned on its side.

But just because he didn't see trouble, it didn't mean they were safe.

Derek didn't know much about these guys, but he wouldn't put it past them to have somebody staked out outside, just waiting for any sign of movements. Those men struck him as that type.

He'd dealt with plenty of dangerous criminals in his job as a lawyer. Just never while he was this isolated in the wilderness. The legal system was usually his battlefield. It seemed much safer right now than their current situation.

He remained on the edge of the room, moving quietly. As he reached the window, he peered out.

Darkness stared back. Of course. He wasn't sure what he had expected.

He grabbed a fire poker and held it in his hands as he opened the door. At least it would be something to defend himself with, if he needed it.

As he stepped out, the old deck creaked under his feet. Nature seemed to grow quiet around him, as if it sensed his presence and waited for his next move.

The outside still smelled like the storm—heavy rain and damp leaves. Occasionally, he heard random drops tapping against the foliage on the ground, the moisture falling from the leaves above. The wind was brisk outside, and the temperature was probably twenty degrees cooler right now than it had been yesterday. Thankfully, his clothes had dried off last night.

Carefully, he walked along the deck, listening for any strange sounds. His gaze scanned the dark woods for any out-of-place movements.

He saw nothing. No one made any moves.

Relief washed through him. That was a good sign.

He continued around the deck, which stretched around the entire house. After he'd been around the whole place twice, he went back inside. If there was anyone out there, they were still hiding and weren't triggered into action by his presence.

Derek hoped that was a good sign.

He looked back up into the loft and called, "I didn't see anybody. And it's not raining, but it is cool outside."

Autumn poked her head over the side and nodded. "Great. Can you help lower Sherlock?"

"Of course." He scaled the rickety ladder and took the dog into his arms. Carefully, he climbed down and set the canine on the floor. Sherlock shook off, almost as if the dog had too much pride to be manhandled like that.

Derek couldn't blame the beast.

As Autumn climbed down, he waited at the bottom, just in case she needed a hand.

Halfway down, one of the rungs broke. She began toppling backward.

Before she hit the ground, Derek reached out. She landed with an *oomph* in his arms.

Her nervous gaze fluttered up to him, and she said nothing for a moment. Instead, they stared at each other, some type of understanding passing between them.

Finally, Derek lowered her back to her feet.

Autumn brushed herself off, obviously flustered. "Thank you. Again. First the boulder and now this."

"No problem. I'm glad I was here to help."

Was that a rush of attraction he felt toward her? Had she noticed also? Sure, the woman was beautiful. But that didn't mean Derek was looking for any sort of romance right now. He had a feeling that Autumn would say the same.

Derek mentally brushed himself off and nodded. "I guess we should get going."

Autumn nodded and rubbed her throat, almost as if she'd felt it, too. "Let's go."

Autumn couldn't seem to get herself together. She attributed it to the fact that the rung on the ladder had broken just as she had stepped on it. That had to be it.

Her jitters had nothing to do with the fact that Derek had caught her. That she caught a whiff of his aftershave. That she'd felt his strong arms.

Was it possible that he could still smell that amazing after all this time in the rain and in the wilderness? She didn't know, but she definitely picked up on his piney scent. And she liked it, whether she wanted to or not.

She cleared her throat, hating the fact that she felt at odds with herself.

"Sherlock will alert us if anybody's hiding and just waiting for us to go past," she said. "If my calculations are correct, the parking lot should take us about an hour to hike back to. My SUV is still there, so we can go for help."

She pulled out her map and showed him their intended route.

"Did you try your radio again this morning?"

She nodded. "I did while you were out. There's still no signal. The towers must have gotten knocked out in the storm. It's the only thing that makes sense."

"The cold front really did some damage, didn't it?"

"It did. I'm nervous about what might be in store for today as well. We're going to need to watch our steps. If either of us gets hurt, I'm not sure we'll ever get back. We can't risk that."

As she said the words, something changed on Derek's face. Maybe reality had been driven home. Maybe he felt more determination than ever.

She didn't know.

They walked toward the door. Before they stepped outside, Derek grabbed her arm to stop her from exiting.

"Look, Autumn," he started. "I really appreciate all the help you've given me, and I'm really sorry that I got you in this situation in the first place. Truly. But I can't go back to the parking lot with you."

Certainly, she hadn't heard him correctly. "What do you mean?"

"I have to find my brother. I can't leave him out there with these men. I have to help him."

"That's exactly what we're trying to do—help him. I just need backup to make it happen."

Derek shook his head. "I'm not sure we have time to get that help. If William is hurt, time is of the essence. I need to get to him now."

Certainly, he wasn't thinking this through. If he was, he'd see the error of his way. There was no good outcome to them confronting those men.

She had to talk some sense into him. "What are you going to do if you do find him? How are you going to help him then?"

He shrugged. "I don't know. I haven't thought all of this through. However, he needs me, and I can't let him down."

Autumn touched his arm, trying to break through to him. "Derek, there's no way you can take on four gunmen by yourself. You're foolish if you think you can. The only thing you're going to do is get yourself killed also." She needed to get through to him before he did something he regretted.

"I know it might sound foolish. I'm usually someone who likes a plan. But what if backup isn't coming? What if we can't get out of this area? Then what? Then we just lost an hour, and we're going to have to come back out this way anyway."

Autumn let him get his questions out. It was only fair to let him voice the thoughts aloud. But she wasn't sure what he was getting at.

Derek shifted. "Look, I'm not asking that you come with me. I don't want to put you or Sherlock in danger. I'm just saying that I won't be able to live with myself if I walk away right now."

Autumn stared up at Derek, not sure if she admired his stance or if she should shake him. But she supposed if she had a sibling or a loved one in the situation, she would do the same. At least she had a gun with her.

The weapon would help them, for a while, at least. And Derek did have a good point about the roads. If they were washed out, which Autumn suspected they were, then going back to the parking lot would serve no good except to get them to a vehicle.

"You don't even know where you're going, do you?" Autumn asked.

The man might be a great attorney, but he didn't seem like the type who could navigate this forest like she could. She knew this land—she'd experienced it. Derek was strong and capable, but it still wasn't safe to send him out alone.

"I was hoping you might point me in the right direction before you left." He stared at her, his gaze intense yet humble. His blue eyes were warm and intelligent. The start of a beard shadowed his face, and his hair was just short enough that it didn't have to be styled.

She hid her smile. "Even if I pointed you in the right direction, you probably wouldn't find your way back to your old campsite. No offense."

"No offense taken," he said.

Autumn had to make a choice. She knew what the right thing to do was. She had to help him. She just hoped that they didn't both end up dead.

"Come on," she said. "I'll take you where you need to go."

He tilted his head. "Are you sure?"

"I'm sure. But if I'm going with you, then we're going to have to set some ground rules. One of those is that we have to be smart here. No sudden moves. No trying to be a hero. We simply try to find your brother and continue to try to get help. Understand?"

He nodded, gratitude evidence in his rolling voice. "I understand. And thank you."

Though Derek didn't want Autumn to put herself in danger, he was grateful that she and Sherlock were there to help him navigate this wilderness. Truthfully, this was the type of place a person might get lost and never be found.

The place seemed vast and overwhelming. He had chosen to use his time at law school studying rather than out in nature. Right now, that seemed like a mistake.

Autumn turned her flashlight on and aimed it at the damp ground. Footprints had been left in the mud there. "What do you say we try to follow these tracks and see where the men went?"

"I think that seems like a great idea."

She leaned down and said something to Sherlock. He barked back at her. Then the dog took off ahead of them, pulling at the leash.

Derek and Autumn followed. As they moved, Derek's senses remained on alert as he waited for any surprises. He knew that those gunmen weren't the only dangerous thing out here. There were also wild animals and hazardous cliffs, not to mention the mudslides and the flooding. So much could go wrong.

He briefly squeezed his eyes shut and lifted a prayer. *Dear Lord, please watch over us right now. Keep us safe. Be with William also. He needs you in more than one way. Protect him. Please.*

They continued to follow those footsteps. Sherlock was a great dog, so intelligent and so good at doing this. It was one of Derek's first times seeing a working dog like this, and he was impressed.

He and Autumn didn't talk as they walked. It was better if they stayed quiet, he figured. Just in case anyone was out there watching or listening.

Not far into their trek, Autumn paused in front of him and raised her hand back to stop him. He leaned over her shoulder, trying to see what was going on.

As she shined her light down on the ground, he saw a little stream.

"This isn't an actual creek, but runoff from the rainwater," she told him. "We need to be careful when crossing this."

Sherlock looked back at them before sniffing in circles.

"What's the dog saying?" Derek asked, certain that something was wrong.

"He lost the trail and he's trying to find it again."

Derek's pulse pounded in his ears as he tried not to lose hope. "Is that unusual?"

"No, it's not. Especially not with the rain like it is. Sherlock is a good search and rescue dog, but he has limitations. I have a feeling this runoff may have covered the trail."

"And if it did?" What did that mean for them finding William? Derek couldn't stop the question from echoing in his mind.

"If that is the case, then we are going to need to recalculate."

He didn't like the sound of that. Everything seemed to be going so well. They'd appeared to be on track to possibly find William. In Derek's mind, there was a chance that they might even arrive at these men's campsite before the sun rose and surprise them.

Now it looked like it wasn't going to happen.

"Can't we just follow the runoff?" Derek asked.

Autumn continued to stare ahead. "It's not safe. It's slippery, and that water is stronger than you might think it is. Plus, with all the drop-offs around us…it could be a death wish."

"What do you suggest that we do?"

She looked up and to the side, as if using her experience to calculate their next step. "If we have lost their trail, then it's going to be hard to figure out exactly where they are. We could wander around out here for days and not find these men. We need to have an idea of where they might be first."

"I agree." What she said made sense.

"The only other thing that I can think of is that we go back to your campsite and see if we can pick up a trail there. It's also going to be difficult, though."

"Doing something sounds better than doing nothing."

Autumn's eyes met his. "There's a good chance that your campsite is completely gone by now, too. I just want to warn you of that."

Derek flinched at her words, even though he knew that they could be true. "It's still worth a try, right?"

She stared at him another moment, almost as if ascertaining that he understood the implications of doing that. He must have passed her test, because she nodded. "Okay, then. Let's do it."

"You know how to get there?"

"I can find my way there. I know it was located to the east. And the sun's going to be coming up soon, so we can follow that. Like I said before, though, we're just going to need to be careful and watch our steps. This is dangerous terrain, even for the most skilled hiker."

Derek was beginning to feel more and more confident that coming across Autumn was an answer to a prayer he didn't even know he had muttered.

But they were far from being out of danger. No, if anything, the worst was yet to come.

SIX

Just as the sun began to rise, filling the sky with a touch of muted oranges and blues, Autumn heard the river rushing in the distance.

Except she shouldn't hear it.

That meant that the banks were overflowing.

Just as she had expected...or feared.

If the banks had spilled over, it was going to be nearly impossible for the three of them to follow these men's trails. She wanted to do what she could to help Derek.

She knew how much his brother meant to him. But another part of her felt like maybe they were wasting their time and needlessly putting themselves in danger. The pull inside her stretched tighter, the tension undeniable.

If only her radio would work, all of their problems would be over. Maybe not *all* of their problems, but a good portion of them. She'd tried it again this morning, but it still wasn't working.

She hoped that Derek didn't get his hopes up too high. The chances that they were going to find William and that he was going to be okay were slim. But she didn't dare to say that out loud. Derek had already been through a lot. She could only imagine the worry that he must feel.

He was a pleasant companion. He wasn't too pushy, nor did he seem to feel like he had to be macho in front of her. She appreciated those qualities.

There were definitely worse people she could be stuck out here with.

As the wind swept over them again, bringing a chill with it, she smelled the incoming rain. They were far from being out of the woods—both literally and figuratively. She tried not to worry what the rest of the day might bring, but she had a feeling it would be treacherous.

"Are we close?" Derek asked.

"We're less than a mile away," Autumn said. "I'm hoping we can find some answers once we get to the campsite. I wish we'd looked for your brother's backpack more while we were there yesterday. If I knew then what I know now…"

"I looked earlier but didn't see it. I'm not sure what happened to it. You think there's some kind of clue inside?"

"He probably had some supplies, for starters. Maybe there was even a clue inside as to why all this happened."

"You mean all this may not have been random?" Derek's steps slowed.

"That's a possibility worth exploring, at least."

"I'm not sure I understand."

Autumn swallowed hard, choosing her words carefully. "I'm just saying that those men sounded relatively smart, and the clothes they're wearing are expensive. I don't think they're the type to just hang out in the woods looking for victims. What if somebody followed you and your brother out here?"

"Why would they do that?" Disbelief stretched through his voice.

"You're the only one who can answer that. Or maybe I should say, your brother is." She glanced behind her and offered a compassionate smile. She knew this conversation couldn't be fun.

"I… I just don't know. I don't want to think about William being mixed up in anything that's bad news."

"I understand that. But we need to be open to other possibilities right now."

She glanced behind her again just in time to see Derek frown. She knew it wasn't easy to hear, but the smart thing was just to share that news with him.

"You're really good with this, you know." He moved a branch out of their way as they continued to hike.

"My husband was also a ranger, and he was an avid outdoorsman. He taught me a lot."

"He sounds like quite a guy."

"He was. I still have trouble believing that he's gone." Autumn's heart panged as she said the words. She hadn't intended on saying them aloud, but she had. She didn't talk about her grief often.

"Losing the people we love is always difficult. I don't know what you believe, but I'm always grateful to know that we'll see them again one day, if they were believers."

His words washed over her. Derek was a Christian,

too, it sounded like. "I believe that with all my heart. Prayer and faith are the only things that have gotten me through the past couple years."

He offered a soft smile. "I understand."

Something about the moment made her bond with this stranger feel even stronger. She couldn't explain it, nor did she want to. But the fact that they shared the same faith would get them far. They were going to have to rely on forces far stronger than themselves if they wanted to survive.

Dear Lord, please be with us now. Give us wisdom. Guide our steps. Protect us from our enemies. Keep us safe from nature.

She had so many prayer requests. If they got out of this situation alive, it would only be by God's grace.

Not much farther, and they should be there.

But as they skirted around a boulder, she heard a strange sound and froze.

All of her senses went on alert.

Trouble was close.

She was certain of it.

As if to confirm it, Sherlock began to growl.

Derek felt Autumn bristle in front of him.

Something was wrong, and Sherlock confirmed it. The hair on the dog's back rose, and his tail shot up ramrod straight.

Autumn's hand reached out, stopping Derek in his tracks.

Derek didn't dare to speak. He knew better than to make a sound. Derek glanced around, looking for the source of her distress.

He saw nothing.

Then why did it feel like they were being hunted?

Autumn put a finger to her lips, indicating for him to remain quiet. Then she began creeping forward, tugging on Sherlock's leash so he wouldn't get too far ahead.

Was it a wild animal? The gunmen? Or something else completely?

He didn't know.

But he could hear the river raging in the background.

Yes, raging.

The river wasn't normally like that. It had been perfect for fly-fishing and wading just yesterday morning. Derek was anxious to see exactly what it looked like now. Would it be one more obstacle for them?

Instead of walking straight on the path they'd been on, Autumn began climbing over some boulders. This route would definitely be more perilous, but she had to have a good reason for it.

Derek trusted her—and he hardly ever trusted anyone. As a lawyer, he'd seen too many good people ruined because they'd trusted the wrong person.

He climbed behind her, watching her carefully, not wanting a replay of his brother's accident.

Every time he thought about it, he cringed. Hearing his brother's leg snap as it had been caught between two boulders…it was something Derek wasn't likely to ever forget.

Even thinking of it now reminded Derek of how much danger his brother was in, with or without those gunmen chasing them. If there was one thing their father had taught them, it was that they always needed to have each other's backs. *That's what family is for,* his dad always said.

Those wilderness trips with their father had made a big impact on Derek. But now this area might be forever tainted in his mind.

They continued to climb across the boulders, and Derek imagined how the large rocks had gotten here, all crashed together in one area.

Again, it just showed the power of nature. It could be a beautiful but formidable foe.

His nerves grew tense at the thought.

You had to respect nature, because you never knew what might happen next.

As if in affirmation, the sun disappeared and dark clouds moved overhead. Thunder rumbled in the distance.

They were in for another storm. That meant they needed to move even more quickly. They couldn't afford to be caught out here again. The results this time might not be as good as they had been before.

Should they try to make it back to the cabin? Or was Autumn's car closer and safer?

He had a lot of questions but no real answers.

Autumn paused and put her finger to her lips again. She crouched down and peered over a boulder, making sure that Sherlock was secure beside her.

As she did, a new sound filtered through the air.

A shout, followed by the sound of a bullet slicing the air.

It was the gunmen.

They were here.

And they had spotted them.

* * *

"They have us surrounded!" Autumn ducked down low, pulling Derek with her. She put an arm around Sherlock, making sure the dog was sheltered and safe.

"They must have seen us coming," Derek muttered, squatting down beside her.

"I agree. They were waiting here for us. I'm not sure why, but we'll have to figure that out at a different time."

He stared at her, his gaze intense. "How are we going to get out of this? Do you have any ideas?"

Autumn glanced around, her mind racing. There was only one direction where the men weren't located.

Behind them.

Where the river was located.

But the dangerous, raging river had rapids that would pull them downstream until they hit Beaver Falls. If they went down the one-hundred-foot waterfall, they wouldn't survive. She was certain of that. But they had very little choice here as to what they could do.

An idea hit her.

"Do you have a good balance?" she asked Derek.

"Not bad. Why?"

"I'm going to need you to follow me. And I'm going to need you to trust me." Autumn waited for his response.

Derek nodded. "Okay, then."

"This way, and stay low," she instructed.

Moving carefully, she maneuvered between the boulders. As she reached the other side, she paused and sucked in a deep breath.

There was the river. It looked even worse than she

had thought it might. Not only were the banks swollen, the land around them seemed to be drowning. To make matters worse, the rocks were slippery, and the thunder above them was getting closer.

The timing couldn't be worse.

Despite that, Autumn knew what she had to do. It was the only choice if they want to survive right now.

But who knew if these men were going to back off? In fact, if Autumn wasn't careful, these guys would follow them. That meant they need to move quickly but efficiently.

Autumn rounded one more boulder, this one close to the river. She looked down. It was at least a fifteen-foot drop down into the water below. But it wasn't just water. It was rocky water. Her body would shatter on those stones.

She shuddered.

Thankfully, Sherlock was great with heights and had no problem walking along the ledges there.

There was no way she would ever endure doing this unless in a dire situation.

A situation like this.

She looked ahead and saw the ledge there. Derek seemed to follow her gaze.

"You're kidding, right?" Derek asked.

"I wish I was. But the ledge is about four inches. If we're careful, we can make it."

"But there's nowhere for us to hide if these guys come after us. We're easy targets."

Her gaze met his. "I have a plan for that. Like I said, you just have to trust me."

Finally, Derek nodded and began inching along behind her on the ledge. As Autumn took another step, the rock beneath her feet crumbled. She pressed herself into the rock wall and caught her breath.

Her heart pounded out of control.

Derek exchanged a quick look with Autumn, and he nodded at her again. She continued edging along the wall. By her estimations, she only had another twenty feet until she reached the area where she needed to go.

But if she didn't time this just right, the gunmen would find them before that.

She resisted the urge to close her eyes.

She couldn't let her fear of heights hinder her.

She had to keep moving, to focus on her goal and not her obstacles.

Dear Lord, help us now. We need You more than ever.

Slowly and surely, they made progress, getting closer to the area that could ultimately be their safe haven. Autumn felt certain that these men did not know about her destination. Unless they were regulars in the area, they would have no way of realizing this place was there.

The only reason Autumn knew about this area was because some college students had been stuck here after drinking too much and then taking a hike. Their judgment had been impaired, to say the least. There'd been an emergency rescue in order to get them out, and Sherlock and Autumn were a part of it.

"They're behind us," Derek whispered.

Her heart leaped into her throat. She glanced behind her just in time to see the men on the rocky ledge.

"You might as well stop running!" one of the men yelled. "We're not going to give up."

"Just keep walking," Autumn muttered, ignoring them. They only wanted to incite fear. She couldn't let them win.

"How much farther?" Derek's eyes were wide with anticipation.

But the gunmen weren't as careful as they were. That meant they were moving faster and gaining time on them. She had to resist the urge to move too fast herself and do something careless.

Sherlock's hind legs began to slip, and he let out a whine. Autumn grabbed the leash to hold him up. As she did, Derek reached down and grabbed the canine's hind legs, planting them firmly back on the ledge.

Relief filled her. She couldn't handle anything happening to her dog. This canine had been her sanity for the past three years, and finding him had been like a gift from God Himself.

Another bullet pierced the air, hitting the rock beside her.

Autumn's heart pounded faster.

She couldn't get to the secure location fast enough.

Because men were gaining on them.

And if they saw where they went...

Autumn shook her head. She couldn't think like that. She just needed to keep moving, to keep her eyes on the goal.

Just then a yell sounded behind her, followed by a tumble of rocks.

She glanced back just in time to see one of the men tumble down the cliff and into the water.

SEVEN

Derek heard the commotion behind him. He looked over in time to see one of the gunmen slide down the rocky cliff.

"No!" the man yelled, his arms flailing.

Derek held his breath as he watched the man hit the water. Immediately, his body was swept downstream in the turbulent rapids. The river pulled him under, making it clear he didn't stand a chance.

"Dear Lord…" Derek muttered the prayer, unsure what else to say, to do.

"We have to keep moving," Autumn said.

Derek glanced at her and noticed that her face looked paler. He had a feeling she was the type who'd stop to help, even if these men were the bad guys.

But not in this situation. In this situation, these guys would kill them.

Maybe they had even more reason for their vengeance now.

One of the gunmen shouted, and all of them began scrambling to try to rescue their friend. They attempted to climb down the rocks.

If they weren't careful, someone else was going to be swept away.

Derek pulled his gaze back to Autumn. She nodded in the opposite direction, reminding him that they needed to keep moving.

That was right. They had no time to lose.

He looked back one last time as the men attempted the rescue.

His heart panged with regret.

The man who'd fallen into the river was now gone, out of sight. His friends continued to climb downward.

Derek knew enough to realize there was no hope.

He, Autumn and Sherlock kept moving.

He had no idea where Autumn was taking him, and he had no choice but to trust her. She hadn't let him down yet.

Several steps later, the cliff ended.

At least, Derek thought it did.

But as Autumn continued moving, he realized it was actually a corner. Autumn carefully skirted around it, staying close to the cliff wall.

He held his breath as he watched the dangerous move.

His lungs deflated when he saw her make it to the other side.

Autumn was okay.

Thank God.

The incident that had just happened with the man behind him had driven home reality. They were in a place where one mistake could cost them their lives.

Derek followed her lead.

After this, he'd have no urge to go rock climbing

again. He had gotten his rush of adrenaline for a life-time on this trip.

As the river wall shifted, Autumn climbed onto a boulder. They were still high up. A safe distance from the water. But she nodded for him to follow her lead, and he did.

A moment later, she stepped into a tree...

No, she stepped into the opening of a cave.

This was where she'd been leading him.

Derek stepped inside behind her. It was cold in here but dry. The space stretched back into a narrow tunnel. He didn't know how far it went, but, here at the mouth, it was wide enough to set up a temporary camp.

Staying here would be an answer to prayer. He'd do whatever was necessary to help his brother and get out of here.

He glanced behind him one more time. He didn't see the men.

Last time he checked, they were still scrambling down toward the river to try to rescue their friend. Hopefully, they wouldn't think to check here.

Autumn studied his face for a minute, almost as if she could read his mind. "That man probably won't make it. I hated to see that happen, but there was no way we could rescue him. It just wasn't safe."

"I understand." He looked around at the cave one more time. He needed to focus on their survival right now. "Do you think we'll be safe here? It seems like they might find us. Those men seemed pretty persistent."

"The cliff is still above us, and you can only see this cave if you're standing at the right angle since the opening right here is so narrow. Plus, a tree covers most of the mouth to this place. I feel like we'll be okay. But we need to keep our ears open, just in case."

"How did you even know this was here?"

She told him about the rescue that she'd done here about a year ago. As she did, Derek pictured it all playing out. He was sure Autumn had a lot of stories to tell from on the job. She seemed to love it.

"I can't even imagine what you see in the field," he said, lowering his backpack to the ground.

"You don't want to. It's the best and the worst of people. Their worst nightmares and their greatest hopes... sometimes." She put her bag on the floor also and let go of Sherlock's leash. Her gaze seemed to access the space.

He didn't miss that *sometimes*. He hoped that he wouldn't have to tack that on to the end of their story. He hoped he would be able to find his brother and that everything would be okay, but he would be a fool not to prepare himself for the worst-case scenario. The men after him were ruthless, and if they had his brother... there was no telling what they had done with him now.

He glanced around again at the dark space. "So what now? What are you thinking?"

"We stay here until the danger passes. Those guys are most likely going to help their friend. In the meantime, we lie low and stay quiet."

"I can do that."

"When we're sure they're gone, we can grab some of the dry wood from the shore. I've got a lighter, so we can start a fire in here. This will give us some shelter when the rain starts to come."

"Okay, let's do that."

Autumn paused, and her gaze locked with his. "After the rain clears, we'll figure out our next step. I'm hoping the towers come back up. I don't know if we're going to get out of this without some backup."

Derek heard the concern in her voice, and a shudder went down his spine. This was life or death, wasn't it? It would only be by God's grace if they were able to get out of it.

But he was thankful they had gotten this far.

Two hours later, the rain continued, just as torrential as before. Autumn knew they were up high enough that they should be safe from the floodwaters. But that still didn't stop the flutters from invading her stomach. The situation had become precarious.

Derek found some wood that was dry enough that they were able to start a fire. The heat was welcome. However, she hoped that the smoke coming out of the cave didn't attract anybody.

Nobody in their right mind would be out in this weather right now. Even though those men knew the general direction in which she, Derek and Sherlock had come, there was no way they could get to them right now.

That was good news.

As she sat by the fire staring at the flames, she tried to focus on everything she had to be thankful for. Starting with the fact that Sherlock was okay.

She reached over and ran a hand down the length of her dog's back. He looked up at her with his blue eyes before leaning into her touch.

"The dog loves you," Derek said as he sat across from her, the fire separating them.

"He's been very faithful and very loyal to me. I can't complain about that."

"No, you can't."

Autumn knew she shouldn't bring this up, but she needed to keep her thoughts occupied. For that reason, she asked, "So you were engaged?"

Derek glanced down at his arms, which rested on the top of his knees, before looking back to Autumn. "I was. She actually left me at the altar."

Autumn's eyes widened. "Man, I can't imagine. I'm sorry to hear that. Did she ever give you an explanation?"

"She said that she felt like marrying me was what was expected of her, and she didn't want to live an expected life."

She watched his steady expression. She couldn't read his feelings on the matter. Was he heartbroken? Or did he agree? "And how about you? How did you feel?"

He released a slow breath. "Initially? I was hurt. I'm a planner. I like to know where things are going. But after a while, I realized her words were true. We were great friends, and friendship is a great basis for marriage. But you also need some spark, some passion."

"I can understand that it was still difficult."

He frowned. "It was. People just expected us to get married. And it wasn't that I didn't love her, nor was it the fact that we couldn't have made it work. But we did feel more like friends than we did two people who were madly in love with each other."

"At least you came to that realization. That's important."

Derek nodded. "It was. My life today doesn't look

anything like I thought it would. But that's just all a part of living, isn't it?"

"Yes, it is."

He shifted, pulling his gaze from the fire to Autumn. "What about you? How did you and your husband meet?"

"We were both rangers. We met when I started working here at this park. We couldn't stand each other at first, and then…one day we realized we actually loved each other."

"Sounds like a nice story."

"It was. Kevin was a good guy. The world lost someone good when he passed away."

"Have you dated since?" Derek visibly cringed as the words left his lips. "I'm sorry. I shouldn't ask these questions."

"No, it's okay. I know we're stuck out here with nothing but time on our hands right now." Truthfully, Autumn didn't really mind talking about it, even though she didn't do it very often. There was something about Derek that made him very easy to talk to. "No, I haven't dated very much since then. I haven't really felt the desire to, you know?"

He nodded, understanding in his gaze. "I know that all too well."

She felt such an immediate bond with this man that it scared her. She wasn't supposed to feel this way. She wasn't supposed to feel anything for anyone other than Kevin.

She glanced outside the cave and noticed that the rain was letting up.

A rumble of hunger sounded in her gut. She was

starving. If they were going to be stuck out here much longer, they were going to need more supplies.

"Do you know what?" Autumn said, suddenly feeling restless. "I think I'm going to peek outside for a minute. I'll be right back."

He nodded and said nothing.

Autumn stepped out and discovered her theory was true. The rain was just a drizzle, at least, for a moment. She glanced around but didn't see any signs of the men. If they were smart, they were long gone by now.

Looking down, she saw something on one of the tree limbs below. Was that…a backpack?

It certainly looked like it.

She called back into the cave for Derek. "I need your help."

He stepped outside, and his eyes widened. "It's William's. The water must have carried it downstream."

"That would be a good thing for us. Did he have food inside?"

"He sure did."

"We're going to need to retrieve that."

What was William's backpack doing here? Derek had no idea about the answer to that question, but he saw this as an answer to prayer. The only thing he wasn't sure about was how they could safely retrieve it without being swept away in the floodwaters themselves.

"If you take my hand, I think I can reach it," Autumn said. "It's there at the rocky ledge, and the floodwater's just beneath it."

"Are you sure that's safe?" Concern ricocheted through him as he imagined how this would play out.

Autumn frowned, though the expression quickly disappeared as if she wanted to hide it. "I think I can do it. We need to try at least."

After a moment of hesitation, Derek nodded. This wasn't just something they were doing for fun. This was a matter of survival. If they were careful...

"I'm going to climb down the side, and when I get to that ledge below, that's when I'm going to need you to get on your belly and to hold on to my hand. I'll stretch out and see if I can reach it. Let's just pray this works."

"I've already started praying." Derek's words were true. He wouldn't stop praying until they were safe.

Autumn offered him a soft smile before beginning her descent down the rock wall. Derek held his breath as he watched, but he realized that the woman was capable. Still, in these conditions, nothing was certain.

Sherlock stood beside Derek, watching Autumn also. It was almost as if the dog was worried as well.

Once Autumn reached the ledge below, she looked up at Derek, her gaze intense and focused. "I'm ready now."

Just as he'd been instructed, he got on his belly and reached forward. He took her outstretched hand and held on tightly to it. Whatever he did, he could not let go.

With one more glance back at him, Autumn reached down.

Derek held his breath, praying their plan would work. She could almost reach the bag but not quite.

"Can you move forward any more and still be safe?" Autumn asked.

Derek scooted forward, his chest pressing into the

rock beneath him. He still had enough leverage to hold him up here, but all this made him uncomfortable. It was too uncertain. He liked things to be black and white, right or wrong, up or down. Everything felt like it was in the balance right now.

"How's this?"

With obvious strain on her face, she reached down again. Her arm pulled in his grasp, and if his grip somehow slipped, he knew without a doubt that she'd go tumbling to her death.

He couldn't let that happen.

Autumn gave one more groan and gave it one last try. Her teeth seemed to grit as her lips pulled back with intense concentration.

Her fingers were mere inches away from that backpack. Maybe not even that much. If she could just reach a little farther…

Derek shifted just a little more, praying this wasn't a fatal error.

As he did, Autumn gave one last burst of effort. Her fingers enclosed the handle of the backpack.

She had it!

But it was too early for to feel victorious.

Derek helped pull her back upright until she was pressed against the ledge again. She handed the backpack up to him, the relief on her face obvious.

"Now if you could help me get back up here, I think I want to stay put for a while," she said.

Derek couldn't blame her. He climbed on his knees to give himself a little more arm room. Then he took her hand and helped her climb up the cliff.

As soon as she reached the ledge where Derek was,

she collapsed. Sherlock licked her face, almost as if he understood what she was feeling.

Derek wanted nothing more than to hug her. How many of these situations were the two of them going to find themselves in? One after another, apparently.

"You okay?" Derek placed a hand on her back, feeling like she just needed human touch to let her know she wasn't in this alone.

She nodded and rolled to her side before lying on her back and staring at the sky. Her breaths came quickly, laced with exertion and adrenaline. "Yes, but I did see my life flash before my eyes back there."

Derek lowered himself to the ground, trying to catch his breath as well. "If there's anybody I had to be stuck out here with, I'm glad it's you."

She let her head fall to the side as she glanced at him and a grin stretched over her face. "I appreciate your vote of confidence."

"I mean it. You're…amazing."

"Thank you." She pushed herself up on her elbows before finally sitting up completely. She let out a long breath before saying, "You ready to see what's inside your brother's backpack?"

The brief amount of relief Derek had felt disappeared. It didn't really make any sense why a new grip of anxiety squeezed at him. But despite the illogical nature of the emotion, it was still there.

What if he found something incriminating inside his brother's backpack? He was about to find out. He prayed for grace and wisdom in the coming moments.

EIGHT

Autumn and Derek waited until they were back in the cave before they opened the backpack.

Autumn raised the bag toward Derek. "Would you like to do the honors?"

He shook his head, his gaze burdened with unseen pressures and questions. "You can go ahead. You know what you're looking for more than I do."

She nodded before unzipping the first compartment. She began pulling out some food. Granola bars. Peanuts. Beef jerky. Water.

"Almost all of it still looks good," she said.

That was a blessing, because they were going to need some more nourishment to sustain them, especially if this lasted much longer.

"We sealed everything in airtight bags to protect it against the elements and so that animals wouldn't be able to follow the scent of it."

That would prove very handy now. Autumn didn't know about Derek, but she was hungry.

She continued to dig into the depths of the bag and found a flashlight, a compass and even a blanket that had been rolled up. It was wet, but maybe they could dry it out. It would come in handy tonight.

Some clean clothing was inside, also packed in plastic bags. Derek could certainly wear some of it, and Autumn might even trade in her shirt for one of the sweatshirts in there. Warm, dry clothing sounded nice.

Really nice.

"Nothing out of the ordinary yet?" Derek said, his voice sounding thinner than usual.

Autumn glanced up at him. He seemed more nervous than she had expected him to be. Did he know something she didn't? Was he hiding something?

She didn't think so. She thought she could trust the man. But she had to be careful still. Too much was working against her right now.

Autumn supposed they were about to find out.

As she reached the bottom of the backpack, her hand hit fabric. There was nothing there.

"It's empty," she muttered.

Derek's shoulders slumped, as if he was relieved, and he ran a hand over his face.

"Why are you so nervous?" She studied his face.

"Nervous?" He shrugged before releasing a long breath, almost as if he had decided he should no longer be fake. "William and I have drifted apart in recent years. But he's always been more of the take-life-by-the-horns kind of guy. If he sees something he wants, he goes after it."

"And that's a bad thing?"

"I've always figured that those traits could go one of two ways. He would either be wildly successful or he'd find himself in a heap of trouble. Unfortunately, both of those qualities can masquerade as the other."

"Wise words." Had William gotten himself into some kind of trouble? She hadn't found anything to indicate that. Not yet, at least.

Autumn glanced back down at the backpack. It still felt too heavy, like she'd missed something.

"Let me just double-check a few more things to be certain," she said. "I can't help but feel there's something else in here."

She looked into all of the pockets and zippered compartments one more time to make sure she hadn't missed anything. It appeared she hadn't.

At the very bottom, she felt a zipper. Her pulse raced. What was this?

"What?" Derek leaned closer, a knot forming between his eyes.

She said nothing, simply tugged the zipper, listening as it buzzed around the bottom perimeter of the backpack.

A moment later, a hidden compartment was revealed. Two Ziploc bags rested at the bottom.

She glanced at Derek before carefully pulling the first one out. Whatever was inside, it was lightweight.

But it had been hidden for a reason.

Carefully, she opened it. She wished she had gloves in case this was some kind of evidence. But these were extraordinary circumstances, and right now she just had to concentrate on survival.

She laid the items out on the floor of the cave and studied them by the firelight. The first was a picture of William with a woman.

"That's his ex-girlfriend." Derek scooted closer to see.

Autumn could feel his body heat next to her. The realization caused an unexpected surge of electricity to rush through her, and she had to catch her breath for a minute.

Why was she having this reaction to the man?

She needed to stay focused.

Autumn picked up the photo and stared at a picture of the pretty blonde. "Nice-looking couple."

"That's Brooke. She looked nice, and she knew it."

Autumn pointed at the dark-haired man in the photo. "You and your brother look a lot alike."

Derek leaned closer. "We do. I've always been told that. But if you look at William, you'll see that he has a sparkle in his gaze. It's like he can't contain that little rakish part of himself that is amused by trouble."

Autumn looked up at Derek, more curious than ever. When she realized how close their faces were, she felt the breath leave her lungs.

She had to get a grip here.

She cleared her throat. "When did he and his girl-friend break up?"

He rubbed his jaw. "Probably four months ago. They'd been together for about a year."

"Who called it off?"

"As far as I know, he did. Said there was too much drama."

Autumn nodded and put the photo down, moving on to the next item. It was a string of numbers that had been handwritten on a torn piece of paper—maybe part of an envelope based on the thin line of dried adhesive on one side.

"Any idea what these numbers mean? It's too long to be a phone number." She counted the numbers one more time. "Too long to be a Social Security number as well."

"Could it be a routing number? Maybe to a checking account?"

Autumn looked more closely. "It's a possibility."

"I wish I could tell you that something was familiar. But I have no idea why William might have brought that information with him."

Autumn pulled out the second bag. It was smaller.

A cell phone. She hit the button and saw it still had some power.

"William didn't tell me he was bringing that," Derek muttered.

"Good to know we have that, at least."

Autumn checked the bottom of the backpack one more time, just to make sure she hadn't missed anything. As she did, her fingers brushed something at the very bottom.

She pulled out another bag, and her eyes widened when she saw the stack of money. She fanned the bills out and estimated that there had to at least be ten thousand dollars here.

"Any idea why your brother would be carrying this much money?" She studied Derek's face. Had she believed him too easily? Was there more to his story than he'd let on?

Derek's eyes looked as wide and surprised as Autumn felt. "I have no idea. It honestly makes no sense to me at all. I could understand if William brought a little cash, just in case he needed it. But carrying that kind of money with you? It's like he was just asking for trouble."

Autumn nodded. Her thoughts were the same.

What exactly was William hiding from his brother?

An hour later, Derek had changed into some of his brother's dry clothing. Autumn also donned a pair of his brother's sweatpants and a sweatshirt. The rest of their clothes dried near the fire, which they sat around right now.

They'd all dined on some of the food in William's backpack. Even Sherlock had enjoyed some beef jerky. The dog was just as hungry as the rest of them, and Derek was more than happy to share their stash of food with the canine. Sherlock had been a lifesaver, and they wouldn't be here without him.

But mostly what Derek was thinking about were those items William had brought with him. He could understand the picture of Brooke. Maybe William hadn't gotten over her.

Maybe all the suspicious contents had been left over from something else?

He might've believed that if it wasn't for the wad of cash in that compartment. A person didn't easily forget about ten thousand dollars in the bottom a backpack.

But Derek couldn't make sense of why William would bring that much money. Was his brother planning some kind of escape? To leave from here and start a new life? To pay somebody off when their trip was over? No matter which way Derek looked at it, it still didn't make any sense.

The unanswered questions caused a throb to begin in his head.

He closed his eyes and leaned toward the fire again. Despite everything that had happened, he had a lot to be thankful for. Starting with this fire. This cave. And Autumn, of course.

The woman stared into the flames right now, her face looking pensive as the flickers of orange warmed her features. But he knew her well enough to know her brain never seemed to turn off. Certainly she was trying to think through possible escape routes for this situation.

All of her law enforcement training couldn't have possibly prepared her for all of this.

Outside, the rain continued to fall. Occasionally, he checked the status of the river. It was still swollen, but it wasn't anywhere close to reaching the cave. That was another blessing.

Autumn had chosen wisely when she'd led them here.

With a sigh, Autumn reached down and grabbed the radio again. "I'll try one more time to see if I can reach anybody. It's worth a shot, right?"

"I'd say so."

She pressed the button and spoke into it. "This is Ranger Autumn Mercer. Is anyone out there?"

She waited as static filled the line.

Derek's stomach dropped. It was just like every other time they'd tried to make contact. Nothing.

But they couldn't give up hope. Eventually those towers would be operational again.

Just then, the radio crackled. Someone said something. Between the static, the words all ran together.

Excitement lit in Autumn's eyes. She jumped to her feet and paced toward the cave's opening. "This is Ranger Mercer—who is this?"

"This is Ranger Tom Hendrix. Are you doing okay, Ranger Mercer?"

"Ranger Hendrix." Relief filled her voice. "I can't tell you how good it is to hear your voice. We're stuck out here during the storm and need assistance. We have an injured man."

"We?"

She glanced at Derek. "I'm with a camper whose brother is injured and missing."

A camper? Something about the professional tone of her voice did something to his heart. He'd felt more like a friend than he wanted to admit.

The thought was ridiculous, though. They were just two people who'd been thrown together in extraordinary circumstances, and nothing more. The sooner he realized that, the better.

"There are also some gunmen out here. They've been following us. I have no doubt they're dangerous. They may even be holding someone captive right now."

"What are your coordinates?" Hendrix asked.

"We're just off the Meadow Brook River."

"I don't like to hear that. The roads have washed out. We're still trying to clean up some downed trees as well. The earliest I can see us getting to you is tomorrow evening, and that's being optimistic."

Autumn's shoulders slumped. "What about a copter? Can you send one of those?"

"Not until the storms die down. It's quite the system going over us. It just seems to be lingering here. The rain will die down but, as you probably know, it's not very long before it starts up again. It's just not safe to be out in these high winds."

"That's what I thought. Are ATVs out of the question as well?"

"They are. We can't make it past the river."

"Okay." Autumn frowned and leaned down to pet Sherlock, who'd followed her.

"At least the towers are back up," he said. "I promise you, we're going to get to you as soon as we can. Is there anything else you need?"

"Just a lot of prayers," she said with a frown. She glanced back at Derek and shrugged, as if making sure he was listening.

"I understand. You've got those. The storm spawned a tornado about three miles west from you. Three people lost their homes. Numerous county roads are blocked. And people are in danger everywhere due to the flooding. It's a bad situation for all of us."

"Just get help here soon as you can, okay?" Autumn's voice filled with compassion.

"Will do. Over and out."

As Autumn lowered the radio, Derek knew she was fighting despair. He saw it in her gaze. In the way she nibbled her bottom lip.

She would probably never speak any of it aloud. And he could appreciate that. But the emotion was still there, lingering in the depths of her eyes. This situation was dire.

She walked back toward him but didn't have to say anything. Her frown said it all.

"I'm sorry," Derek said. "I can't shake the feeling that this is all my fault."

"You and your brother couldn't have known when you set up camp that all of this would happen." She lowered herself across from him near the fire.

"No, I suppose we couldn't. But I still feel responsible." Derek was always the prepared one. How had things gone so wrong? Then again, how could someone prepare for all this?

Autumn offered another soft smile. "We'll get out of this. One way or another, we're going to get through it."

She was still thinking about other people, even in the middle of what had to feel like a crisis of her own. That had to be admired.

Just then, her radio crackled again.

Autumn and Derek exchanged glances before she lifted it to her mouth. "This is Ranger Autumn Mercer. Repeat."

"We are looking for you," a deep voice said.

Something about that voice didn't sound professional, not like another ranger getting back to her. No, the person on the other end almost sounded menacing.

"Who is this?" Autumn asked.

"We will find you," the man said. "And we are not going to give up until we do."

Autumn and Derek exchanged a look.

This was one of the gunmen pursuing them. He'd somehow managed to get hold of a radio and had heard Autumn's conversation with the ranger.

Derek's stomach sank at the realization.

These men knew that Autumn, Derek and Sherlock were stuck out here until tomorrow evening.

The good news was that Autumn hadn't given out their exact location.

Still, things had taken another grim turn.

He began praying for whatever tomorrow had in store.

NINE

Autumn didn't like any of this.

The news just seemed to be getting worse and worse by the moment. They were trapped out here with the men. Despite the treacherous situation, their leader had still found a way to taunt and threaten them.

The man was relentless.

She ran her hand across Sherlock's back, thankful for the dog's presence. Sherlock had always brought her so much comfort, even now. She stared into the fire for a minute, mesmerized by the flames and trying to sort her thoughts.

She picked up the photo of William and Brooke again and stared at it. "Is there any chance that somebody could have grabbed William thinking it was you?"

Derek's eyebrows shot up. "What do you mean?"

"Let's just say this wasn't random. Let's say somebody followed you guys out here. What if they saw William with you? Then they realized they grabbed the wrong person and that's why they're coming after us now."

A knot formed between his eyebrows, and he shook his head. "I'm not sure why anybody would come after me."

"You're an attorney, right?" Her voice perked. Maybe she was on to something.

"That's right." He nodded slowly, uncertainly, like he didn't like where this conversation was going.

"You've certainly made a lot of people mad, at least if you're anything like many attorneys. Lawyers make enemies. Am I right?"

He nodded. "I can't deny that. But I haven't had any explicit threats lately, if that's what you're saying."

She leaned closer. "Let's not think lately. Let's just think at all. Has anyone ever threatened your life?"

"Plenty of people, though I think most of those were just empty threats." Derek let out a breath. "I know that's not helpful, so let me think a little deeper here."

He paused, staring into the fire, and Autumn gave him time to think. Certainly, he had a lot of cases to think through. She didn't want to rush him.

"There was one man I put in prison after a drunk driving episode," he finally said. "He got out last year, though, and I haven't heard anything from him. There was another sailor I had put in prison for murder, but he's in there for life. I can't imagine him coming after me now."

"Anyone else?" Autumn stared at him, hoping they'd find some answers through this conversation.

Derek's eyes widened, as if he'd remembered something. "There was this one guy. He went to jail after beating his wife. I know he was up for parole. But he was definitely angry at me. Said that I had made up evidence and things like that. Of course, I didn't. But this guy was in denial. He honestly couldn't see where he had done anything wrong, even though his wife had plenty of bruises to prove it."

Autumn swallowed hard. Was this the information they'd been looking for? If they could figure out who the guys were and why they were pursing them, maybe they could outwit them at this game.

"What was his name?" Autumn asked.

"Owen Perkins."

"You don't know for sure if he got out on parole, though? Right?"

"I've been out here for the past four days, and my brother and I both made a promise not to bring cell phones." Derek glanced at the device that had been found in his brother's backpack. "Obviously, my brother didn't feel as serious about that as I did."

"I guess he didn't."

"What are the chances that we have service out here?" Derek stared at her.

Autumn shrugged. "Honestly, there's no telling. Service is iffy on a good day. But with the storms we've been having…it's anyone's guess."

He grabbed the phone and hit the button. "I need to figure out what my brother's passcode is."

"You have some good guesses?"

"How hard could it be? I'll try his birthday first." He typed something in and frowned.

It obviously hadn't worked.

"Maybe my parents' anniversary…" he muttered.

Autumn scooted closer. "Any success?"

"No, and one more try and I'll be locked out." He paused and pressed his lips together. "There's only one other possibility I can think of. Let's hope this works.

It's the birthday of our childhood dog, Muffins. William always loved that dog."

Autumn's breath caught when she saw the screen on the phone flicker on.

It had worked.

Her gaze went to the battery level. It only had ten percent left. They needed to use that ten percent carefully. There was only one bar—but at least there *was* a bar.

"Should I search for information about Owen Perkins or should we try to call somebody?" Derek stared at her, waiting for her before proceeding.

"Since I've already talked to Ranger Hendrix, I don't think there's anybody else who can do anything for us. Go ahead and search."

He typed in that man's name, and they waited. The phone was slow to load the search results.

But finally, the page filled.

Derek sucked in a quick breath.

"What is it?" Autumn asked.

He turned toward her, his eyes wide. "Owen was released from jail two days ago."

"You really think he is the one who might be out there coming after us?" Autumn asked.

"I think it's a really good place to start at least."

All Derek could think about was the fact that Owen Perkins had been released from jail.

Owen had always given Derek a bad feeling. Something about the man was off and dangerous.

Was it really possible that the man might be coming after him now? He didn't want to believe it. Yet, at the same time, he wanted some type of logic in this situation. Nothing made sense right now.

He sat by the entrance of the cave. It was his turn to keep watch. Sherlock stayed beside him, even though the dog's eyes occasionally closed. Derek was certain that if the canine heard anything, he would be instantly alert.

All Derek saw right now was darkness and the occasional drips of rain coming from the entrance of the cave. The rushing of the river actually sounded rather soothing. If circumstances were different, maybe he would actually sleep well right now.

But too much was at stake. Too much was on his mind.

He glanced back at Autumn. She'd used the blanket that his brother had been carrying with him. She wrapped it over her and used the backpack as a pillow as she laid near the fire.

He was supposed to wake her up at two thirty so they could trade duty. But he doubted he would. She needed her rest, especially if all this turned out to be his fault.

The two of them had talked before Autumn laid down. They decided first thing in the morning, they would try to track the gunmen again. It was the only way they could think of to locate William.

Once they found wherever these guys were staying, they couldn't make a move. They would need to wait for backup. But maybe, in the meantime, they could get their eyes on William and figure out if he was okay or not.

Derek lifted another prayer. He really hoped that his brother was okay. Every time he closed his eyes, images of William being hurt or in pain filled his mind. He couldn't handle it.

William had never been a great little brother. He mostly thought of himself. But that didn't mean he deserved anything bad to happen to him. Derek had always gone to bat for his brother, and he would do it again now.

But he still couldn't understand why William had brought so much money with him.

Derek thought about that number sequence again. What could that possibly mean?

He had to believe that his brother had packed those things on purpose. The money. The photo. The cell phone. Even the name with the numbers below it.

His brother had obviously known something that he hadn't bothered to share with Derek.

A bad feeling turned inside Derek at the thought. Secrets were rarely a good thing. He'd prosecuted enough cases to know that. But would his brother purposefully put them in danger? He didn't want to think that could be true.

Just then, Sherlock's ears perked. He stood on all fours, a low growl escaping from his depths.

Derek straightened and stared outside, trying to prepare for the worst.

He saw nothing.

But the dog had obviously heard something.

He grabbed his flashlight and shined it outside, trying to find a source of whatever it was that bothered Sherlock.

It was so dark. It was hard to see anything, even with his flashlight.

But only one thought remained in his head.

What if those men had found them again?

Autumn jerked from her sleep.

What was that sound?

Suddenly, she forgot all about resting and warmth and getting sleep.

Sherlock was letting them know that something was wrong.

She scrambled to her feet and grabbed her gun. She hurried toward the entrance of the cave and crouched beside Derek as he shined his flashlight outside.

"Do you see anything?" she asked, one hand reaching for her gun.

"No, nothing. Just darkness, the cliff face and rain. Maybe Sherlock only thought he heard something."

She wished for sanity's sake that she could believe that. "No, not Sherlock. His instincts are great. He's never let me down. Can I see the flashlight?"

Derek handed it to her. She shined it outside as well but, just like Derek said, she also saw nothing.

Tension snaked up her spine. What could have triggered Sherlock? Had those men found them again?

She also knew there were other dangers out here in the nighttime, especially in these conditions. The three of them weren't the only ones who were looking for shelter right now.

So were the wild animals who called this place home. The beam of the flashlight illuminated everything around her one more time. She stopped as something reflected back to her.

Two things, actually.

Two eyes.

Probably about six feet from the cave.

Her breath caught.

"What is that?" Derek whispered.

"If I had to guess?" Her throat went dry. "A bobcat."

Derek stared at her a minute, as if making sure he'd heard correctly. "This isn't good."

"No, it's not." She put her hand on top of Sherlock's back, trying to soothe the animal. "It's okay, boy. Heel."

The last thing she wanted was for her dog to get into a fight with a wildcat. She wanted to keep Sherlock safe just as much as the dog wanted to protect her.

"Derek, go grab one of the sticks from the fire. Try to get one that's burning on the end, if you can. That will scare our visitor off for now."

He didn't argue or ask questions. Instead, he rushed over to do exactly as she had told him.

He returned a moment later with a makeshift torch. Autumn took it from him and held it out at the entrance of the cave. As she did, the light illuminated the bobcat. The creature had come closer. He was probably only two feet away now.

Tension filled her as the implications of the situation flooded her mind. This could be deadly.

She prayed it didn't come to that.

Sherlock let out another low growl. He could sense the danger, too, couldn't he?

Autumn just hoped this worked. She had her gun, but she didn't want to use it on the animal.

There had been a wildcat attack two weeks ago. These creatures weren't above doing that, even though they were usually fairly docile unless threatened or sick.

"I don't think the fire is scaring him," Derek whispered.

"Just give it a minute." Autumn hoped her words were true. Normally, experts said to spray cats with water. She didn't have a spray bottle with her, however.

She'd never actually come face-to-face with one of these creatures. She'd seen plenty of them from a distance. But they usually ran away as soon as they saw a human.

This cat might be desperate, though. Hurt? It was a possibility. But she thought it was more likely that the storm had confused the animal. Maybe floodwaters had wiped out its home. She didn't know. She just knew this cat could not come in this cave right now. It would be a fight for the territory, if it did.

"I think it's still coming closer," Derek whispered.

Autumn agreed. That didn't make sense. The cat should be running away from the fire.

Unless the cat was desperate. Desperate usually meant aggressive.

Dear Lord, please protect us now. I know I keep asking that, but I just can't seem to stop. The danger keeps coming.

"Do me a favor," Autumn said. "Go get one more stick. Maybe this one's not bright enough."

Derek rushed away to do as she asked.

When he got back, she held both of the sticks outside the cave and shoved them toward the cat, trying to scare the beast away.

But the glowing eyes just stared back at her.

She had no idea if this was going to work.

TEN

Derek didn't like this. It was one thing to pit man against man. But pitting man against nature was an entirely different story. And both of those things at once?

It was nothing but trouble.

This whole camping trip had just been a bad idea.

"Let me hold one of the sticks for you," Derek said.

Autumn gave him one, and he extended his arm outside the cave. He held the fire toward the cat, praying that it would scare the feline off.

The cat stood defiant.

In fact, it appeared that the creature was slowly creeping forward. An animal that brave…it was unnerving.

"Do you think it wants our food?" Derek asked.

"It's a possibility. As a matter fact, why don't you go get a piece of that jerky right now?"

Derek had sealed everything back up, but he knew animals had great senses of smell. The beast could be hungry for food and could have sensed it.

Quickly, he unwrapped one of the sticks and brought it back to Autumn. "What are you going to do now?"

"I'm going to throw it away from the cave."

"Won't the cat fall into the river?"

"Bobcats are great climbers. He should able to go down there and retrieve it. He'll be okay."

Derek was going to have to trust her on that. It beat the alternatives—being attacked or having to use one of their last bullets.

As the cat continued to creep closer, Autumn held out the food. The cat paused.

Derek crouched back, half expecting the cat to attack.

The next instant, Autumn tossed the food onto the riverbank below.

He held his breath, waiting to see what would happen.

The cat leaped away from them.

Autumn's plan had worked. But how long would they be safe? Would the bobcat return?

Derek released a pent-up breath. "Can we stay here?"

"I'm hoping that's going to hold that cat off for a while. But we're definitely going to need to stay here just in case. It's not safe for us to travel. It's too dark. Too wet. We have to choose our poison. Face the cat? Or face sliding off into the river?"

It wasn't a choice that he wanted to make.

"If we stay here, we remain on guard," Autumn said. "Unless you need to get some sleep. If that's the case, fine. I can take over duty."

"I'll be fine."

No way was Derek going to let her face this alone. Not if he could help it.

But that situation had been too close for his comfort.

* * *

As they sat at the entrance of the cave, Autumn glanced at Derek.

The man had surprised her.

Most guys liked to be in charge. But he seemed comfortable enough with his own masculinity to let her call the shots. She appreciated that quality about him.

Yet, at the same time, he didn't seem weak. His humility only made him seem more secure. If Autumn had to battle his ego as well as the elements and the gunmen…it would be an entirely different story right now.

She counted her blessings.

She tried to put herself in his shoes. The man had been left at the altar. It couldn't have been easy.

Derek was accomplished. He was handsome. And he was obviously smart.

In some ways, he reminded her of her husband. It was the strangest thing, because, when she looked at Derek, she felt a flutter of nerves sweep through her.

She hadn't felt those things in a long time, nor had she thought she ever would feel those emotions again.

But something about Derek was different. They made a good team. Autumn couldn't say that about very many people.

Just then, Sherlock stood from her side, walked over to Derek and lay down beside him.

Traitor.

Yet she couldn't fault the dog. Seeing that Sherlock trusted Derek only reaffirmed that she could trust him as well. The sight warmed her heart.

At once, a memory filled her. An image of her and her husband sitting in the screened-in porch behind their house. One of their favorite things to do was to sit back there during rainstorms, listening to the drops hitting the tin roof.

She smiled.

Those were the moments she missed the most. The simple times.

Now she sat out there with Sherlock and listened. Something about the sound soothed her. But, if she was honest with herself, it also left her feeling lonely.

"You're looking at me." Derek studied her in curiosity.

Autumn looked away and let out a little laugh. "I guess I was. I'm sorry."

"What are you thinking?"

She swallowed hard, contemplating what to say. "Just that you surprised me."

He raised an eyebrow. "Surprised you how?"

"You seem like a good man, Derek." It was honest but safe and not too revealing.

He offered up a smile. "I'd like to think so. I try, at least."

"Are you ready to return to DC?" She could wonder about his life outside all of this. What did he do when he wasn't working? Did he have a full social life? Was he happy?

"Funny that you ask that." He shifted, rubbing Sherlock's head. "I'm actually at the point in my career where I need to figure out what I want to do next. I thought it was private practice. But the firm I joined keeps me even busier than I'd been at JAG. Sometimes I'd like a slower pace of life."

"What are you leaning toward?"

He shrugged, his gaze scanning the area around the cave. "I'm not sure. There are days when I think that this is the career I want to stay in forever. And there are other times when I would like to get outside DC."

"I can understand that. It wasn't easy for me to leave my old career behind. But it was the best choice I ever made. I never would have met Kevin if I didn't."

"You really love being out here, don't you?"

She shrugged. "When I'm outside, I can usually figure things out a little bit more. Life has a bit more clarity away from the busyness and technology."

"Even now?"

"Even now, believe it or not. There are lessons that we can learn in all kinds of situations in life. Including this one." She leaned forward and rubbed her hand against Sherlock's back, trying not to feel jealous that Sherlock had chosen Derek.

"I agree with you. Very wise words. Seems like you might need a vacation when all this is done."

She let out a little laugh before sobering. "You know, I actually haven't had a vacation in years."

"Not since your husband died?"

"I didn't even take one after he died. I couldn't. The thought of sitting at our house all by myself… I couldn't handle it. So I threw myself into my work."

"And how did that work for you?"

"Maybe the jury is still out on that one. I'm not sure. Some days I feel like I've grown by leaps and bounds, and other days I feel like I'm right back to where I started."

"That sounds like the nature of grief."

The two of them shared a moment of silence, and she felt something pass between them. Did Derek?

She leaned her head against a rock opening, feeling exhaustion washing over her.

She wasn't sure if Derek felt anything or not. But she had other things to think about right now. Things other than romance and romantic feelings. Or if she could possibly fall in love again one day.

But at least she felt some hope.

There was a lot to be said for that.

As soon as the sun rose and the rain let up the next morning, Derek, Autumn and Sherlock departed. They left the majority of their things in the cave and planned on coming back tonight if necessary. Truth was, Derek hoped they were rescued before then. But, if they weren't, at least they had a home base.

As he remembered the events from last night, Derek wasn't sure how much longer that would be the case. Especially if that bobcat came back again. They were intruding into its territory. Was there anywhere that was safe out here?

He wasn't sure.

Just as they had yesterday, Autumn led the way as they climbed the ledge above the river. *Don't look down*, he reminded himself.

Heights didn't bother him, but the sheer drop was enough to unnerve the most brazen person. The rapids almost seemed to taunt them. He was nearly certain the river had swollen even more after last night.

Sherlock looked like he had done this a million times

as he followed behind Autumn. She still held on to his leash, just in case.

The good news was they hadn't run into those gunmen again.

Not yet.

Hopefully not again, though he knew that was wishful thinking.

Near the area where the one man had slipped yesterday, Autumn paused. She reached into a bush on the side of the cliff and grabbed something.

She held up a swatch of fabric. "I think this is a piece of the gunman's shirt. The branch must have caught it on its way down. This will help Sherlock lead us to this man."

"We can use whatever help we can get," Derek said. For a moment, he almost felt like that fabric was like the dove bringing back a twig to the ark. It offered them some semblance of hope.

Finally, the three of them reached the end of the ledge and climbed back onto solid ground. Autumn glanced around before motioning for Derek to follow. That must have meant that the coast was clear.

Still, they remain quiet as they moved through the woods. If those guys were out there, they didn't want to alert them that they were coming.

So far, it was working.

Autumn let Sherlock smell the fabric swatch. After sniffing, the dog began to pull her. A few minutes later, they stopped at the campsite where he and his brother had stayed.

There was hardly anything left. The tent was gone. Water covered the area where the fire pit had been.

"We have to keep moving," Autumn said.

He nodded and continued to follow, trying not to think about the implications of everything that had happened. He was thankful to be alive right now. If he hadn't found Autumn when he did, this might be an entirely different story.

He would probably be dead.

Autumn let Sherlock lead them through the dense, slick forest. They probably walked for twenty minutes, in the opposite direction of his old campsite.

As a new sound filled the air, Autumn turned around and pressed her finger to her lips, motioning for him to be quiet.

Derek knew what that meant. That they were close.

He joined her as she hid behind a tree. As they peered off into the distance, he saw that three tents had been set up.

He drew in a sharp breath when he spotted one of the gunmen who'd been chasing them yesterday. The man sat outside by a campfire, poking it with a stick.

They had found them.

He, Autumn and Sherlock had found a gunman.

Now they needed to figure out what to do from here.

ELEVEN

"Now that we know where the gunmen are staying, we'll be able to lead the authorities back here," Autumn whispered. "We just need to be patient now."

"But my brother..." His voice faded wistfully.

"If we're all dead, we're not going to be able to help him." She knew this had to be hard on him, but they had to be careful.

"Can we stay couple more minutes? I'd just like to see if there's any signs of life." Derek's voice cracked with grief.

Autumn's heart pounded in her ears. She understood his dilemma. Though she didn't want to do anything to put the three of them in danger, she knew this was important to him.

"We'll stay a few more minutes," Autumn said. "Just promise me you're not going to try anything rash."

"I won't. I promise."

She believed him. He'd done nothing to show he couldn't be trusted.

The three of them remained perched in their hiding spot behind the trees. Autumn watched the campsite and saw the one man by the fire. She could only assume that another man had been swept away by the rapids. Still, the third man should have been shot in the shoulder during their first confrontation. That would just leave one more man.

The fight was becoming more evenly matched as time went on. But that still didn't mean that they would be able to take these men. Autumn had no idea how many weapons they had or how much ammunition.

Plus, these men were brutal. They didn't think anything about destroying human lives. That was evident in their actions.

Autumn, on the other hand, couldn't stop thinking about that man who had been swept downstream yesterday. Part of her wondered if she should've done more to help him.

Yet, she knew if she had, they'd all be dead right now. It didn't stop the ache in her heart. As a search and rescue ranger, her desire was to help people, not to destroy lives.

She continued to watch the campsite. The tents these men had…they were nice. Expensive.

Kind of like the camo clothing they wore.

Who were they? If these men really did have as much money as she assumed, that might rule out Owen Perkins. From what she understood from Derek, Owen didn't have that kind of money.

What about that money William was carrying with him? She struggled to put all the pieces together.

A few minutes later, another man left his tent and joined the first man by the fire. He had a sling around his arm.

This must be the man she'd shot.

The two of them muttered things to themselves, things that Autumn couldn't make out. But she had no doubt that they were most likely planning their next move.

Her stomach tightened at thought. She just knew they weren't done yet.

She wasn't sure how long Derek wanted to stay here. They could afford to linger for a little bit longer, as long as they were careful. But being this close was risky.

The wind swept over the area again. If Autumn understood correctly, this would be the last of the system, and the storm should pass over them after this. She could only hope, at least.

The weather had been overwhelming. Without it, they would probably be back to safety right now. Maybe even with William. It was hard to know for sure.

Across the way, a squirrel scampered.

Autumn froze, placing her hand on Sherlock's head and praying the dog remained on duty. Squirrels were his weakness.

Plus, the critter had caught the gunmen's attention.

She watched as the men froze. They glanced around, looking for the source of the movement.

One of men reached for his gun.

They were ready for action, Autumn realized.

She glanced back at Derek. His face looked tense also.

They waited to see what would happen.

Dear Lord, keep us invisible. Please.

She'd never muttered so many desperate prayers before.

Finally, the men finally seemed to notice it was just

a squirrel. They turned back to the fire and their conversation.

Autumn felt her lungs deflate.

That had felt close. Too close.

How much longer would they have to wait? She wanted to gather as much information as she could. But not to the point of putting them at risk.

Thirty minutes later, a third man emerged from the tent.

It was about time.

Autumn's breath caught.

The man hauled someone out behind him.

Derek's brother.

William.

He was alive.

Relief washed through her.

She glanced at Derek and saw his gaze fastened to the scene.

Thank goodness his brother was still alive.

But when Autumn saw the way William dragged his leg behind him, her hope turned into concern. Someone had used a stick and wrapped some cloth around the man's leg.

But he was still obviously in a lot of pain.

His face scrunched, and he let out a moan.

Derek caught his breath beside her, and she placed a hand on his arm. Her touch was partly in comfort and partly in warning. She feared he would act instinctually.

That could get them killed.

He continued to watch. One of the men tossed something to William. It appeared to be a package of food. Maybe an MRE—Meals Ready to Eat.

At least they were keeping William alive.

But even from where Autumn stood, she could see that Derek's brother was in bad shape. His lip appeared to be busted, his eye swollen and his clothes dirty. He had been through a lot.

How much longer would he survive out in these elements?

Autumn had no idea. But she didn't like this.

Derek felt the anger rising inside him. Why were these men holding his brother hostage? He obviously needed medical help. Seeing his strong and confident brother in this condition made Derek feel sick to his stomach. He wanted nothing more than to rush down there and rescue him.

But he knew that would be a bad idea. It would put them all in jeopardy.

Autumn glanced at him. She didn't have to say a word for Derek to know her thoughts.

It was time for them to leave.

They'd already been here too long. One wrong move and...

Autumn looked at him and nodded.

They turned away, cautiously maneuvering through the woods and careful not to say a word.

As they did, the rain started again. Sometimes it felt like it wasn't ever going to let up. At least they had somewhere dry to return to. At least, for now.

They waited until they were a good half a mile from the camp before Autumn turned to him and spoke.

"Now that you had a better look at these guys, did you recognize any of them?" she asked.

Derek had already thought about it and shook his head. "No, unfortunately, I didn't."

"So none of those guys were Owen Perkins?"

"They weren't. Nor did any of them look like anybody I ever saw with him. I'm not sure that he's our guy."

She frowned. "You're sure?"

He nodded. "I'm sure. I mean, Owen could be violent. He might even want to track me down. But I don't see him grabbing some friends and trekking through the wilderness to do that. He's a coward. He is more likely the type who would do a drive-by shooting or try to catch me by surprise."

"If that's the case, then we need to keep thinking. The more we can figure out about these guys, the better our chances of defeating them."

"I agree. I can't stop thinking about it. I just keep hoping that something will make sense. But it hasn't yet."

"And I still think we should consider that maybe it was something that William has gotten himself into."

"If that was the case, why do they keep chasing after us?"

"Maybe they think if they have us that will give them leverage over William."

His stomach clenched again. He didn't like the thought of that. Not one bit.

A hard wave of rain hit them, coming down steady and strong and making it hard to see anything in front of them.

"Stay close," Autumn said. "Unfortunately, this rain started just as we've reached the hardest part of the trail."

He nodded. What part of this process hadn't been hard? It seemed like every time they turned around, they hit a new obstacle.

He supposed he could relate this back to law school. He'd put in long, grueling hours. There were times he'd wanted to quit. But he hadn't. He'd pushed through until he reached his goal.

That's what they needed to do right now.

As they started to cross through the gorge area, Derek held his breath. This would definitely be the trickiest part of the walk back. But there was no way to get to the cave other than this route.

He watched best he could through his blurry eyes as Autumn carefully picked her steps in the rocky area.

Just as she reached the middle of the gorge, he heard a sound above them.

Was that thunder?

Something in his gut told him it wasn't.

He looked up just in time to see a mass of boulders tumbling toward them.

Autumn heard the rumbling and knew exactly what was happening.

She let go of Sherlock's leash and patted his back, signaling for him to run.

She tried to duck out of the way, but it was too late.

The ground disappeared from beneath her, and she began to tumble down the mountain.

As she looked down below, she knew how this could end.

First there was a cliff, and then a river.

Both were likely to kill her.

Swallowing a scream, she reached for something to grab. A rock. A branch. A tree.

But there was nothing but dirt and moving rocks.

The muddy ground around her continued to pull her down, leaving her feeling helpless.

She glanced in the distance one more time. She was only feet from the cliff.

She closed her eyes and lifted a prayer.

As she did, her hand swung forward and she grabbed a...branch?

She wrapped her fingers around it, and her body jerked to a halt. But not before momentum pulled her legs over the ledge.

She was literally hanging on by a thread right now.

Her head spun at the thought of it.

What about Derek? Had he gotten caught up in this, too?

She glanced up a time to see him run down the mountain toward her. Relief filled her. At least he was okay.

But what about Sherlock?

Her gaze traveled to the other side of the mudslide.

Sherlock carefully navigated the rocks as he rushed toward her.

The dog was fine.

Gratitude washed through her.

But she knew she wasn't out of trouble yet.

Especially when she heard the stick crack.

Her lifeline going to break any minute now.

"You've got to help me," she yelled.

Derek reached the ledge and bent toward her, his

eyes assessing the situation. "We're going to get you. Just hang on."

"This branch isn't going to hold me. It's going to break any time now."

He nodded, his gaze serious and intense. "We've got you, Autumn."

Something about the way he said the words made her believe it.

He pulled the flannel shirt from his arms. While still holding on to one arm, he tossed the other end down to her.

"Can you grab hold of this?" he yelled. "We can use it as a rope. I can pull you up."

She stared at the sleeve, her throat feeling dry and achy.

Grabbing ahold of one lifeline would require letting go of the other.

Could she do this?

She had no other choice if she wanted to survive.

TWELVE

Derek's heart pounded in his ears as he realized what was at stake here.

Autumn's life.

He couldn't let her down now. He'd never forgive himself if he did.

"Is your footing stable?" Autumn yelled, her voice strained. "The whole ground is mush right now. I don't want to take you down with me."

Derek kicked his feet against the ground. The rocks beneath him seemed stable.

But he knew Autumn's words were true. One slipup and they'd both be goners.

He looked down at her and nodded. "I can handle this."

There was no time to waste. That branch was going to break any second now.

She stared at that flannel shirt for another moment. Derek knew it couldn't be easy to let go of that branch, that lifeline. It was the only thing keeping her alive. But this was the only way he could rescue her right now.

She drew in a deep breath, as if prepping herself to

take action. The strain on her face grew deeper and her arms seemed to go slack, as if her muscles were weakening.

Finally, one of her hands left the stick. Her whole face was tight with intensity under the pressure of what she had to do. But, as she reached forward, her hand wrapped around the flannel.

Good. This was a good start.

"Hold on to it with both hands," he said. "You can do it."

Derek braced his feet again, ready to hold her up. He hoped this worked, because he didn't have any other plan right now.

Autumn released her other hand and grabbed the shirt. Derek felt himself lurch forward. He caught in his balance and grunted as he shifted his balance.

Autumn didn't weigh much, but momentum pulled them forward, pulled them toward their death.

Derek saw the fear in her eyes, and he needed to re-assure her. "I've got this."

As if Sherlock realized that they needed help, the dog jumped over the mudslide area in one bound. His teeth gripped the flannel shirt, and he helped Derek pull Autumn toward stable ground.

Two heaves later, Autumn was propelled back up on the cliff. On solid ground, she sprawled on top of the rocks beside him.

Derek leaned back and caught his breath as his heart raced in his chest.

That had been close. Too close.

He turned toward Autumn, placing a hand on her back. "Are you okay?"

She looked up, her limbs trembling and her eyes full of relief. "I am now. Thank you."

She turned over and rubbed Sherlock's head. The dog barked, almost as if he understood what had almost happened.

The two of them were quite the sight. They were a team. No one could deny that.

Derek had felt a part of their team the past couple days, and it had been a good feeling.

One he didn't want to end.

Derek wanted nothing more right now than to take Autumn into his arms. It was ridiculous, really. And he knew that.

But, in that moment when Autumn had been dangling over the cliff, he'd realized how quickly she'd gained a place in his heart. She'd been his rock while they were out here, and Derek knew that he would never be the same after this experience.

Autumn pushed herself up on her palms and released one more breath. "We're going to have to think of an alternate way to get back to that cave."

Derek looked up at the mudslide that consumed this section of the mountain. Yes, they would need an alternate plan if they wanted to get back to the cave.

But just how they were going to do that was an entirely different story.

Autumn felt weariness washing over her. That mudslide had taken more out of her than she wanted to let on. Her shoulder ached, there was a gash on her leg, and she was fairly certain her hip was bruised.

Still, she was grateful to be alive.

Thank goodness Derek and Sherlock had been there. If they hadn't been... She pushed away those thoughts. That had been too close.

Her life had flashed before her eyes—again.

She glanced up at the landscape around her and felt exhaustion pressing in. Going on two nights without hardly any rest was finally catching up with her. She only prayed that the backup rangers would be able to arrive today.

But as much as she wanted to believe that would happen, she was also doubtful. Until this rain let up, they were most likely going to be stuck out in these woods with those trigger-happy gunmen.

The three of them had to climb up the mountain and go over the ridge in order to skirt around the mudslide and get back to the cave. She kept telling herself she could do it, but her body wanted to shut down.

Her shoulder ached. A sharp pain went through her knee. Her head pounded.

She felt Derek's gaze on her, studying her, and she tried to pull herself together.

"Listen, maybe we should take a rest," Derek said.

She'd never been a good actor. Certainly, he could see the pain and discomfort written on her face. It was hard to hide.

Even though she didn't want to, she nodded. Maybe a little rest would be a good idea.

They found a boulder that was the perfect height for them to sit down and take a breather. She took her backpack off, grabbed a bottle of water and took a long sip. She then poured some for Sherlock.

Thankfully, the rain had stopped for now, but the

wind coming behind it was chilly. It would have been bearable if not for their wet clothes and shoes.

"I should check out your leg," Derek said, pointing to the spot. "There's a cut near your knee."

She pulled up the leg of her pants and flinched when she saw the gash there.

"We should clean that," he said.

She nodded, trying to hold back her pain. "There's a first aid kit in my bag."

He riffled through the backpack until he found it. Then he poured some water on the wound, patted it dry and put some ointment on it. As the final step, he put a bandage over it.

Autumn felt her cheeks flush when she realized his care and concern.

Derek was a good guy, someone she would like to get to know more once this was all over.

If this ever ended. Sometimes it felt like that wouldn't happen.

"All better," he announced.

She looked away before he saw the growing affection in her gaze. "Thank you."

"So, what are you thinking?" Derek asked, staring off into the distance.

"I'm thinking that when this is all done, I want to take a long bath, read a good book and eat some Chinese food."

He chuckled. "That Chinese food does sound pretty nice right now."

She glanced at him, noticing just how handsome this man still looked, despite their circumstances. She wanted to know more about him, about what he was like outside of these circumstances.

"How about you?" she asked. "Besides reuniting with your brother, what are you most looking forward to?"

He rubbed his head. "You know what? I don't really know. Food sounds nice. Warm clothes sound nice. The only thing about the situation that's been good is—"

"Is what?" Autumn's heart pounded in her ears as she waited for him to finish.

Derek glanced at her. "You."

A surprising wave of delight rushed through her. She'd been hoping he would say that. Because she felt the same way.

The thought of Derek returning to DC, to his condo or house or whatever it was, resuming life as if they had never met...the thought caused sadness to press on her.

So did the thought of her returning to her regular life. Back in her cozy but lonely cabin. Searching for ways to move on after Kevin had passed.

She'd never thought that she was ready to move on, but meeting Derek had changed that.

She realized that Derek was waiting for her response. "I'm really glad we were able to meet also. I just wish the circumstances had been different."

He let out a weary chuckle. "Me too."

"You know, we're pretty high up," she said. "Maybe I'll check one more time to see if we have radio reception."

"Sounds like a plan." Derek took a long sip of his water before pouring some into a bowl for Sherlock.

She pressed the button on her radio. "This is Ranger Autumn Mercer. Is anybody out there?"

She remembered yesterday when the gunman's voice had come over the line. She held her breath, praying that she wouldn't hear that same voice again.

Instead, Hendrix's voice came on the line. "Ranger Mercer, it's Hendrix."

Relief washed through her. "Any updates on the situation?"

"I'm afraid our hands are full right now. The roads are washed out, and we're doing everything we can to get the trees cleared. We tried to send a crew in by foot, but the river keeps stopping us. It's just a bad situation wherever we look."

She pressed her eyes closed. "So you won't be getting to us today?"

"It doesn't look like it, Mercer. I'm sorry. I know the situation is dire. I assure you that we are doing everything we can, though. Are you guys doing okay?"

She glanced at Derek. She remembered seeing William with those gunman. Remembered the bobcat near her cave. Remembered the mudslide and all of the aches and pains she now had as a result.

"We are hanging in," she finally said. "But we'll definitely be happy when we're able to get out of here."

"The rain is supposed to pass this afternoon. After that, I'm hoping we will be able to get to you. Maybe first thing in the morning."

"Thanks, Hendrix. I appreciate that."

"Take care of yourself, Mercer."

As she lowered the radio, she glanced at Derek again. How much more of this could they take? She wasn't sure. But their limits were about to be tested.

* * *

Derek kept listening to the radio. Kept waiting for the gunman to come over the line with another threat. Five minutes after Autumn ended her call with Hendrix, there was still nothing.

Instead, his mind went back to the conversation he'd had with Autumn earlier. She said she was happy that they had met, too. That sent a wave of delight over him. Maybe something good could come out of this situation. He would be a lucky man to have someone like Autumn by his side.

Derek glanced over at Autumn again and saw her flinch.

"You're still in pain," he muttered.

He saw the discomfort written on her face. But he tried not to push too hard. But seeing that cut…that couldn't feel good.

"I'll be okay," she insisted.

"If you don't feel like walking, we can stay here for longer."

She let out a slow breath and glanced around. "It is tempting. I was really hoping that backup would be here. I'm afraid if we go back to that cave, we're going to need to stay there. I don't know if I can manage another trip back this way. I need food. And my leg hurts."

He nodded, knowing that they were both reaching the ends of their ropes.

"We can stay here as long as you need. You think we're safe from those men?"

"I haven't heard them. I've been listening. But we would still be wise to keep our eyes open. The last thing we need is to be ambushed."

"Let me walk to the top of that mountain and see if I can spot anybody. How does that sound?"

"Seems like a good idea."

He patted her knee before climbing to the top of the ridge. From there, he should be able to see what was going on around them.

With the storms that had come through, many of the trees had lost their leaves. That didn't help Derek and Autumn when they needed to hide, but it did help when it came to surveillance.

He scanned everything around them. On an ordinary day, he would be awestruck by the beauty surrounding him. But right now, all of this just felt like a big trap they were unable to escape.

First scan, he saw nothing.

He almost walked back down to Autumn, but he paused. He would look one more time just to be certain.

As he did, he saw something move to the west.

His muscles tensed. Was that what he thought it was?

He ducked behind a tree, just to be certain.

It was.

Two men walked their way. They were at least five hundred feet away, probably. That didn't leave them much time to hide.

He had to get back to Autumn, and he had to get back to her now.

THIRTEEN

Autumn looked up as she heard quick footsteps headed her way.

It was Derek, and his motions looked urgent. She knew that something was wrong. What had he seen?

"They're coming our way," he said. "We need to find somewhere to hide."

Though her entire body ached, she knew she was going to have to put that aside. Her adrenaline would get her through this. At least, she hoped it would.

She pushed herself up from the boulder. She'd been afraid that those gunmen may have heard that mud-slide and come to find out what it was. It looked like her fears were confirmed.

"We could go to the other side of the ridge," Derek said. "Maybe there's somewhere we can hide out of sight over there. I saw an outcropping of boulders earlier."

"I think it's worth a shot. Maybe they won't go over that way."

Derek took her hand. "I'll help you."

She couldn't deny the flash of warmth that rushed through her at his touch. Who would've ever thought that a circumstance like this could have brought about such strong feelings? But it had.

However, this was not the time to think about warm, fuzzy feelings.

With Derek's help, she and Sherlock scaled the top of the ridge. They climbed over to the other side and found the outcropping of boulders he'd mentioned. There was just enough space for them to squeeze in between and to duck down low.

And they were just in time.

Voices floated with the wind.

The men were definitely getting close. In fact, it sounded like they were walking to the top of the ridge themselves to survey everything down below.

"Look at that mudslide," one of them said. "Sure wouldn't want to be caught in that."

Autumn ducked down lower, praying they wouldn't be found as she hugged Sherlock to her chest and whispered for him to be quiet.

"I wouldn't want be caught in it, but I wouldn't mind if those two we're chasing were. And their dog, too."

The men chuckled. Just hearing the sound in the conversation made Autumn bristle. Despite that, she remained down low and out of sight. One mistake could mess up everything for them.

"Do you think Foxglove is going to let us stop looking?"

"Not until he gets what he wants. But he's threatening that tonight will be the night."

"The night for what?"

"The night that we kill this William guy. He's nothing but dead weight at this point. And he didn't carry through with his end of the bargain."

What in the world were they talking about?

Autumn and Derek exchanged a look.

Footsteps came closer, and Autumn sank even lower. Derek rested his hand on her knee, as if trying to offer her a moment of comfort.

She appreciated knowing she wasn't in this alone.

"I don't see them anywhere over here," one of them said. "Who knows where they are by now?"

"Apparently, they're still on this mountain," the other said. "Foxglove heard it on the radio. They're not getting off anytime soon."

"We better find them today then, otherwise our whole plan will be ruined."

"Let's keep looking. Maybe they're back there by the ridge where Frank fell, God rest his soul."

"Do you think he survived that fall?"

"I don't think there's any way he did. Foxglove keeps on talking about how it's the fault of that ranger and William's brother. I think it made him even more determined than ever to find them and make them pay."

"I, for one, am just ready to get out of here. This is a sopping wet, cold, awful place. I'm ready to get back home. I just hope all of this is worth it."

"Hopefully, in the end, it will be. In the end when we're rich."

They both chuckled.

Autumn and Derek exchanged a glance.

These men weren't going to give up, were they?

Derek waited until he was sure the men were gone before he said anything. "Autumn, if we don't act soon, they're going to kill William."

"It doesn't sound like this has anything to do with you, like we suspected. This has something to do with money. Maybe they want that cash that your brother was carrying?"

"If they had wanted the cash, I think William would have just given it to him. My guess is that they want something bigger."

"Would your brother have that?"

"My brother runs a hedge fund. Ten thousand is nothing for him."

Autumn's gaze froze with that thought. "So maybe these men grabbed your brother, hoping to get a large payout from one of his investments. They could've even known who he was and followed him out here just to do that."

"I'm not sure my brother would just hand something like that over, though."

"He might be getting desperate. But I don't like the way the conversation went. It does sound like they are about to take drastic action."

"That's what I thought, too. But how do we help him?"

She let out a slow breath. "Maybe we can come up with a plan ourselves. It won't be ideal. It will be risky. It will be dangerous. But do we have any other choice right now?"

He squeezed her hand. "I don't want to put you in the middle of this."

"I appreciate that. But I am in the middle of this one way or another, whether I like it or not."

Just then her radio crackled.

Both of them froze.

Was this the bad guys? Were they contacting them again to threaten them?

Instead, they heard Hendrix's voice across the line. "Ranger Mercer?"

"I'm here. What's going on?"

"I just ran the plates on that car you saw in the lot. I'm sorry it took so long."

"It's standard procedure to send in a form recording the cars in the lots," Autumn explained. "It helps in case there's ever a missing person's report, among other things."

It made sense, Derek mused.

"What's up?" Autumn said into the radio.

"This is worse than I thought it would be. Those plates belong to Samuel Foxglove."

Foxglove? That was the name those men had used. "That name doesn't mean anything to me."

"He's known for being involved in the weapons trade," Hendrix said. "If you're stuck in the woods with him, then you are in trouble. He's a very dangerous man."

Autumn glanced at Derek. Neither needed to say a word to realize the implications of his statements.

"You need to stay away from them until help can get there."

"Do you have a description of him?" Autumn asked.

"He's six feet tall, dark hair and eyes, a scar across his cheek."

That was definitely the man they'd seen earlier.

"Do you understand that you need to stay away, Ranger Mercer?" Hendrix asked.

"I understand. Over and out."

Autumn studied Derek. He felt her eyes on him.

"Why would your brother be mixed up with Samuel Foxglove?" she asked.

Derek shook his head. "I have absolutely no idea."

"If this man is as dangerous as Hendrix says he is, then your brother really is in big trouble."

That was right. His brother needed help.

But Autumn had just told Hendrix that they would stay away until backup got there.

Derek wished they *could* stay away. But he wasn't sure they had any other choice but to get involved.

At least, *he* didn't have any other choice.

He needed to come up with a plan before those men killed William.

Autumn didn't have to know Derek well to know that his mind was racing.

She didn't have any brothers or sisters, but she could imagine that, if she did, she'd do everything in her power to help them in a situation like this. That had to be what Derek was thinking also.

She shifted her leg, wishing she hadn't gotten hurt. She could still move, but everything was going to be a little bit harder now. Their bodies were wearing down after being out here in the wilderness for so long.

Her mind raced through what Hendrix had told her. *Samuel Foxglove. Dangerous. Stay back.*

She understood all of those things. She knew the implications of the situation that they were in. It could have a very bad ending.

She had to be smart. She had to use her head. But she couldn't completely ignore her heart, either.

"I've gotta go back and help William before they kill him," Derek finally said, his head falling back against the rock behind him.

"I know," Autumn said.

He did a double take at her.

"You know?" Surprise laced his voice.

Autumn nodded. "I'm not sure that help is going to be here in time."

He shook his head. "From what that other ranger told you, it won't be."

"Let's think this through," she said. "If we were to attempt to rescue William, what would it look like?"

He let out a long breath. "I've been trying to think it through, to come up with some type of plan. I keep on trying to think like the criminals that I put behind bars. I keep asking myself what they would do if they wanted something bad enough."

"And what did you come up with?"

He shrugged. "At first, I thought maybe we could wait until these guys were sleeping and cut a hole in the back of the tent."

"Like a bank robbery?"

He let out a soft chuckle. "Maybe. This is a terrible idea. The other men could wake up and…"

"I can see where you're going with that, but I do think we need to keep thinking about other possibilities here."

He turned toward her. "Did you have any ideas? Not that I expect you to be involved with this."

She grabbed his hand and squeezed it. "I'm involved with this whether I want to be or not."

Their gazes caught. "I don't want to see you get hurt,

Autumn. I know we haven't known each other that long, but…"

She squeezed his hand. "I know. I feel it, too."

He wiped a tear from her cheek, a tear she hadn't even known was there.

"You're so beautiful," he whispered. "On the inside and out. I've never met somebody as brave and steadfast as you are."

Her heart leaped into her throat when she heard the sincerity in his words.

Slowly, Derek leaned forward, and their lips met in a soft kiss. For just a minute, all their problems disappeared and were replaced with bliss.

As he pulled away, Autumn felt a soft smile tug at the corner of his mouth. "Maybe we could try that again sometime when I'm not covered in mud and after I've gotten some sleep."

He let out a chuckle, his forehead touching hers. "That seems like a good idea."

They remained there a moment, each enjoying the bond they'd just shared.

But Autumn knew they had other things they had to think about. She pulled back, instantly missing his warmth.

She cleared her throat as she looked up at him. "I guess we really should keep brainstorming some ways to get William back. It's going to be nightfall soon, and that's probably going to be the best time to act."

Derek nodded, seeming hesitant to let her go. "I think you're right. Let's start brainstorming."

But Autumn knew she'd be thinking about that kiss for a long time.

FOURTEEN

Two hours later, Derek and Autumn had a plan.

As they'd sat in the outcropping of boulders, they'd talked through nearly every possibility they could think of.

One idea had risen above the rest. They had very few choices right now. But they might have come up with a plan that would work.

As a moment of silence fell, he glanced at Autumn. She leaned against the rocks, her eyes closed, and rubbed Sherlock's fur. The dog sat beside her, his eyes still open as if on the lookout for trouble.

Autumn looked tired. Exhausted.

They'd been able to get a little bit of rest in the outcropping of boulders. They were going to need their energy tonight.

Derek worried about her. He continued to insist that she could stay here and that he could act on this plan himself. But Autumn didn't want anything to do with that.

She kept saying that he needed a wingman, and Derek knew, in an ideal situation, that would be true. Nothing about this situation was ideal, however.

He'd spent some time scavenging the area, and he'd been able to come across an old rope. Some climbers must have used it. It hadn't been washed away by the rainwaters because it was wedged between two boulders. They would be able to use this to enact their plan this evening.

They'd drunk some water and eaten some energy bars and beef jerky, sharing all of that with Sherlock in the process.

As soon as the sun began to set, Autumn glanced at him. "You ready to head out?"

He nodded. "I guess this is as good a time as ever."

He helped her to her feet, and they began their trek toward William.

"So does the name Samuel Foxglove ring any bells yet?" Autumn asked, glancing up at him in curiosity.

"No, it doesn't."

"Do you think your brother got wrapped up in something involving weapons smuggling?"

Derek shrugged. It had been all he had been able to think about as well. "I suppose it's a possibility. The more I think about it, the more I realize that finding that cash along with the phone and the other objects in his backpack… William must have had something else in mind when he came out here. I had no idea or I never would have been a part of it."

Autumn nodded, moving a little bit slower than usual. Still, they needed to keep their energy up by maintaining a slower pace. There was no hurry to get there. They weren't going to do anything until it was dark.

Even then, they knew their plan was risky. But out

of all the options they had come up with, this was the best plan of them all.

But something else had changed in Autumn also, Derek realized. She seemed more distant. More cautious.

Was it because she was in pain from her fall?

Or was it because he had kissed her?

Maybe it hadn't been the right move. But it had definitely felt right at the time.

Derek would have to worry about that later. Right now, he needed to focus on survival.

He prayed this plan didn't get them all killed.

As she walked down the mountainside, Autumn couldn't stop thinking about that kiss she and Derek had shared earlier.

It had been that blissful. A pleasant surprise in the middle of a not-so-pleasant situation.

But then reality had hit her.

She couldn't bear the thought of falling for someone and then losing them again.

Losing Kevin had nearly wrecked her. And now Autumn was putting herself into a situation where she was falling for a man in the midst of a dangerous, life-threatening situation.

She couldn't do this again. She had to put some distance between herself and Derek. It was better to feel the pain now than it would be later, after her feelings grew even more. After she got used to being around him more. After she became dependent on him as a companion.

Her chest squeezed with sadness at the thought.

She needed to stay focused. To think about their plan. These feelings right now would distract her. Could make her not as sharp or on top of things.

She wasn't confident that her and Derek's plan was going to work.

But it was all they had, she mused as she climbed up a steep incline. Her muscles strained with the action, but she pushed forward. Despite the cold. Despite the dampness. Despite the pain.

Out of all the options she and Derek had discussed, this had been the one that made the most sense given their situation and resources.

A flutter of nerves still lingered inside her. So much could go wrong. Autumn dreaded the thought of facing those gunmen, especially in her current weakened state.

She pushed back some thick foliage, trying to watch her step as the darkness grew deeper.

What if it was still a couple days until rescuers could get to them? They were going to be stuck out here with these men, and they couldn't simply be sitting ducks. They needed to be proactive.

Autumn also knew if this plan worked, that there would still be more obstacles to face. Starting with the fact that William could barely walk. At least, that was the case last they knew.

She continued to lift up prayers for this situation.

Finally, the three of them reached the campsite of the gunmen. They paused a safe distance away so they wouldn't be discovered.

Nightfall was upon them and worked in their favor right now. Autumn could be thankful for that, at least.

She lingered behind a tree and watched as the three

men were sitting around the campfire. William was out there also, but he leaned against a tree, almost appearing like he couldn't even hold himself up. Based on his hunched body, the bandage on his arm and leg, and his sunken eyes, he wasn't doing well.

Meanwhile, the other three men sat around together, looking like they were just friends on a trip together as they laughed and drank.

Just what were they planning? It was obvious by the conversation she and Derek had overheard earlier that the men had planned on killing William tonight. To look at them now, Autumn wouldn't have guessed that.

Something didn't make sense.

She leaned toward Derek. "I'm going to get a little closer. Stay here."

His eyes widened, but he nodded as if he trusted her. "Be careful."

"I will be." Remaining low, Autumn crept close enough to hear more of their conversation. She needed to know exactly what she was getting into. She couldn't lead everyone into an ambush.

"We need to figure this out before the roads open back up," Foxglove said. "When that happens, there's going to be law enforcement all over this area."

"How much time do you think we have?" the man with his arm in a sling asked.

"My guess? Less than forty-eight hours."

"You going to tell us where that money is?" Foxglove asked, turning to William.

"I told you. I hid it in my backpack behind some rocks. But it was gone when we got back there. I don't know what happened."

"He's sticking to his story," Foxglove said.

"That's because it's the truth!" William's voice rose with emotion.

"We have other means of getting what we need," Foxglove continued. "Just wait."

"Your beef is with me. Leave my brother out of this."

"It's too late for that." The third man let out a deep, menacing chuckle.

What did that mean? Autumn wondered. What else was going on here?

Autumn didn't like the sound of this. Exactly what kind of situation were they putting themselves in? Part of her wanted to run, to forget about this.

Then she remembered Derek. She had to do whatever she could to help him. It was clear that these men weren't going to wait until the conditions cleared and backup was able to come and help Autumn out.

If they didn't act soon, William would die.

As soon as darkness completely surrounded them and the men had disappeared inside their tents, Derek and Autumn decided it was safe enough to act.

Derek was surprised that no one had been left outside to guard everything. But that would work in their favor, so he wasn't complaining.

Instead, he and Autumn looked at each other and nodded.

It was time to put their plan in place. He only prayed that everything worked out the way it was supposed to.

Moving carefully, they walked to the opposite side of the camp. They collected as many sticks and branches as they could and leaned them against each other, al-most like a tepee.

They kept adding to the arrangement for as long as they could, knowing that the bigger they could build it, the more effective it would be. Even Sherlock helped, carrying sticks in his mouth toward the structure.

They had to be careful to be quiet, otherwise they would draw attention to themselves and everything would be ruined.

Finally, the construction was set in place. Autumn tied a rope around one of the sticks, and they dragged the cord through the woods as far as they could.

Autumn turned to Derek. "You're sure you're up for this?"

He'd be lying if he said he wasn't a little anxious about how everything would play out. But this was still their best bet.

"I've got this," he told her.

She stared at him another moment before nodding and taking a step back. "I'll be waiting on the other side of the camp."

"I'll get there as soon as I can."

She stared at him one more moment before nodding. Then she and Sherlock walked away.

When Derek was sure they were a safe enough dis-tance from him, he looked down at the rope in his hands. As soon as he pulled on this, everything would be set in place. There would be no going back.

Maybe he should have tried to do all this without Autumn. But he knew there was no way she wasn't going to help. Even if he had tried to sneak off to do this on his own, she would have found him. Certainly, she knew exactly where he would have been heading.

But that didn't bring him very much comfort. The way to solve this problem wasn't by getting more people hurt.

Despite that, he knew that their plan was solid. The only potential hiccup he could see was the fact that his brother could hardly walk. It was going to be much harder to escape with him for that reason.

The good news was they didn't plan on going too far. They would take William back to that outcropping of boulders. Derek hoped that they could stay there until help arrived. The covering was perfect for them, just out of sight to anybody who might be looking.

He swallowed hard and looked down at the rope one more time.

It was now or never.

He let out his breath and then tugged on it.

A loud crash sounded in the distance as the sticks hit the ground.

This was it.

Derek had to move.

As he heard the men scrambling from their tents, he ran back toward Autumn.

He only paused long enough to double-check that the men had run toward the commotion.

All three of them.

This was his chance to grab William and make a run for it.

FIFTEEN

Autumn remained at her perch and watched everything play out.

So far, everything was going according to plan.

The tepee of sticks had fallen, causing a loud enough crash to get the men's attention.

All three of them had hurried from their tents to see what had happened.

That meant that they'd left William alone.

The unknown right now was how long they would stay gone.

Derek and Autumn had built that stack of sticks far enough away that it would take a considerable amount of time to go check things out. But if the men returned to their camp immediately...that could lead to trouble.

From her position, she watched as Derek darted toward the tent where William was staying. She held her breath, watching as he disappeared inside.

Please, Lord...

Part of her wished she could go help, but she knew she'd only get in the way right now. It was best if she remained on lookout, with her gun drawn.

Like she was now.

First sign of trouble, she'd fire a warning shot. If the men persisted, she would take aim at them.

They couldn't take any unnecessary chances out here.

Some people would say that even attempting to rescue William was an unnecessary chance. But they had to do whatever they could.

Autumn held her breath, watching and waiting.

She could only imagine Derek waking up his brother, trying to get him on his feet so they could get away.

His injury might be one of the biggest obstacles that they had to overcome.

Her gaze scanned the perimeter again.

She saw nothing. No one.

Hopefully, it would remain that way for at least ten or fifteen more minutes.

That's how much time they needed just to get William and to get away from here.

Finally, she saw Derek and William emerge. Derek had his arm around his brother, and William's face was scrunched in obvious pain.

This wasn't going to be easy for him, but there was no other way.

The two of them hurried toward Autumn. As soon as they reached her, she'd help escort them away. Right now, she was just acting as security.

Again, she scanned everything around them.

Still nothing.

She continued to pray that it would stay that way.

Sherlock let out a little whine beside her, almost as if

he agreed with her silent assessment. That dog always seemed to read her thoughts.

Finally, Derek and William reached her.

Her heart soared with a moment of victory.

But she couldn't celebrate for too long. They had to move.

"Glad you guys made it." She nodded toward the distance. "We've got to get going. Now."

Derek had never been so happy to see his brother. William hadn't been sleeping when he had gone into the tent. No, he was sitting up, almost as if waiting for more trouble to find him.

Then his face had crashed with relief when he'd spotted Derek.

The two of them hadn't had a chance for a reunion. They had to keep moving.

Helping his brother was even harder than Derek had anticipated. Not only was his leg broken, but those men had shot him in the arm. Though the bullet had only skimmed his skin—leaving that blood they'd found earlier—it was obviously painful for William if anything touched that area.

His brother was also a big guy, and though Derek could handle his weight, it made moving through the forest even more cumbersome.

It didn't matter. They just had to get away from these guys before they were caught.

"I'm Autumn." She glanced at William before her gaze traveled down to his leg. "Feeling okay?"

William shook his head. "No. I got a fever yesterday. I know enough to know that's not good."

No, it wasn't, Derek mused. That probably meant that infection was setting in. If his brother didn't get medical help soon, then he really was going to be in trouble.

Derek let out another grunt as he helped his brother up a rock. Autumn slipped an arm around him also to help out. But her gaze still remained focused on everything around them. They had to be careful here.

Derek glanced back one more time.

Enough time had passed that those gunmen should be returning to their camp soon. Certainly they'd realized they'd been duped. They weren't going to be happy when they found out about it.

That was another reason why Derek and his companions had to continue to make good time here.

"How did you guys find me?" William asked, his voice ragged, like he was out of breath. A thin sheen of sweat covered his skin, and his gaze looked hollow.

"Sherlock helped." Autumn glanced down at her dog. "But these men have also been on our trail for the past couple days. Do you know who they are?"

"Samuel Foxglove." His brother's face scrunched with either pain or disgust—or both.

"Listen, save your breath," Derek said. "We'll talk more when we get to our safe location."

"Safe location?"

"It's not much," Autumn said. "But we have somewhere that should hold us over until backup arrives."

"I was hoping backup might already be here." William let out a moan as they continued to move through the forest.

"The roads are washed out," Derek said. "The storm

did a number on the area, and they're having trouble getting anybody else out here."

William let out a groan. "That's not what I want to hear."

"Believe me, it's not what any of us wanted to hear," Autumn said. "We've got to keep moving."

It seemed the farther they went, the heavier his brother became. William couldn't put any weight at all onto his foot, which meant he was hopping between every other step. He also used Derek and Autumn as crutches.

This was going to be a long and slow way to travel. But they had no other choice right now. Perhaps if they'd had more time and resources, they could have made some type of device to help pull him.

But it was too late for that now.

They just had to move.

Autumn didn't like any of this. She'd known it was going to be difficult to rescue William. But they were moving entirely too slowly.

Though she tried to help, she also needed to keep her eyes and ears open for any signs of trouble. Between trying to assist William and navigating this mountain, she glanced around.

So far, she had seen nothing.

But certainly those men had gotten back to the camp by now. Certainly, they'd realized that William was not there anymore. At any time now, they were going to start coming after them.

Autumn knew the men would be able to move faster than they could. That was going to be a problem.

There was no time to lose.

By her estimations, they had at least another half a mile until they reached their temporary shelter.

That was their best bet at this point.

But she worried if they were going to be able to make it or not.

At least the darkness was their friend.

She knew this area better than almost anyone. Even in this blinding darkness, she had a general idea of where they needed to go.

Those men? They could very well get lost out here.

Was it wrong to hope that they might?

William let out another grunt.

Autumn's heart pounded with compassion. She knew this couldn't be easy for him.

But there would be time to talk to him later.

Right now, they just had to move. The thick trees and steep landscape didn't make it easy, nor did the nighttime that hung around them.

She glanced behind her again, looking for any signs of trouble.

Still nothing.

Besides, Sherlock would let her know if someone approached.

That didn't stop the anxiety from knitting itself in her back muscles.

William let out another grunt. He wasn't doing well. His face looked pale. His breathing was too shallow.

Maybe all of this was a bad idea.

Still, Autumn had known they couldn't leave the man there to die.

"Do we need to stop?" she asked as she felt William's weight pressing on her.

"No," William said through gritted teeth. "I can keep going."

Autumn exchanged a look with Derek. He was obviously worried, too. Tension hardened his jaw.

They continued forward, but with every step, Autumn's anxiety grew.

Why didn't she hear those men yet? They should be following after them by now. Certainly, they'd realized what the plan had been.

That uncomfortable feeling grew in her yet again.

As if Sherlock could read her thoughts, he paused and let out a low growl.

Something was wrong.

Danger was near.

Derek cast her another glance, as if he sensed it also.

They froze, and Autumn held out her gun, ready to act.

But before she could, she heard a click.

And another.

Then another.

"Put your gun down," someone said. "We have you surrounded. One wrong move, and we will shoot."

Autumn knew better than to argue. She slowly lowered her weapon to the ground and waited for whatever was about to happen.

SIXTEEN

Derek sucked in a quick breath. He wanted to glance at Autumn, but he already knew how she would look.

Full of apprehension.

Just like he felt.

How had those men found them? And what would they do with them now?

They had seemed so close to freedom.

Despair threatened to consume him, but he couldn't let it.

Autumn raised her hands in the air. "Don't shoot."

Three men, all armed, stepped out of the darkness.

Foxglove stepped closer to Derek, leering in his face. "You really thought you were going to get away with your little plan?"

Derek raised his chin. "As a matter of fact, yes, I did."

"It's a good thing that we are smarter than you, then. As soon as we saw that wood, we knew something was up. We're not as dumb as you think we are."

"We never said you were dumb," Derek said. "Why don't you just let us go? We could pretend like this never happened."

He knew it was a long shot, but it seemed worth a try.

Foxglove let out a deep, throaty chuckle. "I'm afraid that's not possible. Not until we get what we want."

Derek glanced at his brother, wondering exactly what kind of trouble he'd gotten himself into.

Then he briefly closed his eyes and lifted a prayer that they weren't all going to die right now. They had come this far. They couldn't be defeated now.

"Start moving," Foxglove said. "You can help your brother walk. But one wrong move, and I'm going to pull this trigger." He turned to face Autumn. "And I'm going to start with her."

Derek glanced at Autumn and saw her face looked paler.

And suddenly he knew that this was all a bad, bad idea.

He should have never dragged her into this.

Because he would never forgive himself if something happened to her.

This wasn't the way things were supposed to work out, Autumn mused.

She kept one hand on Sherlock's leash and the other raised in the air as the gunmen led them away.

They had been so close to freedom. So close.

How had those men sneaked up on them without them ever hearing a thing?

It didn't matter now. All that mattered was that it was done.

Now she and Derek had to figure out what they were going to do next.

It was clear that rescuing William was going to be

even more difficult than she and Derek had anticipated. He just wasn't in any shape to walk through these mountains.

If they could survive until tomorrow morning, maybe her fellow rangers would get here in time. But in the meantime…they needed to figure out how to stay alive.

As they continued through the woods, the man shoved Autumn. Sherlock growled, showing his teeth and threatening to protect Autumn.

"It's okay, boy," she muttered, keeping her tone calm.

The last thing she wanted was for Sherlock to try to protect her and for her dog to get hurt in the process. She would do whatever it took to keep her canine safe. He'd do the same for her.

"You weren't ever supposed to be involved in this," Foxglove said.

Autumn knew he was talking to her.

"Funny you said that," Autumn said. "Because you guys weren't supposed to be out here on park property doing anything illegal."

The man chuckled, as if breaking the law amused him. "You're feisty. I like that."

"Let her go," Derek muttered. "It's like you said. She has nothing to do with this."

"I can see he's got a soft spot for you," Foxglove said, mischief rising in his tone. "That will be good to keep in mind."

Autumn felt the tension pull across her chest. It seemed like with every minute that passed, the situation just got worse. Maybe they shouldn't have ever attempted this rescue. Then again, what choice had they really had?

Finally, they reached the camp. Foxglove shoved Autumn forward again, as if to quicken her steps. The thrust threw her off balance, but she caught herself before hitting the ground.

When she looked up at Derek, she saw the anger brewing in his eyes.

She shook her head subtly, letting him know that she was okay and that he shouldn't react. That's what these guys wanted. They wanted an excuse to go ballistic on them. She and Derek couldn't let that happen, though.

"Tie them up to these trees," Foxglove barked. "They obviously can't be trusted."

The men began securing Derek, then Autumn, with some old rope that they wound around their midsections. They attached Sherlock's leash to a hook on another tree and then tied up William to a tree on the other side of the camp.

Autumn watched carefully, trying to see what their next move would be. Would they begin to interrogate them right here, right now? What kind of information did they even want to know?

She remained quiet, not wanting to provoke anyone. The best thing she could do right now was to try to stay under the radar. At least until she got her feet back under her.

She watched as the men huddled together on the side of the camp, murmuring things to each other that she couldn't make out. The man with his arm in a sling was apparently Whitaker, and the third man went by Montgomery.

She made mental notes in case she needed to know that later, after they were rescued.

Because she had to hold on to hope that they would be rescued.

A few minutes later, the trio disbanded, and Foxglove strode toward Derek.

"Where is it?" he demanded.

"Where is what?" Derek asked.

Could they be talking about the ten thousand that had been found in the backpack? That was the only thing that made sense to Autumn. But there was clearly more to this story.

"Your brother owes us some money." Foxglove practically spat out the words. "It's missing. Did you take it with you?"

"I didn't steal any money from my brother, if that's what you're asking," Derek said.

Foxglove pointed his gun at Derek. "But do you know where it is?"

"He doesn't know anything about it." William rushed before his voice became strained. His face scrunched with pain. "It's what I've been telling you. Just let him go."

"I wouldn't have had to capture him at all if you'd give me back the money that's mine," Foxglove said.

"The money you owe him?" Derek repeated, staring at his brother.

William let out a breath and lowered his chin toward his chest. "It's a long story."

"William…what did you do?" Disappointment rang through Derek's voice.

Foxglove chuckled as he paced in front of them. "You really don't know, do you?"

"I have no idea."

"Your brother got into some gambling debt. He desperately needed some money, so he made a deal with me."

"What kind of deal did he make, exactly?" Derek's gaze went to William, and Autumn saw the questions in his eyes. This was all a shock to Derek.

"He helped us set up an account for our weapons trading business. Meanwhile, we paid off his debt. Win-win. Until he disappeared with some of our cash."

Autumn processed everything that was being said. This didn't look good. What was William thinking when he got tied up with these guys?

It didn't matter right now. What was done was done.

Derek listened as Foxglove addressed everyone like a militant leader planning a coup.

"First thing in the morning, we're going to find that money. Until we do, I'm going start picking people off one by one." Foxglove stared at all of them, his gaze unrelenting. "In the meantime, I hope you guys all try to get some sleep. It's going to be a long day tomorrow. At least, for some of you it will be."

He let out a heartless laugh, one that made it clear that human life meant nothing to him.

Derek glanced at Autumn and then at William. How were they going to get out of this one?

He wasn't sure. They were dealing with some dangerous men here.

Now that he'd had a closer look at Foxglove, he realized he had seen the man before.

He and his brother had stopped at a café on the way

here. As Derek had paid, he'd seen a man watching him from across the dining area.

Derek hadn't thought much of it. He'd assumed that the man was a local and had noticed a new face in the area.

But these guys had followed them here. They had followed them through the wilderness, all in a quest to get this money from William. The first chance they had to grab his brother, they'd obviously done that.

What a nightmare.

After Foxglove finished his tyrannical speech, he and his men disappeared into the woods for a moment, talking quietly between themselves. Derek didn't know how long it would be until they were back.

The night was cold and damp. Animals scampered in the background. The wind rustled the leaves. Tree branches clacked together.

When Derek was sure the men weren't listening, he called across the campsite to his brother. "William."

His brother's weary eyes met his, his head barely raising up. "I'm sorry, man. I never meant to get you involved with this."

"What's going on?" Derek continued. He needed some answers. They couldn't wait any longer.

"What Foxglove said was true." William's voice sounded breathless, ragged and lined with pain. "I had big gambling debts. These guys promised to help me. All I had to do was to set up an account for them so they could funnel their money there without penalty. In return, they let me borrow fifty thousand dollars."

"We found some money at the bottom of your back-pack. Is that what they're talking about?"

"No, that money was so I could escape. But I tried to give it to them as a good faith promise. When I got back to the campsite with them to retrieve it, my bag was gone."

"The water must have washed it downstream."

"I figured something like that must have happened. It was the only thing that made sense."

"Why didn't you tell me any of this before we came out here?" Derek asked, disappointment rippling through him. "Maybe I could have helped you out before you had to turn to illegal means."

"I didn't know what else to do. I didn't want to tell you. I knew you'd be upset."

"So you brought me out here basically to say goodbye? Then you were going to take off?" Derek wouldn't put a lot past William, but this shocked even Derek. He'd thought his brother was better than this.

"I know how it probably sounds, but it was all I knew to do. I didn't want to totally disappear without ever speaking to you again."

"That money wouldn't have lasted you very long." Certainly, his brother knew that. He would need access to more funds than that if he wanted to start a new life. And he had to know these guys were going to come after him.

William shrugged. "I was doing my best to get by. I didn't know what else to do. I panicked."

"Why haven't they killed you yet? Why didn't you just tell them?" Something wasn't adding up in Derek's mind. Was he missing something still?

"Like I said, I told them I had some cash in the back-pack, but then the bag disappeared. They didn't believe me. The only reason they're keeping me alive is because they think I know where the money is."

"I know where that ten thousand dollars is," Derek said.

William's eyes lit with hope. "Then you've got to tell them."

Derek feared if he did tell them that information, they would all end up dead anyway.

SEVENTEEN

Autumn listened to the conversation between Derek and William, knowing she needed to stay out of it. This was between the two of them—for now.

As a moment of silence fell, her radio crackled. A moment later, Hendrix's voice came on the line. "Ranger Mercer? Are you there?"

Hope trickled inside her.

She stretched her arm, wondering if she could somehow reach the device. It was on a log, only a couple feet away. Or maybe her foot could kick it…

Almost as if he'd been lingering close to eavesdrop, Foxglove appeared from the woods and glowered down at her. He held a gun in his hands, the end pointed at her.

She glanced back at Derek then at Foxglove again. She knew that one wrong move, and Foxglove would pull that trigger. One of them would end up dead.

"Answer it," Foxglove growled as he picked up the device. "But make one mention of what's going on here, there will be casualties."

Tension snaked up her spine at his ominous-sounding

words. Before she could think too much, Foxglove held it to her mouth and pressed the button there.

Her throat burned as she said, "This is Ranger Mercer."

"Good to hear your voice. You doing okay?"

Autumn glanced at Foxglove again, feeling his burning gaze on bearing down on her. "Doing fine."

"The roads are still washed out coming from the west. But the good news is I think we can get a team in coming from the east."

She glanced at Foxglove again, waiting for his indication as to what she should say next.

"Tell him you're fine and that there's no hurry," he whispered.

"He's not going to believe that," Autumn said. "He already knows that there's somebody out here with a broken leg. He knows that you're out here, too."

His nostrils flared. "Tell him that William has passed away and you haven't had any more trouble. That there's no hurry."

Autumn continued to stare at him, apprehension racing through her blood. She repeated, "He's never going to believe that."

Foxglove leaned closer until he was in her face, his rancid breath flooding her cheeks. "Then make him believe it."

She sucked in a deep breath, trying to quickly formulate her thoughts. She would never forgive herself if she made a wrong move that resulted in somebody getting hurt. She was going to have to play by Foxglove's rules right now.

Autumn nodded, and Foxglove squeezed the button on the radio again.

She swallowed hard before saying, "I'm sorry to tell you that the man we were looking for has been found. He didn't make it."

William's face went pale as he heard those words being said out loud.

"I'm sorry to hear that," Hendrix said. "Where is your location? We'll still get a team in there to get you out and to recover his body."

Autumn glanced around, trying to figure out what to tell him exactly. Before she spoke, she saw Foxglove's raised gun point toward Derek.

Her throat tightened even more.

"I know you have a lot of other things going on," she finally said. "We'll be fine here for a little while longer. We have food and shelter. Take care of whatever you need to. I know there are a lot of people out there who need help."

"I can't argue with that. What about the gunman you mentioned? Any updates on that situation?"

Autumn swallowed hard as she stared at Foxglove. "I haven't heard from them. They must have left."

"That's good news, at least. Listen, our incident report list is a mile long," Hendrix said. "But we'll get to you as soon as we can."

"Like I said, I'm doing fine. Don't worry about me right now. We'll huddle down until help arrives." It pained her for the words to leave her lips. Help seemed so close, and she was sending it away.

"When we get closer, I'll radio you so we can find out your exact location. Sound good?"

"Sounds like a plan. Thanks, Hendrix."

As soon as the radio conversation ended, Foxglove put the radio back on the ground and everyone turned to stare at him, waiting for his next instruction.

"Sounds like we'll be safe here for a little longer." Foxglove paced in front of everyone, still holding his gun. "That's a good thing. Because we're not done yet. We want our money back. The money that was stolen from us."

"I'm not sure how you think you're going to get that out here in the woods," Derek said. "Nobody has any type of internet connection to make any transfers here."

"We'll figure out a way," Foxglove said. "We always do."

Autumn shivered. She heard the pure evil in his voice. And she had no idea how they were going to get out of this situation alive.

Derek felt the tension growing in him. They were at these men's mercy, and there was nothing they could do to save themselves right now. They were literally tied to trees with no weapons and no means of escaping. Even if they somehow managed to untie themselves, there was no way to escape with William. That was clear.

Derek had to think of another plan.

He glanced around.

The men had disappeared into their tents, and William appeared to be passed out against the tree across from them. When everything was silent, Derek turned toward Autumn, anxious to talk to her privately.

Her eyes looked tired. The ponytail she'd pulled

her hair into was crooked and loose. Her clothes were muddy.

But she was still a sight to behold, even in this state.

"I'm sorry I got you into all this," Derek said.

She offered an exhausted smile. "None of this is your fault. The only people that I blame for this are Samuel Foxglove and his crew."

He knew her words were true, but that didn't stop the guilt from flooding him. "What are we going to do?"

She grimaced. "I wish I knew. I'm trying to saw through this rope using the tree bark, but it's a slow process."

"I have been trying to rub it against the tree also. But even if we manage to get these ropes off…" His voice drifted. This had been all he could think about. "I was thinking, maybe you and Sherlock could run for it. I could stay here with my brother and—"

"Then they would end up killing both of you," Autumn finished. "They've made it clear that if we make one wrong move, we're goners. I believe them."

So did Derek. But there had to be something that they could do. They couldn't just sit here.

"I still think it might be worth it for you to try to escape," Derek said. "None of this is your fault. And I know you don't blame us. But my brother stole money. That's what set all of this in motion. You don't deserve to be in the middle of it."

"Derek…" She stared at him, her eyes orbs of compassion.

"It's true." His voice cracked. "You've been a real superstar during all of this. I'd probably be dead right now if it weren't for you. But you don't deserve to be in the middle of the situation."

"Derek…" She tilted her head and frowned.

There was nothing she could say. He knew the truth.

"I need to get you free. You and Sherlock need to go. I'll handle things here and face the consequences."

Autumn didn't say anything for a moment before frowning. "I want to say you're wrong. But unless we have help, I'm not sure any of us are going to get out of this."

At least they were on the same page with that thought. Now they needed an escape plan.

"How's the rope coming?" he asked.

Her teeth clenched as her arms continued to make slight up and down motions. "I think it's getting thinner. I'm doing my best."

"Do you think Hendrix believed you when you said you didn't need his help?" Derek whispered.

She shrugged. "I don't know. He knows me pretty well, so I'm hoping he can read between the lines. But I also know the park service has a lot going on right now."

That's what Derek had assumed also. "Maybe he'll send someone anyway. Wouldn't that be nice? To have a cavalry riding in right now?"

"Maybe. But we shouldn't plan on that. Right now, we only have ourselves."

"I agree."

Just then, Autumn's eyes widened, and she shifted. "Derek…"

"What is it?"

The next instant, the rope fell from around her body. She pulled her arms out in front of her. "I did it."

His heart leaped with hope. Maybe they would get out of this situation. "Now, can you get Sherlock?"

"I can try. I'm not leaving here without him." She stood and started toward her canine.

But before she got there, a click sounded.

"I don't know what you think you're doing," someone growled. "But I would sit back down by the tree if I were you."

Derek looked over and saw Foxglove's face come into focus. The man must have just been watching and waiting for them to make a move. And he had caught them.

The hope that Derek had growing inside him fizzled like a closing argument gone bad.

Autumn stared at Foxglove's gun. She knew without a doubt that the man wouldn't be afraid to use it. But the last thing she wanted was to be tied up to a tree again. Next time, she wouldn't be so fortunate at getting herself untied.

She was certain that they had no time to waste right now. William was fading by the moment, and, if they didn't get him medical help soon, he was going to go septic.

"Get over there," Foxglove said, pointing at the tree with his gun.

Sherlock growled, looking ready to pounce as soon as Autumn gave him the signal.

"You don't want to do this." Autumn raised her hands in the air.

"Don't tell me what I do and don't want to do."

"I'm a park ranger. If you hurt me, you'll face time in federal prison." Her voice sounded strained.

"I'm already facing time in federal prison. And if I let William off the hook, what kind of precedent will this set for other people who try to steal from me? Not a good one. He's made his bed—now he has to lie in it. Unfortunately, he dragged you two into this mess also. Stinks to be you."

"Maybe we can think of a compromise." Autumn raised her hand in the air, trying to look unassuming. She had to use whatever tactics she could think of right now.

Foxglove stepped closer. "There's no compromising here. I need to get what William took from me. It's important enough that I came all the way out here to this wet, remote, nightmarish place to make my point."

"I understand that—" Before Autumn could finish her sentence, Foxglove slapped his gun across her face.

Pain ripped through her skull, and she grasped the area of impact. Everything around her began to spin.

Sherlock snarled, his claws digging into the dirt as he tried to get to Foxglove.

"Autumn!" Derek yelled.

She looked back at him and saw him tugging against his confines. He wanted to get to her, to help.

But it was no use.

No one could help right now.

"Now, do I make myself clear?" Foxglove glowered at her. "There's no compromising. You have no say so in any of this. You're going to do it exactly like I tell you or else."

"Yeah, I get it." Autumn's hand remained on her cheek, which now throbbed uncontrollably. She'd never been hit like that before. In all of her training to be a ranger, she'd never gotten into a scuffle.

Montgomery emerged from the darkness and took her arm. He shoved her against the tree and began wrapping the rope around her again.

"Do it tighter this time," Foxglove said. "And next time, if you get out, we're not going to have a conversation. I'm just going to shoot. Do you understand?"

Autumn nodded. She had no doubt his words were true. "Understood."

"Now, get some rest." Foxglove practically spat out the words. "Because the two of you are going to have a long day tomorrow."

"Why is that?" Autumn asked.

"Because I need a little goodwill offering that's going to assure me that William is going to be able to pay me back my money."

"What's that?" Derek asked.

"You're going to take us to get that ten thousand dollars he brought with him. After that, I'll worry about the rest of the money he owes me. Now, get your beauty rest. Because I am going to take everything you've got tomorrow."

Derek's heart throbbed in his ears. He couldn't believe the man had hit Autumn. More than anything, Derek wanted to bust out of these ropes and get to her.

But he knew that was an impossibility.

Instead, he stared at her from his confines. "Are you okay?"

She nodded, resting her head against the tree behind her. "Sorry. I was close."

"No, I'm sorry. He shouldn't have hit you like that." Anger still burned through him at the thought of it.

He watched as she closed her eyes, and he wanted nothing more than to comfort her.

But he couldn't.

He cared about her. He knew that. But Derek had sensed her pulling away earlier.

Maybe he shouldn't have kissed her. Maybe she wasn't ready for that. Or maybe she wasn't interested.

But Derek knew without a doubt that he cared about Autumn. Seeing her in pain did something to his heart. It almost brought out a primal side of him that wanted to lunge at the men and attack them.

He couldn't do that. Even if he could, it wouldn't be wise.

"What are we going to do tomorrow?" Derek whispered.

"It sounds like we have no choice but to show them where that money is."

"But the hike is treacherous," Derek reminded her.

"I know. I don't like it, either. But I don't know what other choice we have." She closed her eyes and leaned her head against the tree.

Derek could tell that she was getting tired. So was he. Everything that happened over the past couple days was catching up with them. Their bodies—and minds—were exhausted and needed to recover.

What a nightmare. Sometimes, none of this seemed real. He often prayed that it wasn't real, that he would wake up.

But that hadn't happened yet.

Dear Lord, please help this situation. Protect Autumn. Give us wisdom. Don't let our enemies win.

Derek closed his eyes. He knew he should try to get some sleep. Maybe with some rest, he would see things clearly and his reactions would be more thought out.

But there was no getting any rest out here.

Not only was it cold and damp, but there was too much on the line for him to allow himself that luxury.

An invisible weight pressed on his shoulders. He had to figure out what to do to make this situation right before someone else got hurt again.

EIGHTEEN

Autumn's face still ached as the sun began to come up. If she had a mirror, she was sure she'd see a large bruise on her jaw. It hurt every time she opened her mouth to yawn.

The good news was that she was still alive.

She wasn't sure how much longer she'd be able to say that.

Derek was right to be concerned about the hike today. It was one thing to make the trek in your right state of mind, when you've gotten sleep and when you'd eaten.

But the elements, when combined with their sleepless nights and lack of good nutrition, would be even more dangerous.

What were these men really going to do with her and Derek as soon as they had that ten thousand dollars? Would there be any need to keep them around for longer?

For that matter, Autumn was kind of surprised they hadn't tried to take William back to their vehicle so they could attempt to find a computer and he could make some type of financial transaction that way. Then again, she supposed Foxglove and his men knew that the roads had washed out.

If only she could somehow get a message to Hendrix. But she didn't know how she could do that without alerting these men to what she was doing.

She glanced over at Derek. His eyes were closed, though she doubted he was actually sleeping.

When she'd seen the concern in his gaze last night, it had done something inside her.

She reminded herself not to get attached. It was too hard to lose the people that she loved. Although she had been thoroughly impressed with the man, she knew there was a chance that both of them wouldn't be getting out of the situation alive.

She couldn't bear the thought of losing someone else that she loved.

Loved? It was too soon to say that she loved him. Of course. But the feelings she'd begun to feel for him were definitely growing, getting stronger all the time.

She needed to stop them before they went any further. Before she set herself up for heartbreak.

The sound of one of the men talking drifted through the air, and a moment later Foxglove stepped out. His men followed after.

At his instructions, they untied her, Derek and Sherlock. She held her dog back as Sherlock snarled at the man. The canine had always been a great judge of character.

"As far as I'm concerned, that dog is dead weight." Foxglove narrowed his eyes at Sherlock. "One wrong move, and I'm pulling the trigger."

Autumn leaned to the ground and put her arms

around her dog, feeling a surge of protectiveness. She whispered in his ear, "It's okay, boy."

She couldn't bear the thought of anything happening to her furry companion.

Foxglove tossed each of them some water and an energy bar. "Here is your ration for the day. Drink and eat up. You're going to need your strength."

She unscrewed the water bottle and sipped. Then she cupped her hand and filled it with water for Sherlock.

"You're giving your only water for the day to your dog?" Foxglove asked, looking almost like he pitied her.

"I'm not going to let him go thirsty or hungry. I'm not that kind of person."

"If I were you, that dog would've been the first thing to go." His eyes hardened, and he shook his head.

Autumn had no doubt that he'd told the truth. The man lacked any type of moral compass. That's what made him so dangerous.

She took the energy bar and quickly read the ingredients. It looked like it would be safe to give some of this to Sherlock also.

She broke off half the bar and gave it to the dog, who gobbled it up. Then she began nibbling on the rest of it.

As she did, she glanced at Derek. His muscles looked bristled and tense as he stood nearby.

Then her gaze went to William. He was still alive, letting out little moans in his sleep.

But he wasn't doing well.

He needed medical help, and he needed it soon.

More unseen pressure mounted between her shoulders.

"You guys ready to get going?" Foxglove turned back to them, gun still in his hands.

"As if we have a choice," Derek said.

Foxglove laughed. "Now you're catching on. Do I need to remind you of the consequences here?" Foxglove grabbed Autumn's arm and pressed the gun to her temple.

She sucked in a breath. Sherlock growled at her feet, ready to launch at the man.

"Call off your dog," Foxglove said, almost as if he were testing them.

"Heel, boy," Autumn said. "Heel."

Sherlock sat back, but she could see the look in his eyes. A look that clearly said he was ready to attack as soon as Autumn gave him the signal.

Part of her wished she could do that. That she could just tell him to assault the men around her.

But all of these men had guns, and she feared Sherlock would be a casualty. She couldn't risk that.

"Let her go," Derek said, his voice tense with barely restrained emotion.

Foxglove stared at him for a moment before shoving Autumn away from him. She caught herself before she tumbled to the ground.

"I just want to make it clear what will happen if something goes wrong," Foxglove continued.

"I think you've made that abundantly clear," Derek said through clenched teeth. "If you need someone to manipulate William, use me. Not her."

Autumn felt her heart launch into her throat. His care and concern for her were touching.

A tension pulled inside her.

Part of her didn't want to get too close to the man.

She wanted to put up all the boundaries that she could to protect her heart.

But the other part of her knew finding someone who would sacrifice himself for her was a rare gift. She knew she'd be foolish to let him walk away at the end of this.

She didn't have time to consider those thoughts any longer. Foxglove pushed them ahead, and they began their trek to retrieve the missing money.

Anger continued to mount inside Derek.

He wasn't one who got into fistfights. He had always preferred his battles to be of the intellectual kind.

But right now, something carnal rose inside him. He wanted nothing more than to turn all of his rage onto this man until he got his hands off of Autumn.

He reminded himself that reaction would do them no good right now. No good would come of letting his emotions get the best of him.

Autumn led them down the path, back toward the cave where they had stowed the money. Whitaker stayed behind with William.

Foxglove and Montgomery came with them. Both had their guns drawn, just in case anyone made a sudden move.

Autumn said very little as she walked through the trees in between the boulders. But Derek could tell from the way she walked and moved that she was still in pain.

She still hadn't recovered from that mudslide yesterday. The cut on her leg had been pretty bad, and Derek knew she'd hit her hip and shoulder. That, when coupled with Foxglove's attack last night...she had to be in pain. Too much pain.

What Derek wouldn't do to put himself in her place, to switch positions with her.

If only things could happen that easily, with just one wish.

But he knew that that wasn't the case.

He lifted another prayer and watched his steps as he navigated the rocky terrain.

He wasn't sure how long it would take to get to the cave, but he estimated that it would be at least an hour until they reached the old campground area. From there, they'd have to scale the side of the cliff again.

This could end up being an all-day excursion just to get this money.

Maybe, in the meantime, Hendrix would send his men this way, despite Autumn's words last night.

Derek could wish that, at least.

Behind him, Foxglove began to whistle.

The irony of the moment wasn't lost on him. Here was a man who had the power of life and death in his hands. And he seemed so carefree, like it didn't bother him what was ruined in his path of destruction.

Men like these had made Derek decide to be a lawyer. He wanted justice for the bad guys. He needed to see them behind bars.

Ever since his mom had died during a bank robbery when he was younger, he had known he wanted to do whatever he could to stop men like this in their tracks.

As they got closer to the campsite, Derek heard the river. It sounded louder than usual. He knew what that meant—the water was even more volatile than it had been before.

A few minutes later, they reached the campsite and Derek expelled a breath.

He'd thought the banks were swollen before. But now, they were at least eight to ten feet higher than before. The sight of them took his breath away.

Autumn must have been thinking the same thing. She paused near a large boulder and shook her head as she stared at a new inlet that appeared to have formed where the campsite used to be. Water rushed from the mountainside, forming what looked like a new river.

"I didn't expect this," Autumn said.

Foxglove stopped beside her and surveyed the area. "Is this a problem?"

"In order to get to that money, we're going to have take a detour and scale the side of the rock face instead."

Foxglove pointed to the water. "Or we can cross this. We don't have time for a detour."

Autumn shook her head. "It's a bad idea. I don't know how deep it is."

Foxglove said nothing for a moment as he looked around. "There's only one way to find out."

"What are you thinking?" Autumn's voice turned hard, as if she was anticipating bad news, as if she knew his response would be something she didn't approve of.

Foxglove grabbed Derek's arm. "He'll test it out for us."

"No!" Autumn began to reach for him but dropped her hand as she saw Foxglove's warning gaze.

"I didn't ask you for your opinion," Foxglove said.

"You're asking him to die." Autumn's eyes widened with fear. "It's not safe to cross this."

"We'll never know unless we test it," Foxglove said. "If he doesn't make it across, then we'll know we need to turn around and go back."

"If he doesn't make it across, that means he's going to die." Autumn's voice cracked.

Derek stepped forward. "I'll do it."

Autumn's gaze widened even more as she looked up at him. "No, Derek. You can't…"

Derek knew what the odds were. If Autumn kept insisting that Derek couldn't do this, then they were just going to make Autumn do it. He couldn't chance that, and he knew that these guys were not going to back off.

He stared at the raging river in front of him and wondered exactly what was going to happen here. He had no idea how this would play out.

"Derek…" Autumn stared at him.

"It's okay," he told her.

Their gazes met for a moment, and he hoped he didn't have to say a word for her to know how he felt. In these few short days they'd known each other, he had developed feelings that he hadn't known were possible.

Though one part of him told himself to keep this woman at arm's length, the other part of him knew that his life was going to be forever changed after meeting her.

He didn't know what was going to happen today, but he was a better person for knowing Autumn Mercer.

She squeezed the skin between her eyes and looked away, almost as if she had resigned herself to accepting what was about to happen. Foxglove wouldn't change his mind. He'd left no doubt about that.

Foxglove pushed him forward. "Now go."

With one more look at Autumn and a pat on Sherlock's head, Derek stepped into the water.

He sucked in a breath. The water was chilly and came up to his knees.

Even though he wasn't in deep, the pull of the water was overwhelming. The rushing rapid had a strength he hadn't anticipated, like a jet stream roared beneath the surface.

"Keep moving," Foxglove said.

Derek glanced back in time to see Foxglove point the gun at Autumn.

That was what he'd thought. If didn't obey, Autumn would get hurt. He wasn't going to let that happen. Maybe—just maybe—he'd be able to make it across.

He took another step and sank to his waist.

It was definitely deeper than he had anticipated—and stronger.

Derek reached for one of the boulders that still jutted out above the surface of the water. Maybe the structure would help him keep steady.

But as he took his third step, the ground disappeared beneath his feet.

The rapids claimed him and began pulling him downstream, proving they were stronger than he was.

He heard Autumn scream.

He knew how this was going to end.

In a few minutes, Derek would go over Beaver Falls and plunge to a certain death.

NINETEEN

Autumn screamed when she saw Derek's body being swept downstream in the raging rapids. "Derek!"

She knew what this meant.

There was no way to survive what waited at the end of this river.

She started to reach forward, almost as if she might be able to grab Derek. But she knew there was no use. There was no grabbing him. The rapids were too fast, too furious. They'd pulled him away too quickly.

She wanted to close her eyes and pray, yet she couldn't seem to look away.

Derek's body was swept under the water as the river consumed him.

She held her breath, waiting to see if and when he would resurface.

Beside her, Sherlock barked, almost as if the canine had begun to care about Derek just as much as she had.

There!

Derek's head bobbed out from the water.

She released her breath, though she knew this was far from being over.

How much farther did he have until he hit the falls? Three hundred feet?

In water like this, the distance would go quickly.

Moisture pressed at her eyes as the seriousness of the situation hit her.

If only she had more time. More supplies. A team around her who might help.

She had none of those things, only a helpless feeling that pressed on her.

Dear Lord, help us!

She sucked in a breath when she saw Derek catch a fallen log.

Maybe there was hope!

But they had to somehow figure out a way to make it to him.

"Let's leave him there," Foxglove said. "We'll need to find a different way to get to the cave."

Autumn's mouth dropped open. "I'm not leaving Derek there."

He leaned closer, his rancid breath again spilling over her cheek. "You're going to do what I'm telling you to do."

She crossed her arms, a stubborn determination rising in her. It might get her killed, but she didn't even care. She couldn't live with herself if she let Derek die.

"I'm not leaving him," she said.

Foxglove raised his gun again, and she fought the urge to flinch. She braced herself for the pain she was certain would come again. Would he slap her again? Or would he just pull the trigger this time?

"You don't get to call the shots here," he finally growled.

"If you don't have me and you don't have Derek, then you can't find that money," she told him. Derek would be proud. It seemed like a good closing argument. "And that's all there is to it."

Foxglove stared at her before lowering his gaze. "You have thirty minutes. And then I don't care anymore."

She released her breath, feeling a temporary moment of relief. But she knew that would be short-lived.

Thirty minutes? It wasn't enough time. But she was going to have to see what she could do. She was certain Derek would do the same thing for her if the roles were reversed.

She glanced around her and saw that if they backtracked some and climbed over a ridge, they might be able to avoid this new section of the river that had opened up. If they could do that and get to the other side, then Autumn could walk down as close as she could to the shore and maybe reach Derek.

She was going to have to move more quickly than her body wanted to allow.

Every part of her still ached from her fall yesterday. But she could ignore that. For now.

When this was all over, she'd have plenty of time to recover and rejuvenate.

Right now, all that mattered was getting to Derek.

Sherlock seemed to understand exactly what she was doing. The dog pulled on the leash as he led her toward that ridge. The two gunmen followed behind.

Autumn hated to take her eyes off Derek, even if it was only for a few minutes. At least when she could see him, she knew he was okay, that he was still hanging on for his life.

But now that Derek was out of sight, she had no idea if he was okay. What if he couldn't hold on? What if the rapids had already pulled him from that branch and he was heading downstream again?

She shook her head. She could hardly bear the thought of that. She had to remain positive.

Autumn kept walking, kept maneuvering around the large rocks. She finally reached the area where the ground inclined. It was going to be tricky to maneuver through this area, but she felt sure that they could do it.

She watched where Sherlock stepped and then she followed behind the dog. The ground slipped beneath her, threatening her with falling into the water below.

But that didn't happen.

She didn't bother to glance behind her. Foxglove and his crony were going to have to figure out how to get through this themselves. She certainly wasn't going to offer any help. Especially since she'd been given a time limit.

"Don't get too far ahead of us," Foxglove growled.

She glanced back and saw that he was struggling to get through the tricky passage.

No doubt he wasn't normally the type of guy on the front lines of things like this. No, he was the type of guy who did backroom deals, trying to utilize every re-source possible to get as much money as he could. He had men who did his dirty work for him.

The thought of it made her like this man even less, as if that were even possible.

She pressed ahead, navigating her way through the rocks, the water and the elements.

She knew not to try anything foolish. She knew if

she did, those men wouldn't hesitate to pull the trigger. Then both she and Derek would be gone.

Finally, she reached the edge of the river.

Derek was still hanging on to that branch. He was still alive.

Autumn had to figure out a way to keep him like that.

Derek raised his head, trying to keep the water from rushing into his mouth.

It took all of his energy just to hang on as the water bulldozed him.

The rapids were so strong. He couldn't get over just how powerful they were.

His arms gripped the old weathered tree. If it wasn't for this downed foliage, he would be dead right now. He had no doubt about that. But he was far from being safe.

He tried to pull himself down the length of the tree back to the shore, but he couldn't. Not only was he fighting the rapids, but his shirt was stuck. He kept trying to reach back, to pull it off the broken branch that snagged it. But it was no use. He couldn't get it free.

He'd even tried to take the shirt off. But the water pressed too hard against him. It was almost impossible to move at all.

He glanced around. What was he going to do? He couldn't just stay here until he died. There had to be some other option.

He gave another tug, hoping that the fabric of his shirt would rip and release him.

It didn't.

"Derek!" he heard someone yell.

He looked up and saw Autumn scrambling down the shore toward him. His heart pounded into his chest.

She'd come for him.

But just as quickly as his hope rose, he saw Foxglove and his man following behind her. Just what were they planning now? Did he want to know?

She paused near the upended roots of the tree and stared at him, Sherlock by her side. "Can you pull yourself across the tree?"

"I'm stuck!" he yelled. "I tried, but it's no use."

Autumn frowned as she stared at him. Derek could see the wheels in her mind turning, trying to come up with a plan, a solution.

She glanced at her watch, as if time were running out.

What did that even mean? He didn't know. It didn't matter right now.

He needed to keep thinking also.

If he slipped up, he had no doubt he'd be swept into the river and over the waterfalls.

He knew he'd never survive that fall.

He had to try to get his shirt loose again. It was the only solution that made sense.

"Can you get your shirt off?" Autumn yelled.

"I've tried!" he yelled back over the roar of the water. "It's stuck. But I'll try again."

Just as he promised, he tried to work his elbow down, to get his shirt dislodged.

It didn't matter. He couldn't get it off. The water trapped him against the log and hindered his motions.

"It won't work!" Derek called.

Autumn continued to stare, her eyes studying the situation and trying to figure out a solution.

"Maybe I can climb down that log and get you free," she called.

"I can't let you do that. It's too risky."

The thought of something happening to her caused Derek's adrenaline to rush. He could not let that happen. He would rather die himself.

"It's the only solution that makes sense!" Autumn called back.

"Don't do it, Autumn. You're going to get yourself killed."

Even as he said the words, he saw Autumn walking toward him. He saw her pressing on the tree to see how stable it was against the land.

She was going to do it anyway, wasn't she?

Derek needed to think of a way to talk her out of this.

"Autumn…it's not safe. You're going to kill yourself."

"I can't just leave you there," she said. "I won't do it."

"She only has ten minutes to get you out of this or we're leaving!" Foxglove yelled.

Even from where Derek was, he could see the man gloating.

That was why Autumn was glancing at her watch. Foxglove had given her a time limit. The man truly was despicable.

"I can do this," Autumn said, creeping closer. "I can help you."

She straddled the tree and began inching her way down toward him.

"Autumn…" Derek called.

"I don't have any other choice."

"Don't do this." He had to get through to her.

"I'm not going to leave you to die."

She continued to inch toward him, but Derek could see the fear in her face. Anybody would be scared in this situation. She shouldn't be doing this.

Four feet out, the tree shifted. As it did, it pushed Derek under the water. Cold water filled his lungs.

He clawed his way back to the surface and popped his head out, coughing out the water.

Because his shirt was stuck, only his mouth and nose emerged from the water.

Every time a rapid swelled, liquid filled his mouth again.

Derek knew with certainty that he was not going to survive this.

The last thing Derek heard was Autumn yelling his name.

This was her fault, Autumn realized. She'd put weight on the tree, which shifted it. She couldn't continue to creep out unless she wanted to drown him.

Now Derek was stuck under the water, and she didn't know how to fix it.

If she got into the water, too, she knew there was a good chance that she would be swept away with the rapids.

Then she would be no good to Derek.

But she meant it when she said she wasn't going to leave him here.

"Five minutes," Foxglove called behind her.

The man was heartless. She wanted nothing more than to put this man in his place. But this wasn't the time, nor did she have the resources or the leverage to do so.

Right now, all she could do was focus on helping Derek.

She glanced around. There had to be something else she could do.

But she had no idea what.

But she couldn't give up hope.

Almost as if Sherlock read her mind, the dog scrambled down the tree past her. She'd let go of the leash and left him on the shore.

But she had never expected the canine to follow her.

Panic surged through her.

What was the dog doing?

"Sherlock!" she called.

She looked farther downstream at the river. Looked at the rapids there. Imagined her dog getting swept away in them.

Her heart pounded with premature grief.

She could not lose her dog, too.

"Sherlock!" she called again.

But the dog kept walking down the tree, his balance perfect.

What was he doing?

Autumn kept her eyes open and began to pray fervently for his protection. For Derek's protection.

Everything felt out of control right now. Out of her hands. And she didn't know how to fix it.

She liked fixing things. She liked being in control.

But there was nothing about this situation right now that made her feel like she could do anything. She was helpless.

As Sherlock dived into the water, she felt a tear trickle down her cheek. "Sherlock! No!"

Her body sank into the tree as her dog disappeared under the rapids. This was not the way that things were supposed to turn out. She'd been praying so hard for a happy ending.

"You might as well come back to us now," Foxglove called. "It's over."

Could his words be true? Was this all over? Autumn didn't want to believe it.

Her gaze fastened on the scene. Sherlock had gone under the water. What was he doing? Had he already been carried farther downstream?

Seconds ticked passed.

A moment later, her dog's head bobbed to the surface. There was something in his mouth.

Was that…fabric?

The dog went back under water one more time, and Autumn held her breath, watching and waiting to see what he was doing.

The next moment, he reemerged, nudging something with him.

Was that… Derek?

He was barely lucid, but he was free from the branch he'd been stuck on.

Sherlock must have chewed through his shirt and set him loose.

Her heart let out a triumphant cry.

But she knew without a doubt that things were far from being over.

Derek clung to the tree with one arm and Sherlock with the other. He looked like he was barely hanging on.

But the good news was that he *was* hanging on.

Now that he was above the water, Autumn could creep farther down the tree. She began to scoot down the log with both of her legs wrapped around the trunk.

When she got close enough, she grabbed Sherlock from the water. She pulled him onto the log and kissed his wet head. "Good boy..."

She lifted the dog until he was behind her, walking back to toward the shore. Then she turned back to Derek.

How could she leverage his body? She was going to need his help.

She reached forward and grabbed his arm. "You can do this."

He said nothing, but she could see that determination in his gaze. He was far from giving up.

He pulled himself down the tree. Autumn moved slowly with him. She wasn't going to let go of him. She needed to be like his safety harness in case anything went wrong.

Finally, Derek's feet must have hit the bottom. He crawled back to dry land and collapsed there.

But the important thing was that he was okay.

For now.

TWENTY

Derek lay against the ground and let out a cough.

Against all the odds, he had survived. He was on dry land.

And it was all thanks to Sherlock and Autumn. Those two were truly lifesavers.

He had been certain when he went underwater that last time that he was never going to come back up.

Then he'd felt the claws against his back. He'd known that Sherlock had come to rescue him.

He owed both Sherlock and Autumn his life. He just hoped that he had a chance to thank them one day.

Someone kicked his side, and he let out a moan.

"Get up. We're wasting time." Foxglove glared down at him from above.

Derek pushed himself to his feet. As he did, Autumn's worried face came into view. She touched his arm, silently asking him if he was okay.

"We need to keep moving," Foxglove ordered. "We've already wasted too much time."

"He almost died," Autumn barked. "Give him a moment."

"We don't have a minute. You're lucky I gave you as much time as I did."

Autumn glared at Foxglove and kept an arm on Derek. "You okay?"

He ran a hand through his hair and nodded. "I am. Thank you both."

"I hate to break up this reunion, but move." Foxglove shoved Derek, pushing them downstream.

"You need to back off." Autumn's voice rose with defiance. "We're not going to be any good to you if we're dead."

Foxglove only offered a cold stare. "Don't make me repeat myself. Now, where do we need to go from here?"

Autumn glanced around before her gaze stopped at a cliff in the distance. "Up there."

"And how do you propose we get up there?"

"We're going to have to climb. I hope you're ready for it."

Derek dreaded it. His body felt weak. Spent.

But he would do whatever he had to do to keep Autumn and Sherlock safe, as well as his brother. He'd use every last bit of his strength if he had to.

"Move!" Foxglove said.

With one last worried glance at him, Autumn grabbed Sherlock's leash and started toward the cliff in the distance.

Derek followed behind, still coughing up water. The air was cold in his lungs, promising certain sickness.

Nothing about this situation was good.

Nothing.

They trudged down the shoreline, dodging fallen trees and debris that had been pushed over by the water.

Finally, they reached the area where the ground began to climb.

"We'll need to watch our steps in here," Autumn said.

She didn't wait for Foxglove to acknowledge what she said. Instead, she and Sherlock began to scale the side of the mountain. A few minutes later, they were walking on the same ledge they'd traveled a couple days ago.

As he moved carefully, Derek still couldn't stop thinking about how William could have done this to him. If his brother had just made wise choices, they'd never be in this mess.

But Derek supposed it was too late to look back. All he could do right now was look forward and try to fix the wrongs that had already been done.

And right now, he had a bigger challenge ahead of him.

His head was still spinning from that near-death experience. His shoes were wet. His muscles felt strained.

Navigating this ledge wasn't easy on a good day. But right now, it could be even more deadly. He had to pour all his attention into each step.

Autumn glanced back and felt worry pulse through her.

Derek was in no state to navigate this right now. But she knew that Foxglove wouldn't care. The man was determined to get his money, no matter whose life it cost.

The best thing Autumn could do right now was to try to keep a calm disposition and a clear head.

That's what Kevin had always told her.

What would he say if he knew what was going on right now?

He'd want her to be smart.

He would also give his blessing for falling in love.

Her back straightened at the thought.

Where had that come from? It was so out of the blue. Right now, all she should be thinking about was survival.

But somehow the thought that Kevin would approve of a new relationship crossed her mind.

It didn't make sense.

But Autumn did know that when she'd seen Derek out there, his life on the line…that she'd feared losing him, feared letting him go.

Once this was over, maybe they could talk about what was going on between the two of them. Maybe she could make sense of all these emotions she was thinking and feeling.

They continued down the ledge. She was almost to the area where they would need to turn the narrow corner and then navigate into the cove where the cave was located.

The water was considerably higher this time, even more than she'd seen in all her years working for the park. On the other hand, it didn't surprise her.

The storm system had hovered over them for nearly three days, just dumping water on them. As the bigger rivers overflowed, they emptied out in the smaller rivers like this one.

It was no wonder that Hendrix had his hands full right now. She had seen firsthand all the damage that storm had been capable of.

"You doing okay?" she asked Derek quietly. She glanced back to see his expression.

He looked paler than she would like to see, but he nodded. "I'm fine. Thank you."

But his voice sounded weak. His motions looked like they took entirely too much effort.

She had to think of a plan to get them out of this. It was all there was to it.

Just then an idea fluttered into her mind.

Would it work?

She wasn't sure. But it was at least worth a try.

But she was going to have to be very careful if she wanted to enact her plan without any casualties.

Derek sucked in a breath as he heard commotion behind him.

He glanced behind him in time to see Foxglove's foot slip.

Before he slid down the mountain, Montgomery grabbed his arm and pulled him back up.

But Derek saw the flash of fear on the man's face.

He'd thought he was going to die.

Derek understood the sentiment. His life had flashed before his eyes, too.

Part of him wondered what these men would do once they had that money they were after. Would they shoot him and Autumn and leave them in the cave?

He wouldn't put it past them.

Though one part of Derek wanted to be the hero and try to take these guys out, the other part of him knew that would be foolish. It could end up with them all dead. Besides, he didn't have a weapon.

For that reason, Derek thought the best move might be just to be compliant and to be on guard.

He just hoped that assumption paid off.

Just ahead, he spotted the entrance to the cave. Not much farther, and they would be there. They continued to walk, watching their steps, even as weariness pressed into them.

Finally, they reached the entrance.

Autumn moved aside the sapling that blocked the cave's mouth and nodded inside. "The backpack is in here."

"Ladies first," Foxglove said.

Autumn's eyes narrowed with irritation, but she slipped inside. Derek followed behind her, memories flashing back to him. Memories of sitting around the fire inside and talking to Autumn, getting to know her better. Memories of listening to the rain and thunder outside from the cave's entrance, pretending for a moment that everything was normal. Memories of seeing that bobcat outside.

Was it possible that had just happened a couple days ago? The events of this week seemed so surreal.

Foxglove and his man climbed in beside them, and they all huddled near the old fire pit where he and Autumn had kept warm.

But something was wrong.

Autumn and Derek glanced at each other.

The book bag was gone.

"Where is it?" Foxglove growled.

"It was here when we left." Autumn pointed to the ground. "Right, Derek?"

"She's telling the truth. It was there."

"Then what could've happened to it? Because I have a feeling you two are lying to me." Foxglove raised his gun and pointed it at Autumn again. "You led me out here for nothing."

Derek felt the anger growing inside him. He could not let that man hurt Autumn. They'd been through too much.

"Somebody better start talking or I'm going to start shooting," Foxglove said.

"Why don't you put down that gun so we can have a rational conversation?" Derek raised his hands as he tried to talk some sense into the man.

"I'm the one making those decisions," Foxglove said. "Now where is it?"

"I don't know," Autumn said. "I'm telling the truth. It was right here."

Foxglove raised the gun and pulled the trigger.

As he did, Derek dived toward him.

But it didn't matter.

A rumble sounded around him.

Were they facing another rockslide?

And what did that mean if they were inside this cave?

TWENTY-ONE

Autumn heard the roar.

The sound of that bullet must have set off a rockslide.

The last thing they needed was to get trapped inside this cave, especially with Foxglove.

As the rumbles continued, they knocked Autumn off her feet. She hit the slick ground in the cave. She clung to it for a minute, trying to gain her balance.

"We need to get out of here!" she yelled.

Derek grabbed her and helped her to her feet as everyone scrambled toward the entrance.

But was it too late?

She heard the rocks falling down the cliff face just outside the cave.

They emerged and scooted down the ledge just as the rocks tumbled over the cave's entrance. A few smaller rocks skipped and bounced, pummeling their arms and legs.

But the large rocks appeared contained several feet away.

If they hadn't gotten out when they did, they would have all been stuck in there.

Autumn could count her blessings that hadn't happened.

Just as the thought entered her mind, a stray rock plummeted down the cliff. She glanced up just in time to see it hit Foxglove's man.

He tumbled into the basin below, yelling as he fell to his certain death.

"Montgomery!" Foxglove yelled, staring down at his friend.

Derek grabbed Autumn, and his body covered hers as more stray rocks rained down from above.

He was willing to take the brunt of this.

Warmth spread through her. Warmth and concern.

She didn't want anything to happen to him because of her. At the same time, she felt powerless to stop it.

Instead, she stood there, trying to catch her breath. Trying to wait for the next wave of rocks. Trying not to panic.

Finally, the rumbles stopped.

After a couple seconds of silence, they all turned and looked at each other.

Autumn's gaze went to Foxglove's hands.

Somehow, he'd managed to grab his gun in the midst of all that.

She followed his gaze as he looked down into the basin below.

His friend lay there, his body a crumpled mess.

There was no way he'd survived that.

Foxglove turned toward her, anger heating his gaze. "This is your fault!"

"This is because you pulled that trigger," Autumn said. "Don't put this on us."

"Montgomery is dead because of you." He raised his gun again and aimed it at her.

"You do know if you pull that trigger again, then we're all dead," Derek reminded him.

Foxglove remained quiet for a moment. Finally, realization seemed to roll over his features. He snarled as he lowered his weapon. "Where's the money?"

"It's like we said, we don't know," Autumn said. "I don't know what it's going to take for you to believe us."

"Who else knew about this cave?" he demanded.

"Nobody but us…" Her voice trailed off.

"And who?"

Autumn glanced at Derek. "Us and that bobcat."

He snorted. "You're saying a bobcat stole my money?"

"She's saying the bobcat could've come back for food and carried that backpack away from here in the process," Derek finished.

As Derek said those words, Autumn glanced below her. If that cat had come back and gotten the backpack, he probably wouldn't have carried the whole thing back with him to his den.

As if to confirm that thought, she saw a swath of khaki down below.

It was the same color as the backpack.

But she dared not speak the words aloud.

She didn't have to.

Foxglove followed her gaze and spotted the bag. "That's it, isn't it?"

Autumn didn't say anything.

"You need to go get it," Foxglove said.

Derek shook his head. "If we go down there, it's going to be another death wish."

"I don't care. I want to know if my money is in there."

Autumn felt the familiar tension thread through her muscles again. She knew there was no way to talk this man out of it. She also knew that Derek was in no shape to climb down there himself. She was their best bet.

But this wouldn't be an easy feat. She didn't have the right gear or the right shoes to do it.

However, she wouldn't be able to convince Foxglove of that.

Derek felt apprehension ripple through him as worst-case scenarios played out in his mind. Autumn would be risking her life if she did this.

He grabbed her arm. "Don't do it."

"I don't have any other choice," she said, her voice sounding strained but stubborn.

"She's right," Foxglove said. "I'm getting that money one way or another."

Derek squared up against him. "People's lives are more important than money."

Foxglove let out a deep chuckle. "Maybe to you. Not me. Now, I really don't need both of you around. So you can either decide which one of you is going to get that backpack, or you can decide which one of you wants to die first."

Derek glanced at Autumn. He knew without a doubt that this man was telling the truth. He wouldn't hesitate to kill them.

Autumn stepped toward him. "I'll do it."

"Autumn…" Derek's voice trailed off.

"I can do this." Her gaze implored him. "I am our best bet."

He knew it was true. "But…"

She touched his arm. "I'll be okay. But I'm going to need your belt."

"My belt?"

"That's right. It can act as a safety line for me. At least until I can get to this next ledge."

He nodded, not questioning her. "Whatever you need."

With hesitation in her gaze, she glanced at Foxglove one last time, casting him a dirty look. Then she climbed down on her knees and began to lower herself down the rocks. She worked slowly, finding the right footholds to assure she wouldn't slip.

Derek watched, holding his breath and praying she'd be okay. Just as he did the first time they'd had to grab this backpack, he lowered himself onto the ground. Sherlock remained beside him, acting as a sidekick in case he needed something.

Derek released his breath when he saw Autumn make it to the first ledge below. Just one more, and she should be able to reach that backpack.

Now that Derek looked at it more closely, it became clear that that bobcat had come back. He saw the teeth marks and saw how the fabric had been torn apart. There had been some sealed food inside, but the cat must have smelled it.

He glanced around quickly, making sure that the creature wasn't lingering anywhere close.

He saw nothing.

Autumn continued to climb downward. He knew the woman well enough to know she was careful and well thought out. That realization brought him comfort now.

Foxglove, on the other hand, tapped his foot beside him, obviously impatient with how slowly things were moving. He was going to have to wait. There was no other way to get around the situation. But Derek had a feeling the man wouldn't care about that.

Finally, Autumn reached the bottom. She lifted the backpack up and showed Foxglove. "Got it."

"Make sure the money is inside," he said.

Derek prayed that the money was there. If it wasn't, he didn't know how the rest of the day was going to play out.

She opened and riffled through it. A moment later, she pulled out a bag of cash. "Happy now?"

"Throw it to me," he said.

Derek's stomach clenched. What exactly what was the man thinking right now? His gut feeling told him it probably wasn't anything good. Derek and Autumn were just a means to an end, as far as this man was concerned.

"Can't I just carry it back up?" Autumn asked.

"You need both of your hands to climb back up. You know that. Throw it to me."

After moment of hesitation, Autumn did just that.

Foxglove got it and examined the bag for a moment before a satisfied smile crossed his face.

"Good job." He then pointed his gun down at Autumn. "Now, you've outlived your usefulness, and I need to get rid of the dead weight."

"No!" Derek yelled.

It couldn't end this way—and he would give his life to assure that it didn't.

Autumn held her breath when she saw Foxglove had pulled the gun again. He was going to kill her, wasn't he?

But before he could pull the trigger, Derek's leg swept out and hit the man behind the ankles.

Foxglove fell to the ground, his gun clattering on the ledge below.

She continued to watch, hardly able to breathe as Derek and Foxglove began to wrestle.

Derek threw a punch, hitting Foxglove in the face. Foxglove came right back and punched him in the gut.

Both of them were on the ledge, and at any minute, either of them could slip. Or their actions could set off another rock slide.

Dear Lord, help us now.

They struggled to see who could reach the gun first. Her stomach sank when she saw Foxglove grab it. He aimed it at Derek, who raised his hands.

"I should kill you now," Foxglove grumbled.

Derek said nothing. No doubt, he knew there was no changing his mind.

Dread surged through Autumn as she waited to see what would happen.

Foxglove raised his chin, something changing in his eyes. He lowered his gun—but only slightly.

"But I won't," he said. "I like you. You're a fighter. Not like your brother."

Autumn released the air from her lungs and rubbed Sherlock's head.

"You guys could be useful, so I'll give you one more chance," Foxglove muttered. "Don't blow it."

She knew better than to trust a criminal. But maybe they had just bought a little time.

She glanced up at Derek and saw blood trickling from the side of his mouth.

But he was alive. She was thankful for that at least.

"I'm coming up," she said.

Derek looked down at her, climbing on his stomach again so he could assist her.

Autumn knew coming back up was going to be harder than going down. Momentum wouldn't be working in her favor. Plus, her muscles felt tired, spent.

She made it back to the second ledge. But this would be the hardest part here.

Derek lowered the belt down to her, and she grabbed onto it like a lifeline.

"I got you," he said. "I won't let go."

And somehow, Autumn knew that he wouldn't. She trusted him.

She grabbed the belt with one hand and began her ascent with the other.

Derek helped her and pulled at the belt, raising her upward. As soon as her arms reached the ledge, he grabbed her and pulled her up beside him.

She was safe.

For now.

Sherlock came and licked her face.

"I'm glad to see you, too, boy." She rubbed his head.

"Enough!" Foxglove said. "We've got to get back to the camp. I have more that needs to be done. So can we wrap all of this up?"

Autumn and Derek exchanged a glance. Just what was he planning now?

She almost didn't want to know.

TWENTY-TWO

Derek felt the weariness pressing in on him as he walked down the ledge again. With any luck, this would be the last time he would need to do this…forever.

The good news was now they were down to Derek, Autumn and Sherlock against Foxglove. However, Foxglove had a gun, and they didn't.

Derek had expected to see more remorse and mourning from the man after he'd lost his friend. But there had been nothing. That just drove home the point that this man was dangerous and heartless.

Derek's gaze hit Autumn as she walked in front of him, her hand on Sherlock's leash. The dog was a natural out here, not uncomfortable in the least as he scaled this mountainside. Derek was so glad that Autumn and Sherlock were okay. If only he could promise them that they would be okay into the future. But he knew that wasn't a promise that he could make.

Finally, they reached the end of the ledge. Carefully, they climbed around the water that had almost killed Derek earlier.

He shuddered as he remembered those moments.

He'd come close to losing his life. Having that happen had confirmed one thing to him.

Life was too short not to take risks.

Though part of him had wanted to keep people at arm's length ever since his father had died and Sarah had left him at the altar, that was no way to live. No one knew how much time they had left on this earth, and they had to make the best of what we did have.

As soon as Derek got out of the situation—and that was the way he was going to continue thinking about this—he was going to make some changes in his life.

And they *were* going to get out of this. Derek was going to focus on the positive here. This man was not smarter than they were. If it wasn't for the man's gun, he had no doubt that they could take him.

He tried to think through what might happen once they got back to the camp. Obviously, William owed this man more than ten thousand. And Derek knew without a doubt that Foxglove was not going to walk away with any less than that.

It was like he'd said earlier—his reputation was on the line here. If other people that Foxglove worked with saw him as weak, they would walk all over him.

Derek had seen enough drug lords in action to know how these types of people operated. Foxglove was cut from the same cloth as some of those men Derek had put behind bars. He was all about money and power, no matter the cost.

Ahead of him, he saw Autumn was beginning to limp. Her body had been through so much, and she was clearly in pain. He wished more than anything that he could help her.

He crept forward and touched her arm. "Are you okay?"

"It's just my leg from where I hit it yesterday. It's sore, but I'll be okay."

"You don't look okay." He examined her face and saw how pale it was. She was in pain. Scaling the side of that mountain must have only made her injuries worse for her.

"Let me tell Foxglove if we need to stop," Derek said.

She shook her head. "We can't do that. You know he won't care."

"What are you two whispering about up there?" Foxglove asked.

"She's hurt." Derek turned toward him.

"Yeah? So what? My friend's dead. You think I'm going to feel sorry for you?"

Derek felt the anger burning inside him. "Autumn helped to get your money. She didn't have to do that."

"That might mean more if I hadn't had a gun to her head when she did it. It wasn't exactly out of the kindness of her heart." He let out a rough chuckle.

Just then, Autumn moaned, and her eyes implored Foxglove's. "Can we stop? Just for a minute? Please."

Foxglove grunted. Finally, he nodded. "Just a minute then. We don't have time to waste."

Autumn leaned against one of the rocks and closed her eyes, leaning into her good leg and stretching out her other one.

She needed to see a doctor.

So did Derek's brother.

This wilderness was not the place where anyone wanted to get hurt, especially in these conditions.

She let go of Sherlock's leash and leaned down toward the dog, whispering something in his ear. It was obvious how much comfort she found in the canine, and right now it was no different.

Then she leaned back and closed her eyes, almost as if absorbing the sun and hoping it would reinvigorate her.

Derek glanced behind him and saw Foxglove standing there, his gun still in hand, finger still close enough to the trigger to use it if he needed to. As his gaze swerved back toward Autumn, he saw her eyes widen as she looked at something in the distance.

"Sherlock," she murmured, her voice listless.

Foxglove straightened, following the dog with his gaze. "Where is he going?"

"I can run and get him." Derek stepped that way.

"No." She grabbed his arm. "It's too late. He must have seen a squirrel and run off."

Derek narrowed his eyes. In all the time that he had been around Sherlock, he'd never seen the dog do that.

He stared at Autumn for a moment. What wasn't she telling him?

Autumn's heart pounded in her ears. She hoped she made the right choice. She had told Sherlock to go.

She'd whispered in his ear, "Home!"

She knew those words would send him back to the parking lot. She knew the dog was smart enough to get there. Her only hope was that the rangers would be there when he arrived and that the dog could lead them back to Autumn.

She had been quietly sending SOS signals from her

radio all morning. Then she had turned it off, just in case someone tried to reply to her.

It was her last-ditch effort to get them out of here. But she was out of ideas as to what else to do.

Her leg hurt but not as much as she let on. She mostly wanted to stop to give Sherlock an excuse to go running ahead. But, as she looked at Derek's eyes, she saw the confusion there. She hoped to be able to explain all of this to him. Soon.

"Who cares about that stupid dog anyway?" Fox-glove asked. "Let's get moving. One less mouth to feed, right?"

Autumn stood, making sure her face was etched with pain. She wanted to take her time getting back to the camp. That would give Sherlock time to get to the parking lot and for backup to arrive.

She had a feeling that once they got back to the camp, Foxglove had another plan for getting more money. It was the only thing that made sense. If she was in this man's shoes, then she would want to get out of this wilderness as soon as she could so she could arrange some type of way to get the cash that was rightfully hers.

Foxglove shoved Derek forward.

Derek looked back, his eyes narrowed with indignation. But he kept himself calm and in control.

She could appreciate that.

So many people would have lashed out by now. But lashing out could get him killed. It could get them both killed. So she counted her blessings that he wasn't that type.

Yet Derek was still strong. There was a lot of strength

to be found in self-control and in being quiet. She admired that.

She looked ahead. They probably had another forty minutes until they reached the campsite. She prayed for whatever would happen once they got there. And she prayed for William and his injury.

And, of course, she prayed that their plan worked.

Derek was still trying to figure out what had happened between Autumn and Sherlock. Her gaze told him there was more to the story. Had she let the dog go on purpose? Why would she do that? Wasn't it more dangerous for the dog out in the wild than it would be with them?

He didn't know, but he was going to have to put his faith in Autumn right now.

As he got closer to the campsite, the tension in his stomach pulled tighter. He didn't know what was going to happen next or what condition his brother was in. He hated to think about his brother being in pain. Even though William, in some ways, had done this to himself, he still hated to see this.

He had a broken his leg, but William had also been shot in the arm. How was Foxglove expecting him to get out of this wilderness?

Even if they were planning on taking William to a bank or some type of financial institution so he could transfer money, how were they going to justify his appearance when they were there?

It didn't make sense.

William needed to be in one piece. Otherwise, the people working at the bank would have to realize that he was under duress. Not only did he look horrible, but the wound in his shoulder and his broken leg would be a dead giveaway.

Derek's stomach felt even more unsettled than before.

Something was wrong here. What were they missing?

Finally, the camp came into view.

Whitaker ran back toward them. Questions laced his gaze.

"Montgomery didn't make it," Foxglove said.

Derek watched as the man's face fell. This man wasn't as heartless as Foxglove. He actually cared that his friend had died.

"You couldn't help him?" Whitaker asked.

"It was too late," Foxglove said. "He hit the rocks too hard. Ask them. They saw the same."

The man looked at Autumn, and she nodded. "I'm sorry. He slipped."

The man stepped closer to her, his muscles bristling with anger. "Did you do this?"

"She didn't have anything to do with it," Derek said. "Leave her alone."

"You don't get a say-so here," the man said, leaving Autumn and going to leer at Derek instead.

That's what Derek had intended—to take the attention off Autumn.

"I'm just telling you what happened," Derek said, keeping his head up high.

"We don't have time for this," Foxglove said. "We have things we need to get done."

He pointed his gun at Autumn and Derek, indicating for them to go farther into the camp.

Derek searched his surroundings, looking for his brother.

He didn't see him. He waited until he reached the tents to ask any questions. But his brother clearly wasn't tied up to the tree as he had been earlier.

"Where's William?" he asked.

"He's in his tent," Whitaker said before spitting on the ground in disgust.

"Why?" Derek asked.

"Because he was whining too much. Crying about how much it hurt. I got tired of listening to it." The man's nostrils flared.

"What do you plan on doing now?" Derek asked.

"Beats me."

"William…" Derek muttered.

He stepped toward the tent. Nobody stopped him.

Quickly, he unzipped it and peered inside.

His brother lay on a sleeping bag there, unmoving.

"William?" Derek rushed toward him and knelt beside him.

But his brother didn't respond.

Concern rushed through Derek as he reached to check his pulse.

He prayed his brother was still alive.

But he had a bad feeling about this.

TWENTY-THREE

Autumn saw the concern on Derek's face as he rushed inside his brother's tent.

Her heart sank as she waited.

Was William dead?

Her pulse pounded in her ears as she waited to hear what Derek had discovered. She wished she could rush to him, that she could help him. But with that gun on her, she knew she shouldn't make any moves.

Derek stood from the tent and glared at Foxglove. "He's still alive, but barely. He's not even conscious. He needs help."

"Sorry." Foxglove shrugged, apathy obvious in his lifeless gaze. "But he should've thought about that before he got himself into this mess."

"You…" Derek growled, his fists clenched at his side.

Autumn sensed that Derek was about to do something he would regret. She could tell by looking at his eyes and reading his body language that he was ready to charge at the man and tackle him to the ground.

Before he could do that, her arm shot out to stop him.

"He's not worth it," she said. "Fighting him right now won't do any good. It's just going to get you killed, too."

She watched as Derek's intense gaze finally softened. He closed his eyes and looked away, as if reality was finally sinking in.

"You're right," he muttered.

"We've got to get out of here," Foxglove said. "We have some ATVs stashed about an hour west of here. We can get there, then I can get one of my guys to pick us up."

"ATVs?" Autumn asked. "How many of them do you have?"

It probably didn't matter. Because there were only two of these men, and they had three hostages.

That meant that this man had no intentions of leaving with all three of them.

The thought did not make her feel any better.

"We can't leave William here." Derek put his hands on his hips, standing his ground as they stood there at the camp.

"You can come back later and get him." Foxglove brushed him off as he took a step toward the woods.

"He's not going to make it that long."

"Do you want to carry him through this wilderness?" Foxglove stared at Derek, waiting for his response.

Derek knew that wasn't a possibility. His brother was too injured, too heavy. There was no way to navigate these woods with his brother over his shoulders. If he could do it, he would.

"I can stay here with him." Autumn's gaze met his.

Derek knew she was trying to say something. He didn't know what, though. Did she know something that he didn't?

"We're not leaving you here," Foxglove said. "All of us are going. Now. No questions asked."

Derek felt the anger continue to rise in him. "How can you just leave William to die?"

"That's just the nature of this business. He should've known better than to get involved with me."

Derek still didn't move. "How are you going to get his money if he's dead?"

A subtle smile lit Foxglove's face. "I have my ways."

Derek tried to think like this man was, and he could only come to one conclusion—and it wasn't a possibility he wanted to face. But it was the only thing that made sense.

"I'm never going to pass as William, if that's what you're thinking. We've lost touch over the years. I don't know his passcode or PIN numbers. I definitely don't have his fingerprints."

"No, but you have other things that we could use."

Derek shook his head, still trying to figure out what he was thinking. "What does that mean?"

"You'll see soon enough."

He crossed his arms. "No, you want me to live, and it's for a reason. What is that?"

"I said you'll see." Foxglove stepped closer, hatred obvious in his gaze.

Derek's mind continued to race, trying to put things in place. The answers were right there on the edge of his consciousness. He just had to connect them.

"This isn't about William's money at all, is it?" Realization washed through him.

Foxglove didn't say anything, he just waited for him to continue.

"You want my money," Derek muttered.

"Your brother is broke," Foxglove said. "He doesn't have anything to give us. But he told us that you did."

Derek felt his eyes widened. "William wouldn't tell you that."

"But he did. Why do you think we went back to the campsite to find you? It was because we knew if we wanted that money, then we needed to find you."

Things began to click into place in Derek's mind. Now it made sense why these men kept following them. It wasn't to use them as leverage. It was his money.

Derek had saved up a nice nest egg as an attorney. He wasn't one to go out on spending sprees or to take lavish vacations. But he did have a decent savings account in his name.

"I'm not giving you my money." Derek narrowed his gaze.

Foxglove raised his gun and pointed it at Autumn. "I'm sure we can think of ways to make it happen."

"This whole time out here…was it about William or was it about me?"

"Your brother is the one who started all of this. He really did take a loan from us, and he really cannot pay it back. When we found him out here, we knew we needed to think of ways for him to be creative and get that cash. In one of his moments of agony, he said your name. So here we are now."

"Unbelievable…"

"He also said in his moment of delirium that he brought your savings account routing number."

Derek sucked in a breath. That's what those numbers

had been in his backpack. His brother had planned on taking money from his account.

Derek stared at Foxglove as he processed everything. "You're despicable, to say the least."

"Maybe we are. But we're rich. And that's how we want to keep it."

Derek saw the determination in Foxglove's gaze. These guys were planning to keep Autumn hostage until they got the money they wanted. But, if Derek had to guess, they wouldn't keep her alive after they got their hands on this money.

Derek couldn't bear the thought of losing her now.

He had to think of a way to put an end to this.

Now.

As Autumn stood in the middle of the campsite, she listened to the conversation, feeling her jaw drop with every new revelation.

These men had been after Derek this whole time. Everything started to make sense.

She didn't want to think that William would have sold out his brother, but people did strange things when they were in pain. Kind of like an animal who'd been injured. You just never knew how they were going to act out, even to those they loved.

She also knew that this situation would not have a good outcome. No matter which way she looked at it, there was no way these guys were going to let her and Derek walk away.

No, they were both going to be goners.

Not to mention William. Leaving him behind here would be signing his death certificate.

Her thoughts went back to Sherlock. The canine should have gotten back to the parking lot by now. The question was, were the other rangers there waiting for him?

It was a question she couldn't answer. She hoped Hendrix got her SOS. She hoped they could read between the lines and knew Sherlock would be able to lead them back here. She also hoped that the roads were passable.

But still there were a lot of unknowns in that situation.

Most of all, right now she hoped that Sherlock was okay. Letting him go was a bit risky. The more she thought about it, the more doubts crept into her mind.

What if her dog encountered a wild animal? Or got lost?

No, those thoughts were ridiculous. Sherlock was smarter than that.

But stress snowballed inside her.

"We need to move," Foxglove said. "Now."

He took Autumn's arm and began leading her way.

As he did, Autumn glanced back. If they left with these men, she felt certain they would die.

The question was, how were they going to get out of this?

They needed a distraction.

Almost as if Derek had read her mind, he froze and pointed at something in the distance. "The bobcat! He came back!"

As the man looked away, Derek burst into action. He grabbed Foxglove's gun from him, ready to fight for his life.

Foxglove turned and swung his arm, connecting it with Derek's face. As he did, the gun flew to the ground.

Derek reeled back.

As he did, the other man came at him.

Autumn lunged to the ground, trying to reach the gun.

Just as her hands gripped the metal there, Foxglove's foot came down over her fingers and the barrel.

Pain squeezed her.

As she looked up, she saw murder in the man's eyes.

TWENTY-FOUR

"No!" Derek yelled.

If Foxglove got that gun back, Autumn was a goner. So was he.

He dived toward the man. Before he could reach him, Whitaker appeared and tackled him.

Derek kicked the man's legs. Whitaker rolled off him, just in time for Derek to swing his leg out and hit Foxglove's knee.

The man lost his balance and fell to the ground.

As he did, Autumn reached forward, her face straining as she grabbed the gun and sat up. "Stay right where you are!"

Foxglove started to reach for her. When he saw her point the gun at him, he froze.

"Nobody move," Autumn repeated, her voice just above a growl as she pushed herself to her feet.

Foxglove stared at her, his eyes looking dazed. Finally, he raised his hands in the air also. "Let's not be hasty."

"One wrong move, and I won't hesitate to pull this trigger," Autumn continued.

"What are you going to do?" Foxglove muttered.

"Are you going to arrest us? While we're stuck out here in the middle of nowhere?"

The man was taunting her. But Autumn didn't look a bit flustered as she stared the man down.

"You're going to do exactly what I tell you to do." She kept her gun pointed at them and her voice hard. "Derek, tie them up," she said. "We need to make sure they're not going anywhere."

"You don't want to do this," Foxglove said, warning snaking through his voice.

"Don't tell me what I want to do."

"This isn't going to work out the way that you think it is," Foxglove continued, undeterred by her hardened voice. The man looked like he could strike again at any moment.

"I don't need you telling me what I'm going to do or what I'm going to think," Autumn said, her voice unwavering. "Do you understand?"

Derek grabbed some rope and tied Foxglove's hands behind him, working quickly before they could try anything.

"You don't have a plan right now," Foxglove continued to mock her. "If you leave me out here, we're just going to figure out a way to get away. You know we will."

Autumn raised the gun in the air and pulled the trigger.

The gunfire cracked the air, and birds in the trees above scattered at the sound, squawking their displeasure.

"Enough talking," she said. "Do I make myself clear?"

Foxglove quieted.

Derek continued to tie up the men. Just as he pulled the last knot, a new sound filled the air.

"Is that… ?" He straightened and glanced in the distance.

It was.

It was the sound of an engine.

And it was coming their way.

He continued staring through the woods just in time to see an ATV emerge.

Was it more bad guys coming to attack them? Did Foxglove have a backup out there?

He glanced at Autumn, trying to read her expression. She still looked composed and unflappable as she held her gun, waiting for someone to make a wrong move.

More noise filled the air.

More ATVs.

Derek really hoped it was the good guys on their way. Because if this was more bad guys, then he and Autumn were in serious trouble.

As the vehicles stopped nearby, he saw several park rangers darting through the wilderness toward them.

Help was here. Praise God, help was here.

Autumn had never been so glad to see Ranger Hendrix arrive. As the crew took over the scene, she lowered her gun and released her breath.

Maybe this was finally over.

It almost seemed too good to be true.

She watched in the distance as Derek ran into his brother's tent. He emerged a moment later. "He's still alive!"

Two park rangers hurried inside to help. Derek hesitatingly left. There probably wasn't much room to work in there.

A moment later, he appeared beside her. As soon as Autumn saw him, she threw her arms around him, nearly collapsing in his embrace.

"Good job back there," he murmured. "You saved our lives."

"I'm so glad you're okay," she whispered in his ear, pulling him tighter.

She took a step back but reached up and rested her hand on his cheek. She'd have more time to talk to him later. There was so much she wanted to say. Needed to say.

But this wasn't the time or the place.

Instead, Autumn glanced around. Her gaze searched the wilderness, and she held her breath with expectation. A moment later, she spotted another ranger cutting through the forest.

There, on a leash in front of the ranger, was... Sherlock.

The ranger released the dog, and Autumn knelt down onto the ground with her arms open. Her dog ran right into them and began licking her face.

"I knew you wouldn't let me down, Sherlock. I knew it." She held her dog closer, grateful that he was okay.

"That was some quick thinking on your part." Ranger Hendrix paced to a stop beside her.

"So you got my messages?" Autumn asked, standing to talk.

"We heard you sending the SOS through the radio. We tried to get back in touch with you but couldn't. I put everything together and realized that you were in trouble. When I saw Sherlock, I knew we didn't have any time to waste. We had to find you."

"I'm so glad you did."

"Now that we know your coordinates, we're sending a helicopter," Hendrix said, turning toward Derek. "We'll get your brother the help he needs."

"Thank you," Derek said. "How did you find us?"

Hendrix nodded at Sherlock. "That dog led the way. Once we got close enough, we held the dog back, just in case. But he brought us right to you."

Derek leaned down and rubbed Sherlock's fur.

"You're a good boy," he murmured.

"We've been trying to bust these guys for a long time," Hendrix said, nodding at Foxglove and Whitaker. "They're in a lot of trouble with the law."

"They were ready to kill us." Autumn shivered as she remembered how close to death they'd come.

Hendrix frowned. "You guys did well. You survived circumstances that most of us wouldn't have."

Autumn and Derek exchanged a look. The ranger only knew half of it, and it was going to take a while to run through the whole story with him. They'd have plenty of time for that later—once they were off this mountain.

"It was only because we worked as a team." Her gaze went to Derek.

As Hendrix wandered away to assess the scene, Autumn turned toward Derek.

"Thanks for your help out there," she told him. "I mean, we only survived because we worked together."

He shrugged. "I'm still sorry that I got you involved in all this."

"Like I told you before, you couldn't have known what your brother was up to."

"Smart thinking with Sherlock. I wasn't sure what you were doing, but I figured you had a plan. There was no way you would have just let Sherlock go otherwise."

She rubbed Sherlock's fur again. "He's never let me down yet."

Derek leaned toward her. "Autumn... I know this sounds crazy to say. I know we haven't known each other that long but—"

"I know," she filled in for him. "I feel it also."

"You do?"

She nodded. "Initially, I didn't want to feel anything. And when I realized I did, it scared me. I don't want to grow attached to someone, only to have something happen to them. I wasn't sure my heart could handle it."

Derek squeezed her hand. "I understand."

"But when I thought you were going to die out there in the river... I knew without a doubt that I didn't want this to be the end for both of us." She wiped away the moisture that formed beneath her eyes.

A smile stretched across his face. "That makes me very happy to hear. I thought I'd messed things up."

She shook her head. "No, not at all. Once you've loved and lost someone...it makes you look at the future differently."

"I can only imagine." He leaned down and kissed her cheek. "I don't want to push you into something you're not ready for."

"I know without a doubt now that I am ready."

He grinned. "Good. Now...we need to have you checked out, especially that cut on your leg."

She bent her leg and felt the stiffness there. "It's true, but I think I'll be okay."

Derek raised an eyebrow. "After all of this settles, how about if we have dinner together?"

She grinned. "Dinner sounds really nice, especially if it's with you. Maybe even more than one."

"Definitely more than one."

The two of them shared a smile, and Autumn felt warmth spread through her chest. Spending more time with Derek was definitely an idea she could get used to. In fact, she could see herself enjoying his company for a long time.

TWENTY-FIVE

Six months later

Autumn looked up as she heard someone step onto her screened-in porch.

Her eyes lit with happiness when Derek came into view. He'd cleaned up really well. Actually, he'd looked great even when they'd been trapped in the wilderness.

But right now, his jaw was clean shaven, his hair neatly combed away from his face and he wore jeans with a short-sleeve top. Casual but professional. He looked very small-town lawyer.

Which was a good thing, since that's now what he was.

She hoped she looked better also. She was off work for the day but had donned some jeans and her favorite T-shirt. Her cuts and bruises had long since healed. Yet, in some ways, she'd always carry them with her. They reminded her of just how precious life was and how at the worst moments, God could send the biggest blessings.

Autumn stood to greet Derek, and he leaned toward her, planting a lingering kiss on her lips. Warmth spread through her at his nearness—just as it did every time they were close.

"Glad you made it," she said, leaving a hand on his chest.

"Time with you? I wouldn't miss it for anything."

The two of them shared a smile.

Then he leaned down and patted Sherlock on the head. The dog wagged his tail as he greeted him. Sherlock seemed to like Derek just as much as she did.

"Good to see you, boy," Derek murmured. "You've been taking care of Autumn for me?"

The dog barked in response.

As Derek and Autumn sat on the swing, Sherlock jumped up beside them and placed his front paws on Autumn's lap. The three of them fit perfectly.

"You got here just before the rain did," Autumn said, nodding outside.

She watched as the drops began to hit the leaves on the woods that surrounded her porch. They pitter-pattered on the tin roof above, and the pleasant scent of fresh rain filled the air. These were the kind of gentle storms she could handle, much more so than that awful line of storms that had trapped them on the mountainside last fall.

Gently, the swing undulated back and forth.

"I still can't believe you're here." She squeezed Derek's hand, never wanting to let go.

Not only had the two of them kept in touch with each other since their ordeal in the woods, but Derek had ultimately made the decision to take a job as prosecutor here in the county where Autumn was living. He just finished moving in this week.

Autumn had been anticipating seeing him all day today. At work, it had been all she was able to think about. She still couldn't believe he was really here. For good.

His arm slipped behind her, and she leaned into him, feeling totally relaxed.

"I could really get used to this," he murmured.

"I could get used to this, too. And, by this, I mean you being here with me."

He planted a kiss on her forehead before pulling her close again. "Me too. This was a good move."

"You're sure you don't miss DC and the fast-paced lifestyle there?"

"I don't miss it for a moment. I like the slower pace. But mostly I look forward to being with you…and Sherlock, of course."

The dog wagged his tail when he heard his name.

Autumn glanced down at the dog and rubbed his head again. Sherlock really had saved them that day. If he hadn't led the rangers into the woods, who knew what would have happened out there?

"I heard an update today on the case," she started.

"Did you?" Derek moved back just enough to see her face.

"Foxglove and Whitaker are going to be in jail for a very long time. We can definitely be thankful for that."

"That is good news," Derek said. "William is also getting the help that he needs. He's been in therapy, and he's trying to clean up his life, though there's still a chance that he might face some jail time."

"I'm glad to know that that whole situation might have a happy ending."

"Me too." Derek took in a breath and shifted. "In fact, there's something I want to ask you."

Autumn's heart thumped into her chest as she waited to hear what he had to say. She could hardly breathe. "What's that?"

"I know that we both had rocky roads to get here. But as soon as I met you, Autumn Mercer, I knew that you were different from anybody else I had ever talked to. I knew there was something really special about you."

He reached into his pocket and pulled something out. "That said, there's something I want to ask you."

Autumn sucked in a breath as she watched Derek get down on one knee.

Was this really happening? Was it possible that she could find true love twice in her life? It seemed too good to be true.

"Autumn, after Sarah left me at the altar… I didn't know if I ever wanted to look at forever again," Derek started. "I didn't think the heartache was worth it. Though our circumstances were different, I'm sure you can understand."

"I do."

"But when I met you, you brought something to life in me. When I imagined my future without you…it seemed grim."

She waited for him to continue.

"I realized I'd be a fool to ever let you walk away from me. I love you. Autumn Mercer, will you marry me?"

The air left her lungs. She didn't even have to think about her answer. "Yes, I will. I will marry you, Derek. I love you, too."

He slipped a beautiful engagement ring on her finger before rising to his feet. He pulled her along with him and tucked her closer. Their lips met.

As they did, Sherlock barked beside them.

They pulled away and chuckled. The dog jumped between them until he got a pat on the head.

Derek leaned toward the dog. "And yes, Sherlock, I want you to be a part of the family, too. Always."

The dog licked his face.

As Autumn watched all of it, her heart filled with so much warmth and love that she'd never thought she would've been able to experience again.

But she was so grateful that things had worked out just the way that they were supposed to.

And now, against all odds, she was getting another chance at a happy-ever-after again.

* * * * *

Heather Woodhaven earned her pilot's license, rode a hot-air balloon over the safari lands of Kenya, parasailed over Caribbean seas, lived through an accidental detour onto a black-diamond ski trail in Aspen, and snorkeled among stingrays before becoming a mother of three and wife of one. She channels her love for adventure into writing characters who find themselves in extraordinary circumstances.

Books by Heather Woodhaven

Love Inspired Suspense

Visit the Author Profile page at LoveInspired.com for more titles.

SEARCH AND DEFEND

Heather Woodhaven

My flesh and my heart faileth: but God is the strength of my heart, and my portion for ever.
—*Psalms* 73:26

To all my family and friends.
Your unique variety of expertise and knowledge
has been a great benefit to me. Thank you for
responding to my out-of-the-blue texts
filled with questions and what-ifs.

ONE

FBI special agent Alex Driscoll hated undercover work. Pretending to be someone else tied his gut up in knots, especially when he no longer had a partner to watch his back. Tonight, he was playing the part of a chef. His informant had told him to watch for the hand-off of a flash drive to a woman with jet-black hair and a red dress. The private political fundraiser was being held the night after Christmas, though, which meant he'd already spotted thirteen women who matched that description.

"My table wants ours made special order. No ginger, no celery, extra avocado with a light drizzle of wasabi." The woman in front of him raised a heavily jeweled hand. "Too much, and I'll send it back. The rice on the outside, not the inside." She demanded perfection, as did most of the attendees, given they'd all paid two thousand dollars to attend the special event.

"Of course, ma'am." The position with the catering company should've been the perfect cover since he enjoyed cooking, but he wasn't sure he could deliver under the scrutiny of the rich and famous. Sushi was an especially difficult dish to make while keeping watch on the guests. "What led you to attend tonight, ma'am?" he asked as an excuse to look up and scan the room.

Cooking stations lined the back side of the lodge located at the base of the mountain. The building was set apart from the rest of the famous Idaho ski resort. The glass walls on the opposite side of where he stood offered dazzling views of the lit-up ski runs that were closed during the event.

"We support Governor Davenport wholeheartedly." She cocked an eyebrow. "Why else would anyone be here?"

"It's the event of the season." He flashed what he hoped would be his most charming smile. All Alex knew was there was going to be an assassination attempt in the next couple of weeks. The target would be someone powerful, not necessarily the governor. The flash drive Alex hoped to intercept was rumored to contain the name of the target and their itinerary. One of the many women wearing a red dress would be the Firecracker's courier.

He added a dash of black sesame seeds to the top of the roll and handed the sushi plate to the waiter standing by. "What table, ma'am?"

"Seven." She strode off, chin held high, and the waiter hustled after her.

If the Firecracker intended on taking out the governor, he might also be here tonight, discreetly gathering intel on his prey. The same intel Alex needed in order to stop him once and for all.

The assassin's modus operandi usually involved killing the target along with their security detail. Bombs were his choice of weapon. The Firecracker had never targeted a large amount of people at once, like the couple of hundred in attendance now, but Alex wasn't lowering his guard. Every chance he got to slip away, he searched for nooks and crannies in the lodge where explosives might be hidden.

The FBI had no descriptions to go on, no photographs, only that the assassin was in his late fifties. Unfortunately, that meant Alex was surrounded by potential suspects mingling within the party. The lodge was one giant room with floor-to-ceiling windows facing one of the resort's mountains. The other three walls were decorated to resemble a log cabin, a luxury, multimillion dollar one.

At his two o'clock, a man with eyes darting left and right hastily made his way across the room. Under five foot ten, the man was average in height and looks, early thirties. He would've blended in if his right hand hadn't been clenched in a tight fist. Either the man planned to punch someone, or he was carrying the flash drive.

"I heard we talk to you if we want a special order." An elderly woman stepped in front of his station, blocking his view.

Alex looked over her shoulder. "Yes. Shortly. I believe we're out of…" He lost his train of thought as his gaze tracked the man's path. A glittering party clutch sat upright at one of the tables, open and waiting. Six feet away from the table, a woman in red laughed loudly at something another woman said.

"We're out of some ingredients. I'll go and get them from another station. Please check back in a few minutes." He stepped out from behind the station and barely registered the irritated huff. "Pardon me." He jostled in and out of groups in his way, fighting to keep his eye on the one-fisted man.

"Do you need something?" A waiter blocked his path. "You left your station."

"Yes, I need to grab something from another chef. I'll be right back."

Like running through a complicated football play, Alex spun right and darted left to avoid colliding with other guests. There. The man's fist released right over the top of the clutch. The slightest reflection of silver confirmed his suspicions. Alex reached into his white chef's jacket and grabbed the flash drive he'd prepared. Except the woman in red was starting to turn around, no doubt to retrieve the clutch now that the handoff had been made.

Alex had to stall her. He slipped his left foot out, and a man tripped over him, diving headfirst into a group of four. The exclamations drew attention, and just as he'd hoped, the woman in red watched, her brow furrowed. Alex darted behind her, made a one-handed switch and continued to the chef station closest to her table. "I need…salt at my station," he said.

"Then get it from the kitchen. I need mine." The chef scowled before beaming at an approaching guest.

Alex didn't mind at all. Mission accomplished. The woman turned back to her purse, and seeing the flash drive Alex had placed there, closed the clutch and smiled. She hadn't noticed him make the switch. Good. Tonight, they would finally bring the Firecracker to justice.

There were two men staring right at him from across

the room. They had broad shoulders under their tux-edos and matching gaits as they started toward him. Alex didn't think they were the Idaho state troopers that were typically assigned to the governor. The tell-tale wrinkle in their jackets gave him pause. Armed. Unfortunately, Alex had been searched "for security reasons" before being allowed to enter as a chef. His own gun was still in the car.

He darted toward the north wall, making his way around the attendees to get back to his station. A quick look over his shoulder confirmed the men were coming for him. He needed to get the flash drive somewhere safe in case they were associates of the Firecracker.

A woman with caramel hair down to her shoulders, dressed in a shimmering silver gown and strappy heels he'd never imagined she'd be caught dead in stepped into the light.

Violet Sharp, his partner's widow.

Rick Sharp had been killed by the Firecracker two years ago. Violet's face blanched at the sight of him, but she didn't raise a hand or an arm in greeting. Thank-fully, she knew better.

Violet had never been the type to attend ritzy po-litical fundraisers, but grief changed people. He'd also never seen her without her K-9 Search and Rescue dog by her side. She blinked rapidly and broke the unspo-ken connection, turning away to offer a tight smile to a tall, athletic-looking man who embraced her and gave her a little-too-friendly kiss to the cheek.

Alex had hesitated too long. The two men had almost reached him. He continued his path toward Violet and bumped into her shoulder.

"Hey, watch where you're going," the man with her said.

Alex grabbed Violet's elbow as if offering support, all the while dropping the drive into the main compartment of the silver purse hanging at her side. "Terribly sorry, ma'am."

Her eyes widened. "No harm done."

He strode past her, jostling and bumping past other people lest the two men suspect and target Violet. The crowd was getting irritated with him. All the more reason to feign excuses and leave early.

He sidestepped left and reached his food station just as they did.

"Enjoying the party?" the one to the left asked.

"Isn't that what people do?" He shrugged. "I'm not feeling well, though. So I think I'll be leaving early."

"How about we escort you outside then?"

He'd walked straight into that one. "It's cold out there. Looks like snow falling again. How about I—?"

The man to his right flashed open his jacket to reveal a gun with a silencer attached. "Let's go. You wouldn't want anyone else to get hurt, would you?"

Were they referring to someone specific or bluffing? Alex narrowed his eyes. "What you're suggesting would draw a lot of attention. I—"

He'd been focused on the man with the gun instead of the one on the left. His second mistake of the night. A needle pricked through his white jacket and into his arm. He reached out and grabbed the man's hand and yanked the needle back out. The syringe hit the floor, and Alex stomped on it, crushing the vial.

The telltale sensation of heat in his veins and a racing heart rate meant he hadn't pulled out the needle fast enough. He could call out, make a scene, but that might put Violet in danger. As a law enforcement ranger for the US Forest Service, she'd run to his aid. He'd never forgive himself if his decision resulted in her losing her life, too.

"What'd you give me?" he asked. The governor had yet to arrive. The two men were both too young to match the Firecracker's description.

"You're about to find out."

Alex moved to grab the knife on the cart in front of him, but his hand missed the handle and pushed the bowl of chopped green onions instead.

"What did you...?" His voice slurred. His vision blurred. The two men hooked their elbows through his, and he lost his footing. A moment later, cold air stung his face. But his eyes wouldn't stay open long enough to find out where he was going, and he didn't think he'd live long enough to find out.

Violet Sharp could not believe Alex was here. She knew enough of her late husband's work to never wave at another special agent. Ever. If an agent greeted her or waved first, then it was safe. Alex had seen her—bumped into her, even—but he hadn't acknowledged her in a personal way. Her eyes had wanted to follow him when he'd moved past her, but she hadn't wanted to draw any attention to him.

Dark wavy hair, green eyes and only a few inches taller than her, he appeared intimidating in size because of his athletic build. He looked different than the last time she'd seen him, like he was made of harder edges.

In the one second their eyes had connected, she'd

recognized the pain he carried, certain she reflected the same hollow emptiness. Judging by the tension in his jaw, he had felt the same way about seeing her. They reminded each other of the greatest loss in their lives. Rick. The sensation had rocked her off balance. After two years, she shouldn't be so caught off guard by sudden waves of sorrow, but grief refused to follow any rule book.

She also really needed a word with her best friend. Eryn Lane had pleaded with her to come to this party. The only reason Violet had agreed was so that Eryn could have a night out without kids. She'd foolishly assumed the evening would be free of any of the matchmaking attempts her friends had been intent on lately. Eryn had ambushed her by arranging for Violet's high school boyfriend, Bruce Wilkinson, to meet them there.

Every social invitation had become a minefield the past couple of months. It was as if crossing the two-year marker of being a widow had put an Available sign on her forehead. Why couldn't Eryn get it through her head that Violet had no intention of marrying again?

Bruce was regaling them with yet another story of one of his latest business ventures when a current of cold air rushed past her.

"Who keeps opening the door?" Eryn wrapped her arms around herself and turned to find the source of the cold. Two men, one on either side of Alex, disappeared out the back.

"Looks like someone had a little too much Christmas cheer," Bruce muttered. "That guy was bumping into everyone, not just you. And he's one of the employees, no less. If this were my business, I would—"

Violet didn't hear the rest of Bruce's analysis on best business practices. The back of her neck tingled. Something wasn't right. There was nothing behind the lodge but woods. The same woods she'd planned to walk through to get home. "Excuse me, I need to check on Teddy."

She grabbed a napkin from Alex's food station on her way to the coatrack and threw on her wool coat and the boots she'd brought with her. A moment later, she was out the front door next to the parking lot.

Teddy, her Newfoundland dog, sat at attention beside the valet, Daniella Curtis. The sidewalk in front of the lodge had been converted to a red-carpet platform. Daniella managed a podium with little hooks to keep track of vehicle keys.

"Thanks for letting Teddy keep you company." Where Violet went, Teddy went. The town understood that her K-9 never left her side. Leaving him with Daniella had been a compromise after Eryn had expressed her displeasure at bringing the dog along. Even when Violet wasn't on duty with the USFS, she was always on duty for search and rescue. "Has Teddy been a good guest?"

"Of course." Daniella patted the top of the massive dog's head. "He's keeping me from being bored out of my mind."

When Teddy sat upright, he measured over two feet from shoulder to ground. From nose to tail, he was six feet long and weighed thirty pounds more than Violet, though she wasn't about to reveal that specific amount to anyone. Her gentle giant was the best search-and-rescue dog in the area and a loyal companion.

She patted her side. "Teddy and I need to check on something. We should be right back." She set the strappy heels and sparkly purse behind Daniella's podium. She didn't need anything flapping on her person, hindering her speed. "Mind if I leave these here?"

Violet didn't wait for Daniella's answer. She ran around the corner of the lodge. Teddy didn't need prodding. He ran at her side. Plenty of breeds had the sniffing capabilities to work in search and rescue, but Teddy had the type of intelligence that was rare. The back of the building was deserted, but two sets of footprints in the snow led to the woods.

The breeze had faded, and the winter night seemed to be holding its breath. Her time working as Teddy's handler had taught her to pay attention to things she'd never noticed before. She could hear her own heart beating. There was no sign of anyone else rushing after Alex. She had to know if he was okay, Rick would want her to make sure. If Alex didn't want her there, she'd simply pretend she was out walking her dog.

She presented the napkin she'd snagged from Alex's food station. Teddy lifted his nose and made staccato-like inhalations.

"Find."

A whisper was all he needed. His head disappeared into the powdered snow for a split second before popping back up. His golden eyes and brown bushy fur made him appear like a bear, the inspiration for his name, especially in the snow. And right now, he was the happiest bear in the world. He had caught the scent, and he was eager to go to work.

She rushed after him and entered the woods, where

all hint of light from the moon and the stars disappeared. Popping, cracking sounds toyed with her sense of direction. The noise could be footsteps, or it could be sap freezing inside the trees. At only ten degrees, the cold quickly seeped through her long wool coat. Teddy pressed ahead, directing her which way to go.

The powdery snow proved easy to walk across quietly.

"I can't find the flash drive." A male voice reached her ears. "But he's stirring. He got the needle out before the full—"

"Then maybe we make sure he doesn't wake up. Make the call and get our orders."

Violet held out both hands, a signal for Teddy to stop following the trail. She strained to see past the trees. The two men stood with guns drawn over Alex, who lay crumpled in the snow.

A deep, rolling rumble sent shivers up her spine until she realized Teddy was the source. She stepped behind the cover of a thick trunk before the men could see her. She should've realized Teddy knew Alex and could tell he was in danger. A trainer had once told her that people gave off different types of pheromones depending on their intentions. Teddy understood those intentions. If he was worried about what these men wanted with Alex, she was worried.

"What is that?" One of the men looked their way.

The question gave her an idea. Violet made a click with her tongue, and Teddy's gaze shifted to her. She flipped her palm over and raised it to the sky. He lifted up on his hind legs, standing up, a trick they'd been working on for over a year.

"It's either bigfoot or a bear, and I don't want to find out which."

She didn't blame them. Teddy was one of the larger Newfoundland dogs she'd met, and that was saying something. And his growl had the resonance of a wild animal.

"Are you crazy? Put the gun down. We don't have the kind of firepower to take a bear down before he mauls us."

"If he charges, I'm shooting. Bears are beyond my pay grade."

"Leave him. We don't need him anymore anyway. Let's go!"

Violet hastily lowered her hand. Teddy dropped down to his paws but not before he released another guttural growl. The men made quick work of disappearing in the other direction. She counted to ten in case they decided to come back, then she ran for the figure on the ground.

Teddy proved faster and was nuzzling Alex's face when she arrived at his side. Alex had been around often before Rick's death, and he'd always come prepared with treats, ready to win Teddy's affections. Clearly, Teddy remembered.

Alex groaned and reached up, blocking the dog. "No." His voice sounded groggy but clear. She blew out a sigh of relief. Alive. Teddy moved to sniffing the rest of him, no doubt in search of treats.

"It's Violet." She gingerly reached for his wrist lest he attack on instinct. "I won't hurt you. How do you feel?"

He flinched but blinked rapidly. "Violet," he murmured. His heart rate was strong, a little faster than she'd like, but in the normal range. He sat up suddenly. Teddy's tail wagged faster, and he pressed his body into Alex.

"Feel free to hug him to get warm. He holds a lot of heat."

Alex acted as if he was about to take her advice, but instead, he used the quick hug to right himself to standing. He spun around, fully alert. "Where are they?"

"They ran away, leaving you for dead. They thought this bear might finish you off."

He pointed at Teddy. "Him? You?" He ran a hand over his face and exhaled. "Thank you both."

"Do you know what they gave you?"

"A short dose of something to knock me out. Felt like I was going to sleep for a surgery. I don't think they gave me much. I managed to get the needle out of my arm before he got the plunger down."

"Who were they, Alex?"

He shook his head. "I'm not sure yet. I never meant for you to get involved, though. I hope I didn't put you in danger."

"They said they couldn't find a flash drive on you."

"Violet?" A shrill voice called out from the direction of the party. "Are you in there?"

"Do you have your gun?" Alex reached for her arm, steadying himself.

"No need." She didn't want to explain that she didn't carry one anymore. At least, not right now. "That's my friend checking up on me. I left the party when I saw those men dragging you out. Rumor has it you're an employee who drank too much."

A light flickered through the trees. "Get some help." Bruce's voice rang out loud and clear. "There's a man with his hands on her. I'm coming, Violet!"

"I'm fine," Violet shouted. "Just taking Teddy for a walk. One second."

Alex straightened. "I need to stay undercover."

She pointed in the opposite direction of the men. "I think your cover might already be blown. And what do you want me to tell them?" She thumbed over her shoulder at Bruce and Eryn, still aiming lights in their direction.

"I need to be able to move around the town and resort without everyone knowing I'm an FBI agent."

Her throat tightened. "Is this about Rick?" His hesitation irritated her. "The Firecracker?"

He flinched. "You know the name? I thought that information was still—"

"Your superiors interviewed me multiple times when Rick was killed." She shrugged, not wanting to relive the days after, the constant questions and analysis of Rick's last words. "I know the Firecracker was responsible, and that he's still out there."

"I think I've almost got him."

"Then I'll help you in whatever way I can." Maybe she would sleep better knowing Rick's killer had finally faced justice. "I grew up here. I know most of the locals. Just tell me what you need. Who should I tell Bruce and Eryn you are?"

"I need a second." He pulled his white jacket off and flipped it inside out, revealing a black jacket. He removed a black tie from inside a pocket and slipped it over his head. The quick change wasn't anything new to her, as she'd seen her husband practice similar moves for undercover missions, but she was still surprised to see the transformation from employee to party attendee. He brushed off the remaining snow from his legs in one motion.

"Lead the way to your friends," he said. "Before we have more company. My mind is still waking up, but I think I have an idea that might work."

As they neared the tree line, Alex reached for her hand. His fingers, icy from his time in the snow, wrapped around hers. She pulled back, surprised at the gesture, until she realized what Alex must be planning.

She was his new cover.

TWO

Alex slipped on a pair of nonprescription, black-framed glasses as they exited the cover of the woods. The athletic man who had been overly friendly to Violet narrowed his eyes at the sight of them. "Violet? Are you sure you're okay?"

"I'm Alex Ross." He reached out with his right hand to shake theirs. "Sorry if we scared you. I got into town late to meet Violet, but Teddy needed a walk before we went back inside." At the mention of his name, the giant dog leaned against Alex's legs and looked up. "Violet said you're Eryn and Bruce."

Eryn laughed. "And Teddy certainly knows you. Are you two...?"

"It's new," Violet said stiffly. Her hand wrapped tighter around his. "Alex is from Utah."

Alex beamed. He hadn't had time to explain his intentions, but she *had* offered to help in any way she could. She obviously understood. Rick had always said Violet would be better at undercover work than either of them. Knowing her quick wit, Alex had never doubted it. "Long-distance relationships can be tricky, so we wanted to keep it low-key."

There was no one else in the world but Violet who wanted to get the Firecracker behind bars as badly as he did. Rick's death demanded justice. And while still a little groggy, he had realized she would be the best contact he had in town. This way, he could make sure she was safe and have a reason to catch up without attracting suspicion. Rick would've wanted him to make sure she was doing okay. Alex only regretted it'd taken him two years to do so.

"So, you're here on a short visit?" Bruce made no effort at hiding the fact he was evaluating him, sizing up the competition.

"Might be doing a little job hunting, actually. I work in hospitality, so I might get a feel for the resort while I'm here."

"Where are you staying? Oh, never mind. That's a silly question." Eryn laughed, pointing at Violet. "Your mom must be glad someone will finally be staying in the vacation rental."

Violet had a rental? Alex simply smiled and nodded.

"Honey," Violet said slowly. Bruce pulled his chin back in surprise at Violet's use of the endearment. Alex tried not to enjoy the reaction. "It's getting cold," she said. "And late. Sorry to dash, Eryn, but maybe Bruce will keep you company the rest of the night? I'd like to catch up with Alex after his long drive here."

With a jolt, Alex realized he didn't see Violet's dress shoes or purse on her person. "Where's your purse?"

"Oh, I left it with Daniella."

Eryn squinted, a look of suspicion on her face, and addressed Alex. "You've heard about Daniella?"

"He knows I mentor her," Violet answered easily,

tossing aside the test her friend seemed to have wanted Alex to fail. "I'll catch up with you later, Eryn." Violet tightened her grip on his hand and pulled him forward, gaining distance from her two friends. "I'll just grab my stuff, and we can walk to my house."

"You walked?"

"I actually came with Eryn, but I planned to walk home. It's not far. There's a walking path to the east of the river."

"In the dark, in the winter."

"With Teddy." He felt her fingers stiffen, no doubt with irritation. "You might have forgotten, but I'm a trained officer, Alex."

He bristled. "So am I, and they got the jump on me."

She dropped his hand as if it had burned her. They rounded the corner of the lodge. "You're right. Being trained doesn't guarantee safety. For either of us."

She was referencing Rick's death. He struggled to find something to say, but she stopped in front of a podium that had a locked glass case over rows of keys. "The purse is gone."

Alex finally felt warmth in his fingers and toes, but not for good reason. If her purse was gone—

"Daniella?" Violet called out to the dark parking lot.

A teenager with long hair braided down her back appeared behind them with a steaming cup. "Sorry, Stephen got me some cocoa."

The purse and heels were dangling from Daniella's elbow. "I took them inside with me to make sure they'd be safe."

"That was very thoughtful. Thank you." Violet reached for the items.

"You had them with you the entire time?" Alex asked.

Daniella raised an eyebrow. "Well, I set them down for a second. No offense, but a bunch of rich people aren't going to be tempted by Violet's stuff. Maybe the employees, but I kept a watch on them."

"I'm sure it's fine. Thank you." Violet eyed Alex warily as she leaned over and gave Daniella a quick hug.

Alex overheard Daniella whisper, "Who's the guy?"

"I'll tell you later," Violet replied with another whisper before ending the hug. Eryn and Bruce both passed them and reentered the party, waving their goodbyes.

The faster he got the flash drive out of her purse, the better. They strode away from the lodge. "I'll drive you home," he said.

She opened the back door of his sedan, and Teddy made himself comfortable, taking up the entire three seats. She pointed to the passenger side. "Unless you're willing to call this in and find out what drug they gave you, I'm driving."

He'd call his handler later, but calling for backup might ruin their chances of catching the Firecracker. They suspected someone on the target's security detail was helping the assassin.

"Whatever it was, I'm fine now." He tossed her the keys. "But I'm not arguing. You know the area better anyway."

They got in quickly, and she started the car. "I'm surprised Bruce and Eryn didn't recognize you, since you bumped into me at the party."

Alex reached into the console and pulled out his tablet. He slid the adapter into the side, preparing it for the flash drive. "People see what they expect to see." He grabbed the silver purse she'd set over the cup holders. "For instance, did you see I dropped a flash drive in your purse?"

Her eyes widened. "No."

He held up the purse for permission to rifle. She nodded and returned her attention to the road. "The flash drive is going to help you find the Firecracker?"

"Hopefully. There is more than one potential target at the resort this season—"

"Politicians and celebrities love this place."

"We think a member of the target's security detail put their itinerary on the flash drive and arranged it to be delivered to the Firecracker through a series of hand-offs. I managed to switch it for my own with a tracking device." The evening bag opened with barely any effort, the magnetic clasp revealing sparse contents. "I put the drive with the itinerary in your purse in case the men found it on me. One look at the itinerary, and we should be able to figure out who Firecracker is targeting." He frowned. "There's hardly anything in here."

"Dress purses aren't designed with security in mind. My keys and wallet. That's it."

He dumped over the bag and let the two items fall onto the keyboard. "Unfortunately, you're right." His throat burned with sudden indigestion. No drive. Daniella must have set it down longer than she'd implied.

He hit the power on the tablet. He had one trick up his sleeve. "So they got their flash drive back. But maybe they still have the one I slipped them, too."

The tracking software flashed to life. The blinking

dot moved along a road. He breathed a sigh of relief. "They're on the move."

Violet took a left turn.

The dot continued to move. "They just turned from Sunset Strip onto Serenade Lane."

"We're on Serenade Lane." Her voice had a monotone quality.

Alex strained forward. "Then we're gaining on them. Can you speed up?"

She pressed on the accelerator. "Alex?"

He focused on the map. Questions were going to have to wait. "Now they're on Cottonwood."

"Serenade turns into Cottonwood. Alex," she said more sternly. "There's no one but us on the street."

"Then we haven't spotted them yet. The dot is still moving."

She took a sharp turn and stopped. "Is it moving still?"

His irritation spiked. "What are you doing? They've turned on—" He pulled in a sharp breath. The dot had stopped moving, but how could that be? Violet grabbed her purse from him and rooted around in the bag. She frowned and unzipped a front pocket.

His veins felt like they were pumping lava as she held up a silver drive. The same flash drive he'd planted in the woman's clutch.

"Is it possible you made a mistake?" she asked.

He shook his head. "Even if I had—which I didn't—I dropped the flash drive in the main compartment. This was intentional."

"Then you're not the only one with sleight of hand."

His finger shook as he pointed to the front pocket. "Someone is sending me a message."

The Firecracker or his courier had not only seen Alex make the switch, they must have seen Violet, too. All thanks to Alex. He struggled to get the words he needed to say past the tightness in his throat. "Violet, I'm afraid I've put you in danger."

She gripped the steering wheel tightly, trying to absorb the information. Much about Rick's death was still a mystery to her. The scant details she'd obtained had been hard-earned by begging his supervisor, who'd held tears in his own eyes. What she *did* know was that Rick had been collateral damage when a bomb, intended for the Firecracker's target, went off early. She hadn't even been told who the original target was. The only other detail provided had been the assurance that Rick hadn't suffered.

Now the assassin who had killed her husband might have seen what she looked like. Maybe even knew her name? Good. Let the Firecracker understand who he'd hurt by taking Rick before his time. She blinked rapidly, surprised at her own reaction.

Teddy's nose touched her shoulder. The scientist had to be right. He could smell her emotions. Her heart was racing, but Teddy wasn't smelling fear. She couldn't tell Alex her thoughts, though. She'd sound like a maniac.

In danger? If the man wanted to kill her, let him try. Somewhere deep inside, she had always welcomed a chance to come face-to-face with Rick's killer. She'd been praying the same prayer for two years, two months and ten days. The words ran through her mind again, almost on autopilot.

Give me the grace to forgive the murderer, but please give me the chance to see him brought to justice.

Alex studied her. "Violet?"

"I heard you." She offered him a smile. "Where are you staying?"

Alex didn't answer her. Instead, he opened the passenger door and stepped out.

"What are you doing?" Maybe she should've worried more about whatever they'd injected him with. "Alex, this is your car."

"You don't have to use your calm and coaxing voice. I'm fully aware. Just give me a second." He dropped the flash drive to the ground, lifted his foot, and struck the device with his heel. The strength and deliberate force smashed the casing, sending a plastic shard into the car. She flicked it off the passenger seat.

Alex picked up the debris and leaned into the vehicle to get a closer look at it under the dome light. "Need to make sure the circuit board is destroyed in case they made a clone or added their own tracker."

He returned to his seat and closed the door. "Let's go to your place," he said. "I imagine you have several questions, and since I dragged you into this, we need to make a plan. I'd like to see your security system before I call it a night."

She held her tongue even though he kept forgetting that she'd trained as a law enforcement officer, too. Rick had rarely been protective, perhaps because they'd studied together and entered law enforcement at the same time. Her husband had confidence in her abilities from their first day together. Alex didn't seem to share the sentiment.

The only security system she had was a doorbell camera and a few well-placed weapons throughout the house. Her phone was in her coat pocket, but the app would've vibrated had there been any movement near the house. She turned onto the side street leading up the steep hill to her place. "This is why I walk a lot of places."

"Not because you have a natural affinity for the forest?"

She tried to smile at his attempt at levity but wasn't in the mood. "Walking is often faster than using the roads around here, and it's beneficial for Teddy. The forest service manages most of the land surrounding the resort. The resort is within our district, licensed as a partnership. That's why our USFS building is on the main thoroughfare at the base of Ace Mountain."

Her place was set apart from the other houses and condominiums facing the River Run. Nestled into the side of the hill, this section of woods, west of Wood River, led to the Smoky Mountains.

Alex got out of the car after her and appraised the luxury cabin in front of him. Her portion of the building, designed to look like a ski chalet, had tall windows and a balcony that afforded her a gorgeous view of the buttes and peaks that weren't part of the resort. She spent most of her time traversing them with Teddy. Alone. Unless they were on a search-and-rescue mission, which happened more than she'd imagined when she'd moved here.

"I live on the top floor. The bottom level has a separate entrance. It's like two separate houses with a locked door keeping the levels apart. Safe. Especially since the ground floor is empty right now." The floodlights flashed on as she approached the wooden steps of the A-frame.

"You own this?"

"It's the rental Eryn was referring to. My mom actually owns the place. She handed it over to me when she moved to Boise."

"I'm surprised it's empty during peak season."

She snorted. "Not if you read the reviews." She looked down at Teddy by her side. "His middle name isn't Thunder for nothing." She laughed at the shocked look on his face. "I pay the full price for both floors. If I happen to rent out the bottom level, it goes in my pocket. I learned pretty fast that I prefer it empty." She trudged up the stairs. "Though it is nice to be able to offer it when someone really does need a place to stay."

"Like me?" They reached the top platform, and he handed her back her purse.

She lifted the keys out and inserted them into the lock. "Do you really need a place to stay, Alex?"

He tapped the camera placed next to her door, deftly avoiding her question. "Doesn't a camera light usually come on? A red light?"

She left the keys dangling and grabbed her phone. No notifications. Alex was right. Her phone should be chirping with their movements. Teddy's spine stiffened like when he caught a scent. He spun around in a circle, lifting his nose up and down. He touched his nose to the door, barked and then looked pointedly at Violet.

Alex flinched. "His bark sounds like a gunshot. Tired of being in the cold, huh, buddy?"

"Be glad he doesn't bark often." She tried to keep

her voice light, but it trembled. Teddy's golden eyes told her everything she needed to know. She stepped to the side of the door so the window insert wouldn't reveal her location if anyone was still inside. She beckoned Alex. "Do you want to call the police, or is it still best to keep this to ourselves?"

"What is it? What did you see?"

"Teddy's reaction. He's found a scent that doesn't belong here. I think someone might be inside."

THREE

Alex pulled out his gun and scanned the still landscape before turning around. "Why don't you have your weapon out?"

"I didn't bring one."

"You didn't have a weapon when you went after me in the woods?"

"I had Teddy."

"He's not an attack dog." He pressed his lips together. They'd be having a conversation about that later. "Get behind me. I can't imagine the Firecracker could've beat us here, but if I'm mistaken again, I'll be the one paying the price. Are we clear? Stay behind me."

She tilted her head in confusion. "Again? I don't understand."

This wasn't the time to explain he was responsible for Rick's death. "I'm going in."

"You're not clearing the house alone. I have a gun in the back of the silverware drawer, next to the refrigerator."

"You stay behind me, and we'll go straight there. You're familiar with two-man entry?" He wasn't sure law enforcement rangers ever needed to practice such skills.

She rolled her eyes, disabusing him of that notion. "Of course. You clear the door."

He stepped to the other side of the entry and pointed the gun at a forty-five-degree angle. "Ready."

Violet twisted the key in the lock and shoved the door open, giving Alex a clear view of the kitchen and living room's open floor plan. He brought the gun up to chest level as he spun into the room. His gaze swept left to right. "Clear."

Teddy barreled into the room, almost knocking him over. The dog sniffed the floor with such intensity the area rug shifted. In his peripheral vision, Violet slipped past him. He heard the jarring of silverware and the click of a gun being readied to fire. Teddy grew more intent on sniffing the area in front of the armoire. Alex pointed at the hallway and dared a quick look over his shoulder. Violet nodded, her gun at the same forty-five-degree angle.

They worked in tandem, guarding each other's backs, keeping their guns at the ready as they cleared the hallway bathroom, a guest bedroom and, finally, the main bedroom and bath. At least the bedrooms had blinds and curtains, unlike the floor-to-ceiling windows in the living room.

"We need to check the bottom floor, as well. To be safe." Teddy barreled down the hallway. His paws slapped against the hardwood floors, and the sound of his journey echoed against the walls. "I guess I can stop whispering."

She shrugged but didn't lower her weapon fully. "Follow me." She exited the hallway and crossed the living room to a wooden door that had a deadbolt. Teddy sniffed the rug again and stood at attention at the armoire.

"What's in there? Could someone be hiding inside?"

"TV and some drawers below it."

A burglary didn't really seem likely. He'd passed a laptop on her desk in the main bedroom, and judging by dust patterns, the jewelry box on top of her dresser also didn't seem to have been disturbed. He held up a hand, and just to be sure, he flipped open the cabinet. There was a small flat screen television inside. He slid the drawers open and closed. Nothing except for what appeared to be a couple scraps of papers sliding around. He closed it back up. "Any cash hidden anywhere?"

"Very small amount in my fire safe, which I noticed is still on the floor of my closet. You said I might be in danger. Why are you asking about possible theft?"

"There wouldn't have been enough time from the moment you left your purse behind at the resort until now for the Firecracker to have located the house and left before we arrived."

Mere minutes. And even if the Firecracker had been here in Violet's home, what could he have hoped to achieve? Alex kept an eye out for any evidence of the assassin's signature bombs, but there was nothing. "Did you go straight to the dinner from here?"

"No. Eryn picked me up so we could get ready together. I was at her house for a couple of hours beforehand." She adjusted the grip on her weapon. "Continue the search?" At his nod, she flipped the bolt, and they took to the stairs. Teddy stayed upstairs as they searched the lower level, which eased his mind. Unlikely that any intruder had come downstairs, then.

Violet lowered her gun. "All clear."

"I'm going to do a quick check outside. And, I'd like to rent the place. What's your rate?" He nodded at the furnished living area. The resort was completely full, so he'd thought he was going to end up in a hole-in-the-wall thirty minutes away. This was much better, and he'd be able to keep an eye—or at least an ear out—for Violet's safety above.

"You were the brother Rick never had. You know we, I—" She exhaled after the correction. "I would never turn you away." She slipped her gun into her coat pocket. "I'll meet you upstairs to give you the keys." She pointed to the door. "This place has its own entrance."

He exited through the door she'd pointed out. The snow made quick work seeping into his socks and pants for the second time that night. He searched not only for any hidden explosives but also footprints. Nothing. Either Teddy was overreacting or a rodent had made its way into Violet's place. He grabbed his pack from the car and climbed the stairs again. His neck tingled at the doorbell camera. Still no red light at the movement. He gave the box a slight tug and the camera came out of its frame smoothly. The screws were missing, and the back indicated it was no longer plugged directly into the house.

Maybe Teddy deserved more credit. The question remained whether this was related to the Firecracker or an odd coincidence. Either way, he wasn't leaving until he was sure Violet was safe. He let himself in and locked the door behind him.

He set the camera on the counter. "Doesn't do much good without power."

"How'd they detach it without my notifications being set off? I've checked. No camera footage of anyone approaching."

"And nothing is missing in the house?"

"Nothing. I've double-checked. I suppose it's possible a thief tried to get in and couldn't. Doesn't explain Teddy's reaction to the rug, though." She flipped on the lights and pressed a button that lowered drapes over the glass wall. "It's a shame. I love stepping out to the sunlight in the morning."

He tapped the top of the camera. "This is all the security you have, isn't it?"

She offered him a sad smile. "I'm no longer a spouse of an FBI special agent. If you want to get technical, I'm not a law enforcement officer anymore, either. At least, I don't carry a badge. And I no longer live in a metro area. The camera and Teddy have been more than sufficient for the past couple of years."

"You're not still a ranger?" He'd spotted her USFS SUV out front, though.

"I'm the district ranger, responsible for all the employees who manage the three hundred thousand acres of land. It's a promotion of sorts. The law enforcement rangers are all out in the field and in partnership with the county sheriff. It's why I no longer carry a gun."

"Why the switch?"

She sighed, an indicator that it was a long story, best for another time. She crossed over to a kettle on the kitchen counter. "How about some tea?" She opened the fridge and produced two microwave meals. "And dinner. I didn't have a chance to eat."

A quick glance over her shoulder revealed eggs,

bacon, Parmesan cheese and spinach. "You have spaghetti noodles?"

She quirked an eyebrow. "Yes." She pointed at a cabinet to her right.

"Then put those boxed atrocities away. We both deserve a *real* dinner after tonight." He stepped past her. "Might as well get comfortable. We at least need to discuss the short-term plan, starting with tomorrow." He pulled out the ingredients and a skillet and got to work on his fast and easy interpretation of spaghetti carbonara.

"I forgot you enjoyed cooking and being bossy, Alexander." Her teasing glint vanished. Her eyebrows shot up, and her mouth fell open slightly. If he hadn't understood why, he'd have been sure someone had punched her in the stomach. She blinked rapidly, spun away and walked down the hallway.

The memories came fast and furious. He'd teased Rick when he'd heard Violet call him Richard. She used Rick's full name whenever she got annoyed. Violet had responded to Alex's teasing by calling him by his full name, as well. That was probably the last time he'd seen Rick double over with laughter. Inside jokes without Rick here to laugh along with them…

Alex inhaled slowly and exhaled even slower. The pain in her eyes had matched his. Would either of them ever be able to be in the same room without the bitter reminder of what they'd lost?

Teddy brushed up against his legs, panting. "Smell the bacon, huh? Coming up shortly." He didn't make Teddy move as he worked. The weight and heat from the dog against his calves proved oddly comforting, better than a hug. No complicated sharing of feelings necessary.

A moment later, Violet reappeared in emerald green sweats with the US Forest Service logo embroidered on the shoulder. He truly looked at her for the first time tonight. Ironically, she seemed more fragile now than in her dress. Vulnerable.

The question in her eyes caused his neck to feel on fire. He was going to have to tell her. It was part of the reason he'd stayed away, but deep down, he knew he'd never have peace until he asked for forgiveness. The words were stuck in the back of his throat. *It should've been me. We traded places at the last minute. It was my call.* The splatter of hot bacon grease hit his wrist, slapping away the temptation.

"Let's start from the beginning." Violet poured herself a mug of hot water and added a tea bag. She propped her hip against the kitchen cabinet and watched him fry the pieces of bacon. "Why do you think the Firecracker is here?"

"Have you heard of the assassination market?"

"Dark web kind of thing." Her forehead wrinkled ever so slightly. "People make bets on powerful people dying on certain days. Horrible, but it's hard to investigate and prosecute."

"Yes. It's a hit list in disguise. The assassin essentially names his price, or bet, and picks the day or week that it will happen. Except sometimes there are even fewer details than a person's name. Sometimes it's a category like 'powerful political leader dies at a ski resort on vacation.'"

She set down the mug. "Rick thought the market had been defunct."

"The Bureau thought so, as well, until there was a huge cash out in bitcoins a few months ago. The market's still running, albeit harder to track. Do you know who is staying at the resort this season who could be a target?"

He'd never noticed before that her eyes got bluer when she was deep in thought.

"The governor of Idaho seems like a low-power target when I think about the Firecracker's profile," she said.

"Exactly why I'm asking. We can't rule him out, but there is likely a bigger target. We've checked the itineraries of senators and representatives. Nothing. Any ideas of other potential targets that might be here on vacation?"

"No. But I think I can find out."

Violet hung up as the call went to voice mail. Tom Curtis was the busiest man in the valley. He would know who was staying at the resort, the top names. His job was to keep the VIP customers happy, which usually involved the rich, famous and powerful. She had other contacts at the resort she could ask, but most of the famous guests used aliases to register their rooms. At least, according to Daniella, Tom's daughter, they did.

Alex placed heaps of pasta on a plate and handed it to her. "No news?"

"He's a hard guy to reach. We might have to go in person tomorrow night. He's always at the Waller Restaurant, an exclusive restaurant on the top floor of the resort's main hotel."

"How hard would it be to get a reservation? If I get eyes on potential targets and their security details, I might be able to figure this out and request backup."

She inhaled the heady aroma of bacon and Parmesan. "No. Reservations are impossible. Platinum-tier guests only. But…" She sighed. "I have a standing invitation on file for dinner. One I thought I'd never accept." Tom claimed Daniella had gotten her life back on track thanks to Violet. Although Violet disagreed, Tom insisted on thanking her by treating her like a VIP. She'd declined his offer of dinner at the Waller Restaurant, but he'd said her name would be always on the list. "They bring in celebrity chefs on a rotation. It's famous for food and live music, even though the restaurant doesn't technically exist."

Alex beamed. "We need to check it out, then." He picked up his own plate of food. "Guess we're about to have our first date." He winked but must have seen her sudden discomfort. "Bad joke. I'm sorry I dragged you into this."

"I would do *anything* to bring Rick's killer to justice, Alex." Her eyes stung. She crossed the room to the couch and took a seat. "Sorry. My table is still in storage. I don't entertain much anymore."

He crossed the room to sit on the opposite side of her. "I should've asked. Are you already dating someone?"

She laughed. "No. Not even remotely interested. No offense to your choice of cover." She took a bite and let the flavors swirl around her mouth. The man really could cook.

"I was still a little groggy when I made that decision. I should've clued you in, but you picked up my intentions immediately. That's great undercover instinct. You can tell your friends our relationship is much less serious than I implied."

"My friends mean well, but they've been relentless in trying to fix me up lately. It's not that I'm against…" She exhaled, searching for the right words. "I miss sharing life with someone, but no one can be Rick. So why try?" She shrugged. "I guess that means serving as your cover is a win-win for me."

"Win-win? How do you figure?"

She hadn't meant to give him so much insight into her grieving. "You asked why I switched jobs. The experts say not to make big changes after a loved one's death, so I tried going back to work. But on every case, I wanted the suspect to be Rick's killer. It messed with my mind. I no longer trusted my judgment. Teddy picked up on it, too. He started acting confused by my commands. So I decided to throw away the rule book on grieving and change everything all at once. I moved back here and took the district ranger position. It helped. Some. But if my friends stop playing matchmaker because they think I'm taken and I also play a small part in helping take down Rick's killer…"

"Ah. That's what you meant by win-win. Once we get the Firecracker, will you go back into law enforcement?"

"I'm not sure about that. Either way, I think I'd have peace that at least I tried. Having a background in law enforcement and not being able to…" Her voice shook with the frustration that she'd tamped down for years.

"I miss him, too." His fingers fidgeted with the edge of the afghan resting on the back of the couch. "It's why

I switched to undercover work. I want to find the Fire-cracker, sure, but I'm also not ready for another part-ner." His voice had a gruff texture that wasn't there before.

Violet knew if she wanted, they could reminisce in a way that no one else could. The thought terrified her.

He set down his plate on the end table and strode toward the corner where Teddy now rested on his dog bed. "Interesting decor you've got here." The change of subject was a relief, and it probably meant Alex wasn't ready to reminisce, either.

She laughed and popped up on her knees to view the area behind the couch, as well. She'd used her favor-ite frames that had once held photos of her and Rick to fill with photos of other Newfoundland dogs. "It's our inspiration wall." Teddy released a grumbling noise.

"He doesn't sound inspired. This one is just a photo of a statue."

She scoffed. "He's tired. So am I. That's a statue of Sergeant Gander, in Canada. Yes, a dog," she clarified to Alex's raised eyebrows. "World War II hero. A gre-nade landed near the wounded soldiers. He picked it up and ran it toward the enemy." She pointed at the next one. It featured a black-and-white dog mid-dive. "That's Whizz. He saved hundreds of lives as a marine rescue dog. Then, you have an illustration of the nanny from Peter Pan, and the final one is the dog that accompanied Lewis and Clark. All Newfoundland dogs."

Teddy grumbled again. Odd. Maybe he wasn't just tired. "What is it?" The dog jumped up and went to the armoire again. This time, with the lights on, she noted his spine was stiff. "He's found that same scent again."

She got off the couch and walked forward. "Whoever messed with the security camera definitely got inside and spent a lot of time here."

Her skin electrified at the thought of an intruder focusing on the armoire. There was nothing inside but the television and drawers filled with Rick's personal items. Photographs, yearbooks, medals, memorabilia, things that had made him laugh were all stored in there. Nothing of value except to her. Actually, that reminded her there was something in there Rick probably would want Alex to have. She reached out—

"Don't!" Alex crossed the room. "I should've checked behind and underneath before disregarding Teddy's reaction. If the Firecracker—"

"The Firecracker has no reason to kill me, and you said it yourself, there wasn't enough time between the flash drive drop and coming back here. This has to be unrelated."

He didn't answer but took a knee. "Nothing behind here. Let me check one more thing." He got on all fours, and Teddy's head disappeared underneath the armoire along with him. "No, no kisses. Teddy, please."

She fought back a laugh. "You can't get on his level without expecting affection. Can I open it now?"

Alex reappeared, wiping his cheek off. "I suppose it's safe. I opened it once before in the dark. Nothing happened then." Teddy pulled his head back from underneath, as well.

"Okay, boy. Show me what's bothering you." She opened the door. Teddy pressed his nose against the three drawers. One drawer at a time. Her insides felt full of hot lava. "Teddy, sit," she whispered. Her fingers refused her internal demand to remain calm and trembled as she pulled open the first drawer.

Gone. Empty. "Someone took it." Her breath grew shallow and rapid. "Rick's photos." She grabbed the second drawer. Dust. Nothing but dust. "His yearbooks and medals." Her voice hitched.

Alex moved past Teddy at her side. "I thought they were supposed to be empty. I didn't know." He reached over and pulled the third drawer before she could.

Her favorite wedding photo, ripped in two, spun in opposite directions at the sudden motion. Rick's face had a red line drawn through it. A cry lodged in her throat. Alex reached for the second half of the photograph. Violet's face had a red circle around it, but no line.

He straightened and reached for her hand, but she seemed to have gone numb, because she felt nothing but the roaring in her head.

"Violet…" His forehead tightened.

She said the words both of them had to be thinking. "It means I'm next."

FOUR

Alex was a light sleeper on a normal night. After the events of last night, he hardly slept at all. When he did catch a few minutes, his dreams were fueled by memories of Rick looking over his shoulder and saying "I need to talk to you after this. Something about this is starting to seem familiar." The dream always ended with Alex staring at a ball of fire, knowing that his partner was gone.

He sat up straight, sweat rolling down his neck. It was the fourth time in one night that he'd woken up from the same dream. Probably natural given the nature of the case and the time he'd spent with Violet. None of it made sense, though. Sunlight streamed through the blinds. He'd ended up sleeping later than he thought.

Thumping above followed by the sounds of grunts sent him flying out of bed. Those were sounds of a scuffle. Violet was being attacked. He ran barefoot in his navy sweats up the stairs to the connecting door. He grabbed the knob, but it didn't budge. Locked. He didn't think she would lock him out. He pounded on the door. More thumping and grunts could be heard. The small landing with a thin balcony rail prevented him from taking a run at the door.

He descended two stairs at a time and raced for his exit, slipping on his shoes without socks and grabbing his coat. He pulled it on as he ran, arriving at the front entrance to her level within seconds. Also locked. The drapes on the windows were still shaded. Teddy jumped up on the glass insert and barked.

Alex pounded. "Violet! If you're okay in there, I need you to open up in ten seconds, or I'm going to break through. Teddy, move!"

His fingers twitched, tempted to grab his gun and shoot the door down, but Teddy might get hurt. Alex stepped back on the wooden deck. He had room for a running start. This particular door looked most vulnerable at its hinges.

An engine revved up the hill behind him. A silver Jeep pulled up behind Alex's car. Bruce, the so-called friend from last night, stepped out of the vehicle. "She kick you out?" Bruce asked, laughing.

Just great. He didn't have time to explain.

"Alex, was it?"

He ignored Bruce, taking one more step back and focusing hard on the spot he was about to kick.

The door flung open. "What?" Violet's eyes were wide, and her hair was dripping with sweat. "What is it?" She swung her gaze to the driveway. "Bruce?"

Alex fought down irritation, panting from the adrenaline, and turned to Bruce. "One second, please. I need a word with Violet."

She tilted her head, frowning, but opened the door

wide for him. He stepped inside. "You're okay? I heard fighting."

"Fighting? I told you Teddy can be loud when he walks around."

"This was more than Teddy. Thumping, sure, but grunting, fast feet. It sounded like you were fighting off…" He let his words trail off as her face turned a brighter shade of red.

She held a hand to her forehead. "I'm sorry. I thought I was being quiet. Didn't realize sound carried so well down there."

"Quiet about what?"

"Tang Soo Do. It's a martial art. Teddy likes to think he can do the forms, too, so he jumps around a lot. I didn't think you could hear me."

"Practicing forms doesn't usually sound like you're hitting something."

"I have padded targets for practice." She offered a sheepish laugh. "Guess the vacation reviews really do have merit. The floor must not have good insulation. I'm sorry if I worried you."

He blew out a breath. "It's fine. I didn't know that was your thing. New?"

"No. Though I took a break from it for a while. Do you still pitch?"

Alex pulled back in surprise. He'd gone to school on a baseball scholarship, and despite an offer to the minors, he'd decided to follow in his family's footsteps and pursue a career in criminal justice. "You knew about that?"

"Rick bragged that you ensured the FBI softball team won every game."

"Yeah, well, I'm still on a break. Haven't pitched since I went into undercover work."

The light in her eyes dimmed, but she nodded. "Well, again, I'm sorry to have scared you."

Bruce stepped inside, not waiting for an invitation. If she hadn't called the man a friend, Alex would have something to say.

"Everything okay?" Bruce held a white sack with a bakery logo stamped on the front and a bouquet of dahlias.

"Yes, of course." Violet gestured at herself. "I'm afraid I'm not ready to entertain right now."

"Oh, I don't mind." Bruce set the bag and flowers on the counter. "I brought you some muffins." He darted a glance at Alex. "I was hoping to have a word with you alone, as well, Violet."

Alex crossed over to the cabinet, where he picked out a coffee mug and poured himself a cup of coffee from the hot carafe. He needed it more than ever. He turned around and blew on his coffee. "Oh, don't mind me. Go ahead."

Bruce narrowed his eyes while Violet smirked, clearly amused. The man shuffled his feet and stuck his hands in his coat pockets. He leaned forward, leaving very little room between him and Violet. Teddy barreled in between them, threw his front paws on the counter and grabbed the bag of muffins. He ran past them to his bed.

"What kind of muffins were those?" Violet asked, alarmed.

Alex set down his mug and pulled out the treat he had in his coat pocket. He had intended to give it to

Teddy when he came to see them after the case. That reminded him that he'd never found out why Violet had been at the party last night in the first place.

Alex whistled while he removed the cellophane wrapping of the meat stick. Teddy dropped the muffin bag and ran, sliding into a sitting position when his front paws reached Alex's feet. "Good dog." He dropped the treat in Teddy's mouth.

Violet jogged over to retrieve the bag and beamed. "Thank you, Alex."

"I thought he was well trained," Bruce objected.

"Highly," Violet said. "When he knows he's on the job. But he's still a dog." She pulled his food bin out of the pantry. "I got a late start this morning. He counter-surfs if I get behind schedule."

"Can you blame him?" Alex said, unable to keep the grin off his face. He picked up his mug again and took a sip. Bruce looked livid.

"What did you want to talk about, Bruce?" Violet shot Alex a look that seemed to tell him to behave.

"I—I just wanted to make sure you were okay. Eryn and I were talking last night, and…" Bruce leveled a narrowed gaze at Alex. "You never know with internet dating if people are really who they claim to be." He plastered a fake smile on his face. "No offense, man."

"None taken."

"I never said we met on the internet." She smiled but didn't offer any other information.

The man's neck turned another shade of red during the awkward silence. "Sorry. I assumed that was the case since you never mentioned him to Eryn."

Ah, so Bruce was fishing for information, and Violet offered no indication she planned to give it. Alex made a circle motion with his hand, and Teddy, now done with his treat, flopped over on his back so Alex could give him a good tummy rub.

Violet laughed at the dog's antics. "As you can see, Alex and I know each other well, but I appreciate the concern. Thanks for stopping by. I really need to get to work now."

Bruce raised his left eyebrow and turned to Alex. "And you're spending the day out looking for a job?"

"Shadowing Violet, actually. Thought it'd be the best way to get to know the area. Well, that and taking her to the Waller Restaurant tonight." He might've gone too far, judging by the way the vein in Bruce's temple appeared ready to pop.

"The Waller Restaurant?" Bruce repeated, likely soaking in that Alex might be serious competition if he was taking her to the exclusive restaurant. "I'll call you later then, Violet." He gave Alex a quick, challenging glance before he left.

"Wow." Alex lifted the edge of the window coverings and watched Bruce get back in his vehicle. "He's aggressive."

Violet finished pouring Teddy's food into his bowl. "Most competitive person I know. Guess this cover isn't all bad." She straightened, her hands on her hips. "I'm carrying my gun today. Are you really coming to work with me, Alexander?"

At the use of his full name, he held out his hands in surrender. "Okay, I know interrupting your routine must be irritating, but humor me, please. I'll stay out of your hair, but I'd like to check the security of your office. It is my specialty. I also need to know why you were at the party last night."

She crossed the room and opened the drawer next to the silverware. "I was invited. Didn't think I'd go, but then Eryn really needed a night out."

"So, Eryn was the one that paid the two thousand dollars a plate?"

Violet guffawed. "Absolutely not." She pulled out a cardstock invitation and held it out to him. "We both got an invitation like this. 'Come honor the Governor of Idaho.'" She frowned. "It does seem like an odd thing if I stop and think about it, but we thought it was a local event. Two thousand a plate?" She shook her head. "Could it be that locals were invited for free and only nonresidents had to pay?"

Unlikely, but Alex didn't have any theories at the moment. Now that Bruce was gone, he noticed Violet's red-rimmed eyes for the first time. She'd cried last night. "There should be a fundraising paper trail," he said gently. "We can find out."

She poured herself a mug of coffee. "That's got to be what happened. There's no other explanation. Tom Curtis was in charge of the event. We could ask him tonight." She walked down the hallway. "I'm getting ready. You should, too, if you're really shadowing me."

Alex stared into his swirling coffee, processing the information. She'd received a personal threat—as personal as a threat could be. This changed everything. He'd never forget the look on her face after seeing her wedding photo desecrated. The target on Rick's face had to be the work of the Firecracker, but it didn't make sense. What possible reason could he have for targeting Violet on purpose? The invitation, the door camera, taking all of Rick's personal mementos...

None of that fit with the dossier the Bureau had built on the Firecracker. Whatever this was had a personal edge. Teddy pawed his sneaker, likely hoping for another treat. Alex stared into the dog's golden eyes as his own dilemma came into clear focus. He lifted up a silent prayer, hoping that he wouldn't be forced to choose between catching the Firecracker and keeping Violet safe. Violet's safety was top priority, but would she ever forgive him if he let Rick's killer slip through his fingers again?

Violet zipped up her evergreen work jacket and clipped Teddy's K-9 vest around his chest and back before they left. Alex waited outside his vehicle.

"You really don't have to come to work with me. I'm sure you have plenty to investigate on your own."

"It's what a good boyfriend who came to visit would do." He winked and moved to open the passenger door.

Her stomach fluttered from the flirtatious gesture, even though she knew he was only playing a part to keep up his cover. Such an odd sensation, especially since she'd never ever seen Alex as more than Rick's partner. Had he always been so attractive? Best not to think about it. She reached down and patted Teddy's head. "If you're coming with me to work, we all go in my vehicle." She gestured at the white SUV with the forest service logo on the driver's side door. "The back half is outfitted for Teddy's needs. Temperature alarms, fans, even a heated water bowl."

Alex got into the passenger side of the vehicle. He

wanted to talk about the photo they'd discovered last night. She could tell by his frequent side-glances and the way he kept taking big breaths and then closing his mouth. The only way to stay strong was to keep busy, to focus on what mattered.

If Rick were still alive, he would be making the world a better place. She felt the burden to do doubly as much in honor of him. That's why she put in long hours and volunteered. Her work saved lives, and she preferred to stay busy. Rarely was there a free evening like last night where she had time to socialize and think. The holidays stank in that regard. Silent nights were the worst.

"I feel safe here, despite what happened yesterday," she said. "I appreciate your protective nature. I know it comes naturally in your line of work, but it's not necessary." The sun reflected off the two-feet-high snowpack on either side of the road as she made her way down the hill to the town. "Besides, you don't think the Firecracker was in my house. It's probably some two-bit criminal that I or Rick put away. Teddy and I will catch him."

"I can't rule out any possibilities. I've already asked the Bureau to cross-reference any criminals in the area that might've been recently released from cases you or Rick worked on. Want to tell me any more about Bruce?"

"There's nothing to tell, because I'm not interested in him, and he's not a threat." He was recently divorced and seemed to be trying to reclaim his youth. She doubted he had any genuine interest in her, and he especially wouldn't when he realized she wasn't the same Violet he'd once known. "Haven't you had a relationship you regretted?"

"How many dates does it take to qualify as a relationship?"

"If you have to ask, you've never been in one."

"There you go, then." He tapped on his phone, searching for something. She wondered if he was finding anything surprising about Bruce after all. He shifted uncomfortably, adjusting the tight seat belt off his neck. "How's your family? In Boise now, right?"

She tightened her grip on the steering wheel. "My family is doing well." Her mouth dropped when she realized the significance of his question. Alex used to spend a lot of holidays with her and Rick in Utah. They'd always invited her sister, Dawn, to come, as well. "You really want to know about Dawn, don't you? Alex, I hate to be the one to break it to you." She cringed. "Dawn got married this year. Six months ago."

Alex shrugged. "I'm happy for her."

She pulled up to a stop sign and sneaked a peek at his face. Why did it bother her so much that Alex was alone? Many single people had full lives, herself included.

"You can stop with the looks of pity, Violet." He shook his head. "There were never any sparks with Dawn. Honest! On either side, despite what you and Rick wanted." His deep chuckle finally convinced her.

"Well, you couldn't blame us for trying." She made the final turn to the main road, now in the valley. "The double dates would've been such fun." Her voice shook ever so slightly. Caught off guard by the sudden wave of emotion, she faked a smile.

Every question meant to keep the conversation safe brought them back to Rick. The last couple of years, he'd slowly become a taboo subject. Friends and family stopped mentioning his name for fear she'd cry. And now, with Alex, they were talking about him every other minute. She hadn't realized how badly she'd needed to speak and hear his name.

"I'm a little surprised you didn't move to Boise after your mom and Dawn moved there. Didn't you come back here to be near them?"

"At first, yes. It wasn't a conscious decision, but since my mom lost my dad so many years ago, I thought she would be able to help me. I put too many expectations on her, that she would do the work of grieving for me."

He barked a laugh. "Moms are pretty good at fixing things, but not sure she could do that for you."

"Exactly. Being with me while I was so raw was too much for her. Seven years had gone by since we'd lost my dad, and she'd just started to date again. It was only six months after Rick's death that she told me it was time for *me* to get my nails and hair done and find a man."

"I don't imagine that went over well."

She laughed at the memory, even though at the time, she'd been livid. "Let's just say we have a more loving relationship when we live apart. I didn't understand how much work grief takes. Now we'd probably be fine in the same town. We visit each other often."

"I'm glad. I didn't mean to get so personal."

"It's okay. I know you were trying to make polite conversation before getting to the hard questions."

He slapped his knee and shook his head. "Nothing gets past you."

"How's your family doing?" she asked, knowing she sported a giant grin.

"Fine. All serving in public service all over the country and around the world. Same as always. Violet, I really do need to ask—"

"You want to know more about what was taken from the armoire." She'd been prepared for this bit at least. "Everything from the years I knew him. When I moved here, I put most of the stuff from our house in storage, but there were certain things I wanted to keep near me. College yearbooks, photos, notes we shared, that kind of thing. His mother still has all his childhood stuff."

"College yearbooks? You guys met at college?"

"Yes. At a movie night in the dorms. We knew of each other from classes before then, as well, but we'd never really talked until that night. He was actually dating my roommate, Bridget Preston." Her name rolled off the tongue. "She had a magnetic personality. Drew in everyone until you got to know her better. The silent treatment and passive aggression were her tried-and-true methods, but you'd never know what you said or did to cause any of her moods."

She shook her head with the memories as they came fast and furious. "Anyway, she didn't show that night, so Rick sat by me, and we really talked for the first time. That was all. She got wind and was enraged, even though we didn't even share popcorn."

"And she was your roommate? Hard to imagine Rick dating someone like that."

Alex's question reminded her of all the times she'd

needed to sleep on the floor of another friend's dorm because she'd felt like she couldn't relax around Bridget's mood swings. Violet pulled into the parking lot.

"She was the definition of *charismatic*, so I don't blame Rick for being pulled in at first. I even managed to convince myself she was my best friend for a short while. We were both from Idaho. Both majoring in criminal justice. The following year, we were still roommates, but in a shared suite. She started a study group on criminal profiling. We studied most-wanted fugitives from case files our professor gave us. That's when I really started to get to know Rick. We were certain we had fresh insight that might break the cases open."

"Rick was in the study group? Was it kind of like that group of retired detectives in New York that try to solve cold cases over lunch?"

"Exactly, except without any experience. Rick started to feel like Bridget was more in awe of criminals than wanting to catch them. Anyway, he broke up with her before second semester, and Bridget decided it was because of me. So she framed me for plagiarism."

Alex's mouth dropped. "That's usually grounds for expulsion."

"Her intention. She turned in a plagiarized paper with my name on it. Artfully done, I might add. But Rick proved Bridget framed me."

"Hold up." He tapped on his phone.

"Don't bother." She glanced over his shoulder and confirmed her suspicions. "Bridget isn't targeting me. She died a few years back."

Alex froze with his finger hovering over the headline he'd found. She knew what it said. A car crash had sent Bridget's vehicle over the edge of a cliff into Snake River Canyon.

"Rick and I were, in a weird way, thankful for her. She wanted to harm us, but instead, we gained each other." The words reminded her of a Bible verse, but the exact wording escaped her as a small red dot flickered on the dashboard and disappeared.

"Did you see that?" She spun to look over her shoulder, out the back window. Trees surrounded the parking lot of the district office. There was no sign of anyone, though.

"Violet?"

It wasn't a laser scope. It was more likely a reflection from a passing car. All this talk was making her brain susceptible to thoughts of danger. "Nothing," she said, searching again to be sure. The district office parking lot was just off Main Street, but the back end was set in one of the many areas of the national forest that wove throughout the resort area.

Alex scanned for threats as she helped Teddy out of the vehicle, and they entered the offices. Daniella, her mentee and volunteer, had already opened the office and was accepting calls from the public. The young adult gaped at Alex and gave Violet meaningful looks, complete with waggling eyebrows.

"This is my friend Alex. You might remember him from last night."

Daniella's expression as she waved at Alex made it clear she didn't believe he was only a friend. When Alex wasn't looking, Daniella opened her mouth wide and gestured at her shoulder, indicating she thought he was attractive.

Violet tried not to openly laugh. Daniella was so expressive, she made it clear to everyone what she was thinking. Violet checked messages and her schedule at her standing desk while Teddy found his bed behind it and made himself comfortable.

Alex pointed through the windows at the separate garage. "What's in there?"

"Storage and supplies. Extra snowmobiles, ATVs, ammunition and explosives."

His eyebrows jumped. "Explosives?"

"Avalanche mitigation. We make them happen safely before they block highways or put anyone in danger. If the conditions are ripe, recreationists can accidentally initiate them. Don't worry. The explosives are in a separate safe."

Daniella put down the phone. "Sheriff Bartlett is on the line for you. I've transferred the call to your desk."

Violet picked up the phone, not particularly bothered. If it was urgent or a search-and-rescue mission, she would've gotten an alert on her cell. She answered, and the sheriff plowed ahead.

"This is a courtesy call, nothing official, but your friend Eryn Lane is missing. She didn't show up to pick up her kid after morning preschool, apparently. Someone found a spilled coffee cup next to her vehicle on Wood River Avenue. It's not suspicious enough to call in a team yet, but I thought you should know. I've got my hands full now. Talk later." He hung up before she could ask one of a million questions swirling through her mind.

"What? What is it?" Alex stepped in front of her desk. The red dot she'd seen before flashed on the back wall and moved swiftly to the center of Alex's chest. That was no reflection. "Get down!" He dropped into a crouch, and the red dot swung to Daniella. "Get under the desk!" The teenager dived without hesitation.

The dot disappeared. Her heart rate roared in her ears. What was going on? "I thought I saw a laser scope. Did you see it?"

Alex crawled to the window and looked out. "I didn't see anything, but I believe you. Though if we're really dealing with a sniper, they don't usually use lasers."

"Oh, that's reassuring," Daniella snapped from underneath the desk. "I didn't see it, either, though. Is it still there?"

Was she losing her mind? "No. Not anymore."

Alex pointed to the right. "I'm taking the back door. You up for taking the front? Sweep the area and meet me back in here."

They shifted into position, careful to avoid the windows. "Daniella, I need you to stay down until we're clear," she said. "No matter what. If you hear anything, call it in. Teddy, find Daniella." Teddy ran across the room, making his large form fit in the small space between Daniella and the desk legs.

"No kisses, Teddy!" Daniella objected, but Violet didn't hear the rest. The blood pounded in her ears as she swung the door open and scanned the trees. Every step over the pea gravel shot adrenaline up her spine.

"Violet!" Alex's voice rang out.

She sprinted with her hand on her weapon toward Alex's location back behind the garage. He stood to the east, pointing at thick tracks in the mud. The markings indicated someone had come close and turned around and left. "I think the threat is gone, but maybe it's time for us to see if Teddy can catch a scent?"

She felt pulled in different directions. "I'll call in my rangers to investigate. Teddy and I need to find Eryn first. She's my best and longest friend in the world, and the sheriff said she's missing. I'll never forgive myself if anything happens to her."

His eyebrows jumped. "I know the feeling better than most. And right now, I'm worried that something could happen to you. Where you go, I go."

"Then we better work fast." She turned and ran to retrieve Teddy, trying to ignore the way her heart pounded in response to Alex keeping pace at her side.

FIVE

So much for working fast. Violet insisted on dropping Daniella off at home to make sure she was safe. Daniella took advantage of the time to ask how they knew each other and if the town rumors about their dating were true. The young woman had received a few informative text messages while waiting underneath the desk and knew all about their upcoming dinner that night. She could have a future in interrogation methods, and it was clear Violet wasn't used to telling her the bare minimum.

Now Alex tried not to let his impatience show as Violet held the empty coffee cup to Teddy's nose before he walked around Eryn's vehicle three times. At this rate, they'd lose the scent back at the forest service and risk losing their coveted reservation at the exclusive restaurant.

Working several cases at the same time wasn't unusual, but the importance of these two circumstances resulted in a painful knot behind his shoulder blade.

"Sometimes it takes him a bit to find it," Violet explained. "Especially if the scent has been compromised by a lot of people." Teddy's head snapped up, and he turned around and looked directly at Alex. He surged forward, headed directly for him and swerved at the last minute into the forested park across from the coffee shop.

"Good boy," she called. They jogged for several minutes until Teddy stopped, sniffing around. Violet took a deep inhalation but appeared shaky.

"Are you okay?"

"The work can be slow, tedious. It's why we train day in and out. We easily go eight or more miles on a search some days, but…"

"Eryn is your friend."

"Best." The word came out in a whisper. She blinked until her eyes no longer had a watery sheen. Alex hated she was out here. The left-behind cup of coffee was suspicious, but it could be a coincidence. Violet had already lost the love of her life, and now her friend had the nerve to get herself lost where most of the forest and mountain was without cell signal. Getting mad wouldn't be of any help, so he did the only other thing he could think of. Keeping her mind off worst-case scenarios was important. "Why'd you go into search and rescue?"

She pulled her chin back in surprise. "Rick never told you?" He shook his head and trudged after Teddy, who had his nose buried in the snow, apparently debating on where to turn now. "My great-grandfather got confused and walked into a snowstorm. They didn't find him in time. If there had been a search-and-rescue dog in that area, I feel certain tragedy could've been avoided."

"Wow." The change of subject definitely didn't lighten her mood. "And that's exactly what you're doing.

Making sure Eryn's story doesn't end like that. You know she probably just wanted some time to herself and forgot to pick up her kid? I'm sure she's fine."

"That would be very unlike her." Violet kept her eyes on Teddy as they took a sharp turn left and began trudging along the bank of a river. "I actually wanted to start my own search-and-rescue school, but plans changed. Do you like undercover work?"

He laughed, taken off guard by the sudden change in subject. "I guess I don't enjoy adrenaline as much as some. The short answer is no."

"And the long answer? It's just us and the trees right now. We might be out here all day or until I can convince the sheriff to enlist the rest of the search-and-rescue team without waiting forty-eight hours."

He sighed. "Undercover agents have to find what's attractive about the choices criminals make so we can fit in better with them."

Violet's face broke into a smile, and he suddenly felt less cold, trudging in the deep snow. "I can't see you being good at that."

"People can tell when you don't approve of their choices. Wouldn't surprise me if Teddy can smell someone's being disingenuous. I keep finding myself having the same discussion while I'm undercover."

She stopped for half a second and turned to him. "You try to talk them out of their life of crime before you bring the whole operation down. Don't you?"

He rallied his best acting skills in hopes of keeping his neck from turning beet red and shrugged instead. "I may casually point out what else they'd be really good at. Guess it helps ease my conscience. But so far, it's only ever resulted in them doubling down on their criminal activities."

"Does that make the arrests easier?"

"Yes and no. The mission of the FBI is to protect the American people and uphold the Constitution. I can find peace that I've done my job. But I do get tired of hearing all the reasons why their choices are the best way, hearing them disregard the damage they've done to their own lives and the pain they've caused others."

"You have a good heart, Alex." Her warm smile, her bright eyes and the way she said his name all snapped something inside him, and his chest grew warm. He felt unsteady on his feet for half a second.

Rick's words the week before his death replayed in his head. *They say the most successful agents are the ones that have a solid support, a family to come home to at night. Maybe it's time to look at getting yourself that, Alex.*

His mouth went dry. Why was that memory choosing *now* to resurface? He'd only ever thought of Violet as Rick's wife, a friend, a wannabe matchmaker.

Her shoulders dropped. "Teddy's lost the scent, but he's trying to find it again." They trudged in silence for a few minutes until Teddy's tail straightened, and he launched out of sight. "I think he's got it again. Let's pick up the pace."

Teddy barked, and Violet bolted into action. She was sure-footed, while Alex clumsily fought to keep from falling on his face. He had to lift his knees high to run in the deep snow. Maybe he should train in the forest occasionally instead of his daily routine of three miles on sidewalks and pavement.

She passed a wrought iron bridge and suddenly disappeared. "Eryn!"

Alex made it past the bridge and slid down the muddy bank, absent from snow due to the overhead supports. Underneath, Violet was bent over, an ear on Eryn's chest.

"She's breathing. Heartbeat slow but steady. Call 9-1-1. Tell them to send an ambulance to the Bow Bridge."

Alex didn't hesitate, and the moment he was off the call, he realized Teddy sat at attention, a chew toy in his mouth. The dog would need a bath. Mud coated the bottom of his tail as it swished in the muck.

Violet tapped Eryn's cheek, which was also coated in grime. "Wake up, Eryn. I need you to open your eyes." Eryn groaned, but her eyes didn't budge.

"She's been drugged." Just like the two men had tried to do to him. Maybe he was wrong, but his gut wouldn't let the idea go. The rocks behind Teddy extended for a good six feet before the water's edge. The river was maybe twenty feet across before reaching the rocky bank on the other side. "Is the water low enough to cross on foot?"

Violet worked her arm underneath Eryn's shoulders and began lifting her to a sitting position. "Yes. It's part of the irrigation system. The dam opens up in the spring. When it's at peak flow, the river reaches the top of the bank. Eryn, honey, wake up."

Far off, sirens accompanied the sound of water slapping the rocks. He looked in the direction they'd come. "Could we have gone down this bank earlier? Walked along the rocks this whole time?"

"I suppose. Eryn?"

Her friend groaned again and began blinking her

eyes. Violet blew out a breath with a nervous laugh. "Are you okay?"

The woman's bloodshot eyes glanced around, and her face morphed into concern. "Where am I?" She cringed and placed a hand on the back of her head.

"Someone call 9-1-1?" a voice in the distance shouted.

"Down here," Alex hollered. A moment later, the EMTs slid their way down the mud underneath the bridge until they got to the rocks. The sheriff was right behind them as they took over caring for Eryn.

Alex barely registered the questions the sheriff and EMTs asked as he gazed over the area. Whoever drugged Eryn had been careful not to leave tracks in the muddy spots. Perhaps they'd made their way along the rocks instead. But why? The two men at the political party had tried to drug him, but he had thought it was about the flash drive. Was it possible Eryn was tied to the assassin or his target? She'd been the one to convince Violet to come to the party.

He turned to look at Violet's best friend with new perspective just as the sheriff remarked. "That's a whole lot of jewelry on your person, Miss Lane." The sheriff picked up her purse. "And a whole lot pouring out of your bag, as well."

The EMTs ignored the statement and placed Eryn on a stretcher.

"What are you talking about?" Eryn asked. "My kids…"

"They're with your husband," the sheriff said.

"We're separated." Eryn shook her head as if trying to shake free of the fog that Alex knew she had to be feeling. "You're right. He's still my husband."

"We need to ask you some questions regarding the theft that took place at the jewelry store."

"Sheriff." Violet stepped in between the man and her friend. "I don't appreciate the direction of these questions. Eryn's been drugged and very obviously framed."

"Excuse me, Ranger Sharp, but her vehicle was spotted at the scene by security cameras, and a woman matching Eryn's description, albeit wearing a mask, cleared the place out. Unless we discover that this jewelry is truly hers—"

"I've never seen it before." Eryn began to tremble. "Violet, what's going on? I don't even know how I got here!"

Violet squeezed her hand. "Don't worry. We're going to get this sorted out."

The EMT threw a blanket over her. "We're taking her to the hospital now, Sheriff."

"Make sure you get a toxicology report," Alex interjected.

The sheriff turned to him, his left eyebrow raised. "Aren't you the new boyfriend in town? Who works in the hospitality industry? Mind telling me what makes you think—"

"Because I said she was drugged," Violet said, eyes wide. "And he's right. Order one." She nodded at the EMTs. They counted and lifted Eryn from both sides before they carried her up the side of the bank. Alex knew small-town gossip traveled fast, but for the sheriff to already know he was "the new boyfriend" was impressive.

"This isn't federal property, Violet," the sheriff said,

his voice softer. Apparently, he only referred to her by her title when it suited him.

"Please. Let's not get into a turf war. You told me Eryn was missing, and I found her unconscious. I've never seen those jewels on her, either, but we both know she has no motive and—"

"The bank just refused her a massive loan." The sheriff crossed his arms over his chest. "Word in town is she's on the brink of bankruptcy and facing a divorce. I'll make sure we run the toxicology, but you might start getting used to the idea that your friend was desperate enough to do this." He stomped up the muddy hill, leaving Violet shaken and staring at the river.

Alex stepped forward and placed a hand on her back. "Hey. She's going to be okay. You and Teddy found her."

"Someone framed her." Her eyes searched his. "Why would someone do that? They drugged her like those two men did to you, except they clearly gave her a bigger dose."

"I don't know, but I'm going to find out." As he said the words, he racked his brain to figure out a possible motivation. He'd assumed they'd drugged him because the Firecracker or the mole on a target's security detail wanted to make sure he didn't have a flash drive. But why would they set up Eryn as a jewel thief?

Violet's shoulders sagged. "I want to catch the Firecracker, but I don't want everyone in my life to suffer because of that. Do you really think it's disconnected events?"

Alex didn't know what to say. He was certain Violet wasn't seeing things earlier. Someone had shone a laser scope in her office today, but they hadn't taken a shot. Why not? How did it all piece together? He missed his partner more than ever now, and his keen sense for solving puzzles. In fact, he wondered if Rick had died with the final clue to the Firecracker's identity. His very last words played on repeat in Alex's mind. *Something about this is starting to seem familiar.*

Violet's phone rang, and she answered with a lot of nodding before she hung up. "My law enforcement ranger team brought Callie, a German shepherd, out to help. She trailed the tracks behind the garage, but the scent ran cold at the highway."

Another dead end.

The last thing Violet wanted to do was get decked out for the second night in a row. The Waller Restaurant had a strict dress code, and the quick-change jacket Alex had worn the night before wasn't going to cut it. "The level of scrutiny is different than in the dark, in the woods. Besides that, your pants are all mussed up."

He shrugged, standing in the middle of her living room. "I'm wearing a different dress shirt, but beyond that, I don't have many choices packed with me."

She strode into the guest room and opened the closet where she kept a few of Rick's clothes. She told herself she'd brought them into the house for Teddy's sake, to have his scent nearby, but she'd also been known to sink her face into Rick's favorite sweaters during the first few months of mourning. It was probably time to let them go.

The charcoal suit, light blue shirt and silver tie caught her eye. She brushed her fingers over the fabric. It would fit Alex. The men had commented on being the same size when they wore the same exact thing as a joke to a charity dinner. She smiled at the memory, even though at the time, she had been so embarrassed to be seen with them.

Hanger in hand, she moved to leave and froze at the threshold. She'd been avoiding thinking or reflecting on her time with Rick for so long, in the hopes of avoiding the waves of pain. And yet she couldn't escape those thoughts with Alex around. She blew out a long breath. It was getting easier to think of Rick, easier to enjoy those memories. What an unexpected blessing to a horrible week. A week that she hoped would end with catching Rick's killer.

She strode out into the hallway, where she found Alex had taken off his tuxedo tie, loosened it as far as it could go and was trying to put it around a waiting Teddy. Even with the added length, it didn't fit. "Well, can't say I didn't try to help him get with the dress code. Guess he can't come to dinner with us."

She laughed. "Dress code or not, Teddy goes where I go. I'm on call at all hours, but Daniella is scheduled to work the valet parking tonight."

"Daniella? Daniella who was volunteering at the district office? Wasn't she also working the party?"

"Yes. Her dad is in charge of the VIP clientele at the resort. She's taking on as much work as she can this year to save up for college. It's a gap year of sorts for her. She's almost twenty and working hard to get her life on track."

His attention moved to the suit in her hands, and his eyes twinkled with held-back laughter. He held out his hands to accept the clothes. "Good choice. I'm sure Rick would approve." He disappeared to change in the bathroom, and her heart pounded from the words.

Teddy picked up the dropped tuxedo tie and whipped it around like a toy rope.

"Ah, man. That was a rental," Alex said from the hallway. He stepped fully into the light. There was nothing about him that looked like Rick. They may have worn the same-size suit, but their builds were completely different. Where Rick had been athletic in a track-and-field sort of way, Alex was built more like a wrestler. And yet he was wearing Rick's suit. He tilted his head and studied her reaction. "Violet? Are you sure? I can change if—"

"I'm fine," she said past the tightness in her throat. "I'd like to pull out the photo of the two of you from that night, and I can't." She gestured at the empty armoire.

"We'll figure out who took them and get the photos back. We can even postpone if—"

"No. Catching the Firecracker has to be the priority, Alex. It has to be."

He studied her face for a moment before turning. "Let's go, then." They got in the SUV so Teddy could ride in style. Violet started the vehicle, trying to mentally prepare herself to pretend to be on a date.

He pulled his seat belt on and faced forward. "I hate to do this, but..."

"You want to know how much I know about the Firecracker."

"Yes."

She knew the conversation was overdue. It was only natural. If she'd been the one investigating, she'd have tons of questions. "I didn't know you and Rick were working on a case involving the Firecracker until after his death."

"You never talked about it?"

She turned to face him briefly. "You know Rick played by the rules. He might mention what type of case he was working or if something was bothering him, but the details weren't fodder for dinner conversation. At least, not until the case was wrapped up. The last thing he told me about the one he was working was that something about it was starting to seem familiar."

"He said that to you?" Alex's voice rose in volume. "Did he say anything else?"

She startled and felt her eyes widen at his reaction. "That was it. Why?"

"He said the same thing to me…" Alex paled, obvious to her even in the dark vehicle. "But we didn't have a chance to discuss what he meant."

"We actually studied the Firecracker in college, so maybe that's why he said it seemed familiar."

"Really?" His question was full of hope.

"That criminal-profiling group I told you about? The Firecracker was a most-wanted fugitive even back then. He was one we picked to study as a deep-dive analysis. We discussed how we would track him down. What potential mistakes he could make? That sort of thing."

"Did you find any answers?"

She shook her head. "Not that I recall. His age stuck in my mind. I'd guess by now he'd be in his midfifties. But he disappeared for like fifteen years. We thought he'd retired."

"That matches what we have in our dossier, as well,"

Alex said as she pulled into the valet-parking loop and waited their turn.

"Why do you think he came out of retirement?"

"We're not sure. Maybe because of the advancement in explosives. Or he ran out of money."

"How do you know it's not a copycat?"

He smiled. "Good question. We have his DNA from two decades ago and some from a more recent assassination with the same MO. Unfortunately, when we run it, we find nothing that leads to his true identity. We thought we'd narrowed down a group of relatives, but there was no living connection. Maybe he was adopted."

Her phone buzzed, mercifully ending the discussion on her husband's killer. She tapped the button on her steering wheel that synced with her phone. "District Ranger Sharp." If she didn't have time to see the caller ID before answering, she went with her official title.

"It's Sheriff Bartlett." A tinge of static came through the speakers.

"Is Eryn okay?"

"Received the toxicology report." He sighed. "You made the right call. She was injected with something called midazolam. I'm told it's most often used for anesthesia. Miss Lane had enough in her system to keep her knocked out for a good four hours."

"When was the robbery?" Alex asked.

The sharp intake of breath over the speakers indicated the sheriff hadn't realized Alex was on the call, as well. She could only imagine the sheriff's level of irritation. "Since it will be public knowledge soon enough, the time of the robbery was three hours before you and Ranger Sharp arrived at the scene."

"So she was framed." Violet didn't realize her shoulders had made their way to her ears until she relaxed them. Her friend wouldn't be spending the night in jail.

"It would appear that way. Know any reason why someone would want to do that? We're fingerprinting her vehicle now, but it appears to have been wiped clean."

"Eryn is liked by everyone in this town." Even back in high school, she was one of the rare personalities who never offended anyone.

"Other than her husband?" the sheriff asked.

She cringed, unable to imagine Darren as capable of being that diabolical. "I really think they're trying to work it out. They just wanted some time living apart while they're in counseling."

"In my experience, a wife doesn't try to get a loan without her husband if they plan to work it out."

Alex turned and placed a hand on her shoulder as she processed the sheriff's words. What had Eryn not been telling her? They were best friends, but this was a huge revelation and added a whole other level of confusion to everything that had been happening.

She took a deep breath. "Has she been discharged, then?"

"They're keeping her overnight due to the bump on her head, out of an abundance of caution, but she has a good prognosis. Call me if you think of anything else."

"Thank you, Sheriff." She hung up just as it was their turn to pull forward.

"This is a big ask, especially considering the circumstances, but I need you to act normal." Alex searched her face as if looking for evidence she could continue with the plan. "Like you're on a date."

She exhaled. "Except that's not normal. I haven't been on a date in seven years. I don't think anyone will expect me to act normal."

He faced forward. "That can work to our advantage. We'll keep it simple. Maybe slightly more familiar than sharing a casual meal with a friend. No need to fake romantic thoughts."

The last words made the back of her neck tingle. She could never fall for Alex, but the challenge he'd issued to not think romantic thoughts had the same result as if he were to tell her not to think about an elephant. What if she were to hold his hand again or stare deeply into his eyes? The thoughts were awkward enough to make her mouth go dry. But the thought of a cute elephant helped her switch gears as Daniella approached her driver's door with a smile.

"You should've called me. I would've come over and done your hair. No red dots the rest of the day, I hope?" She smiled. "It was just some reflection, right?"

Violet didn't want to cause Daniella any fear, but she also didn't want to lie. "No more red dots. There was some activity near the storage garage behind the office, though. We're still investigating. Keep it on the down low, though. Okay? And don't report in for any volunteer shifts until we have more answers."

Daniella blinked, wide-eyed. "Wow. Okay. Hope your investigation turns out to be a curious raccoon. Does Teddy get to keep me company again?"

"Absolutely." She opened the back door, and Teddy made his way to the spot in front of the see-through fireplace that provided heat for whoever was working the valet booth.

Alex laughed. "He's done this before."

Daniella took the keys from Violet. "He's practically a tourist attraction. I've seen him mentioned in Yelp reviews, but I think that's from the snowmobile safety demonstrations. He likes to ham it up when he's supposed to keep Violet from riding without a helmet."

"I'd love to see that." Alex reached for Violet's hand as Daniella drove away.

Violet took a deep breath and accepted his hand. Nothing romantic here. Just friends holding hands. Except her heart rate didn't believe it. They checked their coats and took the elevator up to the VIP-only floor.

"Just act comfortable and focus on the food. I'll be keeping an eye out for who is here, specifically trying to identify the security detail. If we pinpoint the target and the mole, then we can drop the cover and move in with backup."

"Understood."

"Thanks for helping out, Violet. I really appreciate it." He dropped her hand and briefly admired her curled hair and dress. The focused attention made her insides jittery. "We make a fine-looking pair."

She snorted, and the tension evaporated. Leave it to Alex to make a compliment that included himself. It was exactly the sort of story Eryn would find humorous. They used to share the funniest tales about their dates, and then later, about their husbands. It'd been years since they'd regaled each other with stories, though.

"Are you okay?" He slipped on his fake black-framed glasses.

"I'd like to visit with Eryn before the night is over, but yeah, I'm okay." The elevators slid open. "I can't rid myself of the feeling that Eryn's attack has something to do with me."

"I don't see how that's possible, but maybe once we find out who paid for your tickets last night, we can find out."

She'd forgotten about the tickets. He was right. She needed answers, and she felt certain Tom would be here tonight. Men in black suits, which no doubt hid weapons and earpieces, stood at opposite sides of the restaurant entrance. This time, as Alex reached for her fingers, she was ready.

SIX

Alex scanned his surroundings. The restaurant had no website—it was that exclusive—so this was the first chance he'd had to scope out potential exits. It was located on the top floor of the hotel, with a sharply sloped glass roof above him, and the stars twinkled like he'd never seen before. To the right, a man played soft jazz melodies on the piano.

The hostess beamed at Violet. "Tom was so excited you finally took him up on the standing reservation." She turned to Alex. "Welcome to the Waller Restaurant. Follow me."

Inside, the lighting glowed exclusively from candles. The diners sat at tables within recessed slots throughout the room. Outside, ski goggles and winter gear could hide identities. The restaurant kept the guests' desire for privacy in mind, and the place had been designed to help the rich and famous keep their anonymity. This made Alex's job more difficult. Roughly half a dozen men and two women in suits stood in the corners of the room, scanning the area.

"Are you wearing spy glasses?" Violet whispered.

"I know Rick never had any, but a couple years have passed and technology…"

If only. He slowed his steps, and Violet followed. Alex placed a hand on her back and leaned over to whisper into her ear, an excuse so he could study the diners at the tables on the left. "Not even facial-recognition glasses, unfortunately. Can you pretend we stopped here like this because I had to tell you something sweet?" As he whispered, he spotted the governor at the next table and an actor that did action films, if he remembered right. He didn't recognize the other diners.

He straightened, and she flashed a flirtatious smile that caught him off guard, despite knowing he'd asked her to do so. Her presence so close to his side heightened his senses. Her hair smelled like strawberries and coconut. They caught up to the hostess, who sat them at the farthest inward table on the right, presumably closest to the kitchen, judging by the sounds.

Designed for intimate conversation, the table was only two feet deep and a good six feet from the other dining alcoves. It was easy enough to lean over and chat with your party without fear of being overheard. Speakers in between the tables softly broadcasted the piano music. Everything seemed to have been designed with discretion in mind. As the hostess left them with a list of specials, Violet leaned forward. "Did you notice anyone?"

"Only on the left side. The governor is dining here." He picked up the menu. No prices, of course. "I wasn't able to get a good look at the people on the right. I'll need to find another excuse to pointedly look that direction."

"It hit me that you hardly ever hear about assassination attempts in the news. Are they really that rare?"

"If we do our job well, they're stopped before ever getting a chance to be headlined as an attempt. The Bureau doesn't typically seek publicity for what we do."

"Good point. Don't want to broadcast your methods too much, right?" The music switched to a slow ballad. Violet eyed the floor they'd just crossed. "If you're any good at a waltz, we can cover the entire floor."

He fought a grimace but stood. Violet was right that the dance floor would be the most natural place to stare at others without causing suspicion. If it'd been anyone else, if they'd been on a real date, he'd have declined. Hand-eye coordination came easy until he was asked to move to music.

He offered his hand, which she quickly accepted. As they stepped out onto the floor with four other couples, he kept a good twelve inches between them, with one hand lightly on her waist and the other holding her hand. The only thing he knew to do was get situated in a way he could see the tables on the right.

"Would you like me to lead?"

He shifted his attention to find an amused grin on her face.

"Alex, I don't think people consider standing in place to be the same thing as dancing."

"I guess now is the time to admit I've never waltzed." The piano melody transitioned into what was clearly an arrangement of a classic power ballad by Journey.

"That's good, because no one can waltz to this. Just step side to side and smile. We'll be fine. See anyone of note yet?"

There were no familiar faces at the first two tables. He'd studied multiple lists of potential high-value targets before this assignment. So far, no one matched. "Not yet. I need us to carefully make our way closer to the alcoves with the most guards."

"Okay. Here we go." She pressed against his hand, and they spun around and smoothly went back into casual, side-to-side swaying.

A laugh escaped him, despite the severity of the mission. "Thanks for leading."

"Don't mention it. I love this song."

His eyes dropped to hers for the briefest of seconds. In the middle of the turn, they'd somehow closed some distance between them and were now only six inches apart. "It's not country music."

Her smile broadened, and his breath caught for the slightest of moments. "You and Rick with your country music. No, thank you."

"Too bad. I guess I know how this fake relationship is going to end. I could never be with someone who hates country music."

She nodded. "And I could never be with someone who doesn't like classic rock." The main line of the catchy chorus may not have been about faith, but he couldn't stop his mind from going there anyway. Violet and Rick had been very vocal about their faith. Alex didn't speak much about his, but he was a believer. "Do you still believe?"

She sighed, as if she'd anticipated the question. "Yes. But it doesn't mean that I don't have a heap of questions for my Maker when it's time."

"Same." He truly understood, and he was back to thinking about Rick's death. "Like why—?"

"Exactly." The decisive nod of her head meant she was done talking about that subject. "See anyone? Do we need to spin again?"

Right. Back to work. He studied the tables. "No one is jumping out."

"How do you know? Did you memorize a book of world leaders?"

He shrugged, not willing to admit to her that's basically what he'd done, only he'd studied a computer screen instead of a book. "Don't like to broadcast our methods, remember?"

"Hang on, then." She twisted her waist and pressed against his hand. A moment later, they'd spun across the floor. Alex fought to keep his shoulders from shaking with laughter. "The goal is to blend in, Violet, not draw everyone's attention."

She openly laughed along with him, and their eyes met. A connection like he'd never before experienced with her stole his breath away. She stiffened in his arms and worried her lip. She must have seen something. His gaze flew to the corners of the room. "What? What is it?"

"Uh…not sure. Nothing."

"You have a great instinct for undercover work, Violet. Never disregard anything that doesn't sit right."

"No, it's really nothing… I think I just have low blood sugar or something. Can we sit down? Have you seen enough?"

He had taken a good look around, and much to his disappointment, he didn't recognize anyone in the room except the governor. "Yeah. Let's order. Maybe we can stay until closing, in case someone else shows up."

She stepped out of his hands, and he followed her to their table. "It's slow food," she said once she was seated. "Meaning each table has only one party of guests reserved for each night. Dinner is supposed to take hours. What you see is what you get as far as the diners. The only exceptions come from being on the waiting list in case there's a cancellation." Alex's gaze drifted up to the mirror lining the top of the back wall. It was likely there to help the waiters keep an eye on the whole room at once, but Alex had a pretty good view of the people waiting to speak to the hostess from this vantage point.

A man in a navy suit, sporting a trim beard and the type of self-assured smile that could either belong in high-powered boardrooms or movies approached their table. Violet moved to stand, but the man waved her down. He leaned over and gave her a quick one-armed squeeze around her shoulders.

Alex forced a smile, surprised by the sour feeling in his stomach. Had Rick fought displeasure at seeing Alex give Violet a friendly hug whenever he came over? He doubted it, though there was one major difference. Rick had been 100 percent confident in Violet's love for only him. Besides, Alex had never had a single thought for Violet other than friendship. So what was wrong with him this week?

He was watching out for her safety, and any man intruding in her personal space was a threat. Yes, that was it.

The man turned to him and offered a right hand. A

firm, honest handshake. "You must be Alex. I'm Tom, Daniella's dad. Whatever you said to convince Violet to come to dinner here, thank you. I always keep one table open to fill as I see fit. I've been trying to get Violet to come for ages."

A soft rosy glow he'd rarely seen crossed Violet's features. For a brief moment, she wasn't a US Forest Ranger, his partner's widow or even a friend. She was a woman with beautiful hazel eyes out on a date. He'd never noticed her eyes before. Dazzling. The change in his perception caught him off guard. She really could do undercover work well. That was all.

"I told you it wasn't necessary, Tom," she said.

"Let me thank you in the only way I know how." Tom turned back to Alex. "Violet changed the trajectory of Daniella's life. Probably saved her life, if I'm being honest. Her mother and I can't even tell you." His eyes glistened briefly.

"He's exaggerating."

Tom straightened and placed a hand on his heart. "I am not."

Violet fidgeted with her cloth napkin. "I only mentored her, and by God's grace, she responded. Our personalities just suit each other. I love Daniella. It's my pleasure to spend time with her."

"Whatever the reason, please enjoy dinner tonight. Enjoy yourself for once. On the house." He turned to Alex, and in an instant, the man's face transformed into an expression usually reserved for enemies. "Be sure you treat our Violet right. She works tirelessly for this community, and we want only the best for her." As fast as the dangerous narrowing of eyes appeared, all animosity vanished and he smiled again at Violet.

"Before you go—" Violet held up a finger and leaned toward Tom conspiratorially. "You organized the governor's dinner at the River Run, right?"

"I was the venue contact," he clarified.

"Were the locals invited to come, too? For free?"

His eyebrows jumped, and he laughed. "Not even for you, Violet. Sorry. The event was two thousand dollars a plate."

"I was actually there, though. Someone sent me an invitation. They must have bought my ticket and Eryn's. I'd like to find out who. Is it possible you could get access to that information?"

"I don't touch the ticket money, only the venue contract fees." His brow furrowed. "That sort of thing becomes public soon enough, though, since it was a political fundraiser. If it can't wait, I'd ask the treasurer handling the governor's reelection campaign."

"Oh? Is the treasurer here?"

"Not tonight, but he's a townie. Do you know Chris Sebatke?"

Her mouth dropped. "His older sister used to babysit me. Yes, I know Chris. I'll see if we can reconnect." She smiled. "Speaking of the governor, there's a lot of suits here. More bodyguards than I would imagine for your normal clientele. Is there a senator here, too, perhaps? Secret Service?"

When Alex thought he couldn't respect Violet any more, she surprised him. Smooth.

Tom leaned over and pointed at the menu, as if discussing the specials. "Federal Reserve Police," he said quietly. "Between me and you, they're more cautious than the troopers and Secret Service we've worked with in the past."

Alex's heart went into overdrive. "The Federal Reserve chair?"

Tom's gaze flickered over to him, surprise that Alex had joined the conversation written on his face. He addressed Violet when he answered. "Mark Leonard is on the board of governors but is rumored to be announced as a nominee for the chair next week." He straightened. "Enjoy your dinner."

The moment Tom disappeared around the corner, Violet's eyes widened. Had they always been so vibrant? "That's the type of powerful position you were looking for, right?"

A federal nominee *would* be the type of target the Firecracker would come out of hiding for. There would be a high price on the man's head. This was the type of lead that could help the Bureau stop the assassination in its tracks. The rumored mole would likely be on the Federal Reserve Police detail. Alex would have to tread cautiously so as not to alert the mole, but he'd also need to make sure Mark Leonard stayed safe.

He'd never been this close to bringing down the Firecracker. The strange happenings of the week wouldn't leave him alone, though. The missing photographs, the red dot in the forest service office and the drugging of Violet's friend. He couldn't find a motive to connect them all, and as he took a bite of what was no doubt the best bread ever to meet his taste buds, he was unable to enjoy it. Because with everything going on, how could he trap the Firecracker while also keeping Violet safe?

* * *

This had to be the most uncomfortable meal she'd ever experienced with Alex. Pretending to be in a relationship had seemed easy enough, until they'd started laughing. A shared laugh had never felt so confusing before. She hadn't meant to be silly, but she also had never needed to lead a man in a dance before.

"Did you notice a woman with long black hair and a red dress at the governor's dinner?" His gaze stayed focused on something above her head. Odd.

"That's like asking me if I noticed a candle in the restaurant. There were a lot of women there. Can you be more specific?"

He shook his head and narrowed his eyes, his gaze still above her. She moved to look over her shoulder. "No, don't look at the mirror," he said. "I don't want to draw attention. See if you can casually look over my shoulder to spot who I'm talking about. She's wearing a black pantsuit and standing in line to talk to the hostess. Not black hair this time. She's blond now."

A waiter walked past them with a large tray of plates, blocking the view of the lobby. She strained but couldn't see past him. "Are you sure it's the same woman?"

"Not a hundred percent sure, but if I'm right, that's the Firecracker's courier." He groaned as the waiter returned to the kitchen. "She's gone."

"Maybe she went to the restroom. How about I go find out?"

He paled. "If it's the same woman, she might recognize you. After all, someone did find your purse and switch the flash drives."

The back of her neck tightened. "Which means the

two men who tried to drug you could also be nearby."
She slipped her hand into her purse. "I understand
the danger, but I feel like you keep forgetting that I'm
trained in law enforcement, too. I'm armed this time,
Alex, as I assume you are. She could lead us to the Firecracker now, and we could end this. Let's get our coats
and go find her."

"I don't think Rick—"

"Would want me in danger?" She slipped her purse
strap over her shoulder. "I think we can both agree all
the weird stuff happening this week might mean I'm in
danger already. And let's get something straight. This
resort is on land in partnership with the forest service.
I am a ranger of the forest service, and even though I'm
not currently deputized with the sheriff, like my law
enforcement rangers, I still have authority to arrest anyone who breaks federal laws."

"Are you arguing jurisdiction?"

"No. I'm telling you that Rick knew I faced danger
daily. It's time for you to accept that and maybe allow
me to help." A flash of black behind the hostess podium
caught her eye, and she stood. "I'm going to check the
restroom to see if she went in there. Please let Tom
know we're leaving. Maybe he'll be able to tell you the
name that woman goes by if she's a regular. I'll meet
you by the elevator."

She strode across the restaurant, lifted her coat off
the rack with one hand and draped it over the arm where
her purse dangled. The coat concealed the fact she was
removing her weapon from her purse so she would be
ready to fire, should she need to. The little speech she'd
given Alex wasn't like her, really, but at least it had cast

all thoughts of attraction to the far recesses of her mind. It was time to work.

Thankfully, the area in front of the restrooms was empty. There was no sign of the two men who had grabbed Alex the night before. She hadn't got a good look at their faces that night, but she remembered their builds. She kept the gun pointed at forty-five degrees, still hidden by the coat, and opened the door to the ladies' room with her foot. There were no sounds from inside, except instrumental music playing from the speaker in the ceiling. Moments later, she'd confirmed there was no one in the stalls.

She stepped outside to find a flustered Alex standing with his coat and a large brown bag.

"What's in the bag?"

"Tom insisted you couldn't leave without dessert. He might also want to murder me after I asked about the woman. I think he thought I was trying to pick up another date while out with you."

She fought against a smile, but her lips wouldn't stop twitching. "Nice to know I've got people watching my back."

"I think it's safe to say he disapproves of your first serious fake relationship." Alex looked around the corner. "I don't see the numbers on the elevator moving. Stairs?"

A quick look in his direction confirmed he held his weapon underneath his coat, as well. He followed her gaze. "Do they train rangers to cover their guns like that?"

"No, but FBI special agents married to rangers sometimes enjoy procedural discussions. We picked up tips from one another." They worked in tandem, both angling the opposite direction every time they reached a landing and peeking out at the hallways. Violet tried not to linger on how natural partnering with Alex felt.

"Did you ever help Rick with one of our cases?"

"Like I said, we didn't usually talk about work, but you remember that arson case?"

His mouth dropped. "Rick told me he just happened to know a lot about trees. It was you, wasn't it?"

She shrugged, knowing Rick would've gotten a kick out of seeing the shocked look on Alex's face. "Maybe."

They reached the bottom lobby, and she noticed Alex's shoulders sagged.

"I think it's safe to say we lost her," he said.

"Is it time to shed the undercover role and check the security cameras of the resort?"

He cringed. "Maybe. Though that will no doubt get back to the suits of the Federal Reserve Police. I was hoping to avoid that."

She nodded. "Then maybe I put a call into Stephen. He's Daniella's boyfriend. He works in the security office. I might be able to casually tell him to look out for the woman and two men. He's not the type to ask too many questions, especially since he knows I work for the forest service."

"Thank you. How about we head back then? I think it's time I have a long talk with my handler back at the Bureau. There might be enough here to bring in backup."

They reached the valet parking where Daniella was handing over keys to a couple. Teddy stretched from his spot in front of the fireplace and ambled over to her. "Long day, huh, buddy?"

"He was great, as usual," Daniella said over her shoulder. "Greeted some of the guests who wanted to say hi. Mostly, he napped."

Violet reached down to pet him, and the corner of some stiff paper scratched at her palm. She bent over. "What've you got there, boy?" She pulled the offending paper out from underneath his vest and flipped it over.

The photograph of Rick and Alex dressed in identical suits and goofy grins stared up at her. It was the photo from the charity event that she'd remembered earlier. The same red marker that had circled her face in the wedding photograph now circled Alex's face in this picture.

"Violet?" Alex's cupped her shoulders. "What is it?"

The hand that held the photo began shaking despite her attempts to remain calm. She straightened and held it out to him. He took one look, spun around and stepped in front of her, as if protecting her. Whoever was trying to torture her had gotten close to Teddy. Her heart went into overdrive. "Daniella, describe everyone who spent time with Teddy."

"I don't know." Daniella looked at her as if she'd grown an extra head. "The usual tourist types. Anyone who loves a dog." Her face scrunched up. "Someone gave him one of those big meat sticks he likes."

Alex jolted at the same time she did. "Who? Who gave Teddy something to eat?"

"I never saw who. Only saw he was enjoying one. I was too busy helping guests."

Violet held out her hand. "Throw me my keys."

Daniella's eyes widened, but she did as she asked. Violet patted the side of her leg, and Teddy ran alongside her. He was too big for her to carry, and she needed to get him seen right away.

Alex ran up alongside her. "Taking him to the vet? You're worried about poison?"

"Wouldn't you be?" They reached her vehicle and got Teddy inside.

He sighed and nodded. "Let's go."

She just hoped they could get him help in time.

SEVEN

Alex stared at the photo of himself and his partner in matching suits. It was hard to remember a time that he'd allowed himself to be goofy for the sake of a good laugh. He stuffed the picture back in his pocket, his mind swirling.

He'd yet to reveal his presence to the Federal Reserve Police, but given what had happened with Teddy, Alex requested access to the security footage. Now the Idaho state troopers who guarded the governor knew he was FBI. They had gotten back to him a moment ago to reveal the security tapes of the hallways and portico had been set to loop on footage from the previous night. Security had been breached.

Violet exited a swinging door and joined him in the lobby of the vet hospital. "Doc said he can induce vomiting instead of pumping Teddy's stomach." She let out a shaky breath. "They don't think he was poisoned. They're running a few more tests to make sure he looks good." She sank into the closest orange plastic chair and dropped her head into her hands. "I can't lose Teddy."

He sat next to her and placed a hand on her back.

She wouldn't handle the news of the security footage well. If the cameras could be compromised despite state troopers and Federal Reserve Police working with hotel security, then how could they keep their protectees safe against the Firecracker?

"You won't lose Teddy," he said instead. "We're going to find whoever is doing this and put a stop to it."

She placed a hand on top of his. "Thanks, but you don't have to do that."

"Do what?"

"Promise justice. Because we work in law enforcement, it seems like something we can control, doesn't it? But if Rick's killer can get away—"

"We're going to get him, too, Violet." The words held no luster, though. She was right, yet again. Repeatedly saying he'd catch the killer wouldn't make his promise come true. "At least, I pray we'll catch him."

She gave him a soft smile. "I'll join you in that prayer. But while we wait, I'd like to talk about something else for now. If that's okay?"

He flipped his hand over to properly hold hers. His mind whirled with questions about the case, but for her sake, he strained to find a new subject, at least for a few minutes. "You enjoy mentoring Daniella?"

She casually dropped his hand and leaned back into the chair, wrapping the dress coat tighter around herself. "I don't know if it's the mentoring I enjoy or who I'm hanging out with. I suppose in the back of my mind, I've realized it's the closest I'll get to motherhood."

He vividly remembered Rick discussing their dilemma about starting a family. It hadn't been a matter of if, but when. Rick had told him he'd request a desk position within the FBI once he became a father. Alex had struggled with that news as it meant he'd lose his partner. Now, after years in the field undercover, a desk-jockey position sounded like a dream come true. "You adore kids, if memory serves."

He used to think he'd want a family someday, but if he couldn't even protect the people in his life now, how could he possibly be a good father? Fathers protected their families. They died for them. Alex had sent the friend he considered a brother to his death because of a bad judgment call. Had he been making bad calls while he was with Violet, too?

"I adore the kids I know, at least." She sighed. "Speaking of which, I need to check in with Eryn since we're so close to the hospital. She might like some help with her kids. I don't know what her current arrangement is with her husband."

The back door opened, and Teddy bounded through. Violet and Alex jumped to their feet and went to either side of the dog to pet him.

"I believe he's fine," the balding vet said. "We fed him a small second dinner, and he's doing great. If he shows any concerning signs, you have my number. Don't hesitate to call." The vet leaned down and petted the top of Teddy's head before disappearing into the back again.

Violet straightened. "Ready to go, boy?" She looked at Alex. "Do you mind if we stop at the hospital? Eryn would probably like a chance to thank her rescuer."

"They'll let Teddy in the hospital?"

"Official K-9s are allowed. Besides, Teddy's kind of a celebrity there, as well. He's saved so many lives."

"As have you."

"I wouldn't have been able to without Teddy." They got inside the vehicle, and her phone vibrated. "Official call. One second."

Alex couldn't hear what was being said, but Violet's silence spoke volumes. Her eyes grew wider and her breath shallow. He was about to reach for the phone when she finally said, "Understood. Bring in all LEOs. This is top priority… Yes. Let me know as soon as you know." She hung up and paled.

"Violet?" He knew that LEOs meant she was calling in all law enforcement officers within her forest district. "What's going on?"

"Remember the garage behind my office?"

He held his breath. "What's happened?"

"Our snow ranger needs to confirm, but one of my team thinks we might have some explosives missing."

"Bombs are missing?" He enunciated every word, and his head throbbed with the sudden increase in his blood pressure. That's all he needed. Trying to capture an assassin that specialized in blowing up people, and explosives were missing. At Violet's slight nod, he wanted to punch something. "And they just now discovered this?"

"After the mysterious red dot incident, the rangers were cataloging the storage in the garage. We keep the explosives in a special safe. There was no sign of tampering, so they didn't check the contents first. They're bringing in my lead snow ranger for avalanche control to confirm their suspicions. It's not a simple job. We need him to look over his logs to rule out human error. There are checks and balances. If the log sheet doesn't match the contents of the safe but does match the recent avalanche-mitigation efforts, then problem solved. It's unlikely, but everyone makes mistakes."

"If there are bombs missing, then game over. We fill the hotel with bomb-sniffing K-9s." They'd also lose their chance to catch the Firecracker, but Violet didn't need to be told the obvious.

"I know how serious this is, but I also don't want to create a false panic."

"What kind of explosives? What's the magnitude?"

"The snow rangers use a variety of types based on the conditions and the location. Different needs, different kinds. We have small snow shots. Those need to be manually detonated from a distance."

"How powerful are we talking?"

"You step on one wrong, and it takes off your foot. We use half a dozen at a time, usually. But we also have a fairly new system of remote-detonated explosives. We place those in the harder-to-access mountains. We can set those off no matter the weather or time, so we can limit highway closures."

He groaned. "I'm guessing those are more powerful?"

"Yes. But harder to take and walk away with."

"Except we saw tracks."

"Yes. I'm aware. They're going to call me back as soon as the snow ranger arrives."

"How much does the log say is missing?"

"Enough to set off a few avalanches."

He closed his eyes for a second to ease the pain building in his temples. "I need to let the troopers know—"

"They know." She turned to him. "My snow ranger

notified the police and the troopers before he called me, out of an abundance of caution."

"Please tell me the moment you have confirmation." He needed to phone his supervisor to discuss how to proceed. Even if he was called off the case, he was staying until he could figure out who was tormenting Violet and those she cared about. "You're not going to like it, but—"

"You also want to ask Eryn questions."

He huffed. "That's unnerving, you know."

"Sorry. It's what I would do in your situation. You're trying to figure out the connection and why someone is targeting me and the people closest to me." Her voice shook ever so slightly. "It'll mean breaking your cover, though. Eryn won't believe a boyfriend in the hospitality industry would be asking such questions."

"I'm aware." With the news about missing bombs, staying undercover seemed like the least of his concerns.

She took the first right turn as the hospital parking lot was adjacent to the animal hospital. They parked in the visitors' section and made quick work of getting to the second floor before visiting hours ended.

Eryn Lane, a petite woman with short blond hair, looked small in the hospital bed. She blinked, bleary-eyed, and turned her focus from the television to the doorway. "Violet!" She reached her hands out. Violet and Teddy hustled to her bedside. Teddy waited patiently for their hug to be done and then lightly pressed his paws on the edge of the bed and lifted his head for Eryn to show her appreciation. "My hero."

"How are you?" Violet asked.

"I'm perfectly fine now. They're just taking precautions. I can't thank you enough for proving my innocence."

"I'm sorry you're in this situation. I have a feeling it has something to do with me."

Eryn flinched. "How could that be?"

Violet looked over her shoulder at Alex. His cue. "Eryn, I'm actually FBI special agent Alex Driscoll. I'm here on a separate investigation, but someone seems to be intent on targeting those closest to Violet this week. Can I ask you a few questions?"

"Of course." Her mouth dropped open and her eyes slid to Violet. "You're not really dating?"

"Afraid not. He needed to stay undercover, and that was the easiest ruse we could come up with."

"That's a relief. No offense." Eryn gestured toward him. "I was pretty miffed you'd kept something like that from me." ·

"I think you've been keeping a few things from me, as well," Violet said gently.

Eryn flushed, and Alex could tell they needed to talk. "Let me get a few questions out of the way, and then I'll give you some privacy. Did you pay for the ticket to the governor's dinner?"

"Pay?" Eryn scrunched up her nose. "It was free. I was invited, but I had to RSVP."

"To who?"

Eryn looked up. "There was a phone number on the invite."

Violet blinked. "Mine didn't have a phone number."

"I had to give my name and a few demographic-type details for their stats or something."

Violet's intrigued reaction likely matched his own. There was a lot of information that could be gathered from a demographic survey. "Violet, you didn't RSVP to anyone?"

She shook her head. "No, I went as Eryn's plus one."

"They had her info, though," Eryn said. "I gave it to them since she was my guest."

"I'll need to get that number from you. Last question. Can you think of anyone in town, anyone from high school or your shared past who would have a grudge against you both?"

Eryn frowned. "Are you serious? Is he serious? We were like the two most goody-two-shoes girls in school. Nice to everyone."

Alex turned to Violet. "That seems hard to imagine."

"Growing up in a small town, you don't really have the option to make many enemies. It wouldn't be wise, at least. We weren't exactly doormats, though."

"Anything but," Eryn added.

"Okay. That's all for now." Alex gestured to the hallway. "I need to make a phone call. Mind if I do so in your SUV? I can pull it around to pick you up."

"Sure." Violet handed him the keys. "Teddy and I will join you in a few minutes."

He strolled back through the hospital, deep in thought. If it weren't for the men who'd tried to drug him as well as Eryn, he'd dismiss any potential connection between the Firecracker and the actions taken against Violet.

The photo in his pocket meant that someone knew he was close to Rick. Could this all be about Rick or Violet?

That would make sense only if he was missing something about his former partner's murder. To bring it up again, in detail, was something he'd never wanted to do with Violet, and yet he knew he'd never have peace until he did. She was the one person who might fill in the missing pieces from that day. But if she learned the whole truth about Rick's death, would she ever be able to look him in the eye again?

"You're really okay? Didn't hit your head too hard?" Violet asked, hating the thought of what those men could've done to Eryn.

"Physically, I'm almost one hundred percent. They ran tests and checked me out, and I'm fine. For that, I'm very relieved. The worst part was not knowing how I got there and seeing that jewelry on and around me." Eryn's eyes watered. "There was the smallest part of me that wondered if I was losing my mind."

Violet reached for her friend's hand and held it. Teddy made a noise in his throat that sounded like his attempt at soothing sounds before he flopped down on the ground at her feet. He'd had a rough day, as well, and all because of her. If only she understood who would do such a thing and why.

"What the sheriff said about loans and bankruptcy... are you in some kind of trouble?"

Eryn shook her head and closed her eyes. "No. When I agreed to try separation, Darren talked about selling the house and splitting the proceeds. I don't want to take the kids from the only home they've ever known, so I tried to get a loan for his half of the house to pay him outright."

Her mouth dropped open. "That's so much to take on yourself." Her throat tightened at the realization of the burden Eryn had been carrying alone. Alex had been right. People saw what they wanted to see. And she'd wanted to see her friends without real hurts and struggles. A groan built in her throat. "I thought you guys were in counseling. I had no idea. Why didn't you tell me any of this?"

Eryn turned away, a faint blush on her cheeks. "You had your own stuff to deal with."

When Violet first returned to Sunshine Valley, she'd been newly widowed. She'd practically had a sign on her forehead that read I Can't Handle Any Big Emotions. Not that she didn't care, but she hadn't been able to share anyone's burdens or even their joys. But now?

With sinking dread, she realized she'd made it clear to anyone who knew her that finding love and happiness again wasn't possible for her. Hadn't she said as much to Alex the other night? Who would be comfortable sharing highs and lows with a friend who'd declared that? No wonder they'd been trying so hard to play matchmaker.

"I'm so sorry I've been pushing away any real conversations about the tough stuff." Violet squeezed Eryn's hand. "I want to be here for you the way you've been for me."

Eryn let her head sink back into the pillow with a sigh. "I'd like that. And as far as Darren goes... I think we might have a chance again after all." She gestured at the hospital gown. "This gave him a scare. Not that I'd ever advise getting drugged and left for dead as a treatment for struggling marriages."

Violet pulled her chin back. She'd never imagined anything good could come out of something so horrible.

"Time will tell, I suppose," Eryn said. "Enough about me. *That* was Rick's partner?" Her eyes narrowed, and her eyebrows jumped. "It's more than a cover, isn't it? There's something there." Eryn gasped. "Oh, I see it on your face. There is."

Violet's neck felt like it was on fire. Teddy shifted and pressed against her legs, confirming that her emotions were running hot. "I... I don't know. And even if there were, it would never work."

Eryn crossed her arms. "Why not?"

Violet faltered, surprised by the intensity of the question and how it stumped her. The answer had seemed easy a week ago when all relationships had been off the table. When Rick died, she'd thought she would literally perish from the pain of losing him. Each day that she woke up was a surprise to find that her own heart was still beating and her lungs still breathing without him there.

She'd eventually resumed eating and drinking— albeit less—mostly thanks to her stubborn mom. Grief physically hurt. Her entire body ached all the time. The only thing that had helped her was movement. At first, it was to take care of Teddy, because he relied on her. She'd needed to keep up his training for his sake.

Teddy was miserable without his work, and she knew he missed Rick, too. She could see it in his eyes and the way he held his head. And she'd realized if she kept moving, the pain didn't hurt as much. She couldn't think or feel with as much intensity if she stayed active, working on a problem that was right in front of her.

"The first year was hard, and the second year was harder somehow," she finally told Eryn. "I don't know why it was harder, but I just tried to stop feeling. I don't know when it started getting easier. Sometimes it's a shock to realize I'm not in pain, and other times it hits me like a bolt of lightning out of nowhere, and I fall apart all over again."

"But you seem like yourself again with Alex. I saw it myself."

Her heart jolted with the realization Eryn was right. She had felt like herself with him many times. "He mentions Rick," she finally said. "I didn't know that I craved someone else talking about him. Alex gets how important it is to keep his memory alive, maybe because he misses him almost as much as I do." She exhaled slowly. "He's not holding his breath or looking at me like I'm going to break down if he says Rick's name. It's nice."

"I'm very glad." Eryn shook her head slowly. "But I'm telling you that's not all it is."

Her stomach flipped. "Maybe it's just about finding out who killed Rick and who is putting my friends and Teddy in danger."

"No. I've known you since fifth grade, and while you've changed a lot, one thing remains the same."

Eryn's calm refusal was beginning to infuriate her, and she placed her hands on her hips. "Oh, yeah? And what's that?"

"Whenever you like a boy, you bite your lip. You do it whenever you think about Alex or look at him." Eryn's eyes twinkled.

Violet didn't think her mouth and eyes had ever

grown so wide. "I…" A breath of air that sounded somewhere between a laugh and a gasp escaped. "I do not!"

"You do. You *so* do." Eryn wiped the tears from laughing away. "It's cute. You did it with Leo in junior high, Bruce in high school and the first time you brought Rick home to meet your parents." Teddy lifted his head, watching their interchange carefully. "See, even Teddy agrees with me," Eryn added.

"Don't bring Teddy into this." She found herself laughing while tears escaped out the corners of her eyes. Even amid the frustrating mysteries and danger surrounding her, she'd laughed more this week than in the past two years. The thought sobered her.

"What? What is it?"

"Is it weird that I'm scared to feel…?" She couldn't fully voice what was swirling in her heart and mind.

Eryn reached for her. "Violet, you're not forgetting Rick. And having a laugh or even feelings for another guy doesn't diminish the love you had for him…" Violet's breath caught, and Eryn quickly added, "…will always have for him."

Her shoulders dropped, even her limbs felt lighter. "Hey, you're the one in the hospital. You're not supposed to be helping me."

"I've never experienced loss like you have, but I watched you go through it with your dad. Remember years ago, that summer during college, when you were at my house and that song came on?"

She instantly remembered. It was the song she and her dad always used to dance to. When he'd first passed away, she couldn't hear it without breaking down. But years later at Eryn's house, she'd found herself wanting to dance to it instead of crying.

"You said you could enjoy the memory again. Doing that dance helped you feel closer to that memory."

"I remember." Yet this felt different. She didn't have the words to explain, so she simply offered a smile.

"Eryn?" Darren stood in the doorway with a giant bouquet of flowers. "Is this a bad time?"

Eryn's eyes softened at the sight of him, and she glanced at Violet for a second, as if asking for permission. Violet leaned over and hugged her friend. "No more holding out on me. Both the good and the bad. Okay?" she whispered. "I can take it now."

Eryn's brows rose. "Are you sure?"

"I'm sure. Though no more matchmaking and leave the body-language profiling to the professionals. Maybe my lip was just chapped." Violet winked at Eryn and offered a small wave to Darren as Teddy joined her in the hallway.

She strolled out of the hospital, still reflecting on their discussion. There was a lot of processing to do over the events of the night and the conversation with Eryn. An early bedtime would help her do that. Biting her lip when she liked a guy? As if.

Snow began to fall in fat flakes and hit the tip of her nose. There was no sign of Alex and her SUV. She'd thought he was going to pull up to the entrance or at least be watching for her. His call might've gone longer than expected, or maybe he'd gotten distracted. Good thing she'd slipped into the boots she kept in the vehicle when they'd gone to the vet, or the cold gust of air would've been an unwelcome surprise. She patted her leg, and they rounded the corner, past the streetlight to where she'd parked.

Two figures in the distance caught her attention. Teddy grumbled, and she felt him stiffen beside her. Two men fighting. She squinted. Was that Alex?

Teddy barked, sending shivers up her spine. An arm snaked around her neck. She'd been so focused on the pair of men, she'd missed someone sneaking up behind her!

Hot breath hit her ear. "Someone wants to have a word with you."

A fist lifted, and out of the corner of her eye, she spotted the syringe. She shoved her elbow into the man's side. He barely moved but the interchange stalled him from shoving the needle in her shoulder. She felt Teddy shift behind him.

"Off!" the man shouted.

She stomped her feet and slammed her heel onto his instep. He yelped, and the moment his grip loosened, she stepped forward. Teddy rose up on his hind legs and jumped onto the man's chest, shoving him backward. The man stumbled, turned and ran away just as a gunshot rang out behind her. She spun around. "Alex."

Teddy didn't hesitate. He ran toward the two figures. One of them broke away and also raced off. She sprinted in their direction to find Alex hunched over, and Teddy sniffed him wildly, as if checking him over for injuries. "Are you okay?"

His weary eyes met hers. "More importantly, are you?"

"I think so. He got the jump on me and tried to drug me." She whirled around. "I think he might've dropped the syringe. But I heard a gunshot?"

"My gun. I reached my weapon but when he tried to wrestle it out of my hands, I fired a warning shot into the air. It spooked him enough that he let go and ran." Alex turned on his phone flashlight and walked with her back toward the corner where the syringe would be. The plastic reflected off the beam. "Maybe we can get some prints off this. I don't suppose you have an evidence bag or gloves handy for me to pick it up?"

"I might, in the vehicle." Her voice wobbled, taking her by surprise. She'd spent so long building up a protective layer to keep from feeling too much, and this week was breaking it apart bit by bit.

He reached for her instead of the syringe and pulled her closer. "Are you sure you're okay?"

"I think so."

He looked down, searching her face. "Violet, don't hide your pain from me. You're clearly biting your lip."

Heat flooded her stomach, and she closed her eyes. She hated that Eryn knew her so well. Was she truly attracted to Alex? "It's just a lot to process," she whispered.

He responded by wrapping his arms tightly around her. Her cheek rested against his chest, underneath his chin, and for a moment, all she could hear was the beating of his heart. They stood there quietly, until a bright beam of light hit her squarely in the face.

The sheriff stepped out of his vehicle, pointing his flashlight, as well, at them. "What's going on here?"

EIGHT

The first thing Alex noticed was the sheriff's hand on his weapon as he stood with his door still open. It was a tactical move in case he needed protection. Why would the sheriff think he needed to protect himself against them?

"I was looking for you, Violet. Word around town is you went to the animal hospital and then to see Eryn." The sheriff raised his voice over a gust of wind that carried a burst of stinging snow. As he spoke, two other patrol cars sped toward the parking lot with their lights flashing but sirens off. "En route, I heard about a gunshot behind the hospital. Something you need to tell me?" His eyes remained trained on Alex's side, where his coat had slipped up, exposing his gun.

Violet spun out of his embrace. "I can explain."

Alex stepped in front of Violet, holding has hands up to the sheriff. "I think it's time to properly introduce myself. FBI special agent Alex Driscoll. Two men, the men I suspect are behind Eryn's drugging and likely the jewelry store robbery, attacked us minutes ago. I fired my weapon but didn't hit anyone."

"FBI, huh?"

"I was actually about to call you," Violet added. She turned and pointed at the ground. "They tried to drug me. I'm hoping you can find prints on the syringe."

The two deputy vehicles pulled up in formation behind the sheriff. He held up a hand to indicate they should wait. "Before we continue, I'd like to see your badge, Mr. Driscoll. Nice and slowly, if you please."

Alex complied. Thankfully, he had it on his person today. He'd brought it along in case he needed to discuss intel with the troopers. He reached in his coat with his right hand and produced the badge.

The sheriff reached for his radio. "Stand down. Return to your posts." He stomped through the rapidly building snow and took the badge from Alex. The flashlight beam illuminated the unflattering photo from back when Alex thought a buzz cut suited him. Rick and Violet had been the ones to encourage him to let his thick, wavy hair grow a bit. They'd said it made him look more mature, which had appealed to him at the time.

"You're dating an FBI agent, Vi?" the sheriff asked. Alex had never heard someone call her by that nickname.

Her spine stiffened. Clearly, she wasn't a fan. "It was a cover to help him find Rick's killer, Sheriff."

The man's eyes widened, and he looked between them both. "Did you?"

"Still hoping," Alex said. "We don't know if these unusual happenings are connected."

"The man who tried to drug me said that someone wanted to talk to me." She shook her hands in front of her as if trying to shake something off her person.

"What?"

"The adrenaline and the gunshot… For a second, I thought you'd been hit." Her voice trembled, but she steeled her features. "I'm still going over the details in my mind. But yes, I'm sure my attacker said something to that effect." She squatted, staring at the syringe in the snow. "You have gloves?"

The sheriff removed some from his harness and gingerly picked up the syringe. "This relates to why I came to find you." He slipped the item carefully into a thick bag and stood. "We had another robbery. This time the art gallery. Over a million dollars' worth of art and statues were stolen."

Alex whistled. "I'm surprised a small town has a gallery showcasing items of that kind of worth." In his experience, the art found in small towns usually graced the walls of local cafes and coffee shops, with price tags underneath them.

"This is not a normal small town," she explained. "Our tourists can afford it and often want to buy something while on vacation. It's why we have such a famous jewelry store, as well." Violet turned to the sheriff. "That's not why you came to find me. If you needed the forest service, you'd call my law enforcement rangers. You need Teddy?"

He nodded. "Bruce Wilkinson is missing. His vehicle was found near the gallery."

She released an exasperated sigh. "Don't tell me he's a suspect."

"I follow the evidence." The sheriff gestured at the hospital. "But if this is like Eryn's experience, it might be in Bruce's interest to be found sooner rather than later." He raised his chin into the flurries. "Snow and temps dropping fast. You know I can't call the search-and-rescue team in so quickly and without more information. But since you and Bruce had a relationship—"

"In high school," she said, her annoyance shining through.

"Pretty easy to follow your love life when you've only had one boyfriend and one husband." His eyes darted to Alex. "And one fake boyfriend."

"Why'd I think it was a good idea to move back to my hometown?" Violet muttered under her breath. "Fine."

"I don't think assigning this to Violet is the right call." Alex addressed the sheriff. "Someone is targeting her. They tried to get me out of the picture, and they want to kidnap her. She's in danger, and I don't—"

"That's not your decision to make, Agent Driscoll," Violet said. "I'm used to being in danger as part of my job, and I said I'd do it. Someone is targeting everyone I know, which makes me responsible, and I'd like to catch whoever is behind this more than anyone. Teddy has had a rough night, though." She turned back to the sheriff. "If we don't find Bruce within a few hours, you'll need to call in some officers to take over. Can't you justify it since technically Bruce is a suspect in the robbery?"

The sheriff's lips twisted to one side. "I'd prefer not to do that when I don't think he's guilty, but I'm willing. You know I can't page for a SAR team so soon in this instance. It doesn't fit the guidelines."

"I know." Violet blew out a long breath, and Teddy scooted closer to her.

"Please keep us updated on what you find out." Alex pointed to the evidence bag.

"Will do. Stay safe." The sheriff backed up and took the same route out of the lot as the other deputies. Violet watched them leave until a gust of wind caused her to turn in his direction.

The cold didn't faze him as he was still running hot under the collar. He reached out to touch her shoulder. "You don't have to do this."

"I do."

"I'd rather you pack up and stay somewhere else for the night. Your safety is my priority. You said yourself there are other search-and-rescue dogs. They can find a loophole and call them in early, or you have rangers who—"

"Do you have any idea how overwhelmed search-and-rescue teams are right now? We have millions more people using public lands lately, which is great, but search and rescue is predominantly made of volunteers. They work normal jobs and have lives. They already get paged over a hundred and fifty times a year. Besides, I know the forest land around town the best. The SAR team here trains mostly around the ski areas."

"You work a full-time job, too. You never take a break, do you? It's clear the community loves you because you're serving all the time. You don't have to be a superhero, Violet. Take the rest when you need it."

"Look who's talking. You've been undercover ever since he's been gone, haven't you?" She tapped her index finger on his chest. "You and I are the only ones who understand that the world is void of all the good Rick would have done, all the lives he would have saved and—"

"Of course I understand! But just like the world, the

void in your heart isn't going to be filled if you're exhausted all the time." His words rushed out, full of heat, and he instantly regretted dropping his guard when her face crumpled.

"It's all I have." She blinked rapidly. "It's me and Teddy and the only thing we know to do."

"Maybe it's time we both learn other things. Open up to other possibilities."

Her eyes shimmered in the moonlight. "I'm not sure I can."

He held his hands out. She hesitated, staring at his palms for a moment before placing her hands in his. He wrapped his fingers around hers. "I don't want to insult you by saying I know how you feel."

She glanced down at their hands. "No, but out of everyone else I know, you might come the closest."

"When I look at you, I realize I need to take my own advice. I'm weary of the undercover life."

"Does that mean you're ready to request a new partner?"

He exhaled and looked away. "I don't know. Maybe."

"I understand. Good thing we don't have to try to do it alone, right?"

She was referring to the Lord, he realized. He dropped his head, and her forehead pressed against his. He wasn't ready to pray aloud, but he knew from all the times he'd shared meals at her house that she was lifting up a silent prayer. He asked for the weariness to be left behind, for help in keeping her safe and solving the threats that seemed to surround them. He exhaled, his breath a cloud as he opened his eyes and lifted his head to find her gaze on him.

His mouth went dry. She had a small tear on the side of her cheek, frozen in place. He lifted his hand and gently wiped it away. Her lips parted, and he could only hear the pounding of his heart. She lifted her chin ever so slightly, and Alex drew her closer. He lowered his mouth and—

"Have a good night, Violet."

They pulled apart as if splashed with a giant wave of cold water. A man waved as he shuffled in the snow to a minivan.

"You, too, Darren," Violet croaked. She shoved her hands in her pockets. "I think we should go. Now."

His gut dropped as if a heavy weight had landed in it. What had he done? Had almost kissing her ruined their friendship forever?

Teddy's snoring stirred Violet awake before her phone vibrated. The Newfoundland had located Bruce in one hour flat, so she didn't begrudge him the snores that could rival a lion's roar.

Covered in half an inch of snow, Bruce had at least been in a hefty wool coat. There'd been an empty bottle of liquor beside him and several key pieces from the gallery in his trunk. If the sheriff hadn't already seen for himself that someone had framed Eryn for the jewelry store robbery, he'd likely have hauled Bruce straight to the drunk tank. Apparently, Bruce had been trying to drum up investors, unsuccessfully, for a ski-equipment shop.

Whoever was framing her two friends had done their research. She racked her brain to think of who could want to do this, but her mind kept betraying her need

to focus by replaying the moment Alex had held her in
his arms. The cell buzzed again, refusing to let her ru-
minate. She rolled over to unplug the phone. The first
text was from the sheriff:

Good news or bad news first?

She had a preference for bad news first, but the sheriff hadn't waited for her response to continue texting.

Toxicology report returned. Same as Eryn. Bruce re-
covering. No fingerprints on syringe from last night.

No new leads, then. The phone vibrated rapidly with
a message from Eryn.

I knew it! Darren said he interrupted what would've
been a five-alarm kiss. Sorry for you! Hope you still
got the kiss! I'm getting discharged this morning, and
Darren is moving back in, provided our counseling appointment goes well today. Prayers, please. By the way,
I heard Bruce got drugged the same as me. Is Alex any
closer to finding out who's doing this?

She let the phone rest on the nightstand and fell back
on her pillow, not awake enough to respond. So she
hadn't imagined anything. The whole town would soon
know that she'd almost kissed Rick's old partner. Thousands of tourists might be in town at any given moment,
but locals still kept tabs on each other. They weren't all
gossips, but if it wasn't slanderous enough to keep lips

sealed, word spread. They really didn't need a news-paper, in her opinion.

Her fingers drifted to her lips. What would the kiss have been like? Her heart pounded. The thought of ac-tually falling for Alex was terrifying for a thousand reasons she was too flustered to rattle off, but the big-gest was he wasn't Rick. Maybe she was lonelier than she'd realized. That was her own fault, confirmed by her conversation with Eryn.

Her phone buzzed yet again, and Teddy issued a warbled complaint. She rolled over to stare into Teddy's golden eyes. "Sorry, boy. No one wants to let me rumi-nate on my thoughts and feelings in peace this morn-ing."

The message was from Alex.

Coffee is ready. Officially no longer undercover. Con-tacted campaign treasurer myself. I think you're going to want to hear what I found out.

She hustled through her routine and opened the bed-room door to smell a mixture of bacon, eggs, toast and coffee. She inhaled appreciatively. Much better than the microwave sandwich or cereal bar she usually shoved in her mouth on the way out the door. She avoided eye contact, though, when Alex turned toward her with a full mug of coffee.

"What'd you find out from Chris? That's the trea-surer you meant, right?" She took a sip as Alex held up a meat stick with a question in his eyes. She nodded. Teddy deserved to have one since he'd had to give one up the night before.

Teddy gobbled up the snack greedily before moving to the food bowl that Alex had already prepped. He'd been up early.

"It's your pastor," Alex said. "He's the one that bought the tickets to the fundraiser."

"What?" Violet almost spit out the steaming liquid. She blinked rapidly. "Why would he do that? I know his salary, and it's not enough to be buying parishioners two-thousand-dollar tickets to a political event. Maybe someone else in the church wanted to gift it anonymously and went through him." Even that seemed like a stretch.

"Which is why I've set up an appointment to ask him."

"You can cross him off the list of suspects. Eryn would've recognized his voice if that's who she'd given our details to on the phone."

Alex nodded. "I did track the phone number Eryn called to RSVP to the party. Burner phone. No one answered."

"See? He's not the guy."

"But just as we learned something from talking to Eryn, we might learn something if we ask him a few questions." Alex glanced at the time on the microwave clock. "The secretary set up a meeting in twenty minutes. I thought you would appreciate getting it done before work."

"It's a good thing Teddy and I get ready fast."

"Can I ask you a personal question?"

Her heart pounded. Did he want to talk about last night?

"Why is it so cold in here all the time?" His left eyebrow popped slightly. "Is heat really expensive?"

She snickered, surprised at the question. "Sorry. I guess I'm used to it. It's not a money-saving thing. You don't want to be around Teddy when I don't keep the house cool. Newfoundlands are kind of known for their drool."

He cringed. "Really? I haven't seen him do that."

"Because I don't let him get too hot. Embrace the cold and have more coffee." She hustled back to her room, with a smile on her face. Within fifteen minutes, she'd repacked her gear and the search-and-rescue bag and was ready to go. The moment she shut the vehicle door, though, the awkward electricity between them returned.

"About last night," Alex said. "That, uh, moment in the parking lot. I need to apologize."

Suddenly, it was hard to breathe. She really couldn't handle hearing that their almost kiss was a mistake. Of course, it was a mistake, but she didn't want to hear it from *him*. She wanted to keep her dignity in place.

"Listen. It's fine. I'm sure being undercover can get confusing. For a second, I could believe we were a couple, too." The words rushed out so fast it felt like her ribs were being compressed in a vise.

"No, that's not what I meant."

She took the corner a little faster than necessary and pulled into the church lot. "Oh look, we're here."

"Can we pick up this conversation later?"

Or never would be better. "Sure." But if Alex didn't bring it up again, she certainly wouldn't. They were just two exhausted people who probably hadn't had any real human contact in months. That was all. She exhaled, finally able to breathe freely again.

They stepped inside the church. The early morning quiet of the building enveloped her. The thick carpet and walls managed to turn down the volume even on Teddy's panting. Pastor Sean Stafford rushed toward them with his hand outstretched. "You must be Alex. Welcome!" He nodded at Teddy and Violet. "Nice to see you both again."

Alex leaned into the handshake. "I must say, I'm surprised you know who I am."

"The church secretary filled me in. She keeps her ear to the ground, as they say—"

"And she's married to Sheriff Bartlett," Violet added. She should've known.

"Let me say welcome to the community. Anyone who's a friend to Violet is a friend to us. Mindy thought you might be here to request premarital counseling?"

Her throat closed tight, and Alex had a coughing fit as he took a step back. "No. Actually I'm here on official business. I have some questions about a case."

The pastor waved toward his open office, and they took some seats. "I'd be happy to help, but I can't imagine how."

Violet pushed past her discomfort, even though her cheeks still felt on fire. "Can you tell me why you ordered tickets for Eryn and me—?"

"And Bruce," Alex interjected. He gave her a side glance. "Given the events of last night, I asked the treasurer about his ticket, as well. It will soon be public record that the pastor bought an entire table at the governor's fundraiser."

"But I didn't!" His hand rested on his heart. "There must be some mistake. I don't have that kind of money." Pastor Sean opened the front drawer of his desk, riffled through a few papers and pulled out an invitation.

"That's the same one I received." Violet fingered the paper. His didn't have a phone number or request to RSVP like Eryn's, either. "Turns out they never printed invitations, only tickets."

"I never go to anything remotely political as a rule, so I didn't attend." His forehead scrunched. "How much were the tickets?"

"Two thousand dollars a plate," Alex said. "And there were eight seats at a table."

"Sixteen thousand dollars," the pastor muttered. He waved at someone behind them, and they turned to see the sheriff through the glass wall. "Sheriff, I'm glad you came." He nodded at Alex and Violet. "I was just informed that my name was used to purchase almost twenty thousand dollars' worth of tickets, but I never—"

"And Mindy said the church is missing forty thousand dollars from the general account?"

The pastor nodded at the sheriff's question. "Very concerning."

Violet's spine straightened, and Teddy stood, no doubt picking up on her tension.

The sheriff cast her a meaningful look. "Violet, how come everyone in your circle is one of my suspects this week?"

"Su-suspect?" the pastor stammered.

The sheriff nodded. "I'm afraid so, sir. This is all causing quite the strain in my marriage, too, so we might need a marital counseling appointment after I ask you a few questions." He glanced at Violet and Alex. "Assuming you're done here?"

"I think I have a picture of what happened," Alex said.

Violet stood. "Sheriff, you know this is going to end up being like Eryn and Bruce. It has to." She stared at the pastor with new perspective. He wasn't a thief or a mastermind. Was he? No. He'd have no reason to ever hold a grudge against her or Rick. No reason to steal her husband's memorabilia.

"I'll keep that in mind. Keep me updated on what you two find, okay? I hear there's quite a ruckus brewing at the hotel."

Alex nodded as if he knew what the sheriff was talking about, but she walked in a sort of fog back to the vehicle.

"What's the motivation? Why would someone want all of us at that fundraiser dinner?"

"The simplest reason would be to make sure you were all out of the house."

"That only makes sense if they already intended to also frame every one of us from the beginning." They both settled back into their seats, and she started the engine.

"Perhaps we should rethink this from the beginning."

"It all started with Rick's stuff being stolen. His college stuff…" Her mind was trying to make a connection. It felt like she was reaching out and trying to grab a memory, and she'd almost found it…

The radio in her SUV burst her concentration. "Ranger Sharp?" One of her law enforcement officers rattled off his handle. "You've been requested out at the hotel immediately by Tom Curtis. He says it's an emergency."

She shifted into gear before he signed off. "Buckle up." She flipped on the sirens before speeding out of the church parking lot. Her gut was tied up in knots. There was only one reason Tom Curtis would call her in an emergency. The one person she cared the most about in the entire valley was also the closest she'd ever come to having a daughter. "I think Daniella is in danger."

NINE

Alex stiffened. Violet's adoration for Daniella had been written all over her face every time she'd spoken of her. Whoever was tormenting her had to know that.

"I hate to sound like a broken record," he said. "Whoever is doing this knows way too much about you. Are we sure that your ranger recognized the voice on the phone as Tom's?"

Her gaze darted his way before returning to the road. "He's local. Of course he would. Why would you suggest that?"

"This morning—"

"The 'ruckus' the sheriff mentioned." She took a sharp inhalation. "What do I not know, Alex?"

"I was going to tell you, but I figured we'd discuss it after I had more information. My supervisor dispatched more FBI agents here after our conversation about explosives last night."

"But I told you the snow ranger hasn't confirmed any theft, and the troopers already know—"

"That's not all. This morning, the security cameras picked up a man running through the halls with a black bag over his shoulder. It had an orange emblem that read Danger. Explosives. They're evacuating the lodge as we speak."

Her foot slipped off the gas pedal, and the SUV slowed drastically as they ascended a hill. Her entire face scrunched. "Even if we do discover the explosives were stolen, we don't carry them in bags like that."

Exactly. And Alex also didn't need to explain that the Firecracker would never be spotted so easily. "Given that the security cameras were compromised last night—"

"Whoever is trying to get my attention is better at sneaking around than the Firecracker or…"

"Or someone wanted to make sure the footage was seen to lure everyone out. They wanted the hotel to be evacuated, which is why I'm concerned you're being called there." His heart beat faster. Rick should've never died rounding the corner of that building. The FBI had ruled Rick as a casualty of an assassination attempt gone wrong, but Alex had never understood why there were bombs at that location in the first place.

His mouth went dry. What if the Firecracker and Violet's tormentor were one and the same after all?

"Violet, I know you didn't want to cause Teddy any undue anxiety after the vet last night, but what about now? I think it will be best if we get you relocated. Someone's already been in your house once."

She refocused on the road and took the final turn he knew would lead them to the hotel. "Someone came into the house while Teddy and I weren't there. If they really know that much about me, they'd know I'd have the advantage in my own home."

"They tried to get you outside a hospital, Violet. And

going to the hotel now might be walking straight into a trap."

"If someone wants to talk to me that bad, maybe I should just get it over with so all of this will stop."

He held his tongue. She couldn't really mean she'd *let* them kidnap her. Worry led people to make impulsive statements. After they found Daniella, he'd try again. Maybe even get the sheriff and friends to help convince her to move to a safe place before this escalated even more.

She took another corner without slowing down. The sudden motion didn't faze Teddy. The special seating behind them had been made with high-speed pursuit in mind, or maybe he was so heavy that nothing moved him when he didn't want to be moved. As they approached the hotel, the traffic turned into gridlock.

"Like I said. They've started to evacuate already."

"The entire hotel?"

"They're checking every single room with the K-9 bomb dogs. Once they're sure there are absolutely no devices, they'll allow guests back in. I'm sure there will be some who won't want to return."

She flashed the siren and was able to get around the bottleneck and into the parking lot, though it was pure chaos with lines of cars waiting to leave. Violet swung up onto the curbside. It would be the best spot out of the way.

As they ran toward the entrance of the resort, Alex kept his FBI badge out in hopes they'd be able to get closer. Violet pointed out Tom. His tie was loosened and dress shirt untucked. He was directing employees and pointing at groups of wide-eyed guests with their luggage. He stiffened at the sight of Teddy, held up a hand at the people waiting to speak to him and ran forward. "Violet, I'm so glad you're here. With all these strange things going on, I knew you'd understand the urgency. It's not like Daniella to disappear. She's not like that anymore."

"And security footage?" Alex asked.

"They said it's missing."

Alex exchanged a dark look with Violet. He would need a word with the FBI immediately. They were trusting security footage as reason to evacuate the hotel, and yet it didn't work whenever they actually needed it. He leaned over to speak with only Violet. "Someone wants everyone out of the hotel. We need to consider why, and we need to assume it's the Firecracker running the show."

Her eyes flashed. "Right now, the only thing I'm considering is Daniella's safety. Tom, I need something personal of hers. Can you get something out of her employee locker?"

"They won't let us back in."

"I'll see what I can do." Alex flashed his badge and pointed to the lobby.

The other agent shook his head. "You need to take that up with the special agent in charge."

He was ready to argue there was no time, when Violet interjected, "Tom has run to see if there's something of hers in their car. They carpooled together to work." Her attention shifted to his jacket. "Do you still have that photo? The one that someone stuck in Teddy's vest?"

He pulled it out of his pocket, struggling to focus

while radioed messages were exchanged between officers from multiple agencies. "I don't see how this can help right now."

Violet took the photo, flipped it over and held it out to Teddy. "Ready to work?" The dog sniffed the photo wildly. "He knows my scent, so he'll ignore that." Teddy lifted his head upright and swiveled toward Alex, pressing his nose into his pant leg. "Right, he's got you now. Which leaves..." Teddy sniffed the back of the photo again, and this time, his back went rigid.

"Go to work," Violet said gently.

Teddy dropped his nose to the ground and spun in a circle.

"You don't think Daniella's scent is on the photo, do you? She can't be the one behind all this."

The dog's fluffy tail turned rigid, the tension coming off him almost electric. "No, of course not," Violet said, her eyes riveted on Teddy. "But I think he might've caught the scent of whoever has been toying with us, and I assume that person is the same one who took Daniella."

Teddy vaulted forward.

"He has something!" Alex said.

"Yes." Violet jogged beside Teddy, her attention on protecting the dog in the busy parking lot.

Alex rushed forward. "You focus on the dog. I'll keep you two safe." He held out his badge and waved the other hand to block the line of cars trying to get down the lane and out of the lot. The dog darted right, and Alex sprinted ahead to block a second row of cars.

The dog stopped, turned around in three circles, then slowed his pace. In Alex's peripheral vision, as he was holding traffic back, he could see the slump of Violet's shoulders. Maybe Teddy wasn't so hot on the trail anymore. Or perhaps the person had driven off somewhere.

Teddy stopped abruptly, touched his nose to the back of a black SUV and sat down.

"She might be in here." Violet rushed forward, her hands cupped around her eyes to peer into the darkened windows.

"Stop. Step away." Alex ran over for a closer look. A federal license plate. This was the vehicle that the future nominee for the Federal Reserve chair would be traveling in. "Get Teddy and go back to the resort. Now."

"What? No. Daniella could be in there."

A blinking light caught his eye. Alex took a knee and peered under the SUV. His heart stopped beating for half a second. He had to get Violet away from here, or they'd all be dead.

Violet let loose a shout as Alex lifted her up into the air. She fought against the instinct to take him down. Her head bobbed violently as Alex ran. "Let me—"

He dropped her to her feet. "Only if you keep running. I saw a bomb, Violet. Bomb."

"Daniella…" Her name caught in her throat. "Why didn't you let me look inside first?" She pressed forward, but Alex blocked her. Teddy shoved his head in between them, as if trying to act as a referee. "Just let me check for her." Horns from a few of the cars blared as they were still blocking the lane.

Alex held up his badge at the closest window and placed his other hand on her shoulder. "We need a

SWAT team. Even if she's in there, you don't know if the doors are rigged or if someone—"

The black SUV transformed into a ball of fire before her eyes. The shock wave shoved her backward to the ground. Her head stung, but she flipped over instinctively, hands over her ears, mouth open. A second later, a cacophony of car alarms started, and the earth stopped shaking. Teddy licked her hand. She rose to her hands and knees and gazed into his eyes. "Are you okay, boy?"

Her own voice sounded like it was coming through a sock. Alex's blood-tinged hand dipped in front of her face, offering help. She pushed herself upright, not wanting to cause him pain. She wasn't sure which one of them moved first, but they were wrapped in each other's arms. A pop sounded in her eardrums and the car alarms and sirens tripled in volume. Painfully loud.

"I'm so sorry," Alex whispered into her hair. "I've done it again."

She had no idea what he was talking about. One name ran through her head over and over. Daniella. Daniella was likely dead because of her, and she didn't even understand why.

"Medic! Doc! Somebody!" A man's shouts pulled her attention. Tom jumped up and down, waving toward the front of the hotel, desperate for assistance.

"Why is he calling for help?" She straightened. "Why is he calling, Alex?" Hope reverberated through her entire being. If he wanted a doctor there, at his car, then maybe... She began running with Teddy by her side through the parking lot, ignoring the acrid smell of smoke stinging the back of her throat and eyes.

Tom caught sight of her. "It's Daniella. She's unconscious. I need help!"

A shuddering breath overtook her, and her steps faltered. Alex grabbed her arm, keeping her from a fall. "She's alive, Violet."

Tom likely thought she looked like a lunatic, because she couldn't stop smiling even as her vision blurred. Unconscious meant alive. Daniella was alive!

Violet darted through the spaces between the cars and reached the blue Subaru Forester, with Teddy right on her heels. She yanked the passenger side door open to see Daniella sprawled across the back seat. Tom was on the other side of the car, his door open, as well.

She reached for Daniella's wrist, and a strong pulse hit her fingers. She lifted her face to the sky and mouthed her silent prayer of thanks.

"What is it?" Tom pressed. "What's wrong with her?"

"She's likely been drugged with a sedative," Alex answered. "She'll need to be taken to the hospital, but if she's like the other cases, she'll recover fully. I'll make sure the EMTs head this way!"

"Other cases?"

Violet wasn't sure where to begin. Her throat burned with tension as she took another look at Daniella. The floorboard was filled with trinkets from the gift shop. Tom stooped down to look inside, his eyes full of torment. "She wouldn't have started shoplifting again. That's ridiculous. Why would she jeopardize her future once more?"

"She didn't, Tom. Someone set her up. I don't know why it's happening, but I think someone wants to get to me by hurting those I care the most about." Teddy stuck his head in and nudged Daniella's hand. There was no movement except for the steady rise and fall of her chest to convince them she was still alive.

Violet's stomach vibrated with the tension. Daniella had been so close to the bombing. Too close. What if Tom's car had been next to the one with the bomb? "I'm so sorry. This is because of me, but I won't rest until I stop whoever is doing these things."

Tom's forehead creased in confusion, but he didn't reply. Alex returned and touched her arm. "The paramedics are heading over now. I know you want to see if she's okay, but you have to let others take care of her."

She stood so Tom wouldn't have to witness what was sure to be an argument. "I can stay out of the way of EMTs, but I want be here for her when she—"

"No." Alex's face had a white pallor, and it appeared as if he was going to be sick. "Don't you see? Teddy found the scent of the person who slipped the photograph under his vest. The same person who is so determined to torment you. The one who bombed that SUV. Do you understand what I'm saying?"

She shook her head. The pieces that snapped together in her mind had to be wrong. They had to be. The bombs had been placed in that SUV by an assassin. The Firecracker. "But why?" She hated the way her voice sounded small and afraid.

The paramedics jogged past the car in front of them, headed their way. Violet, Teddy and Alex stepped out of their way. The movement helped her see clearly. People who were still on the premises had gotten out of their cars, some crying, some hugging. Was it out of fear or relief that Alex had kept them from driving any closer before the bomb ignited?

"I don't know why," Alex said. "We're going to figure it out, but right now, I need to get you somewhere safe. He's targeting you, and you can't be out in the open like this, Violet." He glanced over his shoulder where Daniella was being lifted out of the vehicle and placed on a stretcher. "She's going to be okay. The sheriff will ask her if she saw anything. Let's go."

She was a target. His words bounced around in her mind. If she was a target, then anyone close to her might get hurt. Alex was in that photo. He'd be next.

"Violet? Can we go now?"

She nodded and let him lead her and Teddy away from the scene. She barely registered when he asked for her keys, got her and Teddy in the car, and weaved them through traffic, taking alleyways and side streets before parking in front of her place. Once inside, she made sure Teddy drank extra water before she sank onto the couch. Teddy leaned against her shins and placed his enormous head on her lap, staring into her eyes. He thought she needed comfort, but for once, he was wrong. She felt numb.

A plate full of salad appeared in front of her. The last thing she wanted to do was to eat.

Alex sat beside her and offered a smile at Teddy. "Sorry, buddy, but I didn't think you'd be too jealous of our salad."

"I have responsibilities, people to help. I can't let the Firecracker—"

He rested a hand on top of hers. "Take five minutes to eat and try not to think. We have a long day ahead of both of us. Let's refuel before we argue about next steps."

Her lips twitched. There was something comforting about being with someone who knew her well enough to know they were about to disagree. She jabbed the fork into a heap of chopped spinach and romaine. The food tasted like dirt, though. Whether it was due to her emotions or the choice of rabbit food as a meal, she couldn't tell for sure. "I appreciate it. Though I'm eating this under protest."

"You and Rick had the most prepackaged diet I've ever seen. I used to worry you'd both end up with scurvy."

"We weren't *that* bad." She stopped to think about her normal diet. "Okay, maybe we were, but after a long day of work, neither of us wanted to do the cooking."

"Understandable, but I'll feel better if I leave here knowing you have had some real food. You'd probably grow to like it, you know."

"I knew you were an optimist."

His smile disappeared. "Listen, before we move on, I really need to get this off my chest. I should never have even wanted to kiss you—"

His words were like an electric jolt. Instead of being numb, she wanted to run. "Alex. Please. We don't need to discuss it." She couldn't help that her heart skipped a beat at the news he'd wanted to kiss her.

"We do. I've been trying to work up the nerve to tell you this for over two years." His voice caught, sending apprehension down her spine. "It's about the night Rick died. An informant told us the Firecracker was scoping out a building. When we arrived, Rick was supposed to take the west side." He hesitated and dropped his head. "But I knew he had better aim with more sunlight, so I told him to switch places with me."

She struggled to follow what he was saying. "Better aim?"

"We were clearing the perimeter before backup arrived. When Rick rounded the corner on the east side…" Alex closed his eyes and took a deep breath. "There shouldn't have been explosives there. The target would've never gone that way, but—"

"There was a bomb," she finished for him.

"It should've been me. I told him to switch places with me. It was my fault."

She stared at the broken man in front of her, but his declaration was too overwhelming for her to offer him comfort. "Why?" Her question came out in a whisper. "Why are you telling me this?"

He shook his head but avoided eye contact. "Because I could never kiss you without you knowing it was my fault he's gone instead of me. And today you were almost killed, and I can't help but think it was my bad judgment call that…" He inhaled sharply and shook his head. "I just needed you to know."

But she didn't want to know! She stood up rapidly. The right thing to do was to tell him that it wasn't his fault, that she didn't blame him. The only reason he'd told her was because he wanted to feel better. Now, every time she looked at Alex, she'd think if only…

"I'm sorry. If I could go back in time, I would change places with him." The regret on his face was real.

"What's done is done." She strained past the throbbing in her throat. "You were right. It's not safe here.

I'm going to pack." She needed to be alone, or she'd never be able to think straight.

Teddy lifted his head and looked between the two of them. The most expressive dog she'd ever known, his eyes were wide as if to say, "What should I do? Who needs comforting most?" She held her palm out flat, a sign he could stay. She walked down the hall and closed the bedroom door behind her. She didn't want either of them to see what was sure to be an ugly crying session.

Lord, why? She dropped to her knees by the side of her bed and dropped her forehead on the cool sheets. *Chaos.*

That word yet again. She wiped the escaping hot tears from the corners of her eyes but kept them closed. Her memory heightened. Sitting in the common room on orange bucket chairs, the criminal justice study group staring at Bridget after her declaration. "Chaos is the answer," Bridget had said. "Stretch limited resources thin and—"

"So now we all know who to come looking for if you decide to go to the other side and show criminals the *right* way to go about things," Rick had responded with a smug grin on his face. That had been mere days after he'd broken things off with Bridget, and weeks before he and Violet would have their first date. The group had laughed at his comment, and Bridget had narrowed her eyes.

Violet opened her eyes and stared at the light blue walls and the metallic print of the mountains hanging on her wall. Bridget was the type to hang on to perceived wrongs for a lifetime, the type to want to torment Violet. But she was dead. She was dead, wasn't she?

A shadow crossed the metallic print. She moved too late, just as one man clicked the lock on her bedroom door while another came at her with a syringe.

TEN

Alex hadn't meant to cause her more pain. He was sure she was missing Rick with renewed intensity, and she wasn't the only one. He used to sort through his problems with Rick. Not that Rick was one to beat around the bush. If Alex stuck his foot in his mouth, Rick had always been quick to say, "Fix it."

He smiled at the memory. Ironic since this mistake had to do with Rick, and there was no easy fix. His go bag was almost ready, he just needed to repack a few things so that he'd be ready to leave soon. Thumping above, followed by grunts resounded through the floorboards.

Alex glanced at the ceiling, but he wasn't going to fall for that again. She was working off some frustration and anger with her martial arts. Not a bad idea. He felt like punching a few boards himself. Maybe he should've never told her. He certainly didn't feel any relief or newfound peace after having done so, but he'd felt the need to let her know for two years.

She wouldn't want to see him again for quite some time, maybe ever. His fingers shook as he tried to fold his last shirt. Once he got her to a secure location, he was going to hand her security off to another FBI agent. He just needed to convince his boss that she needed protection. The harder job would be persuading Violet that she and Teddy couldn't respond to any search-and-rescue calls for a while. A tall order.

No casualties from the bombing at the lodge were reported, but it had been a close enough call to send the Federal Reserve chair nominee out of town. The welfare of the nominee was out of his hands now, but the FBI would be searching the records of all the Federal Reserve Police to see if they could track the mole there. Given the Firecracker's old-school method of handing over flash drives, Alex doubted they'd find anything.

Teddy barked incessantly, followed by more thumping. Maybe the dog was taking it personally that Violet had closed her door for some privacy. Alex came back to Rick's words before his death. *Something about this is starting to seem familiar.* If it was familiar to Rick, maybe it was something personal. Alex stared through the window at the thick blanket of fresh snow covering the mountains.

Bridget Preston had died, but what if she had made it abundantly clear what the Firecracker should do to never get caught? What if one of the students in the criminal justice study group had taken up the cause? But it couldn't be a copycat case because of the DNA they'd found.

Teddy burst through the door at the top of the stairs, his weight flinging it open. It hadn't been locked, but the movement stunned Alex. The unusual behavior combined with the sound of breaking glass shot adrenaline straight to Alex's heart. He bolted up the steps. Teddy turned and ran ahead of him, jumping and launching his front paws at the bedroom door. "Violet?"

More breaking glass could be heard. "Help!" Her call was hoarse and followed by a grunt.

"Teddy!" Alex swung his arm behind him. The dog understood and shuffled backward. Alex kicked his foot directly below the knob, and the door splintered, swinging open.

Violet face was bright red. An arm wrapped around her neck. She elbowed the man behind her and tucked her chin underneath his hold, slipping out of his grasp. A gun lay on the ground behind the man she'd just struck, but another gun was on the floor in front of the second man, who was currently doubled over in pain. Despite the man's groans he bent over farther, and his fingers were mere inches from the gun.

Alex rushed forward to stop him, but Violet slammed a sidekick into the bending man's back. She spun and issued another kick into the stomach of the man she'd just managed to free herself from. Teddy's deep growl set Alex's teeth on edge as he managed to grab the gun on the floor. He heard rapid footsteps and another bark.

He looked up just as Teddy launched himself at the other man who had just drawn his weapon. The dog grabbed the collar of the man's jacket in his jaws and brought the man down with him as he landed back on his paws. The gun hit the ground and slid underneath the bed.

Alex raised the weapon he'd retrieved and aimed it in the direction of both men. "Enough!"

Movement out the window in his peripheral vision

briefly distracted him. A woman in the trees, pointing a—

The window exploded.

"Violet!" Teddy let go of the man's jacket and moved
in front of Violet. She crouched to the ground, and
Teddy flopped down, his paws sliding underneath the
bed, but his head was clearly too big to fit underneath
the frame. Bullets pinged the wall as Alex ran over to
cover Violet. He only half registered that he didn't see
where either of the men had gone before he crouched
over her. The moment the shooting stopped, he prepared to return fire. He lifted his head to find the men
were no longer in the room, and there was no one visible outside the window.

"I think they ran out the same way they got in," Violet said, breathless. "Through my bathroom, past the
walk-in closet."

"Stay down until we're sure the shooter outside is
gone." Alex still had one of the men's guns in his hand
and his own Bureau-issued one at the back of his waist.
He peeked over the edge of the mattress. The woman in
the tree was no longer there, but she could be waiting
at another location. He ran through the closet, checking
to be sure they weren't hiding behind the clothing, and
into the bathroom. The window above the tub was wide
open. He raced to it, gun raised. There were two hooks
over the windowsill, attached to ropes dangling all the
way down to the ground. They swayed in the breeze.

A house situated next to the woods provided privacy,
but the downside was neighbors couldn't see anyone approaching, even in the light of day. The rev of engines
sounded, and from behind a grouping of trees, three

snowmobiles took off. Two men and one woman, all with helmets on, darted through the trees and headed toward the foothills of the mountains behind the house.

"Whoever shot up the bedroom is gone." Violet stood in the closet, a gun in her hand and Teddy at her side.

"They took off on snowmobiles." He took note of the scratch on the side of her face, the hair that had escaped her ponytail and the sweat gathered on her neck. "Are you okay?"

She leaned over, her hands on her knees, still catching her breath. "What took you so long?"

"Let's just say 'message finally received.' You can take care of yourself."

She coughed a laugh, and her eyes grew misty as she straightened.

"I actually thought you were practicing martial arts before Teddy came and got me."

"You came just in time. I practice for a group attack, but I was starting to make mistakes. My gun was in my nightstand, but they caught me off guard." She patted Teddy's head. "Thanks for the assist."

She lifted a piece of fabric from the dog's mouth and waved it in Alex's direction. "Teddy made sure they won't be getting away this time. Let's go."

Violet led him to the snowmobiles she had parked in the side garage. They were both outfitted especially for Teddy. Usually, she kept one at work and one at home, but on the last late-night mountain mission, she'd snowmobiled straight home for a good night's sleep. She threw a set of keys at Alex and pointed at the helmet. "You've ridden before?"

"Yes, but I think we need backup."

She flipped on the communication in his headset and set it to her shared signal. "Agreed."

Violet picked up her radio and requested backup from dispatch. They'd send one of her law enforcement rangers first, as the forest was on federal land. The snowmobiles were equipped with GPS tracking. "Have him follow my location." She signed off, checked Teddy's harness, and slipped on her own helmet. "At this rate, it'll be hard to catch them. Every second matters. Let's go."

She cranked the ignition and started following the path through the trees. This part wouldn't require Teddy, but if they lost the trail or came to a highly trafficked path, that's where Teddy would take over. The clouds were gathering in the sky and casting a gray pallor over the valley that made it harder to see.

"Can you hear me on this thing?" Alex's voice came through the speaker in her helmet.

She focused on steering around a snow pile that could be covering a small tree. "Yes."

"Now might be the time to let you know I've only ever ridden on marked trails."

"You need to stop telling me things when it's too late to do anything about it." The tension in her shoulders continued to build.

He exhaled through the speakers, and it sounded like he was blowing air into her ears.

"Sorry," she added, knowing he was thinking about Rick's death again, as was she. "This just seems like our best chance to catch whoever is doing this. I'm tired of people I care about becoming targets."

"Noted," he said. "Any snowmobiling tips I should know about?"

She stood up on the running boards as she took a sharp right. "If we're cutting across hills, use the throttle control and your body position to keep the tracks pointed where you want to go. Never ever stop halfway when you're going up a hill." She hesitated. "Unless it's on a sharp cliff where there could be a snow bridge ready to tumble."

"Should I stand up?"

"Only if you feel it helps. I have to do it to compensate for Teddy's weight." She leaned her entire body to the right while keeping her left foot on the running board to make another sharp turn and then settled back on the seat. Her little side mirror revealed the dog happily in his harness.

She had to focus now on the tracks in front of her. So far, the three sets from the other snowmobiles were easy to follow. They were nearing the crest of a hill she knew would be safe, but the snowpack was deeper now, making it more dangerous. "Too much throttle, and you'll drive too deep into the snow, Alex. Too little makes it harder to balance."

"So, no pressure is what you're saying?"

She rounded the top and slid slightly to the left. "Pop the throttle and countersteer."

Alex huffed in her helmet. "At some point, no amount of maneuvering is going to win over a five-hundred-pound heap of metal and the forces of gravity, but I'll do my best."

Fair enough, but she had to think positive while driving with Teddy behind her. The trees cleared out on the next stretch they ascended. A gust of wind blew a light dusting of snow over the tracks. The lines were still visible, but if there was any more snow, she'd need to stop and ask Teddy for help. On a clear day, the expanse of white, much like an empty canvas, would've taken her breath away. Racing across the snow was the closest she'd get to flying, with the occasional bouncing on clouds.

The trees disappeared, and in the distance, boulders and spires poked out from underneath the thick snow like icebergs. If they made a wrong move through the snow here, it could be fatal.

Only one track remained in front of her. Odd. Either the three people had merged and followed the exact same grooves—unlikely—or a pair of them had peeled off. A gust of wind indicated that snow had covered up the trail of the other two.

"Is it just me, or has it gone eerily quiet?"

The engines of the snowmobiles were anything but quiet, but she knew what Alex meant. The sky held no birds, and without trees or other signs of life, she and Alex were exposed. She pressed forward, and boulders rose up on either side of them, offering protection. It felt like being in an alley, except with rocks instead of buildings. The air grew still, no longer blowing gusts of wind.

Was this what being hunted felt like? As if someone was holding their breath, waiting for her to enter into their shot. The space between the rocks narrowed. The carpet of snow resembled a runway leading straight up to the top of the hill.

"Something doesn't feel right," Alex said softly.

She agreed. Even if she was wrong, she didn't want them to crest that hill and find themselves on a sharp decline without protection. "There are some spaces between the boulders up ahead. Let's split up. You go right. I'll go left. Keep heading due north without topping the hill. I'll find a way to round it at an angle from the other side. Maybe we'll cut them off."

"Affirmative."

She stood and placed all her weight on one of the running boards. The sweat from the afternoon's events dripped down her back. Even if she hadn't spent ten minutes fighting off two men with weapons, this type of snowmobiling tested her abilities. Thankfully, they'd practiced it enough. Teddy had learned how to counterbalance with his head, as well.

They made the turn smoothly. She could see the crest of the hill now. With precise movements, she maneuvered to take it at a diagonal. As they reached the top, she saw someone wearing a white snowsuit standing on one of the spire tops, red hair spilling out the back of her helmet. The woman lifted a rifle, pointed at them and pulled the trigger.

Violet swung the handles, making a hard left to avoid getting shot. The snow gave way several inches, and the snowmobile choked, throwing her off. She flipped head over heels and landed on her back. Snow kicked up from every side. She flung her arms and legs out to slow down, but hitting a mound of hard snow took her breath away.

She was sliding down the hillside headfirst at high speed with nothing to stop her but boulders that could take her life. Teddy was skidding mere feet from her, on his back. She fought to spin around so she could see what dangers lay below them, but before she could, something far worse entered her vision. The snowmobile was rolling, bouncing, and heading straight for them.

"I've spotted the men. I'm going after them! Violet?" She heard Alex calling her name through the helmet, but she couldn't answer. She twisted, straining her neck and every muscle in her back until she caught her gloved fingers on Teddy's harness. She kicked a foot out and yanked him toward her, narrowly avoiding the tip of a rock jutting out. Each bump they hit slammed the breath out of her lungs. The snowmobile caught air, lifting up and over them. If it fell on them—game over.

The ground disappeared from her back, and they dropped into thin air. She lost her grip on Teddy's harness, and her hands and legs flailed until she slammed into what felt like a cement slab. Her feet started to sink, and an icy, wet abyss rose up around her. Water poured into her helmet. She felt Teddy's paws against her chest. She blinked rapidly, and the bubbles in the helmet moved enough to see his eyes staring into hers.

A current forcefully thrust them to the side and abruptly changed direction. She was being dragged under by her foot. The snowmobile had dropped in the lake with them, and her foot was caught on the machine.

The frigid waters numbed her body. Teddy was free and floating to the surface. She closed her eyes, and the moment hit her with clarity. If she had told Alex to go left instead of right when they split up, he'd be the one at the bottom of the lake. She understood now the burden he carried. Too bad she'd never have a chance to tell him.

Sleep offered relief to her burning lungs. If only something would stop pulling so hard on her arm.

ELEVEN

Alex swerved, narrowly avoiding plowing the snowmobile directly into a boulder that came out of nowhere. The two men on snowmobiles were getting away, darting through another bunch of trees on the far side of the hill. His snowmobile stalled from the sudden decrease in speed. He slammed his hand on the front of the seat. He'd lost all contact with Violet. They never should've split up. He tried again to reach her. "Violet?"

He stepped off the snowmobile, and his leg sank a foot into the snow. He turned, searching for Violet. Over his shoulder, to the west, a woman with red hair flying out from the back of her helmet and a rifle strapped to her back stood on top of a spire. She paid no attention to Alex or the men on snowmobiles. She was staring at the lake down below.

Below her were two tracks that... Alex's stomach lurched. The tracks disappeared into a wide berth of disturbed snow that led directly to the lake. The lake... Teddy's head broke the surface and then disappeared back under.

"No!" He grabbed his weapon and spun back to the woman, but she was gone.

He shoved the snowmobile with all his strength. *Lord, if ever I needed help, it's now!* He pushed again, and the snowmobile mercifully slid two feet. Alex hopped back on and cranked the motor. Seconds. He only had seconds to get all the way down the hill to the lake and find her. His entire body trembled as he fought to make smart decisions, weaving his way toward the water. He'd be no help to Violet if he crashed. He hit the radio and called for dispatch. "Where is our backup?" His voice croaked. "District Ranger Sharp is down. Medic, we need a medic. Shooters in the vicinity."

He hit a snow divot and momentarily lost control, sliding sideways down the steep run. Remembering Violet's words, he popped the throttle and steered against gravity, standing and leaning in the opposite direction. Mercifully, he came around and straightened. Only a hundred feet to the alpine lake now. The first ten or twenty feet of it had to be solid ice, but the interior section of the blue waters was still visible.

As he reached the ice, he flung himself off the snowmobile and rushed forward. His shoes had little grip as he skated his way to the water. The helmet cast aside, he fumbled for the zipper of his jacket, removing the layers as fast as he could to prepare to dive. The dog's head crested the water as he reached the edge of the ice.

"Teddy!" A hand. The dog held Violet's hand in his mouth. Her helmet bobbed on the water as the dog's powerful strokes headed his way. Never before had he seen a dog's paws work the way Teddy's did. The webbed paws created a current of water rushing behind him. Violet's helmet may have broken the surface, but he didn't know if her nose and mouth were out far enough to breathe. Her body was still immersed in the water.

Within seconds, the dog made it to the edge of the ice. Alex slipped his hands underneath her arms. "I've got her, Teddy." He straightened and fought against the slippery surface to pull her up and onto the ice. The last thing they needed was to both go under. The frozen surface held, and he gingerly laid her down. His fingers shook as he fought to unbuckle the helmet first. The water had already drained from the inside, but as he pulled the gear fully off her head, his ribs tightened at the sight of her blue face. He fought against nausea as his stomach lurched.

Teddy entered his peripheral view, shaking water off his fur. The dog rushed toward Violet, and those golden eyes held the same question that was on Alex's mind. Was she alive?

Alex dragged her by the heels until they reached the solid snow. Rivulets of water ran from her hair and hands. Opening her mouth, he forced all emotion to the back of his mind. He moved her head back and tilted her chin to start resuscitation. She gasped. Her eyes flew open. She twisted to the side, coughing as her entire body began to shake violently.

He knew too much about drowning. No water had been expelled from her mouth. So either her body had fought against the water by forcefully closing her airways, or her lungs had absorbed the water. There was a serious risk anytime the brain was deprived of oxygen, but there was also the danger of the lung tissue swelling and filling with fluid. Alex had no idea how long she'd been under before Teddy pulled her to safety.

They hadn't prepared the snowmobiles with any emergency first aid gear before they left, at least not the one Alex had been driving. He grabbed his coat and wrapped it around her. The woman exuded strength when conscious, but at this moment, she seemed frail and delicate.

She was still wet, but layers had to help. She didn't fight him as he lifted her into his arms, confirming she needed a hospital right away. Even though she was out of the water and breathing, she was nowhere near being out of the woods, both literally and figuratively. Teddy ran alongside him to the snowmobile. The sleigh designed for Teddy was big enough for the Newfoundland and Violet. "I'm counting on you to keep her warm, boy."

The dog rushed forward and slid down next to her without prompting. Alex pushed his hands into his fur to confirm the dog was bone dry underneath his top coat. Amazing. Her eyes flickered open and she groaned.

"Hug him, Violet. Hug him tight. I'm going to get us out of here."

She wrapped her arms around Teddy and buried her face into his fur. How long she'd have strength to do so, he didn't know. And would he even be able to find his way back to town without Violet leading the way? He had to at least try.

A snowmobile crested the mountain top to the east. Alex froze. One lone man sped directly toward him, gliding over the snow. Teddy jumped up to all fours and barked in that direction, but it seemed without animosity. Alex kept his hand on his gun until he realized the man wore a green jacket. A USFS jacket.

The man flipped the front of the helmet upward as he got closer. "I'm Ranger Alatorres. Are you injured?"

"No. I think they shot at Violet, and she ended up in the lake. Teddy pulled her out."

He nodded at the dog. "Where are the shooters now?"

"Two headed west. The other one, I have no idea." Alex pointed at the spire behind him. "She was stationed there with a rifle." He glanced down and realized Violet was unconscious again. Her bluish skin hadn't improved.

The ranger jumped off his snowmobile and ripped open a white packet. He shook an orange square of folded plastic rapidly, and it puffed up. "It's a heated emergency blanket." He unwrapped it and tucked it around Violet. "Better than nothing. We're working on getting more backup here. I need you to head due east. Air ambulance will be landing there any minute. Avalanche risk is too high for them to get any closer to the mountains behind me. Follow me."

Alex didn't hesitate. He'd lost his helmet somewhere near the icy water, so the wind stung his face as he pressed into the breeze and bounded after the ranger. Helicopter blades in the distance confirmed the ranger's words, but Alex feared they might be too late.

Violet's feet and hands had never felt so warm, which didn't make any sense. Her lungs weren't burning anymore, either. Wasn't she in a lake?

"I really don't think the nurse is going to approve." Alex's voice came through her mental fog like a bright light.

She blinked to find Teddy resting on her feet. Alex was leaning over her bed, holding both of her hands between his own warm palms. His attention was focused on her dog, though. "I'm serious, Teddy. If they want to kick you out, that means I'd have to take you, and I'm not leaving."

"Teddy, off," she croaked. Oh, maybe that was a mistake. Her throat didn't enjoy speaking.

Alex flinched and straightened. "You're awake!"

Teddy got off her feet, but the dog attempted to squirm into the small space between her body and the bed rails. He didn't fit. His head reached past her hip, though, and the way his golden eyes widened made him appear so concerned. "I think I'm fine, boy. Can I get some water, though?"

Alex lunged for a nearby stand and brought her a cup of water with a straw. She eagerly drank, and Teddy, seemingly satisfied she was okay, finally hopped off the bed as a nurse entered the room.

The woman raised an eyebrow and huffed. "If you hadn't saved her life, you'd be out on your ear, K-9 hero status or not."

The water took away almost all the pain in her throat. "He saved my life?"

"Along with a few other people," the nurse said, nodding at Alex. "Glad to see you awake." She reached for Violet's hand and placed a device on her finger. The screen illuminated, and the woman smiled. "The doctor will be checking on you shortly, but your oxygen levels are back to normal. We'll need to watch you a bit to make sure you don't have any complications, and then you'll be free to go."

Her memory was slightly fuzzy, but Violet remembered the woman with the gun and the snowmobile barreling after her and...

"Whoa!" The nurse shook her head and tapped a monitor next to an IV bag. "Let's think calm thoughts to keep that heart rate down. In fact, let's check that blood pressure." As the nurse grabbed a cuff and slipped it on the arm without tubes attached, Alex approached the bed.

"That's a tall order," he said.

"Borderline high." The nurse hooked the cuff back to the wall. "Keep the conversation light." She leveled a serious glare at Alex and Teddy before smiling at Violet and leaving the room.

The memory of the water filling her helmet, and her foot being caught, surfaced. "How did Teddy get me unstuck from the snowmobile?"

"You were stuck?" His jaw clenched, and his skin paled.

"A spring had me caught."

"You were missing a boot when I pulled you out." He leaned over and rubbed behind Teddy's ears, and the dog's back right paw went wild, gently shaking her bed. "I guess your inspiration wall really influenced him."

"I told you he has those instincts. And we train in water rescue weekly. It's a little humbling that he doesn't need me to get it done."

The dog made a harrumph noise before he flopped over to the side. He was likely more annoyed that Alex had stopped scratching behind his ear, but the timing made her wonder.

"I think we both need you." Alex's face flamed. "I

mean, we need you to be okay." He cleared his throat. "I know you're probably pretty upset with me still."

Her heart rate monitor was bound to bring a nurse back in soon. He was referring to their conversation before those men had attacked her. That moment at the bottom of the lake wasn't one she wanted to relive, but she understood why Alex had needed to tell her. He moved to stand, his shoulders hunched as if carrying a physical burden of shame, and she reached for his hand. He stiffened, but his eyes softened, searching her face.

"It was my call, my decision to go left through those boulders. I told you to go right. Imagine if I'd told you to go left. You don't have as much experience on the snowmobile, especially a large one equipped like that. And you wouldn't have had Teddy to rescue—"

"Violet, you can't—" He froze in the middle of shaking his head. His forehead creased, and he seemed to be fighting off waves of emotion.

She held his hand tighter, desperate to make sure there was no misunderstanding each other. "You were going to tell me that in law enforcement, you can't second-guess every decision, weren't you?" She pressed forward before he could answer. "I saw the information in front of me, everything in front of me, and I had seconds to react. By God's grace and the training I had to rely on, I made the best decision I could."

Alex turned his face toward the door and started to pull away. She placed her other hand underneath his. "Please, Alex. Hear me on this. I don't need your forgiveness. For all we know, if you had switched places with Rick, both of you could've died that day." Her voice broke. She had to accept the unknown to find peace again. Otherwise, the what-ifs would destroy them both.

His chest rose and fell, and she felt his shuddered sighs as if they were her own. Teddy rested his head on Alex's foot. Alex lifted his chin, looked at the ceiling and blew out a long breath. "Thank you, Violet."

"Thank *you* for saving my life."

He turned toward her.

She blinked rapidly, willing the blurriness away, and an awkward laugh escaped.

His face morphed into a giant grin. "I'm always surprised when you laugh and cry at the same time."

That made her laugh again. She wiped away the tears at the corners of her eyes. "I think I work so hard to hold back my emotions that when one breaks out, they all come out at once."

"All of them?" His hand brushed away hair from her face.

Their eyes locked. "Yes," she whispered. The noises of the hospital faded away as Alex bent over so their faces were mere inches apart. He hesitated before his lips brushed against her cheek.

A knock at the door pulled him upright. Focusing on the doctor at the threshold instead of the keen disappointment weighing on her chest proved a challenge. She barely heard the doctor's questions or registered as he listened to her lungs and told her she could leave after a few more hours of observation. The side of her face still felt warm from where Alex had kissed her. Why did it feel like he was trying to say goodbye?

The chaos of the week began to flood her mind. The moment the doctor left the room, she turned to

Alex. "Before the men broke into the house, I'd started to wonder if Rick's death was intentional, personal. Bridget was obsessed with the profile of a perfect criminal. Chaos was her solution. If a criminal used minor crimes to thin out law enforcement resources, the bigger crime would go off without a hitch."

"She thought the Firecracker was the perfect criminal?"

"No, she thought he could be. She thought the Firecracker's work was the cleanest, the most sophisticated. She admired him. Whenever she got like that, Rick would break the tension by joking that if a criminal started doing what she'd suggested, we'd know to come look for her."

Alex sat down in the nearest chair, his mouth agape. *"Something about this is starting to seem familiar..."*

"That's almost exactly what Rick said to me."

"And me," Alex said in hushed tones.

"Was their chaos like that when Rick was...?" She hated to ask questions about his death, and yet it was a relief to ask someone who might actually know the answers.

Alex's eyebrows jumped. "Yes. Police were overwhelmed that week with a string of robberies." He shook his head. "But how likely is it that someone would remember college—?"

"You didn't know Bridget. She was always suspicious, downright paranoid sometimes. She insisted those qualities would make her an excellent detective."

"She was right, to a point. I've already asked the FBI to reevaluate the copycat angle. We should look at the professor who gave your group the case files to study and any other member of your study group."

"I know it's a long shot, but it might be worth a check."

He hunched over, staring at the floor. "Arrangements have been made, Violet. I'm being called back in."

She stiffened and averted her attention to the ceiling. "Back to the Salt Lake office?"

"Yes. I put in a request before you woke up. I thought you wouldn't want to see me again."

"Obviously, that's not true." Her words came out in a whisper, straining against her tightening throat. She reached for her water and drank, hoping it would relieve the tense emotions, as well.

"I'm doing my best to convince my boss that what's happening with you this week is connected to the Firecracker, but I don't have enough evidence." He gripped the arms of the chair and squeezed, his knuckles turning white. "Since the future Federal Reserve nominee has left, they figure the danger to you has left, as well."

"No evidence? You must be joking. The bombing at the parking lot—"

"The explosives were stolen from the ranger shed. Your snow ranger confirmed that. But I'm trying to tell you that we have no proof of any connection to the druggings and the—"

"What about the laser scope I saw?"

"That's not the Firecracker MO." He exhaled. "We both know someone has it in for you and everyone around you, but we don't have proof it's related to the assassination attempt. It's just conjecture." He splayed his fingers wide, set them on top of his knees and leaned forward, finally looking at her. "Would you consider moving to Boise?"

The question jolted her. She set down the water. "What?"

"It's only a couple of hours away. You'd be close to the Boise National Forest, so you should be able to transfer, under the circumstances. It has a big enough population and plenty of small towns nearby to start your search-and-rescue school."

She studied his pleading expression. Was he trying to tell her he was going to move to Boise, too? She knew the FBI had an office there.

"Your family is there," he added. "Your mom and sister, right? And there's more law enforcement. A city would be safer."

The taste in her mouth turned sour. He just wanted to get her safety off his conscience. He was leaving, and whatever brief wonderings she'd had about a future together vanished before her eyes. "Will you go back to undercover work?"

He twisted his lips to the side. "Trying to change the subject?"

She shrugged.

"No," he answered.

"I thought you still have a couple undercover cases you're working."

"I was taken off those so I could follow the Firecracker lead my informant gave me. They'll turn my absence into rumors of my demise."

"Is it that easy to fake a death?"

His eyes darkened, and he shifted in his chair. "People see what they want to see, hear what they want to hear," he said softly. "I've been wanting to check with the officers who responded to Bridget's car crash and find out more about her death, as well."

The change in subject was a welcome one. She wasn't ready to discuss leaving Sunshine Valley. "I think that's a good idea." The thought that Bridget could've gotten away with faking her own death horrified her. Bridget on the loose without accountability... She'd either be a vigilante or worse, much worse.

If Violet agreed to move to Boise, the people she left behind might be safer, but what if she brought the danger to her mom and sister? The thought of her family brought her mind back to Daniella. Last thing Violet had heard, the girl was still unconscious. "Is Daniella in the hospital? I'd like to see her."

He nodded slowly. "She woke up a few hours ago. I actually need to ask her a few questions."

Daniella had been drugged and helpless in her dad's car, so close to that bombing. And all because of Violet. She dropped her head into her hands. The past couple of years, she had worked so hard at being okay, at staying busy, at living life without needing others. Now she saw that existence as the lie it was. The people in this town were near and dear to her heart, and she'd been fooling herself to believe that she could live without love again. But it was clearly too late.

"I'd like to get dressed and go with you," she said. "Go ahead and make those calls. The faster you do, the faster you can pack up and leave, right?"

He pulled his chin back, then slowly nodded before leaving the room. She hadn't forgotten that Alex's image had also been circled in the photograph. He'd be the next target, she was certain. If they couldn't find the person doing this, she'd never be safe again and neither would anyone she cared about. The faster Alex left, the better, for the sake of his safety and her heart. But if he left, would they lose the only chance that remained to finally capture Rick's killer?

TWELVE

Alex left a message with the Jerome County sheriff's office. The deputy who'd first reported to the scene of Bridget Preston's crash into Snake River Canyon would call him when he reported to his next shift. Patience wasn't Alex's strong suit. He wanted there to be easy answers, but then there was a matter of the DNA left at previous assassinations. They'd even found the Firecracker's DNA at the scene of Rick's death. Could Bridget be working with the Firecracker? The thought that the mysterious assassin could be training others to follow in his footsteps would keep Alex up at night.

Violet stepped out of the hospital room dressed in the extra USFS uniform from her go bag that the rangers had dropped by the hospital when they delivered her vehicle. The level of respect the team had for Violet was obvious in the few minutes he'd spent answering their questions on her condition.

He'd known she was an amazing woman for years, but after holding her in his arms, he couldn't stop thinking of what it would be like to be more than friends. That dangerous and uncomfortable mindset meant he needed to leave town as soon as possible.

Violet tilted her head, studying him. "Everything okay?"

"Yes. No news to report. Waiting on a call back." He gestured with his phone to the end of the hall. "Daniella's room is at the end on the left."

She worried her lip before turning in that direction. The small gesture drove him to distraction. She bit her lip when she was trying not to say something, he felt certain. She never used to do that, at least not that he'd noticed. He made her uncomfortable, and yet he had gone ahead and kissed her on the cheek. He blew out a breath, mentally kicking himself.

Tom sat in a chair by the door, as if serving as a guard. He glanced up, a scowl on his face at the sight of them. Violet winced.

"Tom, I'm so sorry for what happened."

"You didn't do it," Daniella spoke from her hospital bed. "They didn't, Dad."

Tom grunted but remained silent and returned to his book.

"You're awake." Violet beamed at Daniella. "I was so worried about you."

"It was super weird, but I'm totally fine. I'm mostly mad I didn't get to see the SUV blow up for myself. Everyone knows I was there, and yet I can't tell them what it was like because I slept through it."

"Someone drugged you."

She rolled her eyes. "I'd rather not tell people I was drugged, thanks. They might get the wrong idea."

Alex took out his badge and held it out to Tom.

"State troopers have already asked her questions,"

Tom said. "She didn't see anything. Is this really necessary?"

Alex nodded before moving to Daniella. "I'm afraid I need to ask you some more anyway. I'll be looking at it from a different angle than the troopers. Walk me through the minutes you remember right before things went dark."

"Did you see who drugged you?" Violet rested her hand on top of Daniella's shoulder.

Daniella nodded. "No. I mean, I didn't see who did it to me. I was in the parking lot. It was early and still dark, because winter is the worst." She spread out her fingers. "I was about to start my shift but had forgotten my gloves, so I headed back to the car. I saw the reporter, but I don't think she saw me. Then everything went dark."

"What reporter?"

"Um, I forget her name. A woman who writes for *Sunshine Valley Weekly* or something."

"The troopers weren't interested in the reporter," Tom added.

Alex tried his best to smile and nod at Tom, who was clearly agitated. "Could you humor us, Daniella, and tell us more? Do you remember her name?"

"No, but I met her a month ago, so I think she's legit. She was waiting outside the forest service office when I locked up one afternoon." She hesitated and gave Violet a side-eye.

"Why was she there?" Violet pressed. "The smallest details might actually be important."

Daniella blew out a long breath. "Well, it's going to ruin the surprise, but fine. She said you were going to be named Sunshine Valley's person of the year. She just needed to ask a few questions to fill out the piece she's working on."

Alex pursed his lips, pretty sure there'd be no such honor given by the *Sunshine Valley Weekly*. He rapidly typed a set of searches in his phone's browser. Nothing.

Daniella huffed. "Look, she wasn't a scam artist or anything. She already knew all about Rick, and she wasn't creepy. She wanted to know what I liked about working with you—"

Violet offered her a warm smile. "You told her I was your mentor?"

"Yeah. I told her you were somewhere between a big sister and a second mother. Maybe more like a cool aunt."

Alex put away his phone. "Do you remember what she looked like?"

"Long hair. Some shade of brown, but it was totally a wig. I didn't ask her about it or anything. Didn't want to be disrespectful, in case she had gone through cancer or something, but it wasn't the shade for her."

"How'd you know it was a wig?" The courier at the party had black hair, the woman at the restaurant had blond hair and the reporter had brown hair, but maybe they were all the red-haired shooter. He couldn't allow himself to start making assumptions at this stage yet.

Daniella eyed Violet. "Do you want to tell him, or shall I?" But Daniella didn't give Violet a chance to answer. "I style hair for free for my friends. Have my own video channel. Might own a salon someday, but I'm exploring my options. Want to be wise about my skill set and all that."

Violet beamed, and Alex once again felt like his heart was about to explode. He loved seeing the way these two interacted, and he couldn't help but imagine how Violet would be as a mom. Or a cool aunt.

"Was that it, Daniella? Did the reporter ask you anything else?"

"No. I think that was it."

Alex turned to leave.

"I mean, other than asking who else she should interview about Violet."

He spun around. "She asked for more names?"

Violet's eyes were wide. "Did you give her any?"

"I gave her Eryn's name and Pastor Stafford's. I thought they could give better lines than I could. I mean, the best story I could tell about you was how you won the church's hot-dog-eating contest, and then you wanted a bag of chips and soda to finish the meal off." Daniella used air quotes for the last four words. "But I didn't tell that story."

Violet's face turned as red as he'd ever seen it. "I don't normally eat like that."

Daniella smirked and turned to him. "You really need to help her start eating like a human. I worry about her health."

"Working on it," he said with a nod. "I took her to your dad's restaurant for starters."

Tom grunted in response but made no comment. Tom would likely need to be out of the hospital and days from the bombing before he'd be able to smile again.

"Hey! I'll have you know, I ate a salad today." Violet scowled. "Feels like that was a week ago. It's been a long day."

"To be fair, after living a day in her shoes, I can see how she's been able to eat like that and get away with it." Alex wasn't ready to admit how sore his core was after maneuvering the snowmobile in rough terrain. If Violet wasn't complaining, he certainly wouldn't. He tapped his phone where he was making notes. "You gave this reporter Eryn and Pastor Stafford's names. Anyone else?"

"No. She asked me about Bruce, out of the blue, which I thought was weird since that was so high school, but she wanted his last name."

Violet turned to Alex. "That'd be all she needed."

His mind raced. This woman had been in the area for a month, asking questions. Was it possible the events at the political dinner had nothing to do with the Firecracker? Impossible. His phone began vibrating. He looked to Violet, who nodded. He trusted she knew what questions to ask as he stepped out to take the call.

"This is Deputy Griffon. I heard you want to know about Bridget Preston's crash?"

"Yes. You're the one who found the body?"

"No. The body was never found. It was high-water days in Snake River Canyon, but trust me, after falling from the cliff into the river, and judging by the state of her vehicle, no one could've survived that."

Alex felt like punching a wall. "Unless she wasn't in the car at the time." His voice was strained from the tension.

"We did our due diligence, sir." The deputy addressed him with a patronizing tone. "There were witnesses from the crash. Two men, I believe. And part of the flannel she was seen wearing that day was left behind, snagged by a broken window."

"Windows don't break easily."

"They do if remnants of a tree go right through them."

"Thank you for your time," Alex said softly, though his mind was churning over possibilities. "One more quick question. Do you have the names of the two men who witnessed the crash?"

"Uh, yeah, but they were tourists driving through." The deputy went silent for a couple minutes and then rattled off two names, one that ended in Smith, and the other that ended in Johnson. Most likely fake, but Alex jotted them down to have the Bureau trace them.

"Can you remember what they looked like? Specifically, how they carried themselves?" Alex was careful not to lead the deputy, but if he described the men as being two broad-shouldered, wrestler types, they were on the right track.

"It was winter. They had coats on. I really don't remember much."

Alex signed off but jotted more questions on his phone's notepad. Based on his conversation with Violet, combined with Rick's last words, Alex needed to reevaluate the Firecracker's work since he'd reappeared back on the scene. They had DNA from recent cases that was a partial match to the assassinations from twenty years ago, and that had been enough evidence to rule out a copycat. The Bureau had stopped looking for any other differences. Did the hits in the past ten years that they'd credited as the work of the Firecracker also have strings of unusual crime surrounding the timeline?

Violet joined him in the hallway, her eyes wide. "Teddy is the evidence."

"What are you talking about?"

"You said you needed concrete proof to convince your boss that everything happening in town is connected to the assassination attempt. Teddy found the scent on the photograph and led us straight to the SUV. You said it yourself after the bombing."

"Well, yes, but…" Was she right? Was the dog enough?

"Teddy is the evidence," she repeated. "He's a K-9 trained in water rescues, avalanche rescues, and certified in search and rescue." Teddy panted with his tongue hanging out, as if he knew he was being praised. "While we don't work criminal cases, his nose will hold up in a court of law, so it should be good enough for your boss." She eyed him. "Is it enough for you to stay and bring down Rick's killer?"

His heart pounded in his throat. An hour ago, she'd acted like she couldn't wait for him to pack up and leave. She'd seemed to have forgiven him for his part in Rick's death, but then mere moments after that, her eyes had grown distant and cold. Like hanging on to a roller coaster by his pinkie, he couldn't keep up. If Rick were here, he would've told Alex that was because Violet's emotions were impossible to read. How many times had Rick complained about that very thing? Alex had to be certain. "Are you sure you're okay if I stay?"

"After hearing Daniella talk about the reporter, I know we've got to be close to ending this. We might finally have some answers."

"No, that's not what I mean." It was now or never.

He had to lay his fears on the line. "Do I bring you pain, Violet?"

Her hand flew to her stomach as if he'd thrown a surprise punch. The pupils in her eyes grew wide. "Why? Why would you ask that?"

"Because I remind you of Rick. And I know you said I have nothing to apologize for, but that doesn't mean that it doesn't hurt when I'm around."

"No. I mean, at first maybe, but now…" Her eyes had a sudden sheen to them. Was this one of those times where all the emotions were trying to escape, or was she trying not to hurt his feelings? He'd imagined she'd see it as a betrayal to Rick to send him away.

The compulsion to press wouldn't be ignored. "I guess I'm wondering if we can ever be friends, just you and I, without Rick." He cringed, unsure it was fair to have voiced his thoughts aloud.

Her mouth dropped, but a second later, she straightened, appearing ready to answer until her gaze flickered above his shoulder and darkened. The sheriff strode down the long hospital hallway.

"You here to ask Daniella questions, too?" Alex shook his head ruefully. "We should've scheduled appointments. We were round two of questions for her."

"That's not why I'm here." The sheriff pressed his lips together in a firm line and stared down at Violet.

She tilted her head back and groaned. "Please don't tell me another person is missing."

"Also not why I'm here. Though maybe I should be asking you if there will be any more missing persons."

"What?" Alex placed his hands on his hips. What was the sheriff implying?

The sheriff sidestepped Alex until he was right in front of Violet. "Given the circumstances, I'd say it's past time for me to ask you some questions."

Violet offered a half-hearted laugh, but she looked over her shoulder into Daniella's room before addressing him. "Ask away, Sheriff, but maybe tone it down before you make me sound like a suspect."

The sheriff slid his hand an inch toward his holster. "I'm afraid I can't do that."

Violet paced in her own hospital room. At least the sheriff had been willing to move their conversation here. Teddy paced alongside her, despite her assurances that he could sit down. He was keyed up in a way she'd rarely seen, especially when he should be exhausted after rescuing her from the icy lake. He kept his gaze on her face and was clearly worried about her, then. She stopped and patted his head so he would relax.

"Maybe this should wait until Violet has a lawyer present." Alex stood in front of his chair with his arms crossed.

"I'm not taking her in or accusing her of anything. Not yet."

This would be a lot more comfortable if the doctor would discharge her. She was fine. News of the sheriff coming to the hospital to interview her like a suspect would go through town like wildfire. "I have nothing to hide, so let's get it over with. What are your questions?"

"What do Eryn Lane, Bruce Wilkinson, Pastor Stafford and Daniella Curtis all have in common?"

She sank into the edge of the hospital bed. "I think

you already know the answer to that. They all know me, but they all know other people in this town."

"It's a known fact that house values have been sky-rocketing in this area. Word is your mama is gonna kick you out."

Violet barked a laugh. "Sheriff, do you need my mom's phone number?"

"Where did you get your information?" Alex asked.

"The rental never has guests because that's the way you like it. That's also common knowledge. Maybe you're desperate for funds to buy the house."

"I'm a paying guest," Alex said. "And what happened to no accusations? She committed the robberies and framed all of her favorite people while she was at it?"

The sheriff shifted uncomfortably.

"Where are you getting your information?" Violet asked. "The same place you heard stories about Eryn and Bruce and—"

"Like I said, I'm not accusing you of anything yet."

"No offense, Sheriff, but I think we have different definitions of what *accusing* means." She was sure of one thing, though. If the sheriff was spouting this as common knowledge, then that meant this theory had become town gossip. They needed to locate the person who had fanned the flames of the rumors.

"Violet, you're the only one who's connected to everything happening in this town." The sheriff took a step closer to her. "It's my job to get to the bottom of why. If you're holding anything back, now is the time to let me have all the facts."

"You could start with Daniella," Alex said. "She will confirm that a so-called reporter showed up at Violet's place of work, claiming the *Sunshine Valley Weekly* was planning a story on Violet. The reporter needed the names of those closest to Violet. That's your missing link. We find the fake reporter, we find the person behind this. Eryn Lane also had to respond to a sham RSVP for the political fundraiser. When I tracked the number, I found it was a burner phone."

The sheriff turned to Alex and narrowed his eyes. "Is the FBI working on these drugging and robbery cases, as well?"

"Not officially, but I have reason to believe that the same person responsible for all of those things set the bomb today and the bomb that killed my partner."

"Rick?" The sheriff took a step back. "Does the FBI have evidence to back that up?"

"Teddy," Violet said.

The sheriff cringed. "As much as we love Teddy, I was hoping you'd have a little more than that."

Before Violet could educate the official on the validity of her argument, a cheery nurse entered, staring at her clipboard. "Good news!" She lifted her head, read the room and her demeanor shifted into seriousness. "Your final test came back normal. The doctor gave me the go-ahead to start discharge papers. Sign these, and you're free to go."

The sheriff moved to the hallway. "I'll check into this reporter. Stay in town, Violet. You'll be going back to the house or work?"

"She'll be staying at the hotel," Alex answered.

"The hotel?" While she'd resigned herself to not sleeping in her own bed until they'd captured the gunmen, she found the choice surprising.

He turned to her. "After the bombing, they have quite a few openings. I got us adjoining rooms. There are enough troopers still working the scene that I feel it's our safest option in town." Alex gestured at the sheriff. "You must know someone is trying to target Violet, as well. I saw the gunmen myself in her house. A third person shot out her window."

"At your house?" He swiveled to Violet. "Why didn't you file a police report?"

"I called dispatch to send my rangers in pursuit of the men. Maybe I wasn't as clear about why I was pursuing them." She gestured at her arm and the bright pink bandage covering up the puncture from the IV. "I've been a little busy. I'll file a proper report with my rangers as soon as I leave, as the incident happened on forest service land."

"I gave Ranger Alatorres the gun one of the men left behind at the house," Alex said. "He was going to run prints, which I assume happens in collaboration with your office."

The sheriff nodded and crossed his arms over his chest. "I heard about what happened at the lake. My understanding is no one has been found."

His tone set her teeth on edge. Was he insinuating that he didn't believe her? "Alex can corroborate my story. I didn't crash the snowmobile into the lake for fun."

"I'm glad you're okay." The sheriff shuffled toward the hallway but stopped at the door. "I didn't know about a shooting at your house. Resources are stretched pretty thin right now, as you know, so I'll go there and gather the evidence myself."

"I appreciate that."

He nodded before turning away. "I'll be in touch."

Alex stared after him. "Do you trust him?"

"Should I trust anyone right now?"

He looked wounded. "Fair point. Shall we go?"

"Gladly." She reached for her go bag, but Alex picked it up first.

He held up one hand. "I get just how capable you are, but I'd like to help."

"Thanks. After today, I'm not turning down any rescuing." Her cheeks heated, and part of her regretted that she'd been unconscious when Alex had helped her to safety. He must have carried her in his arms.

Alex exhaled a shaky breath. "You'd think in my job I'd enjoy rescuing, but I hope I never have to do it again."

She walked down the hallway with Teddy at her side, mulling over his words. What did he mean by that? If Rick had said something similar, she would've taken it to mean he hoped he'd never see her in danger again. But with Alex, she was unsure. One moment, she thought there was a spark. The next moment, she thought he was kissing her cheek goodbye for good. And then what was all that about being friends? The question still hung in the air since the sheriff had interrupted them. Maybe it was a small mercy, because she had no idea what to say to him yet.

She pulled her shoulders back. How could she think straight about him when he was right next to her? Alex only wanted to be friends and was worried about bringing her pain. Busy and fulfilling work had been enough

in her life until he'd walked in and showed her that she
wanted more. More than friendship.

She inhaled sharply and put a hand to her chest. The
truth was, being *only friends* with him would be painful.
Would Alex ever be able to understand that, or would
he think she was betraying Rick's memory?

"Violet, are you okay?" Alex reached for her shoulder, his own steps slowing to stay at the same pace.
"You're flushed. Should I get a nurse?"

She blinked rapidly. "No. If someone is still out
there, I'll never be free to have friends or anything
else," she added quickly while her courage ran hot.
"They said someone wants to talk to me. If this is personal, my mind keeps coming back to Bridget time and
time again."

Alex hesitated. "There's a possibility she's still alive."

"I knew it."

"I don't want to give you false hope, though." He
raised both his hands, as if trying to slow her growing
optimism. "It's best we revisit all the facts to figure out
other possible suspects."

"Is there something you aren't telling me?"

"They never found her body. The officers think she
was swept down Snake River."

"What if she was never in the car in the first place?"

"They had two male witnesses."

Violet couldn't help but laugh. "Two guesses who
they might be. The woman on the spire… If she's also
the reporter, Daniella would be able to identify her. I
think I have a photograph of Bridget." If they could put
a face to Violet's tormentor, this could all end. Every

law enforcement officer in the area would be keeping an eye out for her within minutes.

Alex raised an eyebrow. "A photo? I thought all your photos were stolen?"

"Just the ones I kept at the house. I have a bin of other photographs in the storage unit. It's a long shot, but I think I still have some from those early college days there, a time before Rick. I know my mom took a photo when I first met my roommate at move-in day. If we have a photograph of her, we might have a photograph of the current Firecracker."

Alex's face lit up. "Lead the way, partner." The air grew heavy with his words. "I... I was being flippant. I'm sorry, Violet. I've stuck my foot in my mouth so many times. I'm so sorry."

She forced a smile. His words confirmed he would never see her as anything but his partner's widow. "It's okay. I know you must miss having a partner." She patted the side of her leg as she started down the hall, and Teddy matched her pace. "I know I rely on mine."

THIRTEEN

Alex's cup of coffee had gone cold. After a mostly sleepless night, he now sat on the floor, his back to the threshold of their adjoining hotel rooms. The trip to the storage shed had yielded two plastic bins full of Violet's college memories. They'd spent hours sorting photographs into piles last night, but they still had no leads this morning. Teddy snored from on top of the closest double bed.

Violet worked on the other side of the room with her bin. They'd agreed to sort photographs into two piles. The photographs with Violet alone or with only males were placed to the side. Photographs with females were in another pile. Alex was to keep his eye out for anyone that looked familiar. So far, nothing had registered.

Flipping through favorite moments in Violet's life amused him, though. Here in all these photographs was the woman Rick had fallen in love with. His gaze paused on her beaming smile, her bright eyes. He looked up to see her stretch across the room and grab another piece of pizza.

"What?" she teased. "I ate those carrot sticks first, like you asked."

"No judgment here," he said.

She rolled her eyes in dramatic fashion before taking another bite. He laughed but couldn't take his eyes off her as she moved back to sorting photographs. This wasn't the same Violet that Rick had married. Sure, there was a lot there that was still the same, her kindness and compassion and brilliance, but grief had changed her. Grief had changed him, as well.

That difference alleviated the guilt he was fighting for being so drawn to her. They could have never been a couple until they'd become these different people. What was he thinking? She wouldn't even agree to be his friend. He had no right to think of her that way.

"Alex!" She kept her head down, focused on a photo, shaking her hand his way. "Come here. I think I've found something."

He jumped up as she stood and shoved a photograph his way. "Recognize anyone here?"

Violet and another young woman with a curly mass of brown hair stood side by side in front of a room with twin beds.

"Is this Bridget?"

She nodded. "Ages ago. On the first day we met. Does she look familiar?"

He studied the photograph. She could be the woman he'd seen, but he wasn't sure. "I would recognize her profile, I think, but I can't really tell from this..." He squinted at the photograph. Was it her?

Violet dropped into a chair, dejected. "That might be the only good picture I have of her. Probably the only one that was ever printed. I think I got rid of the rest.

I wasn't too fond of my memories of her by the time I graduated."

"Understandable. What about yearbooks?"

She shook her head. "No, Rick was the only one who got college yearbooks. I was too cheap for that, and I thought candid photographs were the way to go. Rick wasn't much for using his camera."

Alex laughed, but it sounded as hollow as he felt. He could probably count on one hand the number of photographs he'd taken in college, but he was pretty sure he was in several group pictures, mostly taken by his female classmates. The tension wasn't going to go away until they had a conversation. "Violet, about yesterday…"

She stilled. "I'm not ready to talk about anything personal until I'm sure you're safe."

He pulled back. "Until *I'm* safe?"

"Yes."

"Violet, the last person I'm worried about me."

"Maybe that's the problem! Have you forgotten you were drugged once and almost drugged a second time? I'll never forget hearing that gunshot…" She shook her head. "I don't need another man I—I…" She stood and walked away to the other side of the room, staring at the floor. "I don't need another man I care about getting killed."

She cared. He hadn't realized he was holding his breath. He took a step closer to her. "Do you feel responsible for me just because I was Rick's partner?"

"That's like asking if you've been watching out for me just because I was Rick's wife." Her fists flew to her hips, and she faced him, uncertainty flashing in her eyes. She seemed to deflate. "I mean, that would be a good enough reason."

"You think I'm here simply out of duty? Maybe it started that way, but Violet—" The hotel phone rang, and the shrill noise broke their connection and his courage.

She bit her lip and walked across the room. "Hello?" Her spine straightened as stiffly as Teddy's when he found a scent. Alex covered the space in three steps and leaned close to overhear what was being said.

"It's been a very busy week for you, hasn't it?" the voice asked.

Violet's knuckles tightened around the receiver. "Oh, probably not as eventful for you, Bridget."

A laugh rang crystal clear. "And there it is. What I've been waiting for."

"You wanted me to know it was you," Violet said. The phone was shaking in her hands. Alex reached up and placed his hand over hers. She turned and faced him. He held up his own phone with his free hand and texted the state trooper stationed at the security desk of the hotel.

Violet followed his thumb's movements.

Trace the call currently happening in room 303.

"This makes it so much more fun for the both of us. You may not have Rick's mind, but I figured by now, even *you* would piece it together. With the help of your fake boyfriend, of course. Is he there right now?"

Violet's face transformed from angry to panicked. "Let's keep this reunion about you and me, shall we?"

"Now, that's a good idea. Especially since you're fully recovered from your polar bear swim. Let's get together and reminisce," Bridget said.

"There's a police station I would be happy to show you. We could catch up on old times there. I'll meet you in five minutes."

Bridget laughed. "I had something else in mind, but maybe we'll try your way. Looks like I better get going. See you soon."

The dial tone grated on his nerves. He let go of Violet's hand as she replaced the receiver. "What do you think she meant? There's no way she's turning herself in."

A knock at the door made them both flinch. Teddy barked, which was unusual for him but likely a reaction to their agitation. Alex beat Violet to the door, his hand on his weapon as he looked through the little glass window. "It's the sheriff. Do I have to open the door?"

She sighed. "Afraid so."

The moment Alex opened it, the sheriff looked over his shoulder at Violet. "I need to take a look in your storage shed. Either you voluntarily show me or I get a warrant."

"Bridget." Violet exhaled. She closed her eyes for a second. "I have a feeling I've been framed for something. I just don't know what."

Alex wanted to slam the door on the sheriff, but that would only make the situation worse. "Wait for the warrant, then."

She shook her head. "Whatever is there now will still be there later. Time is not on our side, so let's just get this over with." She turned to grab her coat and slipped her feet into her boots. "Bridget got off easy the first time she tried to destroy me. I never thought she would go this far, but she won't win." She stared into his eyes, and he fought against the impulse to pull her into his arms. "We can't let her win."

"Don't get me wrong, I'm glad you're not putting up a fight, but I am surprised you don't want to know my reasons," the sheriff said.

"Oh, believe me, I do," Violet answered. "I just know I'm going to prove they're all wrong."

"I'll be glad if you can." He harrumphed. "I had a tip called in that you've been seen on security cameras making numerous deliveries to your storage unit this week."

"Is that so? I was there last night with Alex, and there was nothing out of the ordinary."

"Video footage looks pretty convincing."

Alex laughed. "The same type of video footage that convinced law enforcement to evacuate this hotel, which only brought people closer to danger?"

The sheriff's face reddened but he ignored Alex. "I'm here as a professional courtesy, Violet, to make sure this is done right. I could've sent one of my deputies to bring you in for questioning first."

"Understood. Let's get this over with so I can clear my name." She picked up the photograph of Bridget and handed it to Alex. "Take this to Daniella, and see if she can make an identification."

"Teddy and I are coming with you to the storage unit first. Then you can ask Daniella yourself." The forced optimism in his voice confirmed her worst fears.

Bridget was a puppet master. How could the woman hate her this much from their time in college? Was it really all about Rick? Until this moment, she'd only half believed the possibility that Bridget could really have set the bomb to hurt Rick. Even now, she wasn't sure she could admit to herself that someone they'd known could've murdered him.

The drive to the storage shed took only a couple of minutes. Alex got a text and grumbled as he read it. "They were able to trace the call in the hotel room."

"Burner phone?"

"That's the theory. But I've also got good news." He smiled. "Teddy's nose won my boss over. They're sending more agents here tonight to go over everything that's happened this week, from a new perspective. We're going to get her this time. As soon as I've got a team here, we will cover every inch of the national forest with the help of your rangers, and we're going to end this. If Daniella can identify her as the reporter, Bridget Preston will be considered the suspect in an assassination attempt. She won't be able to run."

Her heart lifted, but she was so overcome, she wasn't able to speak. Bridget had been one step ahead of them for too long.

"Help is coming," Alex said, as if understanding her need for encouragement. "This time is different."

She pulled into a parking space. "You won't mind if you're not the one to personally get her?"

His smile was unwavering as he opened the car door and stepped out. He looked over his shoulder. "As long as Rick's killer is brought to justice and you're safe, I'll be happy."

Would he go back to Utah afterward? Her mouth refused to ask the question, though.

"I expect gloves to be used," Alex told the sheriff, who was waiting by the unit. The sentiment was smart, but Violet knew Bridget would never be dumb enough to leave fingerprints. After all, only the Firecracker's DNA had been discovered at Rick's death. If this was all connected, how had Bridget pulled that off?

The sheriff entered the PIN code that Violet rattled off, and the door opened. Diamonds glittered in the morning sunlight. Artistic renderings of the valley along with abstract and impressionist paintings were displayed on top of her covered furniture. A cash box sat ajar with dollar bills sticking out.

"A little overdone," Violet muttered. Despite expecting this was what she was going to face, she still felt her cheeks heat. "Sheriff, you know this isn't me. Do you really think I would use the people I know and care about like this?"

Voicing the question aloud brought her a new sense of horror. That was what Bridget wanted—she wanted all the people Violet knew and cared about to suspect she'd used them.

"It's a little obvious, but I still need to do my job. Surely, you can understand." He nodded as he clicked his radio and asked for backup. "We're going to need to catalog all of this for evidence. Looks like roughly half of everything that's been stolen."

Her mind was still going a million miles a minute, and she barely registered the sheriff's words. Bridget would find vindictive glee in the obviousness of the frame, yet she would want to make sure the charges stuck. How would she be able to do that, though? Even Bridget had to know that Violet wouldn't stop until her innocence was proven. If the woman was the assassin, though, and had been able to plant the original Firecracker's DNA at other assassinations, maybe Violet wasn't giving her enough credit. If she could only figure out what Bridget had planned next.

"Now can I call a lawyer for you?" Alex held up his phone.

She nodded weakly. "Joanne Piper. Though she's not a criminal lawyer, she can probably get me one." A deputy pulled up behind them. The sheriff shifted his hand to his holster where his gun and handcuffs were stored.

Her stomach flipped at the gesture. "That isn't necessary."

"I'm going to have to take you in, Violet. I know this looks rotten, but the more you cooperate with me, the easier this will be."

The last words she exchanged with Bridget replayed in her mind. She turned her attention to Alex. "I told her to meet me at the police station."

"And she said she'd try it your way and would see you soon." His look darkened. "Sheriff, be on guard. I know it's an election year, but even you have to see this doesn't add up."

The officer's nostrils flared, but he refused to acknowledge Alex. "The station is the safest place in town. If you're innocent and we do this right, we can find the real culprit faster. Do I need to use the handcuffs?"

She'd never been so glad her mother and sister no longer lived in the same town. They would've surely been targets, as well. She held up her hands. "I'll go peacefully." How long would it take to ever live down such mortification? She had a feeling Bridget's plans were far worse than simple embarrassment.

Her K-9 stepped in front of her shins with a grunt, effectively blocking the sheriff from approaching. "He's only doing his job, Teddy." She reached for her keys and handed them to Alex. "Take care of him, please. You should probably hold on to his leash. If you have to go back to Utah before I'm released, get Ranger Alatorres to take over his care and training." Her eyes grew blurry. Why did she feel like this was the last time she would ever see Alex and Teddy?

"Of course, but I'm not—" His eyes widened. "Your phone, Violet. Unlock it and let me text Daniella the photo. It'll be faster."

"Enough talk. Let's go," the sheriff said.

Violet shoved her phone into Alex's hands before the sheriff began reciting her rights and the charges. He opened the back door of his SUV and placed his hand on the back of her head to keep it from hitting the roof as she climbed into the hard plastic back seat. Teddy barked, growled and released the most sorrowful wail of a howl she'd ever heard before. How did he know she was going away?

The door closed with a slam, and she saw them through the small squares of wire in the windows. The sheriff slipped into the front seat and started the vehicle. "I really am sorry. I have a feeling my wife won't talk to me for a week after this."

She didn't feel like alleviating his guilt, even though she knew he was doing his job. When she'd picked criminal justice as a major, she'd never once imagined herself being hauled off. Her vision blurred as they drove away from Alex and Teddy. She kept her gaze on them as her ribs constricted so tightly she thought she couldn't breathe. Her heart had just come alive again, only to be ripped out and left behind.

"Please have someone check for bombs at the station before you bring me in." Her voice croaked through the tension. She was ready to face the same death as Rick. She'd imagined what it must have been like for him more times than she cared to admit. *Please don't let me leave this world without stopping her first.* The simple prayer was all her mind could handle as they drove through the forest-lined streets out of town toward the county station.

"You really think this fake reporter is the same person who killed Rick?"

The sheriff's radio burst alive before she could answer. Message after urgent message fired one after another without a pause. An avalanche had blocked the main highway out of town. Multiple vehicles had been caught unaware. Rescue teams were being deployed that moment.

"I can't believe this! Violet, don't your snow rangers watch for these kind of things?"

"You know we do." The conditions were ripe for avalanches, but not in that part of the forest and not the mountain next to that stretch of highway. The slope wasn't deep enough to make it a high-risk area, unless the avalanche had some help. "The explosives," she said simply.

The sheriff was answering his radio and either didn't

hear her or decided not to acknowledge her. "I can't even get you to the station. We're going to have to turn around. Need to get this semi's attention and help him turn around first. Whoa. He's taking the curve way too fast." The sheriff managed to flip his lights on once before the truck's back trailer slid across the highway, folding like a jackknife.

Violet flung her arms up to protect her face as the sheriff slammed on his brakes. A second truck smashed into the back of the SUV. Her forearms struck the metal divider, and she bounced off the plastic seat. The screech of metal overloaded her senses as the vehicle slid off the road. The SUV didn't stop until the hood crashed into an evergreen tree. The sheriff's head hung at an unnatural angle, blood dripping from his forehead.

Hot pain vibrated through her bones as she fought to sit upright. The side passenger door opened and a man in a ski mask came into view. His eyes crinkled. "Let's try this again, shall we? Someone wants to have a chat with you."

He reached for her, and she kicked out her leg. The man grabbed her foot and twisted her leg around until her knee felt like it was going to dislocate. The opposite door opened, and another man grabbed her wrists with one hand. A needle hit her shoulder, and she lost the ability to fight.

FOURTEEN

Alex almost forgot to turn off Violet's pass-code option before the phone timed out. His fingers shook as he forwarded Daniella's information to his own phone. Teddy whined again. "I feel the same way, buddy. We're going to get her back before the day is done."

There he went again. Making promises about justice without being able to guarantee he could make them happen. He pulled the photograph from his pocket and realized he still had the photo of him and Rick, the one that Teddy had used to find the bomb. He needed to get this properly logged as evidence. Unfortunately, he didn't have any evidence bags, so he gingerly put that picture back in his pocket and zipped it closed.

Once he'd captured the photo of Bridget and Violet, he texted it to Daniella, careful to word the question without leading the witness. "Who do you see in this photo?" He signed it with his FBI agent logo he kept for official correspondence.

A quick call to Violet's lawyer, and then he would be on his way to the station. He didn't know if Daniella even had her cell phone in the hospital with—

His cell phone vibrated instantaneously.

Violet was so adorbs in college! The reporter has had some good plastic surgery, and this is no wig. If I had to guess, she's had a lift and some nose work, maybe a little cheek restructuring, but her eyes are the same. Totally her.

A second later, another text followed.

Did I break the case wide open?

He laughed aloud, despite the deputy's strange expression as he still cataloged evidence. No wonder Violet loved Daniella.

Actually, you did. Maybe you should consider criminal justice as a major.

He didn't wait for a response as he ran to Violet's vehicle. Teddy didn't need prompting to jump into his section in the back. "Let's go get her, boy."

They drove the winding, tree-lined road out of town but had only gotten to the town's outskirts when a pileup of traffic impeded their progress. Something wasn't right. Helicopters flew overhead. They headed in the same direction as the sheriff had taken Violet.

Someone wearing orange at the end of the line was organizing traffic. Vehicles began turning around and driving back the direction they'd all come from. This highway was the only way to go east out of town. Travelers would lose two hours going west to take the long way around, but that wouldn't lead him and Teddy back to the police station. Alex pulled over and let Teddy out of the vehicle.

They walked forward until they reached the first vehicle with windows down. "Do you know what's going on?"

"Avalanche ahead. To make matters worse, some semi jackknifed, taking down a police car with it."

Alex's ears roared and he didn't hear anything else. He jogged forward. Teddy slid to his right, his paws gliding over the snow as Alex's feet hit the wet pavement. Despite his arduous training regimen, Alex found himself out of breath as he pressed forward at a faster speed than he'd ever tried. Violet...

They rounded the curve of the highway, and flashing lights rallied him to put forth an extra burst of speed. Two officers saw him approaching and turned, waving their arms at him. He disregarded them, focusing only on the sight before him. The sheriff's SUV was smashed, crumpled into half its size, in between a pickup truck and a forty-foot tree.

He slid across the snow to a stop, searching for signs of Violet. An officer approached with his hands out. Alex shoved his badge in his direction. "I need to see Violet Sharp."

"Was she with the sheriff?"

Only then did he see a man on a stretcher being loaded into an ambulance.

"Yes," he answered weakly.

The officer rattled off something about an escaped suspect. Never before had Alex wanted to punch a perfect stranger. "She's not." He shook his head. There was no time to waste trying to convince the officers. They could sort everything out after she was safe. "We're going to need backup. Get the K-9 officers from the forest service on the trail. Call the rangers and the troopers. She's been kidnapped. No time to explain. Make the calls."

"The resources are simply not available. The avalanche is the number-one priority. I'll make the calls, but until we've got all those people in their cars out of the snow, we've got to focus on the lives we can save now."

The officer turned around and seemed to be explaining to the other deputy what Alex had said. Teddy strained forward, sniffing. He reached the open door of the SUV and whined. When he looked over his shoulder at Alex, his sad golden eyes implored him. The dog wanted to work.

Would the Newfoundland even listen to him? Alex wasn't a trained handler, but this might be the only chance for Violet. "Find," he said tentatively.

Teddy's tail wagged so hard it hit the side of Alex's leg like a whip. He stepped to the side as the dog's head plunged into the snow. Instantly, his back and fluffy tail went rigid. Alex leaned over and unclipped the dog as he'd seen Violet do several times before. "Get her boy," he whispered. Teddy raced ahead, disappearing into the tree line.

"Call the rangers," he shouted over his shoulder. "Tell them we've found District Ranger Sharp's trail and need their help!"

He slid on his back down a small hill to keep up with Teddy. High knees through the snow were going to exhaust him fast. What he wouldn't do for a snow-mobile now.

Thoughts of Violet being with Rick's killer kept his feet moving.

She'd forgiven him for being the one who had survived. That was what he'd thought he needed from her, and while his shoulders had felt the burden lift slightly, the uncomfortable sensation of shame had stubbornly remained. And now it felt like he was about to lose another partner. Her words about their time on snowmobiles returned to him. *Imagine if I'd told you to go left.*

He'd never expected her judgment to be perfect. His gut twisted with the double standard. Rick had certainly never held Alex to that high of a standard. He hadn't expected perfection from Rick, either. In fact, they'd called each other "my trusty old sidekick." As if the person who said it first was the real superhero.

For a joke, Alex had given Rick a six-inch trophy with a faceless man holding a sign that said World's Best Sidekick. From that moment on, they'd played a game where they tried to get that trophy into each other's possession. Using sleight of hand to do it had almost been like a training exercise. They'd each had ownership of the trophy numerous times. Though as far as Alex knew, Rick had the trophy last.

Alex certainly didn't feel like a superhero now. He never had been, though. Snow dropped from a branch overhead and fell on top of him like a wake-up call. He slipped and dropped to his knees. Teddy froze and looked over his shoulders, checking on him.

"Keep going." Alex struggled to his feet. His body might be worse for wear, but he felt a renewed purpose.

He wasn't perfect, no. He was a desperate man. There would never be enough contingencies or perfect plans to avoid evil. He'd finally gotten that through his thick skull. He could only do his best and pray it would be enough.

He trudged forward after Teddy, almost on autopilot. All he desired was to keep Violet safe, but despite trying his best, he had no control over that.

Teddy's trajectory didn't waver. He knew the smell of his partner well. Alex understood more than ever why Violet hoped to help others gain the blessings of search-and-rescue dogs nearby. He wanted to help Violet make that dream come true. His words earlier hadn't been a slip of the tongue after all. He wanted *her* as his new partner, not for work but for life. Was the realization too little, too late?

Teddy stiffened and ducked his head in between two bushes. The snow was almost up to his belly. Alex waded until he was next to him and tried to see what had stolen Teddy's attention.

Roughly twenty feet away, two men sat on snowmobiles. One held binoculars and intently stared at something past the tree line. "As soon as she's done with the girl, it's all warm places from now on. Any minute now, we can join her and head for the helicopter. It's fueled and ready."

Done with the girl? His heart raced, and he put a hand on Teddy. "Shh," he whispered lest the dog decide to growl. He reached for his gun. The men also had weapons, and they were situated in such a way Alex couldn't aim at both of them at once. If he could distract them, he'd feel more confident about taking the pair on at the same time.

Teddy let out an exaggerated breath, complete with the smell of meat sticks. It was almost as if the dog was releasing a whispered bark. Tension radiated off Teddy, but he remained still as Alex kept a hand on top of his head.

"Looks like she's about to wake her up," one man said. "The fun's about to begin."

Alex's gut twisted with the implications. There was a space underneath the bushes without snow. Alex reached down and found a rock about the size of a grapefruit. It would do nicely. His gaze drifted upward to the thick branches full of snow above the snowmobiles. Enough to startle and disorient them if it fell on their heads, as he knew from experience. He lifted up a silent prayer that his pitching skills weren't as rusty as he feared.

"It's about time you woke up." The voice sounded familiar to Violet, but trying to lift her eyelids was a fight. The bright sunshine gave her an instant headache, and she squeezed her eyes closed again. Something about this situation was wrong, but her mind wasn't working fast enough to know what that was. Like reaching through a thick fog to get a coherent thought, she took stock of her senses.

Everything around her was cold and hard and smelled like clean air and pine. She went to move her hand to shield her eyes before trying to open them again, but her arm wouldn't budge. Her balance lost, she tipped over sideways into an ice-cold mound.

Unkind laughter broke through the murkiness of her mind. Her adrenaline spiked, and she jolted upright, now fully awake. A woman with long red hair in a white coat and snowsuit was crouched down, her nose almost touching Violet's. "I'm tired of waiting for you. All I've done is wait for you lately."

"Bridget."

The woman grinned and straightened. She brushed a hand down her hair. "Like my new look?"

"Your new face?" Violet struggled to move into a better position, except her hands were tied behind her back. Her teeth began chattering, and her muscles tightened, trying to get warm.

"Would you have recognized me without our little chat?"

"No." Violet said, staring at her own shoes until they came into focus. She flicked a gaze at the woman. The voice was the same, and the eyes. Bridget had a pout on her face, meaning she wanted Violet to recognize her. Fine. She'd play along. "You're still just as self-centered, though. Would it be better if I called you the Firecracker?"

Bridget clapped. "You *do* remember. See? I knew Rick would, too. That's why he had to go first." She made tsk-tsk sounds. "I blame his obsession with crossword puzzles. Kept his memory too sharp. I knew he'd never forget our time together."

Violet fought against waves of nausea by breathing through her nose. There was no getting out of this alive, but she wanted to die fighting. Maybe she could stop Bridget from taking more innocent lives. She needed time to wake up more, to get the knots untied, but that meant encouraging Bridget's ego to be on display and to talk about Rick's death. "You became the Firecracker's copycat."

Bridget's nostrils flared, and she pursed her lips. "No. I took over for him. Found him on an abandoned ranch before the feds did. They had no idea how close they came, but they gave up too soon. I eventually found where he was hiding on the ranch. I like to think his hairbrush was a gift to me so his legacy could live on—"

"Legacy? Your way of concealing your identity, you mean?" The first knot around her wrists gave way.

"They'll never know the Firecracker had an unfortunate accident when I came to visit him. Like the one you're going to have." Bridget stepped aside.

A set of USFS explosives sat wired together in such a way that they would create a bigger blast than was needed for an avalanche. There had to be at least twice as many explosives here as there'd been underneath the SUV at the resort. Violet forced her expression to remain neutral. Bridget always did thrive on drama, and Violet needed more time. "And when Rick was almost on to you, you killed him."

"It's amazing what a good informant can lead the FBI to do."

In that moment, Violet knew that Rick's death hadn't been an attempted assignation. It'd all been theater, which meant Alex's arrival here must've been orchestrated by Bridget, as well. "You planted tips with the informants. You never intended to carry out an assassination here."

"That's where you're wrong. Rick was a strategic

play. I had hoped to kill Alex first. I wanted Rick to figure out it was me before I killed him." She shrugged. "But Rick was faster to the bomb than Alex, so we never had a moment like this. Believe it or not, I had considered simply ruining your life and letting you live. Guess I've gotten more sentimental than I like to think." Her lip curled. "Oh, don't worry. I'll take care of Mark Leonard before he becomes the federal nominee. Just like I got the delegate Rick was trying to keep me from. It actually helps my reputation if there's one or two who get away. They increase their security, and then I still get them anyway."

She couldn't handle the glee in the woman's voice any longer. "What exactly do you want from me?"

Bridget's face transformed into a sneer. "For you to see that *you* made me the Firecracker. You only have yourself to blame for Rick's death. You'd be nothing without me, but you betrayed me more than anyone. You took away Rick, my friends and my career." She shrugged. "I still thrived, but you needed to feel what it's like when everyone turns against you. And now you know exactly who made that happen. Everyone in your life will remember you as a criminal."

"I've been drugged, so maybe I'm a little slow, but how do you figure? You're the one who tried to ruin my life in college. You're the one who tried to get me expelled." The moment she said the words, she realized it'd do no good. Now she understood what Alex had meant about having to at least try.

"I only tried to help you, Violet. Look at you. I knew, before you ever did, that you were never cut out for criminal justice. Managing forest employees? What a waste of your training, the training *I* could have had. If you hadn't turned on me, maybe you would've spared yourself some pain, huh? Rick would still be alive, happy with me."

Violet ignored the bait. The second knot slipped open. One knot to go. If only her fingers would stop stinging from the cold. She was starting to lose feeling in her pinkie, and pain radiated up her forearms. "Fine. Why'd you take Rick's stuff?"

"I couldn't risk that he'd kept any of our correspondence. I needed to make sure nothing would lead to me after you were gone."

"Hate to break it to you, but he didn't keep a thing."

"You probably burned them. That would be so like you."

Violet forced herself to not roll her eyes. "You don't have to do this, Bridget. You could stop hurting people. Go and live a different life, helping others even."

Bridget flashed a smug grin. "And leave you as a witness?"

"We both know you excel at pretending to be dead. People see what they want to see." As she said the words, she realized that's what she'd been doing the past couple of years. She'd viewed her friends as doing just fine, not having their own problems. And she'd decided to believe she could never experience love and happiness again. She quietly lifted a prayer of thanks that her eyes had been opened.

Bridget had been seeing what she chose to see for years, and her twisted reality had allowed her to justify murder."As if I would believe Miss Perfect Violet wants me to get away with my crimes." Bridget shook her head. "Nice try."

"Of course that's not what I want!" Violet's voice rose, her jaw tight with tension. Her entire being shook, and she struggled to locate the last knot. "I want justice for my husband." Her eyes stung, and her neck felt strangled as she struggled to keep back a sob. "The countless lives he would've affected had he still been alive," she whispered. "But since when did you care what I want?" She finally made herself lift her gaze to look at Bridget again. "You could still stop."

The woman stared at her, and for a second, the Bridget she knew made an appearance. Until a gust of wind blew her red hair back into the breeze. Bridget tilted her head and picked up a rifle off the snowmobile next to her. She approached Violet again and bent over until their faces were mere inches apart. "What people like you will never understand is there will always be those who do the controlling and those who are controlled. I'll never be the pawn again."

Those weren't the only two categories of people, but now that Bridget held the rifle in her hand, Violet had regained her self-control and remained silent.

Bridget straightened. "Besides, I did you a favor. Rick was holding you back. With him gone, you finally realized where you belonged." She smiled. "In a backwoods hole. Like I said, you should never have gone into law enforcement." She exaggerated a fake pout. "Can't say I didn't warn you. Though I have to give you credit, you put up a tougher fight than my men expected. But that only made it more fun for me."

A bark carried over the hushed landscape. Violet

stiffened. She knew that bark, but she refused to look. Bridget straightened and swung around. Violet followed the woman's gaze into the trees to the east. Nothing.

A snowmobile engine in the distance revved.

"That's my cue. My helicopter ride will be waiting for me."

Through the tree line, flashes of a snowmobile appeared. It looked like Alex was driving with Teddy seated behind him, paws on his shoulders. They were coming for her, but they'd be in danger if they got any closer. So far, Bridget hadn't noticed them, and Violet couldn't let her.

Bridget pulled out a small device that Violet recognized as the remote timer to the explosives. She clicked the device and winked at Violet.

Violet finally felt the last knot give and moved to pull her hands apart, but her wrists wouldn't budge. One knot still held. She'd miscounted. Violet buried her face into her bent knees. The only time she'd ever felt this helpless was when she'd found out Rick was dead, and now Teddy and Alex might die with her.

"Ah, that's the kind of goodbye I was hoping to see." Bridget squatted down in front of her and sneered. "You should have never crossed me, Violet."

The woman stood up, clearly pleased with herself. Bridget loved getting the last word, and Violet couldn't let her. She needed more time.

"The thing is, your men were fighting me when I still believed I had nothing to fight for." Violet stared her down, and Bridget's eyes widened ever so slightly, curious. "Imagine how I would fight if I thought I did." Violet slid on her back and kicked her legs against Bridget's heels in one smooth motion.

Bridget's boots flew out from under her. She landed on her back, and the remote flew up in the air and landed ten feet off, disappearing in a snow pile. The rifle slid a few inches away, but Bridget pounced on it before Violet had so much as a chance.

"I've got company. Where are you?" Bridget snapped into a radio.

Static filled the air as a male voice Violet adored answered, "Change of plans. They're tied up."

Despite the pain, Violet couldn't help but smile as she struggled to flip over and get up without the use of her hands. Two figures broke into the open, their snowmobile bouncing over the mountainous slope.

The click of a rifle chilled her bones. "Let's give them a little welcome gift, shall we?"

Though her vision was blurry, she knew in an instant that Teddy and Alex were rushing toward their deaths.

FIFTEEN

Violet didn't wait for Bridget to fire. She slammed into Bridget's torso, and a bullet soared into the air.

Bridget screamed and jabbed Violet underneath the ribs with the butt of the rifle, forcing all air out of her lungs. She hunched over, opening her mouth, with no oxygen to relieve her pain. Five seconds later, her lungs greedily pulled in air. She panted and righted herself just in time to see Bridget hop on a snowmobile and shoot down the fastest route of the mountains, away from the set of explosives at Violet's feet.

Violet took off running, narrowly avoiding falling on her face with each step. Never before had she missed the use of her arms and hands this much. She screamed, "Go away! Go back!" Her voice was weak, and she shook her head as dramatically as she could. They couldn't die saving her.

Fifty feet away, Alex's snowmobile sank into the mounds, and the engine sputtered. He'd choked it. Teddy jumped off the back without waiting for Alex, bounding through the drifts as if to prepare for a happy reunion. "No! Run away!"

Alex did his best to keep up with Teddy until he reached her. Teddy kept running for something and wasn't listening to her for the first time in years. Alex stepped around her and grabbed her wrists.

He wasn't listening to her either. "You have to go. Now."

"Only with you. You'll be much better at driving us out of here on the snowmobile than I will be."

"You don't understand. The explosives! They're on a timer. I don't know how long we have, but it will be any second. She's made her getaway." The ropes mercifully dropped from her wrists and she spun around to face him.

He lifted his face. "Where'd she put the bombs?"

A gunshot rang out. Blood splattered the white terrain around them. Alex's eyes grew wide as he fell to the ground. She felt like her body was moving slower than her mind demanded as she turned to see Bridget perched on her snowmobile with her rifle in hand. The woman returned to her seat and sped off again.

Violet dropped to her knees. "Alex…" She swallowed back a sob. There was no time to fall apart. "Look at me. Where were you shot?" His coat looked intact, but she couldn't tell where the bullet might have penetrated his black jeans. Her focus kept sliding to the blood on the ground.

"I… I'm not sure."

"We have to get you out of here!"

Alex paled, but his eyes weren't on her face. She followed his gaze to see Teddy had picked up the set of explosives in his mouth and had bounded in the opposite direction. She didn't remember screaming, but she heard her dog's name echo off the mountain walls. All she could think about was the other Newfoundland who had tried to get an explosive far from the people he loved. That dog had died a hero. "He can't die!" she cried. She fought to get up, but if she went after her dog, would that mean Alex would die?

Another bullet sped through the air, throwing up snow mere feet from Teddy. Would this woman never give up? The dog didn't so much as flinch. He continued sprinting due west with the package. "Take my weapon." Alex moaned, as if the words took extra effort. She grabbed his gun, stood and sighted down the mountain at where Bridget had once again stopped.

Violet shot off a few bullets, but her aim was shoddy, given the way her fingers fought to grip the gun. The shots were close enough to encourage Bridget to take off on her snowmobile again. Soon, the woman would be too far away for her rifle to do any harm.

"Teddy," she called again, losing hope. "There's a sudden drop-off to the west. He's getting too close." Maybe she could try to find the drift the remote had fallen into, but there had to be at least a dozen, and she couldn't remember which one it was. She moved to dive into the closest one to search. Fingers wrapped around her wrist. Alex had gotten back up.

"Violet, he's trying to save you. Let him do his job." Alex's fingers lost their grip as he stumbled backward, falling into the snow.

He was right, though it was hard to think straight or see through her tears. Her partner's lifesaving instinct would not be deterred, so she had to do her part. She reached for Alex. "Have you figured out where you were hit?"

"Not sure. Upper thigh, I think."

Blood pooled in the snow at an alarming rate. If the bullet had hit an artery, it was game over. Even if it hadn't, blood loss was a serious risk. She leaned over and helped Alex to stand again. "Drape your weight over me. As much as you can. Try to apply pressure to the wound with your other arm."

In the worst three-legged race ever, they rushed back to the snowmobile. Her ribs felt like they were being stretched apart as she maneuvered the vehicle out of the deep pit it had sunken into. "Teddy," she called out again, her voice breaking. "Teddy, please come!"

"He is," Alex said into her ear over the hum of the machine. "He is coming!"

She squinted through the blowing snow. Her beautiful brown dog's fur was flying in the wind. His tongue hung out to the side as he tore through the drifts with the same tenacity as he swam through alpine lakes. He was almost to them! They might just make it—

The earth shook. Alex wrapped his arm around her waist. "Drive!" Sheets of white at the far west edge, just past the drop-off, peeled off the slope and magnified into a giant white plume heading straight for Teddy… and them.

Alex reached around Violet for the handlebars. A cry tore from her throat as they twisted the snowmobile's steering together in a hard left. Even though his chest hadn't been hit, the searing pain at the thought of Teddy caught in the avalanche felt like it would kill him. He had to make the dog's sacrifice worth it and help save Violet.

He kept his head hitched over Violet's shoulder to see, but it was pointless. Tears had blurred his vision. Half a second later, the snow wiped out visibility. Like a hand had grabbed the back of the vehicle and shoved them forward, they flew off the machine. Gravity's cruel game slammed him down, provoking his scream when his gunshot wound was smacked hard. He lost sight of Violet, and snow pelted him for a good twenty seconds before he regained his other senses.

And then there was silence, somehow louder than any of the sounds before. About an inch or two of icy powder coated his face and chest, but he wasn't buried. Teddy had taken the bomb over a cliff of sorts and diverted the avalanche far enough away that they'd survived the explosion. He flipped over on his hands and knees and searched the sea of white. Violet sat up, brushing her hands over her face. She was alive! Her eyes met his, anguish written all over her face.

He diverted his gaze to a hundred yards or so past her to where he guessed Teddy had been. There could still be a chance. Violet followed his gaze and jumped up. "Teddy!"

Alex fought off the waves of dizziness and joined her. His backside was going numb, whether that was a good sign or not, he wasn't sure. For now, he had to help save Teddy.

They stumbled in the deep drifts, falling and righting themselves over and over. "The snow sets like concrete in two minutes after an avalanche. If you're underneath, you have no idea which way is up or down, and which way to dig, but Teddy still has his nose. He should be able to smell, and maybe he'll hear us."

They began hollering for the dog nonstop, crawling over the mounds that were becoming a hard fortress under their hands and knees. Snow sputtered ten feet from Alex's face, smacking the top of his head. A brown paw appeared, followed by the golden eyes he'd come to love.

"Teddy!" Violet began laughing and crying and crawled toward him. The dog bounded into her arms, and she landed on her back with the dog's paws on top of her shoulders.

The sheets of white had settled all the way down the mountain, and far below, he spotted another snowmobile. Only its nose was visible, sticking into the air. Teddy had ensured the avalanche would hit Bridget's escape route. Alex's leg lost all strength, and he dropped into the snow, looking up at the crystal-clear blue sky. If he was going to die, at least his heart was at peace. He just had one more thing he'd like to do.

"Alexander Driscoll, don't you dare die on me!"

He couldn't help but laugh at the use of his full name. "I'm trying my best, Violet, but I need to tell you something."

"Teddy, get him warm." She ran past him to the snowmobile. "Pray the radio still works on this thing."

He only half heard her as the dog lay down beside him, his heavy head on his chest. The static of radio could be heard as Violet sent out an SOS. A moment later, a voice came through.

"This is Ranger Alatorres. Anyone on this line?"

"Yes! This is District Ranger Sharp. Assistance

needed. Special Agent Driscoll has been shot. Medic needed."

"Tell them we need an avalanche dog for Bridget." His leg was regaining feeling again, and he groaned, not realizing what a blessing numbness had been before. Teddy shifted off him and rested at his side. He didn't hear the rest of Violet's hastily worded orders to the rangers, but a second later, her face was above his. "Help is on the way. A helicopter for you, and a German shepherd and handcuffs for Bridget, if she's alive down there."

His breath had grown hot and shallow, but all that mattered was he was with Violet. "I'm scared you won't want to see me again after I tell you this, but I—"

"I love you." She reached for both sides of his face.

He frowned, a little confused but relishing her touch, even if her fingers were freezing cold. "It was that obvious what I was going to say, huh?" Although he was hoping to say it out loud, he was secretly pleased she already understood. "Please know that I would never ever try to replace Rick or diminish his memory. I understand if it's too painful, but I had to tell you."

"What are you talking about?" She blinked rapidly. "I'm trying to say *I* love *you*, Alex." Her breath came out in a staccato rhythm, as if she couldn't get a full breath. "I don't know what the future might hold, but I love you." A tear slid down her cheek.

"You do?" His heart jumped to his throat. "But *I* love *you*."

She laughed. "Well, you don't have to sound annoyed."

"Not annoyed. Shocked." He grinned. "And incredibly grateful." His fingers shook as he slid his hands behind her neck. His eyes searched hers, looking for permission. Instead of giving it, she leaned forward and pressed her lips against his. His heart surged, and a wave of dizziness washed over him, though that was likely from the bullet wound. He hoped for another chance to prove his theory.

Approaching snowmobiles and whirring chopper blades above interrupted the moment. Violet sat up, and Alex held her hand while wrapping his other arm around Teddy. So this was what it was like to want a family. "Violet, before I pass out, I need to ask you a question."

Her mouth dropped open. "What is it?"

"Do you and Teddy have any plans for New Year's Eve?"

Her entire face lit up. "What'd you have in mind?" She gave him a side-eye. "More undercover work?"

"I was thinking more along the lines of a real first date." He patted Teddy. "As long as your partner approves."

Teddy kissed the side of his face, and Violet tilted her head back and laughed. "No kisses! From now on, I'm the only who does the honors." And she leaned over and did just that.

EPILOGUE

Six months later

Violet pulled into the small parking lot of the Military Reserve in Boise. The rustic park was equidistant between her work at the Boise National Forest and the FBI satellite office at the courthouse.

The June air was pleasant, not too cold or hot for a late afternoon. She and Teddy followed Alex's directions up a scenic trail to a spot overlooking the Treasure Valley. Next to a field of wildflowers, Alex was placing a picnic basket on top of a quilt. He spotted them and rushed over. He patted Teddy on the head while pulling her into a hug.

This was her chance. Over the past few months, she'd discovered notes and trinkets in her coat pockets during work hours. Alex used his sleight-of-hand training to leave her surprises to find later at work, and she had been wanting to return the favor. Except, thus far, he'd caught her every time she made a move for his pockets. Today, he didn't seem to notice. She'd finally done it.

He pulled back and did a double take at her smile. "What? You have a twinkle in your eye."

She shrugged. "It's been a good day. In fact, I took an unplanned day off."

He registered his surprise. "Any reason?"

"I received a shipment first thing this morning. Rick's stuff is no longer considered evidence." Bridget had been convicted on so many charges she would never be getting out. Especially since Violet had passed on the news about her finding the real Firecracker at a ranch. They'd reevaluated their DNA leads and taken a cadaver dog with them to the property.

"I wondered when that would happen." He slid his hands to the top of her shoulders, and his eyes narrowed in concern. "How are you doing?"

"I'm okay, really. I'm thankful to have them back." She breathed a sigh of relief at the confirmation that she really meant it. She'd spent hours poring over the photos and notes, and while her heart still squeezed with the memories and the pain of loss, the grief had changed. She no longer felt broken into a million pieces whenever she thought of Rick. Instead, she felt just a little bit closer to him.

Alex watched her closely. "I'm glad. I hope to look at them someday, too. When you're ready." His own smile magnified.

"Funny you should mention that. I can finally give something to you that I'm sure he'd want you to have. Except, I think you already have it."

He raised an eyebrow and pursed his lips. His eyes widened as he patted down his pockets. "You got me, didn't you?"

"I think Rick would've wanted it that way."

Alex pulled out a small golden trophy from his jacket

that read World's Greatest Sidekick. He tipped his head back, and a delicious laugh filled the air. She'd known he'd love it.

A bittersweet smile crossed Alex's face. She understood. Rick would always be missed. Alex lifted his eyes to hers. "I'm impressed." He held up the sidekick trophy. "Though, I know now not to deny this title. There's only one true superhero in our midst."

He gave a knowing glance at Teddy, who wagged his tail in response.

"Agreed."

Alex set down the trophy, unlatched the picnic basket and pulled out a gift bag. "First, a little something for you and Teddy."

She opened the bag to find several framed photographs of Teddy. "They're beautiful."

"I thought he deserved to have his own inspiration wall for other dogs to take a look at." He shrugged. "That is if you still want that property off State Street. The owner has agreed to let you put in an offer before it goes to market."

She gasped and set down the frames to pull Alex into a tight embrace. "Yes!" She'd been working many nights and weekends on her business plan for the search-and-rescue school. She'd been dreaming about that location, which was propped right in between the city and the trails leading into the foothills. "Should I call him now?"

He laughed. "Tomorrow should be soon enough." Alex pulled out a treat from his inside jacket pocket. "And, speaking of Teddy—" he unwrapped it and offered it to the dog "—would you mind if I have a moment alone with your partner? I have something of a sensitive nature to discuss with her."

Teddy flopped down on the quilt and tilted the meat stick with his paws so he could properly enjoy it.

Alex turned back and took her hand. "I'm trying to remain calm, but I have to admit, I'm really hoping you succeeded with a one-handed switch when you put the statue in my pocket."

The little box she'd switched out felt hot in her own pocket. The one time she'd actually managed to pull a sleight of hand seemed very dangerous now. Her cheeks felt on fire, and her heart pounded in her chest. "I didn't look at it. I didn't have an opportunity. It's in my pocket. You want it back now?"

He dropped to his knee. "Would you be willing to open it instead?"

Her breath caught, but she didn't dare hope. It could be something innocuous like a necklace or a pair of earrings.

"This is one of those times you probably already know what I'm going to ask," he said softly.

She pulled out the box, and the black velvet beckoned her. Alex placed a hand on top of the case and flipped it open. The setting sun hit the diamond ring, and beams erupted from the dazzling prisms.

"I know you have a partner in your work, but I'd like to ask you to be my partner in life. I love you, Violet."

She bit her bottom lip, willing her tongue to remain silent until he finished.

He grinned. "You're biting your lip again. I think I finally understand what that means."

"Don't you have a question to ask?"

He laughed. "Violet, will you please do me the honor of being—"

"Yes, I'll be your wife!" The words burst from her mouth, followed by a laugh. "I'm sorry."

"I'm not." He jumped up and turned to Teddy. "She said yes!"

Teddy lifted his head, and if ever a dog could smile, hers did. Right before he returned to his treat, at least. Her vision grew blurry as Alex closed the distance between them. He gently touched her cheeks, his thumbs wiping away the few tears that had escaped. He gently kissed the sides of her face. "I love you," he whispered.

"I love you, too."

He pulled back for the briefest of moments to look at her, his own eyes glistening. Then he kissed her soundly, wrapping his arm around her waist and pulling her closer. A paw landed on top of her shoulder, and they broke apart, laughing at Teddy's attempt to give kisses of his own. Violet wondered at the wisdom of teaching Teddy to stand on his hind legs. She also marveled at the last six months. She and Alex were done hiding from life and love, and their own personal superhero would make sure they kept it that way.

* * * * *

Get 3 FREE REWARDS!

We'll send you 2 FREE Books plus a FREE Mystery Gift.

FREE
Value Over
$20

Both the **Love Inspired**® and **Love Inspired**® **Suspense** series feature compelling novels filled with inspirational romance, faith, forgiveness and hope.

Get 3 FREE REWARDS!

We'll send you 2 FREE Books plus a FREE Mystery Gift.

FREE Value Over **$20**

Both the **Harlequin® Special Edition** and **Harlequin® Heartwarming™** series feature compelling novels filled with stories of love and strength where the bonds of friendship, family and community unite.

Get 3 FREE REWARDS!

We'll send you 2 FREE Books plus a FREE Mystery Gift.

FREE Value Over **$20**

Both the **Harlequin Intrigue®** and **Harlequin® Romantic Suspense** series feature compelling novels filled with heart-racing action-packed romance that will keep you on the edge of your seat.